The books that started it all…and kept you coming back for more!

EXILE'S END
CHEROKEE THUNDER

Come back to Rachel Lee's Conard County—revisit the men and women who draw strength from its blue Wyoming skies…and the bonds of the love they share.

"Rachel Lee's Conard County is a place where every romance reader's dreams come true in the most wonderful of ways."
—Melinda Helfer, *Romantic Times*

RACHEL LEE
has written twelve books for Silhouette in the
Intimate Moments and Shadows lines. In addition to
Destination: Conard County, Rachel Lee brings her
much-loved miniseries to Silhouette's single-title
program with *A Conard County Reckoning,* also
available in 1996. Ms. Lee also contributed to the
1994 Silhouette Shadows Short Story Collection with
"The Ancient One."

Rachel Lee has garnered numerous industry awards.
In 1991 *An Officer and a Gentleman* earned the
Romantic Times award for Best Series Romance,
and in 1993 she won the *Romantic Times* Reviewer's
Choice Award for Best Romantic Suspense with
Exile's End, Book One of the Conard County series, as
well as landing a Romance Writers of America RITA
Award nomination. In 1994, she received two RITA
Award nominations, and more recently *Romantic Times*
named Rachel Lee Best Series/Category Author of
1994. In addition, *Lost Warriors,* also part of the
Conard County miniseries, was named Best Series
Romance of 1994 by *Romantic Times*.

Rachel Lee has lived all over the United States, on both
the East and West coasts, and now resides in Florida.
Having held jobs as a security officer, real estate agent
and optician, she uses these experiences, as well as her
natural flair for creativity, to write stories that are
undeniably romantic.

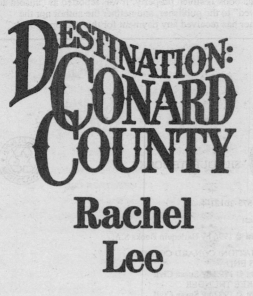

DESTINATION: CONARD COUNTY

Rachel Lee

ISBN 0-373-20121-5

by Request

DESTINATION: CONARD COUNTY

Copyright © 1996 by Harlequin Books S.A.

The publisher acknowledges the copyright holders of the individual works as follows:

EXILE'S END
Copyright © 1992 by Susan Civil-Brown

CHEROKEE THUNDER
Copyright © 1992 by Susan Civil-Brown

Silhouette Books

Published by Silhouette Books
America's Publisher of Contemporary Romance

SILHOUETTE BOOKS

ISBN 0-373-20121-4

by Request

Copyright © 1996 by Harlequin Books S.A.

DESTINATION: CONARD COUNTY
EXILE'S END
Copyright © 1992 by Susan Civil
CHEROKEE THUNDER
Copyright © 1992 by Susan Civil

CONTENTS

Dear Reader,

One of the questions I am most frequently asked is what made me create Conard County. I'm not sure, actually, except that it somehow always existed for me. It was always in my mind and would have been the setting for most of my books even if I had never named the place.

As for the other most frequently asked question: Why Wyoming? Because Wyoming has, over the years, given me some of the most neighborly experiences I've ever had, whether I was vacationing there or just meeting someone from there. Some of the best friends I ever had hailed from Wyoming, and filled me with wonderful stories and wonderful lore that somehow melded into the creation of Conard County. And then, of course, there is the magic I experience every time I visit the state, a magic to be found in mountains, valleys and rivers.

But Conard County is a place of its own, a place born of my wishes, hopes and dreams. My heartfelt thanks to all of you who have made it possible for me to return there for so many exciting visits.

Sincerely,

Rachel Lee

EXILE'S END

To Mom and Dad Brown with love

Prologue

In the shadowed room, a man lay unconscious on the blue sheets of a hospital bed. An IV catheter ran into his left arm. A suction tube ran up into the bandages that covered his face, then disappeared into a hole where a nostril must be. Both his legs were elevated and splinted from hip to toe with stainless steel bars, and bandaged on thigh and shin. His left arm showed scars from recent surgery, paper thin and red.

He had already been through a number of operations, and there were more to come.

The only light in the room came from a baseboard nightlight, which provided just enough illumination to guide a nurse's steps to the bed. In the corner farthest from the small light there was a darker shadow, a shadow with substance. If the man in the bed awakened with clear senses, he might, just might, notice the watcher in the shadows. But he would not awaken. Not yet.

It would be easy to kill him right now. So easy. A little potassium solution injected into the intravenous tube would bring a quick cardiac arrest. Or it would be pitifully easy to smother him with a pillow. Chances were, after all the man

in the bed had been through, everyone would assume he had
merely been too weak to withstand the rigors of surgery. He
had, after all, been through a lot. The thought was pleas-
ing. Yes, he'd been through a lot. Four god-awful, endless
years of hell. Why was he still alive?

But killing him now would be too swift, too easy. He
needed to suffer. He needed to know it was coming. He had
to twist and turn like an insect trying to escape the spider's
web.

The squeak of rubber soles warned the watcher of a
nurse's approach. As the nurse stepped into the room, she
immediately spied the watcher and hesitated.

"You shouldn't be here," she scolded gently. "It's well
past visiting hours."

"I had to come."

The nurse nodded, trying for a pleasant smile. "He'll be
all right. Really. He's remarkably strong. Why don't you
come back in the morning?"

The watcher gave one last look at the bed, at the golden
hair that identified the patient despite the bandages. *Your*
face will be different, but I'll know you. Wherever you go,
I'll find you and stalk you. You're going to learn exactly
what it's like to be hunted. As I am hunted because of you.

The nurse bent over the bed and checked the tubes. Then
she took the man's pulse. When she looked up, she saw that
the watcher had gone.

"I must be losing my marbles," she muttered under her
breath, "but that character was *creepy.*"

And right there and then, she decided to keep a closer eye
on this patient. It was the visitor's eyes, she thought, and,
remembering them, she shivered faintly. Nobody should
have eyes like that.

Chapter 1

He came walking up the dusty drive with a long-legged stride that betrayed a slight, curious hesitation. Amanda Grant saw him while she was weeding her flower bed, and she sat back on her heels, shading her eyes against the bright Wyoming sun. At times like this, she thought, living alone practically in the middle of nowhere seemed like a dumb thing to be doing.

He wasn't dressed the way most people in Conard County preferred. He wore a green army-style fatigue jacket and no hat at all, not a Stetson or even a baseball cap. His hair seemed to flame like burning gold in the bright morning sun. As he got closer she could see that the hair was a little too long, and that he had a full beard, as well.

A stray, she thought. She often saw them along the roads, mostly in the summer, not usually when the first nip of fall was in the air. Homeless, jobless, always on the move. Lost.

Feeling uneasy, she stood and wondered if she should go inside and get the shotgun from the cabinet. The next ranch house was five miles away as the crow flew.

Yes, a stray. He carried a huge duffel, and a knapsack was visible now, slung over one shoulder. Jeans. Black boots. He was getting closer, and she was standing there dithering like an idiot about what to do. Get the gun, she ordered herself. Stand on the porch like some kind of paranoid idiot with the gun and let him know you're ready for anything. Turning, she took a step toward the house.

"Mrs. Grant?"

He was still a hundred yards away as he called her name. Uncertainly, she turned.

"Mrs. Grant, Sheriff Tate sent me."

She seriously doubted any strange, dangerous drifter would have used an opening line like that. She waited uneasily. The stranger came to a halt some distance away, giving her room to run. It was a reassuring gesture, and she relaxed a little more.

"My name's Ransom Laird," he told her. "Sheriff Tate said you were looking for a hired hand. Said you needed the barn roofed." As he spoke, he dropped the duffel and knapsack to the ground. "I'll work for room and board and fifty dollars a week."

It sounded too good to be true. Most of the hired hands in the area wanted twice that or more in cash every week.

One corner of his mouth curved upward in a faint smile. "Why don't you go call the sheriff and check my references? Then we can talk."

Mandy watched Ransom Laird from the kitchen window as she dialed the Conard County Sheriff's Office. He stood with his hands on his hips, head thrown back, face to the sun. Like a man who couldn't quite believe the beauty of the day. She liked that.

"Yeah, I know him," Nathan Tate said, his voice a gravelly growl. "Known him twenty years, Mandy. He was in my unit in Vietnam, and we kept in touch over the years. He's going through a bad spell, and I thought maybe you two could help each other out. He's okay. You can trust him."

"What kind of bad spell, Nate?"

"That's for him to tell, if he wants."

Mandy smiled into the receiver. In this underpopulated area of Wyoming, Nathan Tate was one of the few people who never indulged in the Conard County passion for gossip. "I should have known better than to ask," she said, and heard Nate's gravelly laugh.

"Well," he said, "if I told you about him, you'd have to wonder what I'd said about you. Now you don't have to wonder."

"That's a point."

"You coming into town tomorrow, sweet face?"

"Yes, it's grocery day." Nate called her funny little names sometimes, but he meant nothing by it. He was the happily married father of six daughters, and he took a brotherly interest in Mandy because her husband had been one of his deputies. John Grant had died in the line of duty four years ago.

"Don't forget to stop by the office for coffee, babe."

"Will do."

She stood by the phone for a few minutes longer, watching Ransom Laird sniff the breeze and soak up the sun. Come to think of it, he did look a little thinner than he ought to. What kind of bad spell?

When she stepped outside again, he turned at once, as if he could feel her presence. She hadn't made a sound.

"Okay?" he said, giving her that half smile again.

"Okay," she said gravely. "Room and board and fifty bucks a week for as long as it's agreeable to us both. Your cabin is on the other side of the barn. There should be enough wood stacked beside the cabin to keep you warm when it cools down tonight, but if there isn't you can find more in the woodshed by the other end of the house. You'll have running water over there, but no hot water, so you can shower here in the bathroom off the kitchen. There's a hot water heater in the barn. If you want to install it in the cabin, you can have hot water there, too. Up to you." John had bought that water heater for the cabin just two days before he got killed.

"Fair enough." He bent to pick up his duffel and knapsack.

"Breakfast is at seven, lunch at one, dinner at six."

She watched him walk south toward the barn and cabin. Except for a very slight hesitation, he walked easily, as if he'd walked an awful lot of miles and had learned how to do it with a minimum of effort. She wondered what his eyes looked like. He hadn't yet gotten close enough for her to see. Then, with a tired sort of sigh, she returned to her weeding. The dry breezes of Conard County were desiccating her, she thought suddenly. All the moisturizers in the world couldn't help her shriveled soul.

Less than an hour later Ransom Laird was on the barn roof. Fatigue jacket abandoned, he walked the gambrel roof with the surefootedness of a cat, pausing often to bend and study a rotted area. Behind the barn he'd found the roofing supplies and plenty of one-inch plywood, enough to sheet the roof before laying the new shingles. It was a job that had needed doing for quite some time, but evidently Mandy Grant hadn't been able to afford it until just lately.

The shingling was a job one man could do, but getting the plywood up would be tough. It would need ingenuity and an extra pair of hands. He wondered how tough Mrs. Grant was.

Inside the barn he studied beams and rafters. The damage appeared to be limited to the roof. The rest of the structure was sound enough. In a corner, under a tarpaulin, he found gallons of red exterior paint. So, painting was next on the agenda. He also found a forty-gallon hot water heater, still in its shipping carton, and enough tools to indicate that the late Mr. Grant had been a hobbyist as well as a handyman.

Suddenly a clanging noise reached him from the distance. Glancing at his nondescript, battered but accurate watch, he saw that it was one o'clock. She was calling him to lunch.

The back door was open, so he stepped in without knocking and found himself in a bright, friendly kitchen. It was a big room, big enough to hold a table that would seat twelve, and it spoke of better times, times when this had been a thriving ranch and big families had lived here. It was so empty now that the ticking of a clock in the next room was audible. At the moment, though, it was full of the delicious aromas of soup and coffee. Two places had been set, far apart, with bowls of chicken soup. Next to one place, his, he supposed, was a plate of sandwiches.

"Take a seat," Mandy said. She stood near the stove, her jeans and sweatshirt covered by a bibbed apron. She pointed to the place with the sandwiches.

He smiled faintly, holding up his hands. "Need to wash first," he said.

She colored then, embarrassed by her oversight, and Ransom became unexpectedly aware that behind that grim, cool exterior lurked a woman. Her auburn hair was bound in an unflattering knot on the back of her head, her figure was completely concealed by the huge sweatshirt and apron, but she was a woman. A woman with sad brown eyes. A woman with soft lips drawn into an unnaturally tight line. A woman.

He turned abruptly in the direction she indicated and found the bathroom. He didn't need this. He didn't want this. He stepped on that small, flickering flame of awareness as ruthlessly as he would have crushed vermin.

His hair, Mandy thought, *was* like molten gold. It looked as if it had just been poured from a crucible, then finely veined with silver. He was older than she had thought at first. He would have to be, to have been in Vietnam with Nate. Outside in the sun, he had looked to be around her age, about thirty. Now, up close, she knew he was at least forty. There was silver in his hair and in his beard. There were deep creases fanning away from his eyes. Blue eyes. Eyes the color of the Conard County sky. Eyes that had looked utterly empty except for one brief flare of something as he looked at her. That flare disturbed her.

Narrow hips, she noticed as he turned to walk away.
Narrow, flat hips. Long legs. Broad shoulders. He was tall,
but not too tall. Compact. Lean. Pared to the essentials.
She'd never liked that body type. John had been a little
stocky, with just enough softness to him to make him hugg-
able. This guy looked too hard to be human. He looked as
if he didn't understand the meaning of indulgence. He
looked as if he were unforgiving of himself.

So why was her heart racing suddenly? Why did she suddenly feel warm and weak? Too much sun in the garden, she
assured herself. Too much sun, and not one damn other
thing.

Taking her seat, she waited for him. Some manners
couldn't be ignored, even with hired help.

John. His memory sighed through her mind like the
warm, dry Wyoming breeze. The pain was long since gone,
leaving only a constant, steady sorrow. John's bright brown
eyes, smiling as he walked through the door after a shift,
reaching for a beer with one hand and Mandy with the
other. His hands. His warm, gentle hands, feeling her belly,
feeling the child he would never see, the child that had been
stillborn the day John was buried. The girl child he had
wanted to name Mary after his mother. Both of them slept
now under a cottonwood.

Looking down, Mandy realized her hands were clasped
tightly over her stomach, as if to hold in the ache. John had
been a man to grow old beside. Life with him had been a
gentle, warm, easy flow, a natural progression of days.

"You okay?" The voice was deep, faintly husky.

Mandy looked up into eyes that weren't brown, into a face
that hinted at things that were neither natural nor easy nor
warm. A face chiseled by extremes and harshness.

"Stomach ache?" Ransom asked.

Mandy shook her head, making an effort to unclasp her
hands. "Memories," she said shortly. "Sometimes I remember."

"Yeah." The husky voice was suddenly softer. "Me too."

He pulled out his chair and sat, waiting. Mandy picked up her spoon, and he followed suit.

"I'll need help with that plywood," Ransom said after a moment. "I can get it up there with the pulley, but it'll take at least two people, and it'd be easier with three."

"My neighbor said he'd lend me a couple of his hands to help with that. When do you want to start?"

"Whenever we can get the help."

We. How easily he linked them together. She didn't know if she liked it. But maybe that was how he looked at things. Maybe he was accustomed to team efforts. She was accustomed, after four years, to solitary ones.

"I'll call Tom after lunch."

"I found the water heater," he continued between mouthfuls of soup. "I was thinking. How old is the water heater in the house here?"

Mandy had to think. "At least six years," she said. "It was here when I married John."

"Then maybe we ought to put the new one in here and move the old one out to the cabin. It might save you some money."

She was surprised by his thoughtfulness. She hadn't expected it. "Makes sense."

Again he gave her that faint smile. "I'll get on it this afternoon. I saw paint in the barn, so I'm assuming you want the barn painted, too?"

"If the weather holds."

"The house could use a coat, too."

"Yes." She looked down at her bowl. "Mr. Laird."

"Ransom. Or Laird. Just skip the mister."

"Ransom," she said, trying it out. "Okay. Look, this isn't a working ranch. It hasn't been one in a long time. John went to work for the Sheriff's Department to pay off the debts his folks left. When ... when John died, his life insurance paid off everything that was left. Except for taxes, utilities and food, I haven't got any expenses. That's the only reason I've been able to keep the place."

"You don't work?"

"I work. I'm a writer. It doesn't make me wealthy. It took me a long time to save the money to buy the roofing supplies. Whether I can paint the house is going to depend on my next royalty check. I need help around here. I can't keep up with it all. That's obvious. You've got a job as long as you want it. But major projects are going to be rare."

"Okay." He pushed aside his soup bowl and reached for the sandwiches.

"Coffee?"

"I'll get it, Mrs. Grant. Well, if that's the way it's gotta be, then fifty bucks a week is too much."

She looked up, astonished. "To keep you hanging around here for what needs doing, it's not too much. Everybody else wants more."

He shrugged. "I don't have any needs. No, let me put that another way. I need a place to sleep, some work to keep me busy and enough cash to keep clothes on my back. I don't go for expensive women, I don't spend Friday nights boozing it up, and I don't even have a truck to put gas into. What I need at this stage in my life is solitude and plenty of thinking time. Make it twenty bucks a week and we've got a deal."

"That's ridiculous. I can't agree to that."

"Sure you can. All you have to do is say yes."

"I won't."

Again he shrugged, reaching for the coffee mug by the plate. Rising, he crossed the kitchen to fill it. "Have it your way," he said presently. "The soup was good. It's been a long time since I had any home cooking."

"Have some more."

"Thanks, but I'm full. I haven't had a chance to work up an appetite yet." He returned to the table, sitting back with his legs loosely crossed. "Were you and your husband planning to work the ranch?"

She hesitated. It had been a long time since anybody had mentioned John in her presence, and here this stranger was talking about him as if it were perfectly natural. Well, it *was* natural. John had lived. He'd been a real human being. He had dreamed and planned, and burying him didn't erase that forever.

"We talked about it. It would have been an awful lot of risky debt, though, and John was happy with the department."

He nodded slowly. "This isn't the world's best climate for farming or ranching."

"No," she agreed. "One bad winter could have wiped us out." Rising, she cleared her place and poured herself some coffee. "We wanted to keep the land. For our children." There was a slight catch in her voice, but it leveled out. "It's like owning a piece of the future."

"What do you write?"

She turned, pulling herself out of memory with an effort. Living alone, she was accustomed to drifting into her own thoughts. "Science fiction. Fantasy."

He smiled suddenly, more than a half smile, and for a moment his eyes didn't look empty. "Great. My favorite stuff. Do you use your own name or a pen name?"

"My maiden name. A. L. Tierney."

He straightened. "I know your stuff. I've read all your books." He looked surprised and pleased. "I've got your latest in my duffel right now. You'll have to autograph it for me."

A smile cracked the bleakness of her face. She was aware, suddenly, of every muscle in her cheeks stretching into the unaccustomed expression. "I'm flattered," she said.

The fan of lines by his eyes deepened. "You ought to be. I'm a picky reader. I'm also a cheap reader. Yours are about the only books I buy in hardcover."

He had thawed her a little with his attempt to cut his own wages, but he thawed her even more with that remark. She knew she had fans—she received the nicest letters from them and treasured every one—but this was the first time she'd met one face-to-face.

"Are you working on something now?" he asked.

"Sort of. It's just starting to gel."

"Maybe you'll let me take a peek at it if I'm a good boy."

There was something very boyish in his hard face at that moment, something genuinely eager and interested, and she melted a little more.

"Maybe," she said. "Maybe."

He nodded. "Thanks. Guess I'd better get to work on the water heater."

"And I'd better call Tom," she said, recalled to the reason he was here. "It might be a couple of days before he can free somebody up."

Ransom shrugged. "There's plenty to keep me busy around here. It's been a while since you had a handyman, hasn't it?"

Mandy nodded. "A while."

"Well, I can paint the trim on the barn while we wait for help."

We, she thought as she watched him walk across the hard ground toward the barn. How easily he said it, as if it were a life-long habit. As if being alone were an unnatural state for him. It was the opposite for her. Except for her marriage, she had been alone all her life. During that all-too-brief period of happiness, *we* had been a word to cherish, a warm, lovely, magical sound. It had never come naturally to her tongue. It had always sent a thrill coursing through her, had always been spoken in a slightly reverent voice.

Mandy's mother had given her up for adoption at birth. Her adoptive parents had died in an auto accident when she was only three, leaving her no legacy but her name: Amanda Lynn Tierney. A lonely, solitary child, she had grown up in a long series of foster homes, escaping finally on a scholarship to the University of Wyoming.

There, in Laramie at the rodeo, she had met John. He was in town for the week and swore that from the minute he set eyes on her sitting in the bleachers, he was head over heels. She was much slower. It had taken John fully three years to overcome her defenses, to unlock the barriers around her heart. Weekend after weekend he drove to Laramie, then to Casper after she graduated, to woo her. Little by little the cold, reserved young English teacher melted. And then, one frosty winter morning, she had opened her eyes to realize that her soul no longer lived only on the pages of the book she was secretly writing. It lived, too, in John's presence, in his smile and gentle eyes, in the tender touch of his lips and hands. Without another moment's hesitation, she had picked up the phone and dialed him at home.

"I love you," she had said when he answered. They were married a week later.

She realized suddenly that she was still standing at the kitchen window, and that steady tears were rolling down her cheeks and dampening the front of her apron. She hadn't cried since they laid little Mary in the ground beside John. That had been the last time. The barriers had slammed into place again right after that. Once again her soul existed only within the pages of her books.

Drawing a deep, shaky breath, she lifted the hem of the apron and wiped her face. She had to call Tom about getting some help with the roof. Then she would wash the lunch dishes and go write for a while. She had a crying need to write. It was the only satisfaction she found in her life.

A funny little lady, Ransom thought as he wrestled the water heater onto a handcart he'd found and repaired. Her books were musical, taking leaping, soaring flights of fancy, full of descriptions that heightened the senses, full of adventure and daring. He never in a million years would have believed that A. L. Tierney could be a closed up, locked up, frozen widow. He'd guessed the writer must be a woman; there was more sensitivity in those books than most men were comfortable with exposing. But this woman? This lost lonely soul in the barren reaches of a desolate western state?

He found himself shaking his head and grinned slightly behind his beard. Well, it was far more interesting to think about Mandy Grant's problems than his own.

He got the heater onto the cart finally and paused for a couple of minutes to wipe the sweat off his forehead and catch his breath. Damn, but he was more out of shape than

he'd thought. Evidently it took more than a few months to
come back from years of confinement and poor diet.

Well, they'd told him it would be a while. He was just so
damned impatient these days. He'd missed so much, lost so
much.

The sun felt good on his face. Throwing back his head, he
closed his eyes and let the heat beat on his skin, feeling the
tingle in every cell. And the air. So fresh, smelling of sage
and not one damned other thing. No stinking bodies, no
human excrement, no rotting flesh. Just clean, fresh air and
sunshine.

"Ransom—"

Mandy came around the corner of the barn and halted
dead in her tracks.

He was standing with his head thrown back, face turned
up to the sun, shaggy, molten gold hair scraping his bare
shoulders. He'd cast aside his shirt and Mandy couldn't
suppress a gasp. His shoulders were broad, but his skin was
too pale, as if he hadn't seen the sun in a long, long time.
And there were scars. Angry scars on his back as if—as if—

She couldn't complete the thought. It was too awful.
Rooted, she couldn't move, could only stare. He'd been
sick, she thought. Very sick. Muscle stood out leanly on
him, as if it had been maintained by hard labor on a near-
starvation diet. His waist was too narrow. Too impossibly
narrow.

Suddenly blue eyes the color of the Conard County sky
looked into hers. Empty eyes. She couldn't speak. Nor, it
seemed, could he.

Suddenly he moved, stepping back swiftly into the shadows of the barn. Mandy turned, running as fast as she could
back to the house. When she got there, she leaned against
the kitchen counter, gasping. What had been done to him?
And by whom? And Lord, he must be so humiliated by the
way she had stared at him, as if he were some kind of freak.

"Mrs. Grant?"

He stood at the kitchen door, shirt buttoned, tails hanging out.

"Mrs. Grant?"

When she didn't answer, he stepped into the kitchen.

"You okay?" he asked in that deep, oddly husky voice.

She managed a nod, trying to catch her breath enough to tell him she was sorry, so sorry....

"I'm sorry," he said quietly. "I shouldn't have had my shirt off. It won't happen again. I'm sorry I upset you. The sun just felt so good—"

And suddenly she rounded on him, rage filling her with white heat. "Don't apologize," she snapped. "If you want to walk around with your shirt off, then you can damn well do it! You can sunbathe in the nude for all I care! Just don't apologize. I'm the one who should apologize. I shouldn't— I never would have—I was just so surprised! I'm the one who's sorry. Now forget it."

He stood staring at her, hands clenching and unclenching at his sides. After a full minute he cleared his throat. "I guess I should warn you that my legs are in kind of the same mess."

She closed her eyes. "How?" she whispered. "Who?"

"I can't tell you that," he said quietly. "I'm very sorry you were upset. I really am. I'll go get that water heater now." He paused, hand on the screen door. "Did you come out to tell me something?"

She managed to open her eyes to meet his gaze steadily. "Tom'll be sending over some help the day after tomorrow. If anything, you'll probably have more help than you want."

"Mighty neighborly," he remarked.

"Tom's a good guy. John, my husband, saved his son's life a long time ago. He's been trying for years to do something for me. Guess it's time I let him. He'll feel better."

Ransom smiled faintly. "That he will. I'm sort of like that myself. Now I owe you one."

"Me?" She blinked. "You don't owe me a thing."

"Sure I do. You just treated me like a human being." With a nod, he stepped out.

Well, of all the odd things to say! Once again she found herself standing at the kitchen window, watching him stride away toward the barn. He looked, she found herself thinking, like a guy who ought to be a hero in a fantasy novel. A mysterious man with a mysterious past, a man who had clearly suffered unbelievable horrors.

Molten gold hair threaded with silver. A lost king? Or maybe just an old soldier who'd opposed evil forces . . .

Hardly aware of what she was doing, she wandered into her office, spinning a character in her mind as she turned on her computer and pulled up her chair. Lost love. There had to be lost love, too.

Ransom found her there later in the afternoon. He'd been working on the hot water heater in the kitchen and had simply followed the rapid tapping of computer keys to the office. Standing in the doorway, he allowed himself to snoop a little. Her back was to him as she typed rapidly at the keyboard. On the walls were wild and wonderful fantasy posters and drawings, many of them autographed. Books filled two large bookcases and spilled onto the floor in random heaps. Brawny-chested warriors and scantily clad women stared back at him from the covers. The haphazard confusion showed a vitality lacking in the rest of the house, and it pleased him somehow.

Quietly, he rapped on the door frame. "Mrs. Grant?"

"Just a sec," she said, tilting her head to one side. She typed for another couple of moments and then sat back as the computer drive whirred, saving what she'd just written.

"Okay," she said, turning in her chair with a faint smile. "Sorry to make you wait."

"Sorry to interrupt genius at work, but I figured you'd want the hot water back on before supper, and I need a hand. Do you mind?"

"Not at all." She stood up immediately and followed him to the kitchen.

"I've got to shove the heater into the closet," he explained, "but I can't see the connections when I do it. The fit's too tight. So if you could give me directions?"

"Sure."

He gripped the heater and shoved while she peered into the small closet.

"Another eight to ten inches," she said when he paused, "and just an inch to the left."

"Okay."

He shoved again, wiggling the heater slightly to the left, and cursed as his knuckles scraped the side of the closet.

"Ransom? Are you okay?"

"Just scraped my knuckles." He gave her a small grin through his beard. "Did you ever know a man who didn't curse when he was doing something like this?"

She felt herself smiling back. "No, I guess not."

"So ignore it." He paused, wiping his brow on his sleeve. "Damn, but I wear out easy these days."

"So take a break," she suggested.

"That's more than my ego can take. Come on, where are we now?"

"Two inches back, and maybe a half to the right."

"The right? Figures I'd go too far. Okay, lady, get your nose out of the way. It looks better straight. And cue me as I push this time."

Two minutes later the heater was in place and Ransom was muttering some colorful curses as he struggled with his big hands in the small space to tighten the connections.

"My hands are smaller," Mandy suggested.

"But I'm the hired hand." He bared his teeth as he gave a last, hard twist. "There! Now the gas."

He stretched out on his back, twisting his head at an angle, and reached for the gas fittings. "You've got propane, right?"

"Right."

There was some clanking and banging, a few more swear words, and it was done. He sat up, looking pleased and pale all at once. "Matches?"

She watched him while he lit the pilot, thinking he looked exhausted.

"Ransom?"

"Yo."

"Why don't you knock off for today?" she suggested. "It's almost four anyway, and you look beat."

He turned his head slowly as the gas burner whooshed on. "Did you hire a hand or are you running a convalescent home?"

She couldn't help it; she smiled ruefully. "A little bit of both, from the look of it." And then, in the endless pause before he answered, she tensed, wondering if he was offended. Probably, she decided uneasily.

He astonished her. "Guess so," he said finally. "From the look of it." And he smiled. "Tell you what. You go back to your writing, and I'll cook dinner. I used to be a pretty good cook, and I wouldn't mind trying my hand at it. Okay by you?"

"Sure, if you promise not to get blood in everything." She pointed to his knuckles. Blood was oozing down his fingers.

He sighed and stood up. "Looks like I'm not old enough to be on my own."

"I'll get the first-aid kit," she said.

"It just needs some soap and water."

"Yeah, but this is a convalescent home, remember?"

His surprisingly deep, husky laugh followed her down the hall. She brought the kit back and left him with it. She figured that she would be pushing him too far if she tried to help. A man who'd been through whatever he had was bound to have a lot of invisible scars, too, and making him feel helpless probably wouldn't be welcomed at all.

Back at her computer, in the minutes before she picked up the thread of her story again, she was surprised to realize that the two of them had gone through a couple of potentially emotional crises today. And they'd only just met this morning—and he was just the hired hand.

Biting her lip, she stared blindly at the computer screen. She had felt things today, she realized uneasily. For the first time in four years, she had felt something for somebody besides herself.

Ransom was feeling uneasy, too. It had been a long time since he'd made so much ordinary contact with another human being. She'd even made him laugh, and he hadn't laughed in years.

He set only one place at the kitchen table and called her when dinner was ready. Then he took his own plate and headed back to his cabin. He needed space, lots of space. At this point he still wasn't sure if the events of the last few years hadn't warped him into something unnatural. By himself, in the clean air and open spaces, he could almost believe himself cleansed and whole.

The cabin consisted of one room, comfortable enough for a man or a couple. He looked forward to building fires in the wood stove and cozying up on cold winter nights. He longed to feel the cold again. At the moment, however, he wasn't ready to be confined, even in coziness. He dragged an old wood rocker onto the covered porch and sat with his plate on his lap. The barn concealed him from the view of Mandy's kitchen windows, but over the edge of the gambrel roof he could see the upstairs windows of the house. His privacy was incomplete.

The day was beginning to blend into evening, the autumn chill creeping back into the air. He imagined that some sunsets would be spectacular from here. This one, however, promised to be a quiet fading. The evening star in the west and the moon in the east were both brightening. The sense of space and freedom was a welcome relief.

After his return, they'd kept him in the hospital for three months, putting steel rods in his legs so he could walk again, breaking and resetting his twisted arm. They'd even given him a new nose and cheekbone. The parasites that had ravaged him for so long had almost proved too tough, but the doctors had finally whipped them. Physically he was clean again, and nearly whole. It was his mind he worried about now. His mind and soul.

While they had him confined, trapped by casts and traction on his legs, they'd sicced a psychiatrist on him. First the guy had told him what he could expect in terms of post-traumatic stress and emotional recovery. He'd laid it out like some kind of unalterable plan of operation, and it was a bleak prospect. Then he tried to get Ransom to talk about it. Beyond hours of official debriefing, Ransom had never said a word about what happened, and not even in debriefing had he mentioned how he felt about it. Somewhere, somehow, during his descent into hell, he had severed all feelings. They were in there somewhere, he figured, and sometimes he thought that if he ever started feeling again it was going to be like a nuclear explosion, leaving him burnt to a cinder. He hoped nobody else got singed by it.

But today he had laughed, really laughed. And he had been touched by a small, grim woman's concern for him. Feelings. Normal, ordinary feelings. He wondered if it was a good sign or a worrisome one. Perhaps he could just keep the last few years entombed forever and pick up where he'd left off, ordinary and normal.

"Ransom?"

It was the persistent Mrs. Grant, coming hesitantly across the hard ground. Lately he'd been annoyed any time his solitude was interrupted. He didn't feel annoyed now, however. Surprisingly, the corners of his mouth were stretching into a smile she couldn't see in the twilight.

"Nice evening," he remarked.

"Yes." She hesitated, halting fifteen feet from where he sat. "I just got back from the mailbox," she said.

"Did you walk? I didn't hear a car."

"I always walk. It's about the only exercise I get."

He waited, sensing there was a purpose to her intrusion.

"Um—I got my new book in today. It's not in the stores yet, but my publisher always sends copies as soon as it's off the press. I brought one for you, if you want it."

Damn, she was touching him again, and he was liking it. Some frozen corner of him thawed by a degree or two.

"Thank you," he said, and there was a surprising amount of warmth in his voice, so much that it caught them both by surprise. Rising, he stepped off the porch and accepted the hardcover volume from her. "This is really great," he said, trying to read the title in the failing light. "Really great. Did you autograph it for me?"

She flushed and was grateful the dusk concealed it. "I thought I'd better ask what you wanted me to say."

"Anything you like. You're the writer."

"Um…" She bit her lip. "Let me take it back to the house for a minute. I need some light and a pen."

He could have provided both in the cabin, but he sensed that would make her uncomfortable. Picking up his dishes, he followed her back to the house. In the bright light, the world took on a more normal cast. He washed his dishes at the sink while she sat at the table, chewing thoughtfully on a pen. After a while, she opened the book to the flyleaf and wrote swiftly.

"There," she said, closing the cover emphatically and handing the book back. "Please don't read it now."

So he carried it back to the cabin and there, by the light of a small lamp, opened it to the inscription. Her handwriting was elegant, perfectly formed.

"To Ransom Laird," she had written. "Wounded warriors rise to fight another day, and lost kings return to rule. Parted lovers meet again, and dreams really do come true. Amanda Lynn Tierney."

He sat for a long time staring at the words. She had tried to tell him something without being too obvious. The words, almost banal, skirted something that wasn't at all banal. Funny, he thought. Mrs. Mandy Grant, with her tight lips and sad eyes, couldn't have written that. Mrs. Grant had no faith in such things. A. L. Tierney, on the other hand, had an abundance of it.

Chapter 2

"Morning, Nate," Mandy said as she stepped into the sheriff's dusty, crowded office. She never called him Nate without wondering at the parents who had long ago named him. Nathan Tate wasn't a bad name, but being called Nate Tate had surely caused him some grief in childhood.

"Morning, Mandy." He was a burly man with a permanently sunburned face. Without apology, he was sinking steadily into the softness of middle age. "Is Ransom working out okay?" he asked as he poured coffee into two chipped mugs and handed her one.

"Fine. Thanks for sending him. Tom Preston is sending over a couple of his men tomorrow to help get the plywood on the barn roof."

"Tom would have done the whole damn job for you, sweet face."

"I know. I couldn't let him."

"John saved his kid's life."

"John was just doing his job, Nate. That's how he always saw it."

"Yeah." Nate looked down at his cup. "That's why everybody liked him, Mandy. He never got full of himself. I could use another dozen like him." Sighing, he looked up with a rueful smile. "I'm sure you do enough grieving, babe. You don't need to listen to me. So Ransom is okay?"

Mandy smiled. "He's just fine. I'm glad you sent him. I even think I like him." She bit her lip and then asked, "Nate, what happened to him? I saw his back yesterday."

"His back?"

"It looks as if—as if he'd been whipped, or beaten." She could hardly get the words out. Everything inside her clenched unpleasantly at the memory of his scars.

His mouth tightened, and for an instant his eyes turned as bleak as a winter prairie. "I didn't know. Mandy, you know I don't gossip."

"Yeah." She sighed and sipped her coffee, knowing Nate wouldn't tell her any more. "He's not real well, whatever happened."

"He's convalescing. I know that much."

"I know that much, too." She saw the grimness in Nate's expression. Clearly, she had shocked him with her remark about Ransom's back. Maybe he didn't know much about what had happened to his friend.

"Whatever he's been doing since Nam," Nate said slowly, "it's hush-hush."

Mandy looked up. "Classified?"

"Yep. That's why neither of us will ever know what happened to him."

"Oh." She'd suspected something like that from the way Ransom had said he couldn't tell her who had done this to him. Possibilities flitted through her head, but she probably couldn't begin to imagine the many hush-hush things people could be involved in. There must be all sorts of federal agencies that employed people in such tasks. The Drug Enforcement Agency. The CIA. The Treasury, with its customs agents, and alcohol, tobacco and firearms people.

Nate leaned forward suddenly, appearing to have reached some kind of decision. "I'll tell you a little more, doll.

You're the only other person in this county who doesn't gossip. Besides, you may run up hard against some of the fallout from it, since you'll see so much of him.

"Ransom married about five years back. He fell for some girl in Washington. He wrote and told me all about her, and mentioned that he was planning to get out of the business and settle down and raise a family. Just one more mission, he said. Said he was going to bring his wife out this way after the baby was born."

Mandy set her cup down. "What happened?" Instinctively, she knew it wasn't going to be pleasant.

"Ransom didn't come back from the mission. His wife sent me his personal effects about a month after he vanished, said they'd mean more to me than her. I called her to see if there was anything I could do to help her with the baby. She told me she'd aborted it and was divorcing Ransom."

"My God!"

"I don't know where he was or what happened, except that he must have been some kind of prisoner all those years. And it sure wasn't finished when he got home."

"I guess not." She knew the pain of losing a baby you never had the chance to hold. She couldn't begin to imagine how it would feel to know your baby had been deliberately killed. "How long has he been back?"

Nate shrugged. "I'm not sure. He called me for the first time in April. Said he was stuck in the hospital and that they were piecing him back together. That's when I made him promise he'd come for a visit. I expected him to be a guest for a week or two, Mandy. I didn't expect him to come hiking into town like he did, looking for work. To tell you the truth, this isn't the Ransom I used to know. That guy was driven, aggressive. I always figured he'd wind up the top dog in some big agency."

"He probably just needs a breather, Nate," Mandy said reassuringly. "I mean, whatever he's been through must have been terrible, and then to come home and find out he didn't have a wife or a child—"

"Yeah." Nate turned toward the window and sipped his coffee. "One of my buddies was a POW in Nam. It took him a while to get his feet under him when he got back. By the time he got it together, he was divorced. Four years is a long time. A man can be changed forever in a lot less time than that. And it can take a hell of a long time for him to find himself again."

A hell of a long time, Mandy thought. Especially if you had been a prisoner and had been mistreated.

They talked for a while longer in a general way about the weather, the upcoming Harvest Dance, the approaching county elections. Nate was standing unopposed as usual, but the county commissioner seats were being hotly contested.

"Marge has got her raspberry preserves put up again," Nate told Mandy as he walked her to the door. Marge was his wife of twenty-four years. "Said she put aside the jars you asked her for last spring."

"Guess I'll stop by and get them on the way home. See you in a couple of weeks."

At the door he smiled down at her, touching her shoulder. "You need anything at all, you just holler."

"Thanks, Nate." Standing on tiptoe, she brushed a friendly kiss on his cheek, then stepped out into the sunshine.

She had taken only two steps along the sidewalk when she had the overwhelming feeling that someone was watching her. She turned immediately, expecting to see Nate or one of her other acquaintances, but among the many people walking on the street, she recognized no one.

Turning toward her truck again, she came face-to-face with Micah Parish, the man who had replaced John as deputy. He was an enigma, a half-breed who wore his black hair to his shoulders despite local prejudices, and who seldom had anything to say. All anyone knew about him was that he was a career military man who had served with Nate in Southeast Asia. And that he was a good, if taciturn, deputy.

"Morning, Miz Grant," he said politely, touching the brim of his Stetson hat.

"Good morning, Deputy." Mandy hesitated, suddenly aware that in the last four years she and Micah Parish had passed many of these aloof greetings, but had never exchanged anything more. Perhaps he felt she resented his taking John's place. Perhaps, unconsciously, she had. Suddenly it seemed important to let him know that any resentment on her part was gone. "Maybe you should call me Mandy," she suggested with a tentative smile. "Four years seems like an awful long time to go on being so formal with one another."

Micah Parish smiled even less frequently than he spoke, but just now one corner of his mouth hitched upward and made him look a little less remote, a little less chilly. "Reckon I'll give it a try, Mandy. If you call me Micah."

Satisfied, she smiled broadly, bid him good day and headed for her truck. First she would go to Marge Tate's for the raspberry preserves, and then she would go to the supermarket. It sure was a pleasant morning.

This time when she felt the back of her neck prickle, she ignored it. Micah Parish was probably watching her walk away.

"Nate," the woman had called the uniformed man who had come out of the building with her a few minutes ago, unwittingly identifying Ransom's friend. The woman was of no significance beyond pointing out the sheriff, nor was the deputy with whom she had just spoken. The sheriff was the one to watch. Sooner or later Ransom would turn up here, because Nathan Tate was an old friend. It was pleasant waiting here on the sun-drenched street, so pleasant that patience was easy to come by.

Two hours later Mandy was pulling up to the house with enough groceries to feed her and Ransom for a couple of weeks and a dozen jars of raspberry preserves on the seat beside her. Just as she was braking at the back door, something under the hood exploded loudly and white smoke billowed everywhere.

"Damn!" she swore, pounding her hand on the steering wheel. Just what she needed.

Suddenly the truck's door flew open and strong arms seized her, pulling her from the seat and carrying her free of the clouds of smoke.

"Mandy! Are you okay?"

She looked up into Ransom's concerned face as they emerged into the brilliant noon sunlight. This was absurd, she thought. He was carrying her as if she weighed nothing at all, like a hero out of one of her books.

"I'm fine," she said drily. "The truck's not. I think that was my radiator."

She watched as his concern was transformed into embarrassment. He had reacted like a man accustomed to life-threatening situations. It had never occurred to her that she might be in danger. It had never occurred to him that she might not be. She didn't have the heart to embarrass him further by asking him to set her down, so she simply waited.

And had time to realize that he smelled good: musky, soapy, masculine. And that his chest was hard, and regardless of whatever he'd been through, his muscles were like steel just now, holding her effortlessly. And his mouth, largely unnoticed because of his beard, was firm and well-shaped. She stared at it, her gaze fixated. Time seemed to stand still.

Slowly he slackened his hold and let her feet slide to the ground. Mandy was aware of every single hard contour of his body as her legs slid downward against him. Too thin, she thought, but every inch a man.

"Sorry about that," he said with a faintly sheepish smile.

"Don't be." Carefully she stepped away. "I always wondered what it would be like to have somebody come dashing to my rescue and carry me away to safety. Now I know."

"Silly, huh?"

A smile caught the corners of her mouth, softening her whole face. "Only because it was a radiator and not a bomb.

The effect was the same." Turning, she looked at her still-steaming truck. "Double damn!" she said in exasperation.

"Your only transportation?"

"Yeah."

He put his hands on his hips. "I'll look at it when it cools off, Mrs. Grant. I used to be a passable mechanic."

"Mandy," she said. "Call me Mandy. Guess I'd better get the groceries in before everything thaws." *Used to be,* she thought. She wondered how many *used to's* there were in his life.

Mandy spent a singularly unproductive afternoon. Waking from a long sleep, she thought uneasily when she realized she was back at the kitchen window for the fifth time, staring out at Ransom as he worked under the hood of her truck. Never in her life had she been so conscious of a man's physical attributes or her own sexuality as she was right now.

Funny, she thought, leaning against the counter, staring frankly at the way Ransom's buttocks stretched the worn denim of his jeans as he bent over. All these years she'd believed that she was either undersexed or that sex was overrated. With John it had been a comfortable, warm, affectionate experience, and with his death she thought she'd buried her meager desires. Suddenly her desires were very much alive and not at all meager.

Now, here she was staring at Ransom as if he were a pinup. That was something she'd thought only men did, but here she was looking him over like . . . She flushed and left that thought incomplete. Instead she wondered what his skin would feel like under her hands.

Shrugging, feeling like a silly kid, she shoved her hands in her jeans pockets and went outside. Drawn, like the moth to a flame. The uncomfortable thought crossed her mind and then vanished as Ransom looked up from beneath the truck hood and smiled.

"You blew a radiator hose," he said. "No big deal. The explosion was a backfire."

"Not the radiator?"

"Nope, just a coincidence. The carburetor needs some work, but I can do that. It'll cost you maybe seven bucks for a new hose. I can jury-rig it until you can get to town."

The afternoon was warm, and perspiration plastered his shirt to his back. He would have taken it off if she hadn't been there. The thought made her even more uneasy. It reminded her of the scars. The suffering.

"That's a relief," she managed to say. "I was figuring two or three hundred dollars."

He straightened, wiping his hands on a rag. His blue eyes settled on her, growing thoughtful as they passed over her face. "Did you see Nate in town?"

She nodded, feeling herself color faintly.

"How much did he tell you?"

Her eyes widened. Apparently this man didn't miss a detail.

He shrugged, giving her a lopsided smile, as if to say it didn't matter. "He doesn't gossip. Much. But I figure you're bound to be curious, and he's bound to be concerned, and between the two, there's going to be some talk."

He tucked the rag into his back pocket and paused, looking out over the prairie toward the blue line of the western mountains. "Beautiful country," he said. "Nate doesn't know much, but he's always been good at putting two and two together. It's why he's a good cop." Slowly his eyes came back to her face. "I guess we both spent the last four years in prison."

A soft gasp escaped her. It was true, she realized. But not exactly. She hadn't been living in a prison but inside a fortress. And she wanted to stay there, so what was she doing out here, talking to this man who kept making her feel things?

"So," he said softly, "what were you thinking when you were standing at the kitchen window?"

For the second time that afternoon, time stood still. Mandy didn't even breathe. And then, hardly believing what she was doing, she reached for his shirt. It was unbuttoned, exposing a chest covered with fine golden hair. Carefully, she pushed it off his shoulders. He was holding his breath, too, she realized. He was rigid, taut, motionless. When she had pushed it to his elbows, she walked around behind him. Still he didn't move a muscle. He might have been made of stone.

She made herself look at the crosshatch of scars as she pulled his shirt the rest of the way off. She was sure he must feel her eyes on his back as if her gaze were fire. Then, freeing him of the shirt, she balled it up and hurled it across the yard.

The muscles of his back jerked sharply, but he didn't move. Reaching up, she laid her palms flat against his shoulders, lightly, soothingly.

"I told you," she said quietly, "that you didn't have to wear your shirt. Enjoy the sun, Ransom. You haven't had any in a long time."

Turning, she walked back to the house.

He didn't show up for dinner that evening. It was just as well, Mandy thought. She still couldn't believe what she'd done, and she didn't know how she was going to look him in the eye. Any way you looked at it, taking a man's shirt off was a blatant invitation, no matter how it was intended. And she wasn't sure herself just how she *had* intended it. She had felt possessed.

In fact, to come right down to it, she didn't know what was happening to her. Waking from a long sleep, she had thought earlier, and it was the best description she could think of. That or recovering from paralysis. It was as if something compelled her to reach out to Ransom. First the book and then that little scene this afternoon. Maybe she just recognized a kindred spirit, a fellow paralytic. But that didn't explain the swift rush of sexual feeling she'd had.

Damn, she thought, and buried herself in her office. Damn, damn, damn. John had awakened her once with his slow, gentle persistence, but it had been nothing like this. This was fast, somehow out of control. Dangerous. She couldn't let this happen. Somehow, she had to get a grip on herself before she got hurt.

"Mandy?"

She was sitting in the near dark, a small desk lamp illuminating the computer keyboard, the light from the display casting an amber glow on her face. She swiveled her chair quickly and saw Ransom standing in the doorway, a shadow.

"Ransom!" The exclamation escaped her. Something coiled inside her, a tension she didn't know how to name. She'd never felt it before.

"I knocked," he said. "You didn't hear. I knew you were in here. I saw you through the window when I came walking up."

She managed a nod. If her mouth got any drier it would stick shut forever.

He took one step into the room. "I got to thinking about—hell, I just wanted to tell you to forget it. I figured you were maybe worrying about it...."

He couldn't find the words to explain, but she understood anyway. He was telling her not to be embarrassed, that it was okay. He had understood how she would be feeling. It amazed her, his sensitivity.

"I thought you were mad," she admitted, her voice little better than a croak. "It was...it was..." She couldn't find the words, either.

"It's okay," he said. "I understand. I understood. I didn't come for dinner because—I wasn't mad, Mandy."

"Okay," she said. Words were so inadequate sometimes, she found herself thinking. A traitorous thought for a wordsmith, but she and Ransom were both communicating more with what they weren't saying. "Thanks for telling me." She managed a brief, brittle laugh. "I *was* worrying."

"I figured. I feel like I kind of know you. Because of your books, I guess." He paused, edged a little closer. "I was...I was *touched*. I haven't been touched in a hell of a long time."

"Me either." Understanding somehow that it was not easy for him to admit such a thing, that it made him feel exposed, she felt she owed him similar honesty—especially since he was forcing himself to admit his feelings in order to ease her embarrassment.

"I know." He sighed. "Anyhow, I didn't take it wrong, so don't worry."

She drew a deep breath, cleared her throat. "Have a seat. If you want." Now, she thought, was her chance to make sure he hadn't misunderstood *anything,* despite his assurances.

He looked around in the dark and picked out the easy chair. John had often sat there in the evenings when Mandy got carried away with her writing. She didn't mind Ransom sitting there.

"I'll tell you a little story," she said slowly. "If you want to hear it."

"I do, but only if it begins with 'Once upon a time.'"

She smiled at that. She liked the way he thought, the way he defused the moment.

"Okay. Once upon a time there was a princess born to a queen who was fleeing from her enemies. The queen couldn't keep the baby princess, so she gave her up to a nice rancher and his wife, who promised to cherish the princess forever and gave her a new name to protect her from the queen's enemies. The nice couple kept the princess safe and loved for a few years, and then they were killed by an awful dragon. So the little princess was passed from family to family in the community. Nobody ever wanted her for very long, because she was an odd child with odd fancies of being a lost princess. And the princess never knew who she really was. She only *believed.*"

Ransom drew a long breath. "Poor little princess," he said softly.

"She didn't feel poor, precisely. But she felt very, very lonely, as if something were missing, as if she didn't really belong. And she learned very rapidly not to care, because every time she cared, she lost the people she cared for. And always, always, she had the conviction she was someone else. You see?"

"Yes."

"So she grew up with her head filled with fairy tales. She created worlds where people didn't go away forever, where she could be herself, her real self, and people loved her. All of which made her even odder. She became a teacher eventually, because she loved words, but there was always a sense of waiting, as if at any moment her own people would discover her and claim her.

"One day, at a great tournament, a knight saw her and fell in love with her. The princess found him to be all that was gentle and kind and honorable, but she was afraid to care for him, because she was convinced, you see, that every time she cared for someone, an evil wizard cast a spell to take that person away from her. It was the only explanation. The princess tried to tell herself it wasn't true, that it was just a silly fancy, but there wasn't any other possible explanation."

"I can see why she felt that way," Ransom said, very softly.

Mandy shrugged a little. "Well, the knight was persistent. He wooed the princess for three years, and one morning the princess woke up and discovered it was already too late. She cared. It had happened when she wasn't looking. So she rode off to the knight's castle, and her days were filled with warmth and happiness. And then the evil wizard found out about her happiness and her knight and her unborn baby, and he cast a spell on them all."

Ransom drew a sharp breath, but he said nothing.

"The princess vowed she would never care again. It made her an even odder person, I can tell you. But still, inside her, was the belief that someday, somewhere, she would be found by those who would love her and protect her from the wizard. Someone would recognize her eventually, someone who would know how to defeat the evil wizard."

She paused, turning to stare at the computer screen, where amber words glowed at her.

"One day a warrior came walking up to the nearly deserted castle. He was battered, nearly broken. He'd fought a great many evil wizards, and the marks were all over him. The princess saw him and knew immediately that he had suffered as much as she had had and more. He gave her a little courage, and the princess cared. Just a little. Not enough to draw the evil wizard's attention, mind you. She wouldn't risk that. The warrior had suffered enough, and so had she. But she cared just that little and wanted very badly to heal the warrior so far as her small herbs and potions might help. She wasn't quite sure how to do that, but she offered him shelter and tried to let him know his wounds touched her. That she understood he wasn't a battered, beaten warrior, but that he was in reality a lost king who would eventually come into his own. And being the odd person she was because of her odd life and her odd notions, she went about it in a rather odd way."

Holding her breath, Mandy looked back at him, grateful that the dim light made it almost impossible for either of them to read the other's face.

"The warrior," she continued, "had a kind heart and put up with the princess's odd ways. Unfortunately, I can't tell you how the tale ends yet."

"I can tell you the next paragraph," Ransom said quietly.

"You can?"

"Sure. I happen to know the warrior." He pushed himself out of the easy chair and caused her to gasp by kneeling right in front of her.

"The warrior was touched," he said. "Touched more deeply than he had been in years. It moved him that the princess who had lost so much still had enough compassion to care about his wounds. He was wary of the evil wizard, though, so instead of taking a warrior's vow to protect the castle forever, he simply took the princess's hand in his." As he spoke, Ransom took both of her hands. "And he told her that as far as he was able, he would help her out. And he sealed the promise not by swearing fealty, but by asking for the princess's colors to carry on his lance. This was a small thing, and wouldn't attract the wizard's notice.''

And as he spoke, he leaned forward and touched his soft, warm lips to hers. Just a touch. Just enough to waken a sleeping heart to a half-sleeping state.

"And then the warrior got quickly to his feet, because he hadn't carried a princess's colors in a long time, and he wasn't really sure he was quite up to it yet, and he bade the princess good night and went out to the stable to sleep with his horse, determined to do nothing that might hurt the princess.''

He leaned forward again, kissing her a little more firmly, yet demanding nothing. His lips moved warmly against hers. Then he stood up.

"Goodnight, Mandy.''

She sat in the dark long after he left, realizing he had just returned the gesture she had made in the yard that afternoon. They had laid soothing hands on one another's scars.

Four of Tom Preston's men arrived at seven-thirty the following morning to begin roofing the barn. By eight the yard was full of hammering, banging, swearing and joking. Convalescent or not, Ransom worked and joked as hard as anybody. When the men trailed into the kitchen for lunch, a huge meal of roast beef, potatoes and apple pie that Mandy had slaved over all morning, she noticed he was pale and his hands trembled. There wasn't a thing she could do or say about it, however. Taking a cup of coffee, she slipped away to her office, leaving the men to enjoy their meal without a woman hovering over them.

At five, with a roar of pickup engines, Preston's men left, and silence returned to the ranch. The barn roof was completely sheeted with plywood and tar paper, and packages of shingles had been distributed at neat intervals. From here on out, Ransom could finish the job alone.

He stood with his hands on his hips, his legs splayed, staring up at the roof. It had been a devil of a long time since he had felt such a sense of accomplishment and satisfaction. He could easily get addicted to living like this, he realized: hard physical labor with visible results, open spaces, neighborly people.

"Ransom? You want some coffee or a beer?"

Turning, he saw Mandy poking her head out the back door. "In a minute," he called back. "I want to clean up first." And what a luxury that still was to him, to be able to step into a hot shower and clean clothes. One thing for damn sure: he'd learned to appreciate the small things.

Half an hour later he stepped into the kitchen, hair still damp, and accepted a beer from Mandy, who was putting together a meal of hot beef sandwiches from the lunch leftovers. She stole a glance at him from the corner of her eye.

"You kind of pushed it today, didn't you?" she remarked.

He leaned back, crossing his legs loosely at the ankles. Behind his beard, the corners of his mouth quirked. "I'm still upright," he replied.

"I'm not paying you enough to kill yourself with overwork."

"No danger of that." He sipped his beer. "You're new to this hired help business, aren't you?"

"What do you mean?"

"You treat me like a guest. Or a friend. I can almost feel the guilt radiating from you when I work. Ease up, Mandy. I'm doing what I want to, and I'm happy with the arrangement. And you aren't underpaying me."

With a fork she lifted slices of beef from the simmering gravy and laid them on bread. He was right, she supposed. She was uneasy with the situation, and that was stupid. She was, after all, paying him exactly what he'd wanted for the job.

"You looked worn-out at lunch," she said. "I know it's none of my business, but I was worried about it." She put the steaming, gravy-drenched sandwiches on the table. "Just promise me you'll break when you need to. Then I won't have to worry, and I'll leave you alone."

He let her see the smile he was feeling. "I promise. I *do* have some common sense."

Mandy sat across from him, not nearly so far away as at the first meal they had shared. "Broccoli?" she offered, passing the plate. "John always said I was a natural mother hen and that I worried far too much. He used to tease me about whether I was born this way or if it was teaching that did it to me. He never did make up his mind. And I'm still a mother hen." She looked up with a small smile. "I'll try to curb the impulse."

"You'll get over it when you realize I'm practically indestructible," he said wryly. "Even *I'm* a little surprised at how durable I am."

Her eyes dropped. He wondered how those eyes would look soft and warm with longing. "I bet," she said after a moment. "*Very* durable, from what I can tell."

"There, you see?" he said, gently teasing. "I don't claim to leap tall buildings or be faster than a speeding bullet. I just hold up. I'm like that old pair of jeans you can never throw away because they just won't wear out no matter what you do. They look like hell and you can't wear 'em to town, but you can crawl on concrete in 'em and they just won't tear."

A chuckle escaped her. "I get the picture. I'll shut up."

He shook his head slowly, catching her eye. "I don't want you to shut up. I don't mind your mother-henning. It's sort of nice, actually. But every time you do, I'm going to look at you and say, 'old blue jeans.'"

She laughed outright, and her sad brown eyes sparkled for the first time since he'd met her. She was pretty, he thought suddenly. He hadn't noticed it before. Quietly pretty. And he had the sudden conviction that she had the potential to be beautiful. Not all the time; not like an actress or a model. Just sometimes, at very special moments. It required some effort to return his attention to his plate. No, he told himself, he didn't need this. Not at this stage of his life.

"If you keep feeding me this way, Mandy, I'm going to be back up to my fighting weight in no time."

Her gaze was drawn to him again. His fighting weight. Ten pounds heavier? Twenty? She couldn't imagine him any other way than he was right now, missing gauntness only by a hairbreadth. Her palms suddenly burned with the memory of how his skin had felt beneath them. Smooth. Warm. Boy, did she have it bad!

"How about you?" he asked conversationally. "Is your new story coming together?"

"I think so. A little at a time, at any rate."

"What's this one about?"

Hesitantly at first, then with increasing confidence as he displayed interest and asked questions, she talked about her ideas. As she spoke, they grew clearer in her mind, and almost before she knew it, the entire story was falling into place.

They finished dinner and washed the dishes together, still talking about her book. As naturally as if they did it every day, they took coffee into her office. Ransom sat in the easy chair. Mandy perched on her steno chair and put her feet up on the edge of a desk drawer.

And still she talked. A dam had broken; words rushed forth. This was A. L. Tierney, Ransom realized, the woman who existed behind Mandy Grant's defenses. She emerged as if from a chrysalis, hands moving descriptively, eyes shining. She was caught up in the excitement of her vision, brought to life by a fantasy. Released momentarily from the evil wizard's spell, she dared to share herself.

"I like it," he said when she at last fell silent, head cocked thoughtfully as she considered her newborn story. "How long does it take you to write the book once it comes together?"

"A few months for the first draft. That's the easy part. Rewrites are the killer."

He was a little amazed. He couldn't imagine that writing the first draft of one of her wonderful books could be easy. But that, he supposed, was the difference between a writer and a nonwriter.

"Your books were the first ones I asked for when I could read again," he said suddenly, instinctively understanding what it would mean to her. "I'd read *Talespinner* when it first came out, and I loved it. So when they asked me what I wanted to read when I was recovering, you were the first author I thought of." He saw her face soften perceptibly. He wished she could look soft like that all the time.

"John never read it," she remarked. "He was tickled for me, but he wasn't much of a reader."

"So you couldn't talk your stories over with him?"

"Not really. He encouraged me, and he was proud of what I did, but it wasn't something we shared." She sounded factual about it, not sad or disturbed. "More coffee, Ransom? I think I want some."

He followed her to the kitchen, and while she made a fresh pot, he stepped out onto the porch. The night sky was beautiful, scattered with bigger, brighter stars than he'd even seen.

"Mandy? Come on out. The sky's beautiful. I wish I had a telescope."

"I have one somewhere," she said, coming to the screen door. "Maybe it's in the attic. I'll look for it tomorrow."

The springs groaned as she pushed the door open and came to stand beside him at the rail. The night air had grown chilly, and she wrapped her arms around herself as a shiver took her.

"Here," Ransom said. He stepped behind her and drew her back against his chest, covering her arms with the warmth of his own. For an instant she resisted; then he felt her relax and lean back against him.

He was so warm, she thought, and it felt so good to be held again, even casually. She had nearly forgotten how good it felt to have arms around her. Somehow she just plain couldn't heed her mind's warnings that this was dangerous. It was only for a couple of minutes, after all. Surely she was entitled to be held for just a couple of minutes. What harm could it do?

His voice was a low, husky rumble just above her head. "Thank you," he said.

"For what?"

"This. Night after night I went to sleep imagining myself standing free under the stars, holding...holding a lovely woman."

"Your wife," she said softly. For some reason her heart squeezed.

He sighed. "Damn Nate. Yeah. Only as time dragged on, I knew it wouldn't be her. I knew she wouldn't stick it out for long. Certainly not that long."

"I'm sorry, Ransom."

"I'm not. Not after what she did."

Mandy said nothing, uncertain whether he would be upset if he learned she knew about his child.

His arms tightened fractionally. "I knew it was over. I knew it for a long, long time. So I replaced her."

"With whom?"

"Whom?" He chuckled softly. "Your English degree is showing, A. L. Tierney. Nobody real. A dream. A fantasy. A sweet, sweet fantasy. My priorities got turned around. Nothing I used to think was important seems important now. And things I didn't think much about have become very important."

"I can see how that might happen," she said when she sensed he expected a response. "It would be weird if you weren't affected."

"So they tell me. They also tell me I'll have nightmares for years and all kinds of hang-ups. So far I haven't even had a dream, let alone a nightmare. I think I got nightmared-out a long time ago."

"Maybe."

"But I didn't get dreamt-out. Funny, but the dreams are starting to come again. Not sleep dreams. Life dreams."

"Then you'll be okay, Ransom."

"Like old blue jeans," he said.

Mandy smiled into the dark. "Like old blue jeans," she agreed.

"You, too," he said. "You're old blue jeans, too."

"I'm afraid I have a few holes."

"Nah. Faded a little bit here and there, maybe. So am I. But not worn out, Ms. Tierney. Not worn out."

She noticed his use of her maiden name and wondered if he had somehow sensed the dichotomy that was so much a part of her nature. Again his arms tightened, just a fraction more, but responding to the implied invitation, she let her head fall back against his shoulder, and together they watched the stars.

"Nice," he said a while later.

"The stars are really bright tonight," she agreed.

"I meant you, Mandy. Holding you. It's nice. It feels just the way I hoped it would all those years."

She caught her breath. "Ransom?" Suddenly, she had to know, even if it meant flirting with danger.

"Yeah?"

"Was that your whole fantasy?"

"No. But I have no intention of asking you to fulfill a dream, so relax." He paused. "However, it's been a hell of a long time since I held a woman, and I'm either going to have to let you go or kiss you."

Her heart started to hammer so hard that she felt almost breathless. She knew he would let her step away right now if she made the slightest move. She also knew that if she stayed where she was, he was going to kiss her. All her self-protective instincts were suddenly muffled, distant. A warm, hazy heat filled her. "I'm a great believer in dreams coming true." *Liar,* said that small, objective voice in her mind that never shut up. You believe in dreams in your books, but not in life. Not in life.

Slowly, very slowly, he took her shoulders and turned her to face him. "Are you?" he asked, his husky voice soft.

"I believe in warriors and princesses and lost kings, don't I?" Her voice was hardly more than a whisper.

"And evil wizards," he reminded her gently.

Holding her breath she raised her eyes. His face was a pale blur in the little bit of light from the stars.

"And evil wizards," she admitted. "But maybe there's a talisman—"

"No talisman," he said almost grimly as his arms closed around her and drew her carefully against his steely length. "No talisman. Just hope."

He lowered his head and touched her mouth with his. His beard was surprisingly soft, silky, his mouth warm and gentle. Aching for the caress, she let her head fall back and let her arms find their way around his waist. A too thin waist, but it hardly mattered suddenly as his heat and strength filled her senses. His tongue found hers with a surety that seemed to proclaim that he already knew her this way from another time, another place, that he knew exactly how she liked to be kissed, how she liked to be cradled. There were no false starts, no tentative movements. It was knowing. It was right.

Mandy felt safe. Security washed through her, along with the rising tide of pleasure he elicited in her. His arms sheltered her so securely that all thoughts of evil wizards and spells vanished. She clung, hands creeping up his back to his shoulders, crossing ridges of scar tissue that could be felt even through his shirt, crossing them gently like a familiar, cherished landscape. One hand found his silky molten-gold hair, sliding into it. He fit her perfectly, she thought dreamily. Not too tall or too short. Just right.

"Mandy." One of his arms held her shoulders; the other was wrapped around her waist. He held her tightly, pressing his cheek to hers. "Sweet Mandy," he sighed, and rocked her gently side to side. He made no effort to conceal the need she had aroused in him, but simply waited for it to pass away into tenderness.

"Ransom?"

He could hardly hear her, even in the silent night. "Yes?"

"That was absolutely the nicest kiss anybody's ever given me."

His embrace was suddenly almost fierce, and the softest of chuckles escaped him. "For me, too, Mandy. We'll have to try it again sometime."

"Definitely."

As he released her, she stepped back, and he could see the softness of her face. He hoped suddenly that no evil wizards were watching.

"Have you ever felt," she asked, "that you've lived before?"

"Often," he acknowledged.

She cocked her head, regarding him steadily. "Then maybe I'm not crazy."

"Crazy?"

"I feel as if we go back a long way. A very long way. I hope the karma's not bad." She reached up suddenly, touching his cheek with gentle fingers. "Thank you. Sweet dreams. You deserve them."

The screen door slapped closed behind her, and then the kitchen light went out. She hadn't locked him out, he realized. She hadn't barred the door against him. Hell, she hadn't even closed it. That was an awful lot of trust for a scared princess to be showing in a wounded warrior who'd walked into her castle just three short days ago.

Smiling, he opened the screen door and pulled the inner door shut before he turned and headed back to his cabin. Every time he thought he had her pegged, she turned around and surprised him again.

Chapter 3

Mandy hardly saw Ransom over the next week. He spent long hours on the roof laying shingles and took his meals with her in quick silence, never lingering for a cup of coffee afterward. He was filling out rapidly, she noticed, growing sturdier by the day, and the sun was returning the color to his face and torso. As for his withdrawal, she was at once relieved and disappointed. They'd moved too swiftly, she felt, strangers who had somehow touched one another too deeply for their brief acquaintance. Perversely, however, she missed his easy companionship. After four years of solitude, the brief taste of friendship had left her hungry for more. And that was why his withdrawal relieved her. Surely she had learned that caring only meant pain. Surely she didn't need to learn that all over again.

On Sunday she walked over to his cabin to ask if he wanted to go to church with her. As she rounded the barn, she saw him cutting across the fields and heading out into the open spaces. He needed a horse, she thought. For that matter, so did she. She'd sold the horses after John's death because there just didn't seem to be any point in all the work and expense when she was sure she would never want to ride again.

On the way to church, she considered the idea and felt herself smiling. They definitely needed horses. Loners both, they needed to be able to gallop off away from everything. A warrior especially needed a horse. She felt bubbles of laughter rising in her throughout the service, and afterward a couple of people remarked on her high spirits, wanting to know if something nice had happened.

Nothing had, she thought, driving home. Nothing had happened except that incredibly, wonderfully, she was simply glad to be alive. The autumn days were perfect—dry, clear, with just a hint of crispness in the air to make an invigorating contrast to the sun's warmth. Her marigolds still bloomed riotously around the house, but the first frost was fast approaching. Now, she thought, now was the perfect time to saddle up and ride out to see the last wildflowers, the last green leaves, the last lovely blaze of dying summer.

So she called Tom Preston. She thanked him again for his help with the roof and assured him that Ransom was handling the shingles just fine on his own.

"Actually, Tom, I have another favor to ask, if you don't mind."

He chuckled. "I been waiting a long time to do you a few favors, gal. Fire away."

"I've decided I want horses again. I don't know a thing about judging horseflesh, though, or tack, for that matter. I was hoping you could advise me."

"I'd be delighted, Mandy. What kind of horses do you have in mind?"

"A nice, gentle lady's mount for me, and something suitable for Ransom to ride fence on."

"Fence, huh? You thinking about starting a herd?"

Mandy blinked. She *was,* she realized. "I guess I am," she said after a moment. "John and I used to talk about it a lot." On long winter evenings when dreams were spun out of the gossamer of love and hope. So much, so incredibly

much, had been lost. She closed her eyes momentarily
against remembered pain.

"John would have made a great rancher, Mandy. It was
in his blood." Tom's voice had softened a shade, just a
shade, as if he'd guessed the direction of her thoughts.

"Well, I don't know if it's in mine." Her voice was steady,
hiding, as she had always hidden, the depths of her feelings. "I have all winter to think about it. In the meantime,
I thought I'd have Ransom take a look at the fence and see
how much I need to do. Then I'll have to figure out if I can
afford it."

"Some things are never affordable," Tom said drily.
"You just have to afford them anyhow."

She smiled, and some corner of her mind noted that it was
getting easier to do that. Just a little easier. "But I don't
have to, Tom. I'm not into it yet. As it is, I never mind it if
a neighbor's cattle stray into my grazing land. I'm not sure
they'll feel the same if mine do the straying because I haven't
mended my fences."

He laughed. "Good point. Well, if you want horses, I can
send over a couple today. Tack, too. If you like the looks of
them, you can have the kit and caboodle for a song."

"Tom, I can't—"

"Sure you can. I was trying to sell off a few head anyhow. Never ceases to amaze me how much a horse can eat
over a winter. And the kids don't come home like they used
to, Mandy. I just plain don't need to keep 'em hanging
around eating their heads off."

"Fair market value, Tom. I insist."

"Mandy, you wouldn't know fair market value if it stood
up and bit you on the nose. Tell you what. I promise to give
you a deal that's fair to us both. You want me to have Jim
bring them over?"

Ransom hiked back into the barnyard that afternoon
feeling better than he had in a while. He'd walked long
enough and hard enough to stretch every muscle in his body
and to beat back his private demons with weariness. It oc-

curred to him that he owed Mandy an apology for his withdrawal over the past week. He'd kissed the woman, after all, and then had pulled back so far into his private hell that she must be wondering if she'd somehow disgusted him.

As he rounded the corner of the barn, he found Jim Preston, Tom's oldest son, off-loading a gray horse from a trailer. Mandy stood a few feet away, holding a chestnut horse by its halter. She was laughing. She was actually laughing, with her head thrown back and locks of auburn hair falling loose from her habitual bun. Ransom came to a dead halt, unable to believe the transformation in her.

And then Jim Preston laughed, too, as the horse he was leading sidled and bumped him. Ransom saw the gentle way Preston looked at Mandy. Was that the way the wind blew? Shoving his hands into his jeans pockets, he sauntered up to them.

"Ransom, look!" Mandy's eyes were bright as she saw him. "Aren't they beautiful?"

"Beautiful," he agreed, a smile briefly softening the bleakness of his blue eyes. "You two going for a ride?"

Something flickered quickly over Mandy's smiling face, so quickly he couldn't interpret it. He was left with the impression that she was somehow disappointed, but before he could weigh the feeling, Jim spoke.

"Not me, Ransom. You. And what's more, you get to muck out their stalls every morning. It's two less for me to tend to." He smiled at Mandy. "Let's get them saddled and you can try them out, Mandy. If you like them, I've got the bill of sale right here."

Sale? She was buying horses? Ransom stared openly, watching the way she stroked the chestnut's nose. Damn, she looked so happy!

"You're getting horses?" he asked.

She smiled and nodded. "This beauty's for me. I hope you know how to ride, because you're going to spend an awful lot of time on that gray's back."

Ransom turned to look at the gray gelding. Good, deep chest, sturdy legs. A durable beast, like himself. "I am, am I?"

"Fences need mending," Jim said, grinning. "Help me saddle 'em, Ransom. I'll show you how."

But Ransom surprised them both by hefting the chestnut's saddle and readying the mare for Mandy as competently as if he'd been doing it for years.

"Right now," Jim drawled to Mandy, "I'd lay odds he knows how to ride, too."

She laughed. "I'll tell you something I've learned already. Jim, there's nothing Ransom doesn't know how to do."

Ransom's blue eyes flashed a sudden smile at her over the horse's back. "I'm just a great pretender. Come on, Mandy. Mount up so I can check the cinch and adjust the stirrups."

He gave her a little boost with his hands, and then she was in the saddle for the first time in years. She was almost too impatient to wait while Ransom fiddled with the stirrups. Finally he stepped back, and she cantered out of the yard, laughter trailing behind her.

"You better saddle up the gray and go after her," Jim said to Ransom. "Looks like she won't be back for a while. Here's the bill of sale. Tell her Dad'll stop by later." He started to turn away as Ransom tucked the folded paper in his breast pocket, but he turned back.

"Ransom?"

Ransom looked over at him.

"That little lady hasn't laughed in better than four years. A lot of us would be obliged if you'd see to it she stays happy."

"Fond of her?"

Jim smiled faintly. "A lot of us were real fond of John, and she made John real happy." He looked past Ransom to where Mandy was riding slowly. "She came to church smiling this morning. It'd be nice if she kept smiling."

"Am I being warned?"

Jim grinned suddenly and stuck out his hand. "Hell, no," he said, shaking Ransom's hand firmly. "Just asking you to keep a friendly eye on her. We've all fretted about her being alone out here. There's wildcats out there, Ransom. All kinds. Reckon you know that as well as anybody. Maybe better. And Mandy's about as naive as they come."

It was true, Ransom thought as he saddled the gray and Jim drove away. Her defenses had sheltered her, and she was naive in some ways. But there were other ways in which she wasn't at all naive. In his opinion, Mandy didn't need nearly as much protecting as Jim Preston seemed to think.

He caught up with her about a quarter of a mile from the house.

"You *do* know how to ride." She smiled as he pulled up beside her. "I'll keep the mare for sure. What do you think about the gray?"

"Strong and healthy, and his mouth hasn't been abused."

"Jim says he's a trained cow pony. That may come in useful. Guess I'll go back and tell Jim I'm keeping them both."

"Jim left. Said his dad would come by later. Here's the bill of sale."

Mandy took the folded paper from him and looped her reins around her arm so she could open it. "Eight hundred dollars! He must be joking! The tack must be worth four hundred!"

"It's used," he pointed out.

"So? It's been well-cared for. And these horses are young."

"A gelding," Ransom said. "You can't breed this pair."

"Still—"

"Mandy, something tells me you can argue yourself blue in the face and Tom Preston still won't accept a penny more. In fact, I'm willing to bet it's galling him to take even that much."

She released an exasperated breath and stuffed the bill of sale in her breast pocket. "I can't let him do this. It's not right."

"Fine. Take the horses back. And while you're at it, slap his face so he gets the message."

She turned her head sharply and found him looking grimly ahead. "What do you mean?"

"The man wants to do something for you. Why the hell don't you just let him? In fact, why don't you try putting yourself in his shoes for a minute? You're the writer. Use your imagination."

They rode on slowly, neither of them speaking. Mandy's pleasure in the day had vanished. First Tom gave her the horses at too low a price, and now Ransom was annoyed with her. And what right did he have to be angry at her, anyway?

Plenty, she admitted glumly. She was the one who had put their relationship on a more personal footing than employer and employee.

From the corner of his eye, Ransom watched the expressions play over her face. She wasn't laughing any longer, and he felt like a royal cad. And then she surprised him yet again.

"You're right," she said with a rueful smile. "I'm looking a very kind and generous gift horse in the mouth."

"It's hard sometimes to accept things from people," he said after a moment. "There was a time when I would have reacted the way you just did."

"But not anymore?" Unconsciously she leaned toward him in her saddle, hoping to learn more about him.

"No. Where I was the past few years, none of us would have survived without one another. You come to realize that no one is completely independent. And you also realize that it's our willingness to help one another that makes humanity special. Or at least some of us." *Some of us are just masquerading as human. Some of us aren't human at all.*

She looked down thoughtfully. After a while she said, "You amaze me, Ransom."

"Why?"

"You're not at all bitter."

He laughed then, a harsh, jarring sound. "Oh, I'm bitter, all right. Very bitter about some things. Just not about everything."

Not knowing how to respond, she chose silence, leaving it to him to decide if they would converse and what about. She was contradictorily eager to hear more and terrified of what he might say. In her books she often painted visions of evil, but she suspected they weren't nearly as terrible as the evil that real men could do to one another.

Eventually he spoke. "How come you decided to buy horses?"

"Because it's autumn, because the day is perfect, because every castle should have a couple of horses in the stable for peculiar princesses and stray warriors. Because I need to ride like this. Because you probably need it, too. Because my fences need work after all this time. And because I'm thinking about starting a herd. If I can afford it. A small start. No debt."

"A herd. How small?"

"I'll have to see what I can afford and whether I can afford the loss if I fall flat on my nose. What I know about cattle ranching you could probably write on the head of a pin with a ballpoint pen."

He smiled at that, turning his head to look fully at her. "I know something about it."

She drew rein, twisting in her saddle to look at him. "Tell me," she demanded. "What do you know, and how?"

"I was raised on a cattle ranch in Montana. About the time I went off to college, my dad was ready to throw in the towel. Cattle ranching's not an easy thing to do, especially when the winters are harsh. He lost the ranch eventually."

Mandy nodded and sighed.

"Sheep, on the other hand," he said slowly, "might be a better idea. Wool's back in fashion, for one thing. You can shear the suckers every spring and not have to replenish the herd every time you make a little money. Beef prices stink these days."

She half smiled. "Not in the supermarket."

"The rancher gets little enough of that."

"Sheep," she repeated thoughtfully. "I'd probably be the laughingstock of the county."

"Who cares? The only thing is, your neighbors'll want to lynch you if the sheep stray. They crop the grass so close that the cows can't graze after them."

"That's the point of a fence."

She was considering the idea, he could tell.

"Ransom?"

"Yo."

"If I get into this, are you going to stick around and help me out, or am I going to find myself with a herd and no advice?"

"How do you know my advice is any good?"

Her brown eyes met his fully. "It's just this absolutely crazy feeling I get about you."

"What feeling?"

"That you don't shoot off your mouth when you don't know what you're talking about."

"You haven't known me very long," he reminded her.

"I've known you forever," she said, and then rosy color bloomed deeply in her cheeks. Touching her heels to the mare's side, she took off across the wide open Wyoming spaces. He took off after her, enjoying every minute of the chase. It had been a hell of a long time since he'd galloped wild and free across open ground.

The chestnut had quarter horse in her somewhere, Ransom thought as he urged his own mount all out. The cow pony, on the other hand, had more endurance but less speed. When he at last caught up with Mandy, she had dismounted beneath a cottonwood beside a stream.

"John and Mary are buried beneath a cottonwood," she said as he reined to a halt beside her.

"Mary?"

"Our baby." Her back was to him. He couldn't see her face, but she sounded calm, reflective. With a creak of leather, he dismounted, wrapping the gray's reins around a bush. A well-trained horse would stay anywhere you dropped its reins. He didn't know about these two yet.

He walked up behind Mandy, taking the reins of the chestnut from her slack hand and looping them around another bush. Standing a foot behind Mandy, he said, "What happened?"

"She was stillborn. They didn't know why. The hospital wanted to take care of it, but I couldn't let them. John had wanted her so badly. She's buried beside him." She turned slowly, and although her face was calm, wet trails of tears ran down both cheeks. "She was born the day he was buried. I like to think John has his daughter."

"I'm sure he does." Very carefully, he drew her into the circle of his arms and gently pressed her head onto his shoulder. "Poor little princess," he whispered.

An unsteady sigh escaped her, and she gave in to the comfort of being held. It amazed her that Ransom could feel compassion for her after what he'd been through. He was an amazing man.

"I sometimes think," she said presently, "that life is a passion play we write for ourselves. Life after life we come back to learn, to experience. And in the perspective of eternity, it doesn't much matter whether you experience joy or sorrow, only that you taste it all, learn from it all." Again she sighed. "And I ask myself sometimes why the devil I wrote this script. It hasn't been a heck of a lot of fun."

"Maybe," he said softly, "you saved the fun for last."

"Do I sound crazy? Am I crazy?"

His arms tightened around her, and he battled an urge to pull the pins from her hair and discover the fully glory of those shiny, confined locks. "You don't sound crazy, Mandy. People ask those questions all the time. Your answer sounds more reasonable than most."

"How do you explain what happened to you? What do you tell yourself? What did you say to yourself all those years?"

"Somebody set me up." His voice was suddenly harsh. "That's reason enough."

She shivered against him. "You were betrayed?"

"Exactly."

"By a colleague?"

"And a friend."

She tilted her head back, looking up at him, ignoring the fact that his hold on her had become almost painful. This man had courage, she thought. So much courage. If only she could understand how he remained strong and compassionate in the face of such things, she might be stronger herself. "How do you cope with that?"

"What are you after? Cope with what? That people are imperfect? That a friend sold me out? I was in a position to be sold out because of choices I'd made over the years. I knew all along that I had a dangerous job. Betrayal was just one facet of a filthy business. I wasn't shocked to find myself the victim of something I'd seen happen to others. Human nature being what it is, I was just a random target."

"Random target? Do you believe that much in chance?"

She felt him draw a slow, deep breath. Gathering her courage, she met his gaze.

"When I look at you," he said, his blue eyes intense, his voice low, "I don't believe in chance at all. There's no way on earth I can believe chance led me to you."

His blue eyes came closer. His breath warmed her lips. Weakened by sorrow, tired of her isolation, Mandy gave up her internal battle and closed her eyes, offering herself to his kiss. His perfect, so right kiss. Their lips met, touched, caressed—and retreated.

"I'm riding a wild bull," he whispered, tasting the corners of her mouth. "Sometimes it's all I can do to hang on."

"I know." She understood. Somehow, she understood. She could almost feel it in the air around them, a coalescing wildness like a building tempest. Things were sliding rapidly out of control for her. For him.

He answered her with another kiss, this one deeper, searching. So knowing, she thought hazily. His mouth and tongue were so knowing, evoking feelings not even John had elicited. His arms molded her to him, every contour of their bodies fitting perfectly, and his burgeoning hunger pressed against her shamelessly. There was no shame, not for either of them.

"You feel so right, so good," he whispered, trailing his mouth across her soft cheek. And he gave in to his need, raising a hand to pull the pins from her hair.

"I'm riding that bull, too, Ransom," she said as her hair cascaded down her back, the pins falling carelessly into the grass. His fingers slid into the silky waterfall, combing it gently.

"Hold me, Mandy. Please."

Her hands slid from his chest, one rising to wrap around his neck, the other sliding under his arm around his back. She held him tightly, yearning to comfort him as he had comforted her. Now tenderness seemed to crystallize in the air around them as they kissed yet again, holding at bay the hunger of their bodies, cocooning them against wants and needs and longings—holding at bay the approaching storm. It was enough to hold and be held, to kiss and comfort. One by one her hand traced the ridges of his back, and her gentle touch was like balm to him.

They rode back to the house side by side. Only when they dismounted in the yard did Ransom break the soothing silence between them.

"A couple of battered old warriors," he said softly and brushed the lightest of kisses on the top of her head. "I'll see to the horses."

In the kitchen Mandy started making a dinner she more than half expected Ransom would never show up to eat. It was too late in the day to prepare the elaborate Sunday meal she had planned, so she made thick cold roast beef sandwiches. John had always been secretly pleased when her writing carried her away to the point that she forgot about dinner. Left to his own devices, he would have eaten soup and sandwiches as a steady diet. She wondered if Ransom was like that.

Ransom. Suddenly the afternoon washed over her, and she leaned against the counter, gripping the edge of it tightly and closing her eyes. They'd done it again, she thought. Once again they'd reached out to each other and crossed emotional barriers. They were a couple of people who knew better, yet couldn't seem to resist the temptation.

He'd wanted her body. He hadn't been able to conceal that. Even the memory of his desire stirred a coiling, warm heaviness in her. And she wanted him, too. But out there beneath the cottonwood, they had both wanted something more: the comfort of another person's caring. And that was an even greater danger than the yearnings to feel his skin, his weight, his hunger.

She would have felt a whole lot better if he'd tried to seduce her. That she could handle. Long ago she had realized that for men, sexual need and emotional need were entirely separate. In younger days her cool unapproachability had made her enough of a challenge that men overlooked her ordinary physical attributes. Ages ago she'd learned to handle those advances gently but firmly. Ransom's emotional needs were something else altogether. The last thing on earth she wanted to do was add to his pain.

But worse, far worse, than the reluctance to hurt him was her own growing sense of panic. She recognized the feeling; it came over her any time she sensed that her emotions were becoming involved. It closed in on her like a thick, suffocating blanket, darkening the corners of her mind and making the air too thick to breathe. The first tendrils of caring had put down roots in her heart, and she felt exactly as she would have if she had found her foot caught in the train tracks and, while trying to free herself, had looked up to see the train was almost upon her.

"I see you found the telescope," Ransom said as he stepped into the kitchen. He had seen it on the porch.

She whirled around, startled by his voice, but there was something in her face that went beyond surprise. Fear. He knew it as intimately as he knew pain. He recognized the look, scented the faint metallic odor of it on her. She was terrified.

"Mandy? What happened?" His first thought was that someone or something had threatened her. Immediately his posture altered; she saw him crouch ever so slightly, ready to spring. His eyes scanned the kitchen swiftly, missing nothing. "Mandy?"

"Nothing," she croaked. "Honestly. Nothing." She stared, seeing in his reaction the harsh reality of the life he had lived. He lived on a knife's edge. My God, how could she have let him come so close? He was a walking, talking promise of pain!

Ransom straightened slowly, not entirely reassured, and his blue eyes searched her face. Evil wizards. Suddenly he understood. The wise thing would have been to let the moment pass, let things fall slowly back into unthreatening casualness. He couldn't do that. He couldn't even pretend to ignore the fright in her eyes.

"Mandy," he said again, and before she could react, he gathered her close, tangling his fingers in her hair, drawing her head to his shoulder.

"Please," she said faintly, her voice muffled against his shoulder. "Please. Don't."

"Shh." He rocked her soothingly, as if she were a small, frightened child. One hand rubbed her back gently; the other brushed her cheek, her temple, her hair. "Don't be so afraid," he murmured. "Even when a princess is under an evil curse she's allowed to have a champion."

"You'll go away," she said almost inaudibly. "Everyone goes away. I don't want to depend on anybody. I don't want to care about anybody."

"I can't promise, Mandy. Nobody can make the kind of promise you need."

"I know." She sounded so lost and forlorn that he ached. "That's why I don't want to care!"

He scooped her up, startling her, and she instinctively wrapped her arms around his neck, afraid of falling. In silence he carried her from the kitchen into her study, where he settled down on the easy chair, taking her onto his lap. His arms were tight around her, denying her escape.

"My wife," he said presently, his voice sounding strained, "was in my line of work. We, uh, worked on a couple of projects together and became friends, I thought. In our business, friends weren't easy to come by."

Her own fears receded as she listened. His heartbeat was steady beneath her ear, but she could feel tension coiling in him. The ache in her now was for him, she realized. Dear God, it was already too late. Closing her eyes, she waited for him to continue.

"I, uh, didn't have any relationships with women over the years, because it didn't seem fair. I admit I had casual encounters, but I never went any further, because my job was dangerous, and I seldom knew from one minute to the next if I might be called away for an indefinite period."

When he was silent for a long time, she spoke softly, keeping her eyes closed. "Your wife was different." She knew he was remembering terrible things. The memory of pain was growing almost physically in the room around them. Instead of shying away from it, she felt driven to share it.

"I thought so." His voice had become mechanical, toneless. "She lived the same life. She understood. I didn't have to explain. She didn't have to explain. Between projects, we often got together for dinner or a show. Anyhow, eventually we became lovers. I guess I needed to know that somebody was waiting at home when the mission was done. Life didn't seem quite so empty."

She nodded her head against his shoulder, telling him she understood. Oh, indeed she understood. Loneliness was a devouring beast with harsh claws, and people would do insane things to evade it.

"Karen got pregnant," he continued flatly. "We got married. It was—I was—Mandy, I don't know if I can explain it. A child. *My* child. Suddenly I wanted out of the business. I wanted a home. I wanted to watch my child grow. Karen talked about abortion. She didn't want to give up her career. She was a lot younger than I was, a lot less worn out by all of it, I thought. For her it was still exciting.

Anyway, I talked her out of it. I told her I'd raise the baby, she could keep working. It would cost her nothing but a temporary leave of absence. Our bosses were perfectly willing to go along with that, so we went ahead.''

He drew a long, deep breath. "There was a mission I couldn't pull out of. Everything had been planned. If I didn't go it would have meant—'' He caught himself. "Sorry, that's classified.''

"It's okay,'' she said quietly. She didn't want to hear this, but somehow she *had* to. "I get the picture.''

"So I went. I was supposed to be gone a month. I was gone four years. Karen aborted the baby and continued working. She was—'' He cleared his throat once, then again, squashing down the jagged pain that always came when he thought of his lost child. "She was a double agent.''

"Oh my God!'' She sat up, staring at him, at the cold mask his face had become. She knew what was coming, knew it was going to be one of those things so vile that every feeling, every thought, would rebel against believing it. "She—''

"Yes.'' The word was clipped, short.

"Oh, Ransom.'' Casting aside all caution and fear in her pain for him, she threw her arms around his neck and hugged him as tightly as she could. This man knew betrayal in its deepest sense. He had mentioned that he'd been imprisoned for four years, but to think that he had been betrayed into that horror by his own wife! It was impossible to grasp the enormity of it. It made her own fears seem laughable by comparison.

"I, uh . . .'' He was having trouble forcing the words out. "When I escaped and made it back, it became obvious. She'd been suspected, but there was no proof. What I had to say about what happened, well, the picture was clear to everyone after that. She was—she was—'' He choked, unable to say it.

"Ransom?'' Her hands cradled his face gently. "What?''

"Sanctioned," he blurted at last and buried his face in the curve between her neck and shoulder as shudders racked him repeatedly.

Sanctioned. Officially murdered. The word hung in the air for a long time as Mandy held him, staring blindly over his head into the dark. It was too much to comprehend. Like most people, she knew in a vague way that such things happened, but the reality of such a world was confined to movies and books. Ransom had lived in it. Good Lord, the scars, the wounds, he must carry on his soul! Her chest was so tight that she could scarcely breathe.

Gradually he stopped shuddering. She could almost feel the massive amount of self-control he exercised in calming himself. And he hadn't said one word about his feelings. Not one.

"I'm sorry," he said, sounding breathless. He raised his head from her shoulder, and she released him. He let his head fall back against the chair, closing his eyes.

"Don't be sorry," she said. With her fingertips, she touched his face, tracing the line of his brow, his nose, his chin. His beard was soft, silky, short, and through it she could feel other scars. His face had been ruined, too, she realized. Overwhelmed by it all, she sought out each scar with her fingers and then pressed a kiss on it, as if it would help. As if anything could help.

"Ransom?"

"Hmm?"

"How old are you?"

Once again he brought his arms around her. "Forty-one."

"It's been a long haul."

"Mmm."

"Why did you get into the business?"

He sighed. "After Nam, I couldn't seem to quite settle into real life. And I suffered from a dangerous combination of youth, idealism and a desire to make a difference."

"Did you? Make a difference?"

"Nobody makes a difference on that level, Mandy. If we're lucky, we make a difference on a one-to-one basis."

Her fingertips found another scar just behind his ear and paused there. "I'm finding this difficult to comprehend."

"I'm not sure I comprehend it, either, and I lived it."

"I can't bear to think what each of these scars means." Things inside her shriveled and clenched at the merest thought of how he must have suffered.

"That's over with. Don't worry about it."

"But I do." She bit her lower lip. "I'm mother-henning again. Tell me to shut up. But I have an almost uncontrollable urge to check you over from head to foot and assess the damage. Just like a hen checking over a chick who got into trouble."

At that a muffled chuckle escaped him. "I'd be glad to oblige you, except I couldn't answer for the consequences. I'm not damaged that way."

Color burned in her cheeks, and she had to battle an impulse to hide her face. Right now, though, other things were far more important than a little sexual reference. "I've noticed. How bad are your legs? You said they were nearly as bad as your back."

He hesitated. "You've seen enough. You've heard enough. I don't want you to remember any more. I shouldn't have dumped this on you."

"People need to dump. I'm willing. Tell me about your legs or I'm going to have to look for myself. I can't stand this."

"Pandora," he cautioned quietly.

"Ransom..." Her tone was warning.

"The backs of my legs look like my back. I had to have them broken and reset with steel rods so I can walk. Enough?"

Her throat ached as if it were caught in a noose. "Finish," she said tightly. "All of it."

"I had to have my left arm reset, too. And my face is a miracle of plastic surgery. Mandy—"

"What else? All of it, damn it."

"Nothing major. A few assorted scars from cuts and burns."

With a swiftness that astonished him, she slipped from his lap and hurried out of the room. Several minutes later, she still hadn't returned. He searched the house for her and failed to find her, so he looked outside. He found her in her garden, on her knees in the dark, digging up her marigold plants.

"What are you doing?" he asked, though he had a pretty good idea.

"Working out a boundless rage," she said tonelessly. "I was raised not to throw things."

"Those plants—"

"Will die in a few days anyway." Shoving viciously with the trowel, she dug up another.

"Mandy." Bending, he yanked the trowel from her hand and pulled her to her feet. "You'll be mad at yourself tomorrow. Don't do this."

She struggled against his grip. "I'm mad at the whole world right now. Being mad at myself sounds like a breeze by comparison. Let me go!"

"No. I shouldn't have told you. I shouldn't have upset you. My God, I'm so sorry."

"Stop it!" she shrieked. "Stop it."

"Mandy—"

"Shut up! I've been scared and hurt my whole damn life, and none of it's been under my control. I *want* to be mad. I want to be furious!" She tried to break free of his hold. "I want to shout and scream and smash things! I've had it. Had it! Do you hear me? I'm through! Finished! I'm not going to creep around anymore. I'm not going to be afraid anymore! If I could get my hands on those bastards who hurt you, I'd kill them. Kill them!"

"Mandy. Oh, Mandy." His voice sounded broken, and his arms were like steel around her as she struggled and pounded wildly on his chest. "Oh, my God, what have I done to you?"

Exhaustion ended her rage, leeching it from her until she hung limp in his arms, an occasional sniffle her only sound.

"All done?" he asked grimly, scooping her up for the second time that evening. She didn't answer. Her head lolled as he carried her back into the house and up the stairs to the bedrooms.

"Which one is yours?" he asked. A slight motion of her hand answered him. Carefully he set her down on the wedding ring quilt that covered the narrow bed. Its narrowness made it obvious that she no longer slept in the bed she had shared with John.

"I'll be back in five minutes," he said. "I expect to find you under the covers. If you're not, I'll undress you myself and put you there. Your choice, Mandy."

She managed it. When he returned with hot chocolate in two steaming mugs, she was under the covers, quilt drawn to her chin. Sitting on the edge of the bed, he slipped an arm around her shoulders and raised her.

"Drink," he commanded, and she sipped the warm, sweet liquid, too tired to argue, even when she realized the chocolate was laced with brandy. He must have found the bottle left over from Christmas four years ago.

"I'll be right here all night," he said as he eased her back onto the pillow.

"Go home," she whispered. "It's over now." Indeed, everything inside her felt as if it had shriveled, died and crumbled into dust.

"I'm not leaving you alone." He brushed her long, dark hair gently back from her face. "From time to time, a warrior keeps a vigil. It's good for the soul. Sleep, Mandy."

Chapter 4

He stayed with her all night. She slept restlessly, troubled by vague nightmares, and each time she opened her eyes he was there, sitting in the chair by the bed, watching her.

"Ransom," she mumbled the last time. "Go get some sleep."

"I'm okay," he answered quietly. "Sleep, Mandy."

When she woke again it was nearly dawn. Through the lace curtains at her window she could see the faint brightening of the eastern sky. Ransom's head had settled onto his chest and he was dozing. A fist squeezed her heart, and tears sprang to her eyes.

Suddenly his eyes snapped open, meeting hers. "Mandy?" he said softly, a question.

"I'm okay. For heaven's sake, get some sleep." Her voice was choked with unshed tears.

He shook his head slowly.

"Ransom, please." A tear spilled over.

A look of anguish passed over his face. He bent suddenly, yanking his boots off, and then he stood, unbuckling his belt and flinging it aside. Mandy watched, wondering, but not at all nervous.

He lay beside her on top of the quilt and drew her into the circle of his arms, bringing her head to rest on his shoulder. "There," he said quietly. "We'll both sleep."

It was late morning when she opened her eyes again. Ransom was sleeping deeply, his arms wrapped securely around her, hers wrapped around his waist. Her head was pillowed on his chest, the sound of his heartbeat strong in her ear.

She didn't dare move for fear of disturbing him, so she lay still, watching the sunlight move across the room as noon approached.

He was courageous, Mandy decided, as she thought over the painful things he had revealed last night. At first she had heard his tale filtered through her own fears, but now, in the bright morning light, she understood why he had told her. He was showing her that in spite of betrayal he was prepared to face the risks again. In comparison she felt like an abject coward.

Or maybe, she thought with a catch in her breath that she felt in her heart, maybe he had been telling her that he was just as scared, just as reluctant, as she was. And certainly with more cause.

"Morning." His voice was husky with sleep as his arms tightened.

She turned her head and met his blue gaze, saw the concern there. Searching rapidly through the dusty corners of her battered soul, she found a smile and offered it to him.

A pent-up breath escaped him as his eyes wandered over her face, measuring, gauging, until at last his attention settled on her mouth. "Amanda," he whispered. "Amanda Lynn."

The last person to call her that had been an angry second grade teacher. This was different. This was a recognition. Suddenly she was filled with courage.

As if he sensed it, he tugged her gently upward and brought her lips to his. His mouth opened beneath hers, asking her to explore its smoky, hot depths. How good he tasted, she thought, her kiss swiftly growing bolder. He let her lead, pressing for nothing, not even moving his hands against her back, though she could feel his growing tension.

"Ransom," she whispered. "Ransom what?"

"Ransom Richard," he answered huskily, tugging her mouth back to his.

"Ransom Richard Laird," she murmured, tasting his lips, his tongue, in short, sweet kisses. "A warrior's name. Ransom means son of the shield."

"Mandy." His control was shattering. She could feel it and didn't care. Explosions of need hammered her. Desire shot through her in electric ribbons. Never had she imagined such wild feelings really existed. It appalled her to think her fears might have prevented her from ever knowing this. It was nearly too much. He tasted so right, smelled so right, felt so right. This was her script, the one she had dreamed of since youth.

"Mandy." Her name was a groan, and he took command, kissing her deeply, tugging at the quilt until it vanished. He pulled her over him so their bodies met from head to toe, and he caught her face between his hands, taking her mouth hungrily, pillaging the warm sweet cavern as if he wanted to slip wholly into her.

She moaned softly against his lips and began to tremble with a need so great it threatened to rip her apart. Against her she felt his readiness, and it increased her excitement. Involuntarily she moved against him, pressing, and this time it was Ransom who groaned deeply. His hands flew from her head to her hips, pressing her closer yet, grinding himself into her softness.

"Yes, yes, yes," she chanted in a whisper. "Ransom..."

His hands suddenly swept down, then up, dragging the flannel nightgown upward with them, exposing her skin to his touch. Fire. His touch was like fire. She burned for him, flamed for him, resented the denim that lay between them.

A shiver racked him, and then, abruptly, he grew still and rigid. For an instant he didn't move, and she lay confused, dazed.

"Mandy." Swiftly he tugged at her gown, yanking it down, turning her with him so they lay side by side. He cradled her gently, the only sound their ragged breathing as the world gradually righted itself.

A long, long time later she raised confused eyes to his. "Sweetness," he said softly. "You are sweetness and purity. Amanda Lynn Tierney, I'd kill myself if I ever saw regret in your eyes because of anything I did."

"But..." He had awakened in her a sweet, savage wanting, and she wanted to tell him that she wouldn't regret, couldn't regret—yet some wise corner of her mind knew she would do precisely that.

He saw the flicker of understanding in her eyes and laid a gentle finger across her lips. "Now hush."

He finished the roofing that afternoon, and Mandy wrote like a demon. As page after page filled her computer screen, she knew she was writing this one for Ransom. This was his book, the story she would give him.

Her fears haunted her, too, dark shadows looming in the corners of her mind, but she bravely ignored them. Difficult though it might be, she had at last found something worth all the risks and terrors. She told herself she would deal with those demons one at a time and vanquish them. She would become whole for Ransom.

It was, of course, much easier said than done. Her momentary courage felt like a small, uncertain candle flame in the dead of the darkest night. Superstitiously, she could almost feel threat thickening the air around her. Somewhere along the way she had definitely developed the conviction that Amanda Lynn Tierney had no right to be happy.

When he stepped into the kitchen at dinnertime, they stood staring at one another for a long moment, recognizing the changes between them, the fears, the uncertainties, the needs. And then he held out his arms to her and she went into his embrace eagerly, turning her face up without hesitation.

"Sweet Mandy," he murmured, kissing her once, twice, three times. He hugged her tenderly until she stirred, muttering that dinner would burn.

"Ransom?"

His fork halted halfway to his mouth. "Hmm?"

"Are you going back to your old job?"

He searched her face closely and was amazed to see not fear, but a kind of sad courage. It was as if she wanted to measure the dimensions of an inevitable pain, accepting that there could be no escape from it. Slowly he set the fork down and pushed back his chair. Coming round the table, he pulled out the chair beside her and sat, claiming both her hands.

"I'm on six months' convalescent leave," he said slowly. "I don't have to decide until it's up."

"You haven't decided yet, then." Her brown eyes were huge, her lips compressed to still their quivering.

"I'm not sure," he said truthfully, hating himself for each word as he spoke it, knowing they struck her like blows. "I don't want to go back, Mandy. But I can't lead a purposeless existence."

"Nate said you were a driven man." She looked so brave that something inside him seemed to be breaking.

"That's not it. Not really. I just have to feel I'm accomplishing something worthwhile. It doesn't have to be my old job. In fact, I'd much rather it wasn't."

"What kind of purpose do you need?"

He shrugged. "I'm trying to figure that out."

"You were planning to quit before," she said quietly. "Nate told me. You told me."

"To raise a child." He nodded. "I think about that a lot. That might be purpose enough for me." He looked down at her hands and saw that they were trembling. Then he lifted his gaze to hers and considered asking the question that had been tumbling around in his head like an obsession since dawn when he had lain down beside her and taken her into his arms. In his entire life there hadn't been very many people he trusted enough that he could actually sleep in their presence. Mandy had enlarged that very small, very select group. "Will you go to the Harvest Dance with me?"

Tom Preston's men had mentioned the dance when they had helped with the barn roof. It was an annual event, they'd said, that gave the local ladies a rare chance to get duded up and spend the evening with men who for once didn't smell of horses, cattle and manure. Ransom had laughed along with them, but since dawn this morning it had become important to him to see Mandy "duded up." To see her smile and laugh. To see her carefree for just an evening.

Her eyes widened, and color drained from her cheeks. For an eternity she said nothing at all.

He understood, or thought he did. She felt they were tempting fate already, but this must seem like a step into the jaws of disaster. It was a superstitious attitude that he didn't completely understand.

He understood conditioning, understood how a person could become distrustful or afraid to take risks. A person's mind and soul could react exactly the same way to a bad emotional experience as they did to touching a hot stove. What he couldn't wholly understand was Mandy's apparent conviction that it was some kind of personal karma to lose everything she loved. Ransom was a firm believer that men were the captains of their fates, and that everything in a person's life could be traced directly to decisions made or not made. The universe wasn't out to get Mandy Grant. She had simply experienced the inevitable losses of life in a way that made her feel cursed. The random chances of life, for her, had come to seem like fate or destiny, an Evil Wizard. Personal. Directed. Deliberate. Somehow he had to change her mind about that.

But now, right now, he could see the flare of fright around her delicate little nose, see the dilation of her pupils, see the rapid rise and fall of her breasts. She was scared, but she

wasn't running. She was, he saw, fighting for courage.
Fighting to triumph over herself.

The sight of that struggle had an unexpected effect on
him. Protective instincts that had been buried so long he had
forgotten he had them suddenly rose in an almost painful
rush. "Forget I asked, Princess," he said gruffly. "I forgot
about the Evil Wizard."

Her eyes were huge, wounded, hungry for understanding
and warmth, and yet terrified of what the consequences
might be. "It's silly," she whispered. "This is all so silly...."
She wriggled free from his hold and fled the room, leaving
him in solitude to ponder just how silly it all was.

After a while Ransom stirred himself to clean up the dinner dishes. Silly? he asked himself. Maybe, maybe not. He'd
been having the strangest fancies ever since he met Mandy
Grant. Fancies of knowing her from elsewhere, of destiny
and plans and eternal schemes. He'd never for one moment
felt she was a stranger to him, and somehow neither had she
after the first hesitancy. He could tell. They reacted to one
another with an intensity that spoke of old acquaintance.

Pausing, he leaned his hip against the counter and stared
out at the night. When had he first met Mandy Grant? Not
when he walked up the drive to her house. When he read her
first book? No, even then there had been a familiarity. He
had the oddest sensation that he'd been seeing her face in
dreams since childhood. He felt a sense of recognition that
extended far beyond the past two weeks. Never in his life
had he responded to another person on so many instinctive
levels.

So what did it mean? Finishing the dishes, he turned his
feelings around in his mind but could make no sense of
them. A psychiatrist would tell him it was the result of his
experiences of the past several years. He wasn't emotionally stable. Hah! He tossed the dish towel across the kitchen
to land on top of the washer. He even knew exactly where
he would find her this very minute.

Closing his eyes, he recalled the dreams and fantasies he'd
had during his imprisonment. The woman hadn't had a

face. He'd never seen her clearly. But he'd felt her and heard her, had known her need for him. Mandy.

Suddenly he was galvanized. Striding across the kitchen, he headed not for her office but for the living room. Somehow, he knew she'd fled there.

Mandy was trying to read a book when he appeared in the room. She sucked in a sharp breath as she looked up. He looked like an ancient warrior, she thought as the lamplight gleamed on his golden hair, battered and bloody, but not beaten.

"Amanda Lynn Tierney," he said firmly, "you and I have centuries of uncompleted business to take care of."

She held her breath now, staring wide-eyed, something rising wildly in her, acknowledging him and his words.

"I may have slipped my trolley," he continued, "but by God, we're going to finish it this time, this lifetime. You and I are going to the Harvest Dance next week. And that's final."

The funniest smile curved her lips. "You're as crazy as I am, Ransom."

Suddenly he felt like laughing. A real laugh. The first real laugh in a long, long time. "I know. Isn't it great?"

She laughed with him, because the sound was so wonderful, so infectious, because it did her heart so much good to see this man laugh. But behind her smile, behind her laugh, foreboding took root. It was dangerous to care. Tragedy took everyone she cared about. It was dangerous, but she cared anyway. It was too damn late.

Tom Preston stopped by a few days later to see if Mandy was pleased with the horses, and with a great show of reluctance accepted her check. Standing out in the yard, he watched Ransom scraping industriously at the barn as he prepared to paint.

"Looks like you got yourself a hard worker, Mandy."

"Seems so."

"I don't mind telling you I asked Tate about this guy when I heard about him. Said only good things."

"There are only good things to say."

Tom's gaze grew speculative, and he looked from her to Ransom. "Are you coming to the dance this year?"

"It appears so."

"With Ransom?" He hardly needed to see her nod, and his smile deepened. "We all loved John, Mandy, but it's troubled us to see you alone and sad for so long. Guess I ought to go over and meet the boy."

"He's not a boy, Tom," she said as she walked with him over to the barn. "Far from it."

Ransom saw them coming from a distance and hastily pulled on his shirt, buttoning it rapidly. He didn't want Mandy to have to face the looks he knew would result if word got around about his scars, especially since he was willing to bet gossip was already rife.

He shook Preston's hand cordially and endured the older man's measuring look without any discomfort.

"Mandy tells me you're bringing her to the Harvest Dance," Preston remarked.

"I plan to."

"Well, you'd better be prepared to undergo an inquisition. Everyone's been curious since they heard Mandy hired a hand, but you come to the dance and you'll have to endure the prying of every biddy in Conard County."

Ransom laughed. "I've survived worse."

"Reckon you have. That's a hell of a big job you're fixing to do." He indicated the barn.

"I've got plenty of time."

"You need to be looking at the fence, too, if Mandy means to start a herd. Sheep, she said."

"That's right," Mandy affirmed.

"Good idea." Preston's look became mildly speculative. "What do you know about ranching, Ransom?"

"I was raised on the Rocking L in eastern Montana. My dad went bust one winter."

Preston shook his head sympathetically. "Seen too much of that in my day. A couple bad winters in succession just about puts anybody under. Ever raise any sheep?"

"Some. Our neighbors did. They survived the winters."

Preston's face relaxed into a grin. "You're gonna need help."

Ransom glanced at Mandy, wondering if this conversation disturbed her. Preston was acting as if they were married and Ransom was running Mandy's ranch. It made him uneasy. It didn't bother Mandy, though. She looked as if she were used to it. Seeing his concern, she smiled almost impishly at him. He grinned back.

"I'll cross that bridge when I come to it, Tom," she said smoothly. "I'm not committed to anything yet, so I've got all the time I need to work things out."

The hint was subtle, but Preston picked up on it. He laughed good-naturedly, commented on the lateness of the first frost and headed back to his truck. When he was gone, Ransom put down the scraper and came to Mandy's side.

She tilted her head, smiling up at him. "How's a beer sound?" she asked.

"Like heaven." He followed her into the kitchen. "Are your neighbors always so nosy and chauvinistic?"

She laughed. "Sure. Come on, you claim to be ranch-bred."

"It's been more than twenty years. Guess I forgot. Doesn't it rub you wrong?"

"Why should it? This was John's spread. I'm a city girl in the minds of the folks around here—Casper being the city to them. They know I don't know much about it, and I'm not dumb enough to pretend I know what I don't. You're the rancher in their minds, not me. They're going to want to know how much you know so they can decide if I'm going down the trail to disaster or possible success."

"What if they decide it's failure?"

"Then I'll hear enough dire warnings to make Cassandra sound like an optimist."

He laughed at that, accepting the icy beer she handed him.

"I need to go into town this afternoon," she said presently. "I'm down to my last disk and my last twenty sheets of computer paper, and Dan Riley phoned to say my new keyboard is in.''

''Great,'' he said, leaning against the counter and tilting his head back as he swallowed beer. ''Can I invite myself along? I'm in desperate need of a barber.''

''Sure.''

But he caught a moment's hesitation and was troubled. He didn't know how to bring it up, however, so he held his peace. Finishing the beer, he crushed the can absently and started to go back to work.

''Ransom?''

He looked back.

''What's wrong?''

Turning, he leaned back against the counter, splaying his legs and pulled her up against him for a long, deep kiss. He was sweaty from his labors, but the smell was fresh and good. She leaned into him and gave herself up to the wonder of Ransom Richard Laird. For now her warning, frightened voices were silent, as if the magic of this tenderly budding relationship had smothered them. The past few days had seemed to exist out of time, in a land of perpetual sunshine.

His hands moved gently over her back, and his tongue brushed fiery patterns over the warm sweet interior of her mouth, drawing her into him, deeper and deeper.

''Ransom,'' she sighed, and his hands slipped downward, cupping her soft bottom. Slowly, oh, so slowly, he lifted her against him, showing her what she did to him. And just as slowly he raised his head and looked into her eyes.

''Amanda Lynn,'' he said softly, ''you've got me in the palm of your clever little hand. So, before I make a complete ass of myself, maybe you'd better tell me why you weren't at all sure you wanted me to come with you this afternoon.''

She flushed a cherry red and hid her face in his shoulder. In spite of himself, he smiled. ''Come on, Mandy. My secrets are obvious right this minute. Share yours.''

She shook her head.

Bending, he brushed a kiss on her ear. His breath sent a shiver coursing through her. "I'll torment you," he warned gently.

"You do already," she sighed, too far gone in the pleasure of his touch to care that he knew it.

"Mandy."

She tilted her head back but couldn't quite meet his eyes. "I have a doctor's appointment."

His hands tightened on her bottom. "What's wrong?" he asked sharply.

"Nothing." Her head ducked. "I was just going to get . . . you know."

"What?" And suddenly he understood. He caught his breath and held her so tightly that she finally complained she couldn't breathe. He gentled his grip and pressed his cheek against hers.

"No," he said. It might have been twenty years since he'd left, but he remembered all too clearly what a small community was like.

"No what?"

"You can't go into that gossipy little town for that. I won't hear of it. The whole damn county will be discussing your morals and we haven't even—I won't hear of it."

"I don't care." She stuck her lower lip out mutinously.

"I do. Damn it, Mandy, I won't have you discussed like that. I won't."

"But what if—" She could hardly believe they were discussing this, however circumspectly. She certainly couldn't bring herself to say it right out loud.

"Then I'll take care of it." He would borrow the truck and drive into the next county to buy condoms, but he would not, absolutely not, allow Mandy to become the subject of gossip.

An aching tenderness filled her, and she at last dared to meet his eyes. No longer empty, they shone with gentleness. They blazed with it. She reached up to clasp his face.

"Ransom?"

He almost smiled. "I'm listening, Mandy. Parts of me may be preoccupied, but my ears are wide open."

"John never liked—" Again color flooded her face and her eyes dropped. No amount of effort could bring her to say out loud that John had hated to use condoms.

But he understood what John had probably disliked. "As a temporary measure, it's not bad. Don't worry about that. Not that of all things, princess. In a minute, when I'm sure I can stand without my knees giving way, I'm going to let you go. And you're going to call and cancel your appointment. I'll stand right here until you do."

"Here." Mandy tossed Ransom the keys as she joined him at the truck.

He smiled, the creases by his eyes deepening. "Are you sure you're ready for this? I haven't driven in years."

"It's like riding a horse, Ransom. You never forget. Besides, these country roads are a great place to get back in shape."

Also, she was feeling a little too edgy to drive. She couldn't believe she and Ransom had discussed what they had earlier, especially when they weren't even lovers. Closing her eyes, Mandy remembered a discussion on the same subject with John. Three months after their marriage, he'd brought it up with a great deal of foot-shuffling and hemming and hawing. She'd never forgotten his embarrassment and had intended to handle matters this time so that it never needed to be discussed.

She stole a glance at Ransom. He drove as he did everything else, with easy confidence. As if he felt her attention, he turned and gave her a slow, lazy wink.

"How short are you going to cut your hair?" she asked. He was dressed in a fresh chambray shirt and almost-new jeans. No longer did he look out of place, as he had when he first arrived. As naturally as breathing, he'd assumed the local coloration. A chameleon. The thought jarred her.

"Why?" he asked. "Are you attached to my long, shaggy locks?"

"Sort of," she admitted.

He reached out and patted her leg. "I'll leave enough for you to get your fingers into," he teased. "If you want to."

She did want to. She very much wanted to plunge her fingers into his impossibly soft golden hair. Her gaze dropped to his forearms. His sleeves were rolled back, and fine golden hairs glinted against his tanning skin. And there, just under his left sleeve, she glimpsed a long, thin scar, still faintly red. From when they repaired his arm, she guessed. Inevitably, her eyes dropped lower to his lean, hard thighs.

"I'm blond there, too," he said.

Her eyes leapt to his, and she watched him smile as a hot blush flooded her cheeks.

"You're so lovely when you blush, Mandy. I just can't seem to resist teasing you."

Suddenly he braked the truck right in the middle of the dirt road. Twisting in the seat, he caught her shoulders gently and drew her closer, until they almost touched.

"Do you like what you see, Amanda Lynn?" he asked huskily.

Mesmerized by his blue eyes, she nodded mutely, embarrassment forgotten. Her heart had begun to beat with a steady throb, a pagan drumbeat of anticipation and hunger. So fast. He made her feel everything so fast and so intensely.

"I'm glad," he whispered, brushing his warm lips lightly against hers. "I like what I see, too. Very much." Impossibly, his eyes were smiling. "I steal looks at you all the time, and I wonder, too. And I'm enjoying every single moment of anticipation. If anybody had ever told me that someday I'd wallow in going crazy from temptation, I wouldn't have believed it. But here I am, tempted beyond belief, and I'm in absolutely no rush to put an end to my misery."

Not even John had made her feel as desirable as Ransom did right then. A small sound escaped her, and she slipped her fingers into his beautiful golden hair as he pulled her into him for a yearning kiss.

He tasted her hunger and returned it, but it still wasn't time. She cared for him, he knew, but most of her heart was still securely sealed behind fortress walls. With Mandy he wanted no half measures. If they ever made love, she was going to give herself wholly, without hesitation. She was going to know that the princess had been claimed by her knight.

"I love your hair," she said a short while later as they sat cheek-to-cheek. Her fingers played at the nape of his neck. "Don't you dare cut it all off."

"Just enough so I don't look like a middle-aged hippie."

A little gurgle escaped her. "Sorry, your expression isn't vague enough. You look too dangerous. Like a Viking. Are your ancestors Nordic?"

"My father was of Danish and Scottish extraction, and my mother was a Russian émigré."

"Really? She came from Russia? Do you speak Russian?"

"Fluently." And it had sure caused him enough trouble. It was on the tip of his tongue to ask about her family, but he caught himself. Poor little princess. She would never know those simple but important things about herself. He tightened his embrace.

"Do you speak any other languages?" she asked.

"A few, some so unusual that I can't tell you without revealing classified information."

Her eyes darkened, and he wanted to kick himself for reminding her of the many things she had to be frightened of. Gently, she pulled away.

"We'd better get going or you'll never get your hair cut and I'll never get my supplies."

While Mandy took care of her purchases, Ransom hit the barbershop across the street. A real, old-fashioned, genuine barbershop. He hesitated a moment, wondering if he might get his head shaved after all. Back east, you couldn't find a barber of any kind anymore, and certainly not one as old as this geezer. He would wind up with a military cut for sure.

"Howdy," he said to the barber.

"Howdy," came the answer, the measuring look. "What can I do for you?"

Ransom smiled. "You can save my life. I'm in desperate need of a little barbering, but my girl's threatening to kill me if I cut too much off. Do you think we can find a compromise somewhere between broken heart and effeminate?"

The barber's laugh was wheezy but genuine. "Step up, young fella. I ain't never ruined a romance yet."

The barber was naturally nosy, but Ransom had years of experience in answering such questions satisfactorily while revealing nothing. The old man got sidetracked on to something else finally, and Ransom relaxed.

Thirty minutes later he stepped out onto the street with the haircut he wanted and his beard neatly trimmed. Shoving his thumbs into his pockets, he strolled up the street to the Conard County Sheriff's Office. Mandy had said she would meet him there. He hoped Nate was around.

Halfway there, the back of his neck prickled and a warning heat settled between his shoulder blades. It was a preternatural instinct, honed by years on the edge. He hesitated midstep, convinced that somebody was watching him. Staring at him. Paying attention to him.

But that was ridiculous. He was believed to be dead by almost everybody in the world. Only his family and a handful of people at the agency had any notion that Ransom Laird had returned from the dead. None of them would advertise his whereabouts. And folks here didn't know who he was or who he had been, at least not enough to pass the information on to anyone who might actually care. After almost five years he should be forgotten, anyway.

Probably just some curious person wondering who the stranger in town was, he told himself. He was no longer an active agent. He didn't need to get paranoid every time someone looked at him. Forcing himself to ignore the sensation, he continued down the street.

The instant he entered the sheriff's office, he spied Nate and Mandy in Nate's office.

"Hey, Tater!" he called, and watched several deputies go from shock to laughter. Even Mandy smiled.

"Ransom, I'll kill you, you son of a gun," Tate growled. "I managed to keep that under wraps for twenty years." But he grinned and slapped Ransom's back while dragging him into his office.

"Tater," Mandy said, eyes twinkling. "I like it, Nate."

"It'll be all over town by tomorrow," the sheriff said ruefully. "Ransom was lucky. We used to call him King."

"King? Why?"

"King's Ransom," Nate explained with a smile.

She glanced quickly up at Ransom, and he caught her faint, secret smile. He knew exactly what she was thinking: *Lost kings return to rule.* He winked at her.

Nate spoke. "I was just inviting you and Mandy to have dinner with Marge and me before the dance next week."

Mandy and Ransom exchanged looks. Ransom nodded slightly.

"We'd love to, Nate," Mandy answered.

"We?" Nate brightened. "You mean all this matchmaking's for nothing?"

Ransom chuckled. "I already asked Mandy to go to the dance with me."

"Well, son of a gun. Wait 'til I tell Marge!"

The sun was low in the sky by the time they headed home.

"Is my hair okay?" Ransom asked as he turned off the highway onto the county road.

Smiling, Mandy slid closer and ran her fingers into the hair on the back of his head. "Well..." she said, drawing the word out.

"Damn, I told that barber my girl would kill me if he took too much off."

She laughed softly and blushed wildly, feeling younger and more alive than she had in years. "You didn't!"

"I did. And he told me he'd never yet ruined a romance."

A romance! His choice of words made something inside her turn all warm and weak. And for once all her fears failed to rear up and castigate her folly. "Well, he hasn't ruined this one."

He pretended to sigh with relief. "So it's okay?"

"It looks nice. You had your beard trimmed, too. Now you look like a yuppie."

"A yuppie!"

Suddenly, with an explosive sound, the windshield shattered into a web-work of cracks. Before Mandy really registered it, she was lying facedown on the bench seat. Ransom's weight was pinning her, his belt buckle cutting into her ear as he sheltered her body with his. Simultaneously he hit the brake, bringing the truck to a screeching, choking halt.

"Don't move," he said sharply, his voice low.

"I wouldn't dream of it," she said breathlessly. "Not when you consider where my head is." What the devil was going on?

For an instant she felt him stiffen. Then she gasped as he gently nipped her bottom. "There are possibilities in this position," he whispered back. "I knew you had guts."

"Guts?"

"Shh."

Guts? His meaning trickled through her slowly, stiffening her, accelerating her heart. The shattered windshield, his protective posture, his insistence on quiet. She knew exactly what he was thinking. The hair on the back of her neck prickled.

A very long time later he whispered her name. "Mandy?"

"Mmm?"

"I'm going to get up very slowly. Stay where you are, no matter what."

Galvanized, she reached behind her and managed to grab a handful of his shirt. "No."

"Shh. I know what I'm doing."

She supposed he did, but it didn't make her feel any better. "Please be careful."

His arm slipped under her, squeezing her waist, and then, to her utter amazement, she felt him kiss her bottom. The feeling that trickled through her had nothing to do with fear.

"Absolutely," he whispered. "I want to explore these possibilities a whole lot further."

Slowly he levered himself off her, keeping low. "Slide off the seat and get as far under the dash as you can. Quietly."

She obeyed, crouching into the small space. She could hardly bear to watch as Ransom sat up and peered out the side windows. Then, moving cautiously, he opened the door and slid out.

Nerve-stretching minutes passed in utter silence. Sunset passed into dusk, and finally she had to bite down on her knuckle to keep from calling out for Ransom. She should have known. What kind of fool was she? The minute she started to care, the minute she became involved, disaster struck. She fought to swallow a wild laugh as it occurred to her that maybe she ought to wear a garlic necklace to ward off evil.

"Mandy?"

Suddenly he was there, a shadow against the darkening sky. A muffled sound escaped her. In her relief, she forgot everything else, including her sense of self-preservation. Battling her cramped muscles, she struggled up on the seat and crawled across it to throw her arms around him. He caught her close.

"It's okay, princess," he murmured, stroking her mussed hair gently. "It's okay." But he didn't sound as if he believed it.

The windshield was shattered so badly that they couldn't see through it. While Ransom searched the toolbox in the back of the pickup for a crowbar, Mandy held the flashlight for him.

"What is it, Ransom?" she asked finally. "What caused it?" All the time she had been hunched on the floor of the truck, wild speculations had filled her mind. None of them seemed real, however, not even in the face of the shattered windshield. Nothing, that is, except evil wizards and good old-fashioned karma. She should have known better than to let herself care.

Moments ticked by in silence before Ransom answered shortly, "Buckshot."

Mandy drew a sharp breath, and he looked up at her. "Just some kids fooling around, Mandy. They're probably even more scared than we are." He turned back to the tool-box.

"Sure." She didn't believe it. The beam from the flash-light quivered, then steadied. "Ransom, kids around here don't play with guns. There's no need. Most kids are shoot-ing by the time they're eight, and they own their own guns before they're twelve. It's not like the city, where Dad's gun is a big temptation." She bit her lip, recalling that he'd grown up in similar circumstances.

"I'm sure it was an accident," he said firmly. He found the crowbar and stood up in the bed of the truck. "Mandy, I found the spent shell. Just kids, probably looking for birds, and one of them tripped. I'm willing to bet they don't get a wink of sleep tonight." Bending, he grabbed the side of the truck and jumped down. When he hit the dirt, he staggered to one side and cursed.

"Damn it," he said shortly. "Somebody tell me how the hell steel legs can hurt."

Mandy bit her lip harder and followed him around to the front of the truck. "Ransom—"

He rounded on her. "Mandy, just think! In real life as-sassins don't use buckshot and shoot through windshields! They stalk their quarry and use high-powered rifles with sniper scopes or something equally effective. The worst—the absolute worst—that could have happened if that shot had penetrated the window is that one of us might have lost an eye."

"Okay." Her voice was thin, the word clipped.

Muttering an oath, Ransom threw back his head a mo-ment, closed his eyes and drew a deep, steadying breath. Then, without another word, he moved her away and bashed out the windshield. When he finished, Mandy dug out the whisk broom she kept in the glove box and swept pebbles of glass from the seat and hood of the truck. She would not, she told herself, cry. Ransom had been short with her because he hurt, and besides, she knew better than to care, didn't she? No, she would *not* cry.

"Mandy."

Suddenly she was caught up in a huge bear hug.

"I'm sorry I snapped at you," he said.

All her hurt seeped away. "Do your legs hurt a lot?"

He sighed and kissed her cheek. "Count on you to be more concerned about my legs than the fact I snapped at you."

"You snapped because you hurt. I've been known to do that myself." She rubbed her cheek against his, savoring the softness of his beard. "Just forget it."

He lifted her into the truck and climbed up beside her, reaching for the ignition key. He hesitated for a moment, then leaned back, sighing.

"Mandy, can you humor an old warrior?"

"Sure." She turned to look at him, wishing the starlight was brighter.

"I really do think it was accidental, but I'm sitting here trying to battle twenty years of highly developed instincts. Will you please put your head on my lap and keep down while I drive?"

Her heart raced, whether from a sudden return of fear or the thought of resting her head on Ransom's lap she didn't know. Scooting over, she lay on her side and put her cheek on his thigh. As soon as he had the truck rolling, his right hand came to rest on her shoulder.

"This position has possibilities, too," he remarked, giving her a gentle squeeze. "Tell me the reasons why I shouldn't explore them."

She knew he was trying to distract her, but she was already distracted enough by her own awareness of his proximity.

"Mandy? Come on, give me all the reasons."

"Shut up. I'm too distracted to think."

A brief laugh escaped him. "Me too. I don't suppose you could move a little closer?"

In the dark, she blushed. "What happened to your instincts?"

"They're being superseded by an even older set."

Mandy knew exactly what he meant.

Chapter 5

Back at the house, Ransom pulled up right by the kitchen porch and turned off the ignition. His right hand clamped Mandy's shoulder, holding her where she was.

"Mandy. Humor me further."

"Okay." Wickedly, she nuzzled his thigh with her cheek. She heard him draw a quick breath, even as she drew one herself. What had gotten into her? Reaction to her fright? Or simply the warm, drizzly sexual feelings he awakened in her with such ease?

"Not that way," he said softly. "It's killing me to say that. Damn. Mandy, stay here while I check things out. My other instincts are still driving me crazy. Along with you."

She wiggled onto her back and tried to make out his face. "What's going on? You said it was an accident."

"It was. I'm sure of it. But I'm a trained—never mind. Just let me act out my craziness for a few more minutes."

"Which craziness?" Some devil was driving her into provocation, and even as she spoke she was a little shocked by her own boldness.

"The warrior craziness," he said firmly, but his hand strayed toward the swell of her breast, not really touching, but hinting. "Mandy?"

"Yes, Ransom," she said, suddenly breathless and past caring. "Act out your craziness. Either one. Both. Whatever."

A choked sound escaped him, and his hand touched her cheek briefly. "Stay here. Don't move. Don't make a sound. I'll be back in a little bit."

She lay there for at least ten minutes, unable to believe she had said the things she had. They were both crazy, she decided. Stark raving mad. It was easier, however, to consider her own mad behavior than to speculate about what it was that worried Ransom enough to make him act so cautiously. She had the uneasy feeling that his arrival had brought her into contact with an alien world. She couldn't imagine the darkness he must have known, and she didn't want to imagine that darkness invading her sanctuary.

"Mandy? Come on. Let's get you inside."

"But my stuff's in the back."

"I'll get it. You just get your rump inside."

While he carted in the boxes of paper and disks and the keyboard, Mandy started throwing together a quick meal. They were going to have to talk about these instincts of his, she decided. The warrior ones. She didn't miss the fact that he bolted the back door when he brought the last box in, or that he had already drawn all the curtains.

"Well," he said, returning to the kitchen after carrying the keyboard into her study, "I guess you can't decide whether to be scared to death or not."

"I was just going to mention that. Your behavior isn't exactly consistent." In fact, his behavior was giving her butterflies of dread in her stomach. She didn't want any more violence in her life. None. Never again.

He dug a beer out of the fridge. "I really believe it was an accident, Mandy. I'm not kidding about that. But I've been trained for years to check everything out thoroughly, not to make any hasty assumptions. My life has depended on that training more than once. Old habits die hard. Anyhow, everything seems to be kosher, so I was overreacting. Okay?''

It was hardly okay. Watching him take his precautions had reminded her of things she had been close to forgetting, little things, like the cost of caring.

She put a bowl of tuna salad and a loaf of bread on the table. ''Would you mind making your own? I'm tired tonight, for some reason.''

''No problem.''

''I'll heat some soup.''

''Forget it.'' He caught her hand gently and pulled her to the table. ''Sit down. Let me take care of dinner.''

''Ransom—''

''Cut it out,'' he said, pressing her down into the chair. ''What's the matter? Cycles of the moon? Or are you just furious with me?''

Her eyes flew to his face. ''I'm not mad at you!''

''Good. So what's on your mind?''

He stood over her, hands on his hips, waiting.

She gestured helplessly. ''I don't know. I'm confused. I'm tired. I feel kind of sad. I'm scared but I'm not. I don't know.''

''Frustrated.''

She held her breath, looking down at her hands. ''Oh hell, why not? That, too.''

''Look at me, Mandy.''

Slowly she looked up at him. He was magnificent, she found herself thinking. He looked like a well-barbered Viking warrior.

''Would things be easier for you if I packed my duffel and took off in the morning?''

The question hung in the air between them. Ransom stood as silent and still as a statue, awaiting her answer.

''Probably,'' she said finally. ''But I don't want them to be easier. Sooner or later I'm going to have to deal with all this anyway.'' That much was obvious to her now. Her sanctuary had been invaded, and whether the warrior left now or later, his presence would leave its mark.

He gave a slow nod and pulled out a chair near hers. "How do you like your sandwich?" he asked, reaching for the bread. "Lots of tuna?"

"I can make it."

He turned, giving her an expressionless look. "Look, Mandy. My patience is wearing pretty thin right now. Don't argue, just answer."

"Just a spoonful of tuna, please."

She watched him make the sandwich and suddenly realized a couple of things. He looked tired, very tired. Beneath his deepening tan, he was pale, and there were lines of strain in his face. His mouth was compressed. She'd never seen Ransom's mouth compressed before.

"Ransom? Are you still hurting?"

He finished making her sandwich before he answered. "I shouldn't have jumped out of the truck, I guess."

"Did you hurt something?"

He shook his head. "Don't think so."

"Can you take anything for the pain?"

"Old blue jeans," he said suddenly.

Mandy blinked, then recalled the discussion they'd had last week about old jeans. "Cluck-cluck," she answered.

He flashed her a small smile. "I have codeine if I need it. I don't need it, though. It'll pass off."

"Cycles of the moon," she said slowly.

He turned, studying her face, then laughed. "Okay. Pax."

"Pax," she agreed.

Much later, it was obvious to Mandy that he had no intention of returning to his cabin that night. He joined her in the study while she wrote, and from time to time he would get up and walk through the house with a slow, measured tread. The last time he returned from prowling, she swiveled her chair and faced him.

"Ransom," she said.

"Yes, ma'am?"

"Are you trying to figure out how to tell me that your instincts, the warrior ones, are telling you to sleep here tonight?"

"Actually," he said with a small smile, "both sets of instincts are telling me to sleep here."

"There's a sofa bed in the living room and two guest bedrooms. Take your pick."

"Ouch."

She couldn't help but smile. "That's my best offer."

"I'll take it. Are you through writing?"

"For now."

"I made some hot chocolate. Can I interest you?"

"Just let me exit the program."

He returned with two cups just as she was switching off her computer. He set them down on the table by the easy chair and without a word drew Mandy firmly onto his lap.

She was surprised to realize there wasn't an ounce of resistance left in her. She was scared, but this was one moving freight train she couldn't step away from. It would end one way or another, but she couldn't bring herself to end it unborn. That was as scary as anything else, this lack of the will necessary to protect herself from certain pain.

So what? asked a little voice in her mind. She was thirty years old, too old to believe that another Ransom Laird would ever show up in her life, too old to believe that she would ever have another opportunity like this. The man touched her in so many ways that she was afraid to analyze it. He offered her glimpses of something beyond the ordinary, glimpses of light and life and color. Maybe, maybe, if she accepted his offering just once she could savor the gift without paying too highly.

"That's better," he said, when she was settled. He handed her a cup. "Careful, it's hot."

His free hand rubbed her arm gently. "You know, it's amazing, but just a couple of weeks ago I felt like I had hardly a friend in the world."

"You had Nate," she remarked.

"Nate and a few others, but that's not what I mean."

"I know," she said after a moment. "I know. Friends but not friends. Different levels of intimacy and understanding."

"Exactly. I don't feel friendless now, Mandy."

His blue eyes caught and reflected the lamplight. He was so close, Mandy thought. Hard beneath her, strong against her. If she moved two inches their mouths would meet. "I don't either," she answered softly. And that was absolutely the scariest thing of all.

His stroking hand paused, squeezed her upper arm, resumed its gentle caress.

"Tell me," she said, "what you were doing in the sixth century."

"Invading England with the Danes?" he suggested.

"Wasn't that the eighth century?"

He shrugged. "What were you doing in the sixth century?"

"Waiting for the twentieth. I spend all my time waiting. I'm beginning to think I'm the greatest time waster in eternity."

Leaning forward, she put her cup on the table. Everything inside her quailed at the realization that she was going to take this step for no better reason than that she would always regret it if she didn't. Surely, she told herself, the price of a single taste of heaven was something she could live with, for she certainly couldn't live with the price of passing it up. Gathering together every scrap of her courage, she said, "I'm through waiting."

Their eyes locked. For several heartbeats the universe stood still.

"Just tell me one thing, Ransom."

"Shoot."

"Is there somebody out there who wants to kill you?"

His face was suddenly inscrutable. "Not that I know of. I've been out of action for a long time, Mandy. Does it make a difference?"

She regarded him steadily. "No," she said finally. "Not now. In the long run, it might. I hate to think anybody might want to hurt you. But right now I wouldn't care if you were an inmate on death row." And that was downright terrifying.

He set his mug down. "Now *you* tell *me* something."

She nodded.

"Are you sure about this? Because, by God, if you're not, I'll understand. What I won't understand is if you regret this."

She drew a deep breath and expelled it slowly. "I think we've both got plenty of scars and wounds. I'm not looking to collect any more, and I'm not looking to inflict any."

"What were you doing yesterday, Amanda Lynn?" he asked softly.

"Waiting."

"And what will you be doing tomorrow?"

"Living." And hurting, too, probably, but she blocked that thought.

He smiled then, a gentle, warm smile. "I intend to see to it."

He kissed her tenderly, questingly. She responded without hesitation, welcoming the shaft of delight that plunged through her. She was committed now, and she threw restraint aside gladly. He made her feel so incredibly, wonderfully alive. He reminded her that for every pain, life offered a pleasure, if only you had the courage to reach for it.

His mouth was warm, tasting of chocolate, and it claimed hers with that beautiful rightness that only Ransom gave her, as if her mouth belonged to him, had been created for him, and his for her. The kiss deepened, and Mandy's head fell back against his cradling arm. His other hand stroked her gently, from her back to her hip and outer thigh, then up again. Slowly. His caress and kiss were deliciously slow, as if they had all the time in the world.

He smelled so good, she thought as her hand slid up his hard chest to his neck and then into his hair. Sun-kissed, musky and chocolaty. His beard was wonderfully soft against her cheeks and fresh smelling.

"Sweet, sweet Amanda," he whispered, raising his head a fraction. "You feel so good, taste so good. You fit so perfectly on my lap. I could almost spend eternity like this."

"Almost?" Her voice was a sigh.

"I'm only human after all," he said with a hint of laughter in his voice. "I'll succumb to temptation sooner or later."

"I'm all for succumbing," she answered, just as his mouth found hers again, this time in a sinuous, suggestive kiss that ignited the warm glow in her to an aching flame. "Oh, Ransom," she sighed. "Oh..."

Waves crashed in Ransom's head. Ocean surf pounded in his veins. He had thought he knew the dimensions of desire. Now he discovered he had only begun to explore them. Patience and gentleness escaped him. Panic lanced him. Abruptly he tore his mouth from Mandy's and hugged her tightly, stilling her. Her ragged breath was a warm torment against his neck.

"Mandy." Her name was an almost inaudible croak. He was trembling. God, how he was trembling! "Mandy." This time he found his voice. "We'd better not." Little in his life had been as difficult as saying those words.

Her hand made a convulsive movement against his chest, curling into a fist, pounding a single, painless protest against him. "What's wrong?" She sounded strained.

"Me." Closing his eyes, he battled for control. "It's been so long, and I want you so much. I don't want to frighten you. I'm like a bomb about to go off."

A minute passed, then another. His pulse slowed, and his panic became fear of another kind. And then Mandy raised her head.

"Ransom, if you don't want to frighten me, then you won't."

"You don't know—"

"You're right, I don't know. But I'm not afraid to find out."

"I want this to be perfect for you."

Mandy cupped his cheek and kissed his chin. "Perfection is an illusion. Why don't we shoot for it another time?"

She slipped from his lap and headed for the door. "Figure out what you really want. Me, or the illusion of self-control. I'm going up to bed."

The gauntlet was thrown, and he could almost see it lying on the floor.

Between them, he thought, they had enough devils and demons to do justice to one of her books. They needed to walk with care around each other in order to avoid treading in sore places. Ransom was exquisitely aware of the need for caution and delicacy in his relationship with Mandy, and right now he had the feeling he had transgressed.

She was right about the self-control, though. He was always in control of himself, if nothing else. It was why they had never been able to break him. He set very high standards for himself, standards he never sacrificed. Now he was close to losing that control, on the edge of sacrificing some of those standards, and she had challenged him to do it.

Could he go to her and take the one risk he had never taken? Could he take the risk of what he would see in her eyes later? Did he trust her that much? She had as good as told him that she trusted him implicitly. All he had to do was trust her in return.

Upstairs, Mandy had climbed into the king-size bed in one of the guest rooms. Tense, with a growing sense of disappointment, she waited. She understood, though. She had crossed enough hurdles of her own that she could sympathize with Ransom. This particular hurdle, she guessed, had taken him by surprise.

Ransom never came. Giving up finally, Mandy switched off the light and lay staring into the dark. Maybe he was right, she told herself, trying to ignore the slow, steady throbbing of her body. Maybe neither of them was prepared to be so vulnerable to another person. Ransom didn't want to lose control, didn't yet trust Mandy enough to come to her stripped of everything but his need. And if she was honest, she would admit that she'd had second thoughts almost from the instant she left the living room. She was coming to care deeply for Ransom, and in spite of her determination not to let her neurotic fears overwhelm her, she was nevertheless terrified. He would go away sooner or later, and she just didn't know if she would be strong enough to handle another loss. If she made love with him, her emotions would deepen. She didn't have a single doubt about that.

So let it ride, said the sane, sensible portion of her mind. Let it ride. It was too soon to know if she should risk this step.

But, oh, how empty her body felt, how she ached for his strength and weight. How alone and vulnerable she felt without him.

The feelings that Ransom had shelved for better than four years were shrieking to be let loose. He was up before dawn, and the pearly gray light found him splitting wood behind the barn. He had absolutely no intention of letting those feelings free. All his life, self-control had been the only thing that protected him. As long as he was in control of himself, no one else could control him. Once, just once, he'd relinquished some of that control for the sake of an unborn baby. That lapse had cost him dearly. Once he had trusted. It was suddenly apparent that he wasn't ready to do that again.

Sweat made a fine sheen on his skin as he split log after log. His breath rasped in the chilly morning air, drying out his throat. The demons were at the gate, and he didn't dare let them in. If once, just once, he allowed himself to feel any of the anger and anguish of the last four years, he might fall apart like Humpty Dumpty, never to be put back together again.

And then there was Mandy. Last night she'd offered herself without reservation, and he'd rejected her. It couldn't have made her feel too good, even though he'd told her that his reasons had nothing to do with her. He wasn't so much afraid of the strength of his desire for her as he was of breaching the dam. How could Mandy be expected to understand that? She couldn't, of course, so this morning she was probably feeling hurt and possibly humiliated.

So explain it to her, he told himself, swinging the axe once more in a savage stroke. Tell her you're sitting on a volcano of backlogged feelings. She'll understand.

Maybe, maybe not. At this point he wasn't even sure himself what he was afraid would happen if he let loose. He just knew it wouldn't be pretty.

"Ransom?"

Mandy's voice pierced his preoccupation. Altering his swing, he buried the axe head in the chopping block and then straightened slowly. Pulling a rag from his pocket, he wiped sweat from his face and neck.

She was behind him, and the knowledge made his back prickle. Shirtless, he was mercilessly exposed, and even though she'd seen his scars twice before, even though she'd made it plain they didn't repel her, he wasn't comfortable with it. He turned.

Mandy drew a deep breath as the full morning light bathed Ransom's face and chest, setting his hair on fire.

"You're so beautiful," she whispered.

Something in Ransom cracked, rupturing a fault so deep he knew he would never patch it. Instead of the furies he'd expected, however, there was a flood of warmth so healing that he caught his breath.

"I'm sorry," he said, surprising himself.

"What for?" Mandy asked. "We've both been racing headlong into something we're not ready for. I've been trying to convince myself I'm not frightened when I really am. And you—well, you're just not ready to trust enough to let go. I'm glad you pulled back, Ransom. I'm afraid we both would have regretted it if you hadn't." Turning, she headed back to the house, calling over her shoulder, "Breakfast is ready."

He admired her dignity. He didn't feel very dignified himself, standing there shirtless, covered with sweat, his muscles trembling from an attempt to smother the rage that sat like a cold lump of lead in his stomach. He didn't dare let it emerge. But didn't he have every right to be angry?

Muttering an obscenity, he turned toward his cabin. The least he could do was clean up a little and put on a shirt before he went to breakfast. He didn't want to think about any of it, but the fact was, he was beginning to wonder if he'd been crippled in ways that went far deeper than skin and bone.

A short while later, crossing the hard-packed earth to Mandy's kitchen door, he saw the missing windshield of her truck and was reminded of yesterday's events. Damn, he was slipping if his own inner turmoil could put something like that out of his mind. He'd clean forgotten about it.

"We'll have to do something about your windshield," he said to Mandy as he stepped into the kitchen. The screen door slapped shut behind him, and he closed the inner door against the morning chill. The kitchen was warm, quiet, inviting. Mandy sat at the table, a half eaten plate of scrambled eggs before her.

"Your eggs are cold," she said calmly. "I'll heat them in the microwave."

"Don't bother. It's my fault for dawdling." He pulled out his chair and sat across from her. At least she hadn't retreated to the far end of the table again. "About that windshield. Do you have insurance?"

"Against being shot at?"

He grimaced. "Against vandalism. Call it vandalism. It was an accident, damn it. I'll take it into town this morning and see about getting it fixed." It would give him an opportunity to make a phone call where she couldn't hear.

"There's no rush. I'll just call my insurance agent and tell him what happened. We can take care of it whenever it's convenient."

"It's also apt to turn into winter at any moment, and it'll be damn cold driving without a windshield, Mandy."

She shrugged. "Have it your way." What was eating him?

He ate the rest of his breakfast in silence. It was only as he pushing his chair back from the table that he looked at her. "I'm sorry," he said for the second time that morning. "I'm sorry about last night, and I'm sorry for being so angry this morning. Sometimes I just . . . get angry."

Her head tilted, and her expression gentled. "I guess I can see why you would. Forget about it. I will."

"Thanks. I'll take care of that truck now. Is there anything you want from town?"

Mandy shook her head. "I've got everything I need. I'll call ahead to my agent and tell him you're coming."

He moved around the table and bent over her, tilting her head up for a kiss. "It'll pass," he murmured. "I promise to come home in a better mood."

That was probably why he wanted to go to town, Mandy thought as she watched him turn the truck and head down the driveway. To get away until he got a grip on his anger. Well, if anyone had a right to be angry, surely Ransom did.

The drive to town cleared Ransom's head more than chopping wood had. Maybe it was the wind blowing in his face, or maybe it was just the silence and sunshine; whatever, he felt almost human by the time he pulled up in front of the sheriff's offices.

Nate was buried in his office, burrowing his way through the mounds of paper that came with his job. He always put it off until the last possible minute, preferring to be a lawman rather than a clerk, but at least once a month he paid the piper. Ransom's arrival was a welcome distraction.

"If I didn't know better," Nate drawled as he leaned back and peered up at Ransom, "I'd say you look like a man with weighty things on his mind. Where's Mandy?"

"At home."

"Pull up a chair, son," Nate invited. "Do we need the whole posse, or will I do?"

Ransom half smiled and folded himself into a chair. "You'll do, Nate. You always did."

"So what's up?"

"I came into town to get the windshield on Mandy's truck replaced. Somebody shot it out last night when we were driving home. Buckshot."

Nate let out a low whistle and leaned forward. "Did you see 'em?"

"Nope. I told Mandy it was just some kids, that one of them had probably tripped and the gun went off by accident."

"But you don't believe it."

Ransom shrugged. "Hard to believe it was anything else. But it's also hard to believe it was a couple of kids when I didn't see any kids. Unless kids in these parts lie low and deliberately shoot at passing vehicles."

"Never had anything like that in all the years I've been sheriff." Nate rubbed his chin. "If it was an accident, you would have seen the kids fooling around by the road."

"That's how I figure it. I would have seen *something*."

"But nobody who seriously wants to hurt somebody tries buckshot through a windshield."

"That also occurred to me."

Nate regarded Ransom steadily. "You think it was a warning."

"That's the only thing that makes sense. The question is, what kind of warning, and who sent it? People in my business don't play that way."

"You think somebody's trying to scare Mandy?" Nate sounded disbelieving. "Look, man, John Grant engendered a lot of goodwill in Conard County. Everybody who knew him had a lot of liking and respect for him, and most of that feeling applies to Mandy, as well. Folks around here would do just about anything for her if she'd let them."

"I wasn't seeing it quite that way," Ransom said, with a quick shake of his head. "No, I think I'm the one being warned. The question is, why? Would somebody have reason to want me to move on? Maybe somebody with a personal interest in Mandy?"

"Mandy's gone out of her way not to encourage that kind of interest since John died. It kind of surprises me that she's interested in you, if you want to know the truth. Even if that weren't the case, you're talking about a sick mind. I'd like to think I'd have at least some suspicion if one of the folks around here was unhinged."

"You feel you know everyone that well?" Ransom asked.

"I've lived here all my life," Nate answered steadily. "Except for three years in Nam, at any rate. A sheriff's a politician as well as a lawman, Ransom, and there's not so many people in this county that I haven't gotten to know them all one way or the other over forty-odd years. I can't say for a fact that none of these folks would do such a thing, but I feel I'd have some notion of it if one of 'em was weird like this."

Ransom folded his arms across his chest. "So you tell me what you think is going on. I admit that twenty years in my line of work can make a man paranoid, but so can buckshot through a windshield."

Nate laid his hands flat on the desk. "Are you sure you didn't bring one of your own problems with you?"

"I told you, people in my business don't work this way. A high-powered rifle would be more their speed, and they'd aim to kill, not frighten."

"So maybe somebody wants to play a little cat and mouse with you, make you sweat. I admit that calls for a weird kind of mind, but I can see someone from your business thinking that way a hell of a lot easier than I can see one of my neighbors pulling a stunt like this."

Ransom shook his head. "I don't like it, Nate. That's too easy. In the first place, I've been out of action for the last four-and-a-half years. Only a handful of people know I'm still alive, and the official word among the handful who do is that I'm taking a medical retirement. Anyway, I've been gone so long that I'm not a threat to anyone."

"Somebody thinks you're a threat," Nate said gruffly. "What're you going to do about it?"

Ransom yielded a heavy sigh. "Not a whole hell of a lot, Nate. Not a whole hell of a lot."

"Why not?"

"Just what am I supposed to do? Without any idea of what's going on, anything I do might be exactly the wrong thing."

Nate scowled. "You damn well better be careful. And you better look out for Mandy, too, or I'll be nailing your hide to the barn wall."

"Nothing's going to happen to Mandy," Ransom said grimly. "I can promise you that much. I won't let it."

After he left Nate's office, he hunted up a pay phone and placed a long distance call. The person who answered listened without interruption as Ransom spoke. When he fell silent, the voice on the other end said, "You're officially on leave." In other words, since he wasn't on a mission, he couldn't expect any help. The next sound was that of a phone being disconnected.

Ransom was in the act of slamming the receiver into the cradle when he realized he was being watched. That tingle on the back of his neck was unmistakable. Instantly, he spun around to catch the watcher.

There wasn't a soul in sight.

Not yet ready to believe his eyes over his instincts, he scanned the windows of the surrounding buildings for a sign, any sign, that someone was staring down at him. That was when he noticed the five-year-old child in the window of the convenience store. Relieved, he released his breath.

Damn, he was too much on edge. That was dangerous. He had to stay calm enough to act, not just react. Calm enough to think, weigh and plan. Calm enough to deal with the fact that he was utterly and completely on his own. Usually he was on his own only during a mission, when he always knew who and what he was up against. This time was different. This time he was looking into the dark, and he didn't have an idea in hell who was out there waiting for him.

Hell!

Well, if he didn't accomplish anything else today, he could go into the next county and get some condoms. If things got out of hand again, at least he would be able to protect Mandy from that much.

It was after four when Mandy heard the truck pull up outside. She caught herself just as she was rising from her computer and sat back down again. Considering the odd mood Ransom had been in that morning, she decided it would be better to let him look for her in his own good time. A few minutes later, when it was evident he wasn't coming into the house, she forced her attention back to her writing. Whatever had been bothering him that morning was clearly still working on him.

At five she started dinner, wondering if she were wasting her time. Maybe he was as unnerved as she was by their precipitate rush toward intimacy. Good grief, it had taken her nearly three years to get this close to John.

The thought set her back on her heels. Her hands started to shake, and her mouth went dry. What was she thinking of, to let her feelings grow so swiftly, and for a man about whom she knew so little? He was just a drifter, pausing briefly in her life while he healed. In no time at all he would go back to his job and his other life and leave her once again in solitude. How could she risk her hard-won peace this way?

"The truck is fixed, Mandy," Ransom said from behind her. The slap of the screen door punctuated the sentence.

"Thank you." The words were muffled, difficult to say with parched lips and tongue. To still their trembling, she clasped her hands on the counter in front of her.

"Something wrong?" His booted feet halted right behind her.

"No. Nothing."

He didn't believe her. Strong, hard arms closed around her from behind, folding across her stomach just below her breasts. His warm lips found the vulnerable side of her neck, right below her ear, and a helpless shiver passed through her in response.

"Are you mad at me?" he asked, his warm breath caressing her ear.

"Of course not," she managed to say. Mad? There was no room for anything else with all her panic. Why was it that every time he touched her, her common sense flew out the window? Her hands were shaking now for a different reason, and all she wanted to do was turn around and melt into his embrace.

"Then look at me," he demanded quietly.

She turned within the circle of his arms because she was helpless to do anything else. She was starved for the sight of him, the look of him, the Viking warrior harshness of his bearded face.

"What scared you?" he asked gently, tracing her cheek with a gentle fingertip.

"How do you know I'm scared?" The words were little more than a rush of breath.

"I can smell it on you," he said bluntly. "I can feel it in the way your heart is racing. Are you afraid of me?"

Not even in a desperate need for self-preservation could she tell that lie. "No."

"Then what?"

"Me," she admitted, her head dropping.

He understood. His hand left her cheek, and both arms tightened around her in a comforting embrace. With her face pressed to his hard chest, with his masculine scent rich in her nose, Mandy knew a sense of security that was as utterly irrational as it was undeniable.

"I'm scared, too," he admitted, closing his eyes and pressing his lips to the top of her head. God, yes, he was scared. He was forty-one years old, and for the first time in all those years he felt ties forming, strings that were binding him, tugging on him. He was being pulled to Mandy in a way that was steadily limiting his options. All day, ever since he'd left Nate's office, he'd been telling himself that it was time to move on. Something was wrong, somebody was after him, and he didn't want to risk any harm coming to Mandy. Yet here he was, holding her once again, knowing damn well that not all the furies of hell could take him from her side. Not yet. Not yet.

She was, he was sure, feeling the same way. It was as if neither of them could survive the wound of ending their relationship, even though they both were convinced that the damage would only be worse if they waited. What a hell of a situation.

"Dinner's going to burn," she said faintly against his chest.

He let her go reluctantly.

That night, Ransom didn't sleep worth a damn. He let Mandy think he had returned to his own cabin, but instead he chose to maintain his vigilance over her. She never locked her doors, once a pardonable omission considering where she lived, but pardonable no longer. He made a mental note to tell her first thing in the morning that she had better start locking her doors. He had avoided such discussions because he didn't want to alarm her, but now he acknowledged that had been a dangerous decision.

Until he saw her bedroom light go out, he waited outside, listening and watching. When he was certain she must be asleep, he let himself into her house, leaving the chilly, empty night behind. He could have stationed himself in the living room, but it had been a long time since he had stood night guard-duty, and he wasn't sure he could count on his battered body and mind to stay awake. Instead he sat at the kitchen table, on one of the uncomfortable oak chairs. He made coffee and sat in the dark waiting. Watching. Listening.

And remembering. That was the damnable thing about the long, empty hours. His mind filled the void with images, and those visions were too often unwelcome memories. In the dead of night he discovered just how many appalling memories he had. Surely that said something about him. Well, hell, he already knew it was time to reevaluate himself.

He also found himself reviewing rusty skills in his mind and considering how he might best secure Mandy's castle against intrusion. Nate could do little except keep an eye out for strangers in the county and tell his deputies to stop by the ranch a couple of times a day. For full-time guard-duty there was only himself, and after so many years he doubted his abilities.

There had been a time when he had been confident that if he slept, he would wake at the first sign of anything untoward, no matter how subtle. During his days as a captive, however, he had learned to sleep deeply and let nothing disturb him. It had been a survival skill, and, like most of his survival skills, he had learned it well. So well that he wasn't at all sure anything short of a nuclear attack could wake him.

How long could he keep this up? He asked himself the question and had no answer. He was being foolish, he guessed. A man had to sleep sometime. Nevertheless, he couldn't stand the thought of sleeping while Mandy was sleeping, because she would be defenseless. Someone had to watch over her.

That meant he was going to have to devise a means of safeguarding her while he slept. In the long, lonely hours of the night, he forced himself to consider Mandy's protection and shied away from other thoughts.

Somewhere deep inside, he knew he had become a hunted man. Who was after him, or why, he couldn't begin to fathom, but with gut certainty he knew that someone was hunting him, toying with him like a cat just before the kill.

And with equal certainty he knew he had to protect Mandy. He had led them to her, and they wouldn't forget her if he vanished. No, they would try to use her, and he couldn't expose her to that.

So he sat in the chilly hours before dawn and wondered what the hell he was going to do. The warrior had led the damn evil wizard right to the princess's walls.

Chapter 6

An unusual fog bathed the dawn in pearl gray mists. From the window of her bedroom Mandy looked out to discover that she couldn't even see as far as the barn. In fact, she could hardly see the ground below.

It was as if they had been plucked from the planet and set in some alien world, she thought whimsically. Whimsical or not, the sensation created by the thick fog was eerie and unnerving. Evil. She turned from the window suddenly, feeling the back of her neck prickle with fear. Ridiculous, she scolded herself. Your imagination has always been too vivid.

The morning's damp chill had penetrated the entire house. She washed up swiftly and climbed hurriedly into a thick, warm jogging suit, a baggy navy blue number that she loved for its comfort and warmth and which did absolutely nothing else for her. She'd had it for years, and John had teased her about it being a security blanket. Maybe it was. It certainly felt like armor against some of the malevolence she sensed in the morning.

She found Ransom in the kitchen making coffee and frying bacon. One look at him and she knew he hadn't slept a wink. Not a wink. Did he really think he could fool her?

As she stood in the doorway of the kitchen, a storm whipped through her, sweeping away a mountain of illusions to which she had been stubbornly clinging. She couldn't escape life. Not really. She had buried herself as far out and as far away as she could get, and life had simply walked right up to her door and dragged her back into the game. A truly dangerous game, to judge by Ransom's attempts to dissemble for her.

Her knees turned to water and her mouth became as dry as cotton while she contemplated the reality that lurked beyond her fortress walls. Fortress walls that she had apparently built from the diaphanous stuff of fantasy rather than substantial brick and mortar.

Almost stunned, feeling as if she were standing brutally exposed on a high, windy precipice while cold winds threatened to topple her over the edge, she turned away and headed for the shelter of her study. She had thought she didn't ask much of life. How much, after all, was it to want to simply be free of hurt and terror? Too much, evidently.

Perhaps, she found herself thinking almost numbly, if she couldn't escape the hurt and fear, then maybe she was an utter fool to pass up the joy and pleasure. But her every instinct for self-preservation recoiled from that concept. Caring made the pain even worse.

She might conceivably have spent the entire morning staring numbly at her computer while she tried to cope with her shattered illusions of safety, except that once again life refused to let her hide. The unexpected sound of a car coming up the driveway dragged her out of her preoccupation.

Must be Nate, she thought, or one of his deputies. They were the only people who stopped by without calling first. Glad of the distraction, she hurried out to the kitchen in time to find Ransom setting breakfast on the table and Micah Parish, one of Nate's deputies, climbing out of his dusty Blazer parked near the kitchen door.

Opening the inner door in greeting, Mandy watched the deputy come across the dusty, hard-packed dirt to the porch steps. Other deputies had come to check on her before, but never Micah. She guessed he *had* thought she resented him, and she was suddenly very glad she had spoken to him the other morning.

Micah had come to town four years ago, just after John died. Mandy still remembered him getting out of a battered old pickup and crossing the sun-drenched main street toward Nate's office. She had been there to pick up a box of John's personal effects, and she had watched Micah Parish's approach with a fascination that had briefly pierced her grief. He had been wearing desert camouflage, and Nate, who had served with him in Vietnam, hired Parish, newly retired from the army, on the spot.

"Morning, Micah," she said as he reached the lower step. "Do you have time for some breakfast?"

He mounted the three steps and gave her one of his small, rare smiles. "I've got plenty of time, Mandy. Thanks. Is Ransom around?"

"Ransom's doing the cooking," Ransom said from right behind Mandy. She felt him, felt his heat. Just knowing he was there, right behind her, and that all she had to do to be in his arms was take a step backward, nearly erased her awareness of everything else. Ransom broke the spell by reaching around her to unlatch the screen door. "Come on in, Micah."

That was when Mandy realized that these two men knew each other. There was something in the way their eyes met— Ransom's so blue, Micah's so black—that spoke of understanding.

"How long have you two been acquainted?" she asked.

Ransom looked down at her with a faint smile. "Since Nam."

No further explanation seemed to be required. Even if it had been, she didn't think she would get it. Sensing that if she pushed she was going to run up against a couple of stone

walls, she held her peace for the time being and helped
Ransom finish putting breakfast on the table.

Men could be the most frustrating creatures, she found
herself thinking a few minutes later. Two women friends
who hadn't seen each other in years would be talking up a
storm. These two men didn't say a word. Instead they ate in
a silence that somehow seemed more companionable than
any conversation she had ever shared.

Not until he had finished the last bite did Micah speak.
"Nate figured you'd be getting pretty sleepy around about
now."

A smile nudged one corner of Ransom's mouth. "Nate
figured right. More coffee?"

"Thanks."

Ransom refilled all three mugs. As he did so, he looked
at Mandy, looked her right in the eye. It was a look that
seemed to see all her uneasy and contradictory thoughts and
feelings.

Disturbed, she looked away. "Why did Nate think Ransom would be getting tired?" As if she didn't know. It was
suddenly, painfully apparent that Ransom had spoken to
Nate and shared concerns that he had refused to share with
her. *Kids fooling around in the grass, my foot!*

Micah looked at Ransom as if for permission to answer
her, and Mandy suddenly resented it. This was her home,
her life, and these men had barreled into it without so much
as a by-your-leave, bringing all their violence and ugly games
with them. She set her mug down with a sharp crack and
rose, drawing their eyes to her.

"If I'm not old enough to hear it, intelligent enough to
understand it and trustworthy enough to be told, then I
guess I'm too young, too dumb and too unsteady to be involved. This is my home, gentlemen. Take your problems
elsewhere!"

Ransom caught her in the hallway outside the kitchen.
Grim-lipped, he wrapped an arm around her waist and
hauled her into her study. There, he leaned back against the
closed door and tugged her into the V between his legs,

pressing every inch of her torso intimately to his. And then he kissed her. Violently. Savagely. Like a Viking warrior claiming an unwilling captive.

And just as suddenly, before she could do more than register an explosion of internal heat, he lifted his head and glared down at her. His voice was little more than an angry whisper.

"If I thought my leaving would keep you clear of this," he growled at her, "I would have been gone two nights ago. Unfortunately, princess, any chance of keeping you out of it was gone the minute they found me."

Her wits seemed to have scattered to the four winds before the fury of his kiss, and it was a moment before she collected herself enough to whisper, "Who? Who are they? What do they want?"

He shook his head, every line of his face bleak. "I wish I knew. I wish I had even a foggy idea. I made a call yesterday and couldn't find out a damn thing. The simple fact is that this shouldn't be happening, because only a handful of people have any idea I'm alive, or that I'm here. I've been out of action so damn long, there shouldn't be anyone who wants me, anyway. I've spent the last day and a half racking my brains trying to figure out who could possibly have a score that big to settle with me. Anyone else would have long since forgotten me."

Helpless to stop herself, telling herself she ought to still be angry, ought to feel somehow betrayed, she reached up and touched his face. At the moment all she seemed capable of knowing was that this man was pursued by demons he couldn't seem to shake. The injustice of it was bitter bile on her tongue, and she felt helpless to console him. Unable to tell him these things, she simply said, "What now?"

"I guess Nate asked Micah to spell me so I could sleep. Other than that, I don't know. I just plain don't know, Mandy."

He looked so tired, so... defeated, somehow, as if this were the last straw. Maybe for him it was, after everything he'd been through. He was, after all, just beginning to recover from his last battle, just beginning to find his feet and his direction and his purpose. Aching for him, Mandy leaned into him and wrapped her arms around his waist. With her cheek on his chest, she listened to his heartbeat.

"It's okay," she said pointlessly, the soothing, meaningless incantation of a person with nothing else to offer in the way of comfort except caring. "It's okay." A hard little kernel of resolve began to grow in her. She had no idea how she was going to find the courage to do it, but somehow, some way, she would stand beside Ransom through this. He'd been alone long enough, she thought.

When they returned to the kitchen a few minutes later, Micah was waiting for them as patiently as the earth and trees. He looked up impassively, not even by the minutest flicker of a muscle betraying what he might think.

"You get some sleep," he said to Ransom. "I'll spell you. And then between us maybe we can come up with something."

The fog clung throughout the day. Every time Mandy looked up from her work, gray ghosts swirled slowly beyond the windows, pressing inward. The gloom invaded her writing until finally she had taken an entirely different turn in the tale than she had planned to. Uncertain whether the turn was right or wrong for the story, she gave up in disgust.

Micah made it clear he wasn't a guest and didn't want to be treated like one. He wandered in and out of the kitchen, accepting nothing but a mug of coffee from time to time. He spent most of his time outside, prowling. Patrolling. Guarding. Evidently it was good enough for Ransom, because he slept a solid eight hours.

Mandy was cooking dinner and had persuaded Micah to take a seat at the table when Ransom finally made his appearance. His hair was wet from a shower, his shirttails hung out, and he was yawning hugely as he stepped through the door.

Micah grinned faintly. "You sure needed that, man."

"Yeah." Smothering another yawn, Ransom headed for the coffeepot. "I went out like a light."

Without the least bit of self-consciousness, he startled Mandy by bending to kiss her cheek as he reached for the coffeepot.

In that moment, as color flooded her face and her heart skipped a beat or two, Mandy envied Ransom. He saw what he wanted and he went for it. He didn't analyze every little thing to death the way she did. No. He wanted to kiss her, so he kissed her, and to hell with Micah and the rest of the world. Why couldn't she be a little like that?

Ransom joined Micah at the table, turning his chair so that he could sit sideways to the table and stretch out his long legs. He looked so damn relaxed, Mandy thought, watching from the corner of her eye as he crossed his booted legs at the ankle and smothered another yawn. As if everything were perfectly normal. As if he weren't being hunted.

His first words dispelled that illusion. "Did you get wind of anything today?" he asked Micah.

Mandy's hands froze in the process of stirring the browning meat and onions. A moment later she started stirring again, not wanting either of the men to know how intently she was listening.

"Mebbe," was Micah's laconic answer.

Maybe? *Maybe?* When Micah said nothing to elaborate, Mandy had to restrain an urge to turn on him and demand an explanation. She didn't know Micah well, but she knew him well enough to know he wouldn't say a word he didn't choose to.

After an endless pause, Micah spoke again, dropping his rare words like pebbles into the pool of silence. "Show you after supper."

In the silence that Micah seemed to carry with him like a cloak, Mandy realized just how accustomed she had become to Ransom's companionship at the table. The two of them always talked, always discussed the day's events, and often discussed more momentous things, things like memories and past events, things like hopes and feelings.

Micah short-circuited all that. Anyone would have had some effect on the direction of Ransom's and Mandy's conversation, of course, but she doubted anyone else would have cast a pall of complete silence over them. Micah clearly felt no need for casual speech and appeared utterly unperturbed by the silence. If Ransom was disturbed, he showed no evidence of it, seeming to find the lack of talk completely normal.

It was a mark of the changes in her that Mandy did *not* find it either unremarkable or normal. In fact, it seemed downright unsociable. The only alternative, however, was to make conversation simply for the sake of filling the silence, and that she refused to do. After all, the only safe, neutral topic would be weather, and, like most writers, she had a horror of the trite, even if she *did* occasionally have to resort to it.

After dinner Micah complimented her cooking and then pushed his chair back from the table. "Come on, I'll show you what I found. Then I gotta get back and take care of my livestock."

He led them outside and toward the front of the house. Just before they reached the corner of the porch, he stopped beneath the living room window and hunkered down. Ransom hunkered down beside him, and Mandy peered over Ransom's shoulder.

Micah reached out and pushed aside a marigold plant. There, in the softer topsoil of her garden, she saw a footprint. A small, fresh footprint.

"Too big for Mandy's foot," Micah remarked. "Might almost be a man's size eight or nine. Figure it was someone weighing maybe 130, 140 pounds."

Mandy's heart had begun to beat rapidly, a nervous, unhappy tattoo. "And just what do you think someone was doing in my marigold patch, Micah?" There was, of course, only one thing they could have been doing, but it was so outlandish and outrageous, she wanted someone else to say it.

Micah looked at Ransom as if for permission, then said, "Reckon they were looking in your window, Mandy. Ground's too dry away from the flower beds to tell if they looked in any other windows. Or where they might have come from."

She was suddenly cold in a way that had little to do with the evening's chill. Straightening, she rubbed her arms vigorously, torn between a desire to walk away from this into the house and a need to hear whatever might be said between these men. The fog was creepy, she thought, as icy fingers of fear danced along her spine. It would be dark soon. She had never been terrified of night in her entire life, but now, suddenly, she dreaded the approach of darkness.

"Let's get you inside."

Ransom's voice startled her, and she looked toward him to discover that he had risen and was studying her closely. "I'm fine," she lied.

"Like hell." One corner of his mouth lifted in a humorless smile. "You look like someone just walked over your grave." He slipped an arm around her shoulders and drew her close to his side as he turned to face Micah. "Thanks, Micah. I'll call you later."

Micah nodded, touched the brim of his Stetson hat to Mandy and strode off toward his Blazer.

"Come on, princess," Ransom said gruffly, and guided her toward the kitchen porch. When she stumbled over something, he simply swept her up in his arms and carried her.

"Put me down, damn it," she protested, somehow managing to sound as if she didn't mean it.

"Just as soon as we get inside. You know, I always wanted to be a knight in shining armor and rescue some damsel in distress. I can get used to this."

She scowled. "Don't. I'm not interested in being anybody's damsel, in distress or otherwise."

"I know." The teasing note vanished from his voice as they stepped into the kitchen. Gently, he lowered her feet to the floor. When he was sure she was balanced, he slackened his hold and with one finger tilted her face up to him.

"Day by day," he said quietly, "I get stronger. Little by little, I mend. And more and more, I feel like a man. Especially around you, Amanda Lynn. Especially around you." Bending, he covered her mouth with his.

It was a kiss that was astonishingly gentle, that made unnamed, unknown places in her heart and soul ache with a keen longing. A sound escaped her, a soft sorrowful sound like the mournful note of a dove, a sound that spoke of unfulfilled hopes and dreams, of losses and disappointments. Her hands rose and dove into the golden silk of his hair as pain and yearning warred within her. Why? she wondered dazedly. Why was everything that mattered always denied to her?

Ransom pulled away suddenly, but before she could protest, his purpose became clear. He closed and locked the door, switched out the kitchen light, then scooped her up again. He carried her into her study, and once again she found herself on his lap. And once again he tilted her face to his so that his mouth could seek the softness of hers.

As night gathered around the house, something else gathered around the two of them. Not quite passion, not quite hunger, not quite... Not quite. It was a promise more than a fulfillment, an intent more than a deed.

"Ah, princess," he sighed raggedly against her mouth just before his tongue made a provocative foray into her silken heat.

He knew how to kiss. Nobody, Mandy thought dazedly, nobody ought to be able to cast such a stirring spell with a simple kiss. His tongue stroked hers in a supple, evocative rhythm. Slowly. Deeply. Tenderly. There was nothing demanding, nothing harsh or hungry or cruel; there was only a gentle invitation. And he kissed as if the kiss were itself the consummation. There was no hurry, no sense that he wanted to move on, or that this was merely a step in a journey. No, his kiss was the beginning and end, a pleasure he savored with undisguised enjoyment.

From time to time he paused, lifting his head so they could catch their breath, and then he scattered small, soft, warm, loving kisses on her cheeks, her chin, the tip of her nose.

"Amanda Lynn," he whispered once, achingly, and then bent to steal her breath yet again.

A wizard's spell, she thought dazedly. A mage's enchantment filling her with a burning ache that made her insides throb in a slow, deep demand for more. She felt, but could not prevent, the rise of her hips, the instinctive undulation that signalled her need. Lifting, she sought relief and found only temporary surcease as her thighs clamped together.

He felt the slight movement of her bottom against his lap as she responded to her woman's nature. Awe struck him, causing him to tear his mouth from hers to look, to see that she was indeed so needy for him. He was a good lover, he had always satisfied his partners, but he had never brought one to this kind of response with only a few kisses. Touched, humbled, he was also frightened. Too much. Too soon. He wanted her willing compliance, not her seduction. Her seduction would wound them both.

Bending his head, he kissed her once more, but differently, with a gentler, more comforting quality. He wrapped his arms around her more snugly, tucked her into the sheltering curve of his torso and soothed her tenderly.

He wanted this woman with a terrifying ache that went deeper than the hot throbbing of his loins. He wanted her, but he had no right to take her. Not so long as he was hunted.

Mandy might have been embarrassed, except that Ransom held her so tenderly, as if she were incredibly precious to him. He trailed soft kisses along her jaw until at last she let go of her body's tension and relaxed against him. When she gathered courage to open her eyes, she found him smiling down at her, his blue eyes warm like summer skies.

But neither of them said anything. They trembled on the verge of discovery, but neither of them dared look over the edge.

"I'm afraid."

She said the words aloud at last. Standing with her hands submerged in soapy dishwater, acutely aware that Ransom was prowling the house like a guard again, even as he made occasional stabs at helping with the dishes, she admitted her fear. Saying it, facing it, helped a little. But only a little.

Ransom's arms closed around her waist from behind, and he pressed his face warmly against the side of her neck. "I swear," he whispered huskily, "I won't let anything happen to you, Mandy."

"That might not be entirely under your control," she replied a little unsteadily. Nor was it her biggest fear.

"They'll have to kill me first." There was no huskiness in that statement. It was a simple, flat declaration of fact.

She believed him. *That* was her biggest fear. And that was the yawning gulf between them. In that instant she became sharply aware of who and what he was. Stepping aside, she reached for a towel to dry her hands, then turned to face him.

A warrior. A man whose life was shadowed by violence and blood. A man who had lived by the sword. A man who might now die by it.

Closing her eyes against the sudden grip of pain, she found John's memory waiting for her. John had been a warm, loving, gentle man. Vividly she could recall the tenderness of his nature, the way children had instinctively trusted him. Gentleness and kindness notwithstanding, he had been torn from her by the sword of violence and hatred and fear, by the sword of the world men had created with their savage natures.

Now she opened her eyes and faced Ransom, who watched her narrowly with both concern and an elemental distrust. Elemental because she was sure it was a deeply ingrained part of his nature. When had he last been able to trust anyone? Certainly he couldn't even now.

Every line of him spoke of hardness and harshness. He made no allowances for himself, she sensed, but always demanded he live up to some high ideal. An ideal of being tougher, harder, faster, smarter. An ideal that encompassed honor and duty. An ideal that would make him step between her and any kind of danger. An ideal that would make him die in the place of others.

John, too, had shared that ideal in his own gentler way. *A greater gift hath no man....*

And heaven help the women who loved these noble, honorable protectors. These warriors on the side of right. These guardians of civilization. These men who were prepared to sacrifice everything to protect the flame of decency. God help them.

Once again she turned, away from Ransom this time. She understood these men because her tales were full of them. She recognized some part of them inside herself, comprehended their devotion to what they saw as their duty. She respected them, she honored them, but dear God, she didn't want to care about one of them ever again.

"Mandy?"

"Forget it," she said. "Just forget it." The dishes could wait. Everything could wait. Turning on her heel, she tossed the towel aside and headed for her study. There, at least, it was all fantasy. The pain wasn't real.

The fog was unnatural, Ransom thought. It was nearly midnight, and he left the house to prowl around outside, to look for anything untoward. He wasn't a man who believed in ghosts or magic or other supernatural things, but this fog, natural as he knew it must be, still *felt* unnatural.

Well, he thought, as he moved with a silent stealth he had feared he might have lost, this weather would sure make a great background for one of Mandy's stories. It would be easy, too easy, to believe that some evil wizard had created this fog to dull his senses and block his vision, to conceal the approach of sinister things in the dark.

He grinned into the teeth of the night, amused by his own fancifulness. The amusement didn't last long, however. He had read Mandy's expression earlier in the kitchen, and he had a good idea of where her thoughts had strayed. She was scared again, emotionally scared. Strange, but he didn't think she feared for her physical safety nearly as much as she feared emotional pain.

Nor did he have any right to cause her *any* kind of pain, physical or emotional. That was what his presence here had done, though. Damn!

And his conversation on the telephone with Micah a couple of hours ago hadn't helped any. Nate had warned all his deputies to keep an eye out for any strangers in Conard County, but other than the usual snowbirds headed south, no strangers had been sighted. That didn't mean there weren't any, of course, but without a hint about where to begin, there was little any of them could do.

All the combined skills and experience of Nate, Micah and Ransom had yielded no better plan than to be vigilant. Hell!

Nor were his contacts in the agency any more helpful. In theory, beyond a small handful of highly trusted, highly placed persons, no one knew that Ransom was back from the dead. Even in the hospital he had been shielded behind a false identity.

Still, like a green fool, he had come to a place where he had ties in the form of Nate Tate, a public figure. But it had never entered his head that anyone in the world might be trying to find him, never entered his mind that he might need to exercise discretion. That made him a complete and total fool, he guessed, albeit a forgivable one.

The unforgivable part was that he had jeopardized Mandy.

He would have muttered a string of obscenities, but long practice kept him quiet. If someone was watching or listening in this fog, they mustn't be able to detect his passing.

Like a gray wraith, he slipped through the swirling mists in total silence.

Mandy heard Ransom come in a short while later. She couldn't sleep, and when she had heard him go outside, any desire to try had vanished. The relief she felt upon hearing his return absolutely staggered her, and without another thought she pulled on her bathrobe and hurried barefoot down the stairs.

She found him in the kitchen making yet another pot of coffee. He stood in the dark at the stove, the blue of the propane flame the only illumination. It was eerie, she thought as she paused on the threshold. The blue glow reminded her of the magic she often described in her books, and it shrouded Ransom in unearthly light.

"Can't sleep, princess?" His query was soft as he turned his head to look at her.

There was a stillness in him that blended with the night, a quiet that was more than superficial. She sensed, as surely as if she could read his mind, how acute his senses were right then, how preternaturally alert he was at that moment. She would have had no trouble believing he could hear the swish of her flannel nightgown against her thighs.

"I . . . heard you go out," she said, because she couldn't speak her real thoughts. Thoughts about his magnificence, his virility, his sheer masculine impact at this moment. Thoughts about how much his safety had come to mean to her.

"Just checking things out." His voice remained little more than a whisper, as if he didn't wish to dull his senses with sound. "Everything's okay."

She took a hesitant step into the kitchen, wondering if he wanted her to go, or if perhaps he wanted her to stay, wishing she had the simple courage to reach out for what she wanted the way he did.

Instead, he reached out for her. In a straightforward gesture of invitation that made her throat tighten, he held out one arm, asking her to step up against his side and into his embrace. And when she did, his arm settled around her shoulders, making her feel both safe and welcome.

While the coffee perked, they stood together in the silence and said not a word. He smelled of the night air, and of man. The combination was enticing, and she rubbed her cheek against the side of his chest like a contented cat. His hand tightened a little on her shoulder, a gentle gesture of pleasure and encouragement.

"So we just wait?" she asked finally. "Just wait for somebody to take another potshot at you?"

He sighed and rubbed her shoulder. "Damned if I can think of anything else at the moment." He squeezed her, then released her so he could turn off the flame and poured a couple of mugs of coffee.

Mandy accepted the coffee and waited, missing the comfort of his arm, but unable to ask him to hold her. For a moment he was both silent and motionless, and then he said, "I guess we could sit in the living room."

Why the living room? she wondered as she led the way through the darkened house. The curtains there were drawn, shielding them from any prying eyes, but she understood when he took her mug and set it on the coffee table.

"Come here," he said as he sat beside her, and the next thing she knew she was lying full length on the couch with her head cradled on his lap. He lifted his booted feet to the coffee table and settled back, sipping coffee and stroking her arm and shoulder.

"You don't really want that coffee," he murmured. "It'll keep you up."

Keep her up? What the hell did he think *he* was doing by putting her head on his lap and stroking her? Every nerve ending in her body had suddenly decided to wake up and join the party.

Just as she was trying to decide if it would be wiser for her to return to bed or give in to her hammering impulses, Ransom reached for the clip that bound her hair and released it.

"I don't know how you can sleep with your hair caught up that way," he said quietly.

She didn't know how she could possibly sleep now that it wasn't. His fingers had slipped in among the long silky strands and were gently massaging her scalp, easing tensions she hadn't been aware of and replacing them with new tensions. Sensual tensions.

"Just close your eyes, Amanda Lynn," he murmured. "Just close your eyes."

How long, he wondered, was he going to able to endure this? Time and again she turned to him with a trust that stole his breath, then turned away again in fright. She wanted him, there was no doubt of that in his mind, but that wasn't enough, not for either of them.

With a self-control that astonished him even as he exercised it, he continued to stroke her hair and scalp soothingly, to caress her shoulders reassuringly. With the strength that had carried him through his captivity, he ignored his own needs and the ache of his body for satisfaction.

And gradually the tension seeped from him and something reminiscent of contentment replaced it. He had been alone in the dark with his demons for a long, long time. As one small, frightened woman slowly sank into sleep against him, he at last found some surcease.

Chapter 7

"Don't move."

The growled command followed hard on the heels of a disorienting sense that she had heard something in her sleep. An instant passed as she struggled to place herself and then remembered that she was lying on the couch with her head on Ransom's lap. But Ransom's lap was sliding away.

"Wha—"

"Shh," he whispered sharply. "Stay where you are, Mandy. Just stay. You're safe here, and I don't want you in the way." Safe because nobody in a million years would look for her on the couch at this time of night when the house had been completely dark for hours.

"But what—" She pushed herself up on one elbow and fell silent as she realized an orange glow was coloring the tall curtains on the barn side of the house, and that a deeper orange light seeped around the edges of the curtains. "Fire." The word slid out on a sharply expelled breath. Fire was a deadly threat, and it could leap to her house in no time at all. They needed the hoses, the . . .

"Mandy, stay put. Just pick up the phone and call Nate and tell him we've had an explosion."

Against the fiery glow, she saw Ransom move toward the hall and the kitchen.

"Ransom—"

He whirled then and came back to her, seizing her shoulders to gently shake her. "Listen," he commanded, low-voiced. "It was an explosion. That means it may have been deliberate. I'll do what I can to control it, but you stay here and call Nate. Promise me, Mandy, or so help me I'll stay here with you and we'll both watch it burn to the ground."

He meant it. He meant every blessed word, she realized. "I promise." How she loathed saying those words. It was *her* ranch that was in danger. Her property, her life.

She called Nate at home, rousing him from slumber, but he came instantly alert.

"I'll get help out there," he said swiftly. "You stay in the house, Mandy. I mean it. You do exactly what Ransom says."

Why, she wondered numbly, did the whole world seem to think she was utterly helpless? She wasn't.

Her promise to Ransom fulfilled, at least technically, by her phone call to Nate, she was suddenly galvanized. In the dark, with the familiarity of long years, she ran upstairs and dressed in heavy overalls, boots and a denim jacket. From her bedroom window she could see that it wasn't the barn after all, but Ransom's cabin that was burning.

The meaning of that penetrated her like an icy cold dart from hell. Refusing to give in to sudden tremors and fear, she clattered back down the stairs and headed out the kitchen door to help fight the fire.

She had taken only one step onto the kitchen porch when strong arms seized her in an iron grip. She gasped, ready to fight for her life, and then sagged with relief as Ransom's familiar scent filled her nostrils.

"Damn it!" His growl was barely audible over the roaring crackle of the cabin's destruction. "I told you to stay put!"

"The fire—"

"The cabin's a dead loss. All I can do is make sure the fire doesn't spread. Damn it, Mandy, the person who set the fire might still be hanging around!"

The person who set the fire? Disbelief exploded in her mind like a nuclear blast, and for an instant she was empty of all thought, empty of everything except the blinding white flash of shock.

"Mandy?" Ransom felt her stiffen against him and in consternation tried to read her expression. He could understand that she might be horrified, shaken, scared, furious—there were a dozen things she could feel that wouldn't concern him at all. Her silence, her unresponsiveness—that was something to worry about.

Finally she started to breathe again. "They might still be here?" she repeated quietly, lifting her gaze to his.

Grimly he nodded. "That's right. And they might be looking to make more mischief." He didn't say what kind of mischief, because he figured her imagination was good enough to fill in the blanks—and if it wasn't, then he didn't see any point in alarming her further.

She drew a deep breath. "Well, then," she managed to say steadily, "you sure as hell shouldn't be out here. Come inside."

"The fire—"

She shrugged. "You're worth more than a damn barn." Then she hesitated, remembering the livestock in the barn. "The horses?"

"I let them out into the corral." He had felt a lot of things for this woman. He had felt awed by her talent, touched by her concern, impassioned by her kisses—so many things. Right now, however, he felt admiration. He wouldn't have guessed that she would prove to be so cool under fire.

And right now, with all the dignity of royalty, she took his hand and tugged him back into the kitchen with her.

"We can watch the fire just as well from here," she said calmly. "Or even better from upstairs. Which is the better defensive position?"

"Well, I'll be damned," he said, giving voice to his admiration. "Upstairs would be better."

By the time Nate arrived with the volunteer fire fighters, the cabin had collapsed inward on itself and burned like an immense bonfire. They began hosing hundreds of gallons of water onto it from the pump truck, but only to keep the flames from spreading to the surrounding buildings or the tall, dry grasses beyond the packed earth of the yard. There was little hope of putting it out before it burned to embers, and little reason to, since everything that mattered was gone.

Needing to be useful in some way, Mandy dug out the huge coffee urn she and John had used when they threw a barbecue, and made coffee. Then she started making sandwiches, mountains of sandwiches. Those volunteers were apt to be at this for hours.

Feeling hollow inside, she watched as Nate, Micah and Ransom drew apart to hold a low-voiced discussion. They were excluding her, and she tried to muster some resentment. After all, she *was* involved. Ransom had made that clear when he said it wouldn't make any difference if he left now. He meant, of course, that they might try to use her against him, and she knew with deep certainty that Ransom was honorable enough and decent enough to make it possible for them to get to him that way. Of course, they—whoever *they* were—could also use Nate or Micah against him.

She didn't doubt for a moment that Ransom was acutely aware of those possibilities, and she was sure he damned himself for coming to this place and endangering his friends. He was that kind of man.

Her throat tightened, and she forced her attention back to the burning cabin, a visible orange and yellow inferno. The thought she had been avoiding since she awoke to the fire suddenly shouldered its way past all her defenses.

What if Ransom had been sleeping in the cabin?

Maybe, just maybe, he might not have had time to get out. The explosion must have been the propane tank blowing. It might have been the trigger for the entire fire, or it might have blown after the fire had been burning for some time. Either way, Ransom might never have known. He might have died.

Closing her eyes tightly against a sudden shaft of angry pain, she leaned against the counter and battled for calm in the middle of the hurricane.

The world would be a poorer place if Ransom was lost. She believed that as surely as she knew that her own life would be poorer without him. He had brought a touch of magic into her life. He had brought the sound of laughter to her. He had moved her and awakened her. He had made her care.

He was also a man whose every step was apparently dogged by a curse of violence and destruction. Whatever she might feel for him, however much she might care for him, she could never endure the violence of which he was a part. The violence that was so much a part of him.

It was nearly noon by the time the last volunteer fire fighters staggered out of the yard. After she had personally thanked the last of them, Mandy dragged herself into the kitchen and collapsed wearily at the table. Nate had long since gone to work. Micah, however, stood guard over the smoking rubble while Ransom went to the corral to look after the horses. With a sigh, she put her head down on her arms.

Ransom's voice roused her. "Nate is asking the arson investigator to come out here."

Mandy raised her head, and she saw him standing just beyond the screen door. "He told me. Let me get you some coffee."

"Stay put." He pulled the door open and stepped inside. There he halted and stared at her.

He was covered from head to foot in soot, and he smelled like smoke and sweat, but she had never in her life seen anything or anyone she wanted as much as she wanted Ransom in that instant. Her desire pierced her like daggers of glass, and yearning clawed at her, but fear was ice in her veins.

He saw the fear. He smelled it. And he figured he couldn't put up with any more of this crap. He *wouldn't* put up with any more of it. Until the lady made up her mind where she stood, he was out of the game. He had, quite simply, reached the last straw with a lot of things, not the least of them Mandy's flip-flopping feelings toward him.

There was another survival skill he had learned and learned well, and as simply as flipping a switch, he closed off his feelings for Mandy. Eventually, he found himself thinking with all the detachment of a third party, he was going to pay a price for walling off parts of himself. And as soon as he thought it, he gave an indifferent mental shrug. He had survived things that would have driven other men mad simply because he could cut off his feelings. The piper hadn't caught up with him yet, and considering recent events, he might well be dead before the payment came due.

Without so much as a sigh, his face grew shuttered, his expression bland. Mandy saw it but was too tired, too saddened, too frightened, to wonder at it.

"Let me get you coffee," she said again, struggling for the energy to rise.

"Forget it." He turned toward the hallway. "I need to use your shower, and then I have to go to town."

"Ransom, you need rest. Micah and I will watch over things. You get some sleep." Even in her fright at what this man might mean to her, she couldn't ignore his needs.

"I need something to wear," he said flatly. "Every damn stitch of clothing I had with me is now nothing but soggy ash." He looked at her. Reluctantly, it seemed to her. "The book you autographed for me is gone, too."

He said that last almost thoughtfully, as if he were testing some idea for validity. What was wrong with him? she wondered groggily. Why did he seem so distant?

He saw the confused questions begin to form in her expression, so he turned and left her before she could get started. Damned if he was going to sit still for the third degree from her—or from anyone else, for that matter. He'd had it. He had absolutely, positively *had it!*

His clothes were filthy, stinking and sooty, but he didn't have a change, and anyway, he'd been filthier in his day. He needed the shower, though. *Damn!* God bless America and the hot shower. If he'd had to make a list of what he missed most in captivity, a hot shower would have been near the top, right after freedom and a warm, soft woman. Mom and Apple Pie was a myth. The truth was more like Michelle Pfeiffer and Hot Water.

Except, he thought as he turned his face into the hammering spray, it wasn't really Michelle Pfeiffer he wanted. Not then. Not now. Karen had had that kind of delicate beauty. The stuff of men's dreams. She had also been the coldest bitch it had been his misfortune to encounter. No, what he wanted was the kind of beauty that reached the soul. The kind of beauty a man could warm his heart on for fifty or sixty years.

Scrubbing his head savagely, he thought about the blatant fear he had seen earlier in Mandy's eyes. She'd looked as if he had brought the dragon to her palace gate. And he guessed maybe he had. But, damn it, did she have to look at him as if he *were* the dragon?

That was when he realized he was furious. Enraged. Wrathful. Hell, there wasn't a word to encompass it. He could have chewed nails, punched holes in steel. He felt as if he were verging on a core meltdown.

Dusk had fallen by the time Ransom returned to the ranch.

"Everything's okay," Micah told him as soon as Ransom climbed out of the truck. "You want me to hang around while you take a nap?"

"Naw. Thanks, Micah, but I'm not sleepy. I'll probably crash tomorrow."

Micah searched his face, then nodded. "Yeah," he said. "Yeah." They both knew about anger, real anger. "See you in the morning, man."

"Thanks, Micah. I mean it."

"No problem."

The kitchen door was open in defiance of the evening's chill, and golden light spilled forth, beckoning with a promise of warmth and welcome. Just an illusion, Ransom thought as he paused at the foot of the porch steps. There was no real warmth or welcome in there.

Mandy was frightened, and during the course of the afternoon he had wrestled with himself enough to acknowledge that she was entitled to be afraid.

After all, she had lost every damn thing she had ever loved. And solitude, genuine emotional solitude, was the best fortress in the world. He ought to know. He'd lived like that for nearly twenty years, locked away from everything human and hurtful. And on his one foray into the light, he had found it an illusion.

So why the devil was he trying to step into the light again, and why the hell was he condemning Mandy because she was afraid to?

Because he was stark, raving mad, of course. Because everything inside him had been one great big jumble of confusion ever since he had learned he wasn't going to die after all. For four years he had believed himself to be a dead man. Surely he couldn't be expected to play Lazarus and then act as if nothing had ever changed?

"Ransom?" Mandy stood in the door, silhouetted in the golden, inviting light. "Ransom, are you all right?"

Damned if she didn't sound as if she really cared. "I'm fine." His tone was flat.

"Dinner's ready."

With feet that seemed to be encased in lead, he climbed the steps and entered the kitchen. Distrustful of the deepening night behind him, he closed the inner door and locked it.

"I made your favorite," Mandy said. With a swift glance, she took in his spanking new jeans and shirt, and the two General Store bags he carried that appeared to be full of clothes.

She sounded as if it were a perfectly ordinary evening. That surprised him, jarred him. He dropped his bags in the corner and stepped over to the table. Watching her place the hot beef sandwiches on the table, he wondered why everything seemed wrong.

"Ransom?"

She was frowning at him now, worry evident in her brown eyes, in the set of her mouth.

"Ransom, are you all right?"

"I . . . don't think so." He was surprised to hear himself say it, surprised to realize it was true.

She flew to him instantly, as if she weren't afraid of him at all, and touched his forehead and cheeks. "You feel warm."

"I'll be okay. I'm just tired." Somehow he didn't want her concern.

"Would you rather go lie down?" She looked worriedly up at him. "I'll save your dinner for later. I put fresh sheets on your bed. Go on. Lie down."

Fresh sheets on *his* bed? Until that instant he hadn't realized just how much of a trespasser he had felt in her house during the last couple of days. So she thought of it as *his* bed, did she?

She followed him, fluttering like a nervous butterfly. He wanted to tell her not to flutter, not to worry, to just go away because he would be okay as soon as he slept, but the words didn't want to come out.

And then he remembered he was supposed to be watching over her, that if he slept she would be unprotected. He hesitated halfway up the stairs, then felt her hand in the small of his back, pushing him on.

"Bed, Ransom. Now."

"Mandy . . ."

"Upstairs. Go on. Damn it, you're too big to carry."

He took another upward step, noting that his legs felt heavy, too heavy. "Promise me," he said around a disobedient tongue, and halted, refusing to move another step.

"Anything, if you'll just get to bed."

"Promise... Call Nate. Tell him I'm sick."

Because he was. He knew it suddenly and certainly as the first shiver ripped through him. Time was running out fast. Now he knew what he was in for. More by strength of will than of body, he climbed the last stairs and headed to the bedroom.

"Nate," he said again as he slumped onto the bed.

"I promise. Ransom, what is it?"

He forced out one last word just as another shiver gripped him and rattled his joints. Between clenched teeth, he said, "Malaria."

Poor Nate, she thought as she dialed his number. The man was probably wishing her and Ransom into the next county. Last night he had lost his sleep; tonight she was going to disturb his dinner.

"Sheriff Tate."

"Nate, it's Mandy. I'm really sorry to interrupt your dinner...."

"Hush, sweet face. Dinner's over, and you're never any trouble. Is something wrong?"

Nate had such a wonderful voice, she thought irrelevantly. So soothing and reassuring. "Ransom wanted me to call you and tell you he's sick. Malaria, he said."

Nate muttered an unprintable word; at least, it was a word *her* publisher considered unprintable. "Okay, doll. First it's chills, really bad chills. You'll probably need every blanket you've got to warm him. Then he's going to have a really high fever. He might get delirious from it."

Mandy bit her lip. She didn't know a darn thing about real illness. She was never ill, and John had been healthier than a horse. "Do I need to try to keep the fever down?"

"Yeah, I guess. You might try to get some aspirin into him. And find out what kind of medicine he's been taking for it so I can tell Doc Randall when I round him up."

"You're getting the doctor?" That was such a relief.

"Absolutely. Now run and ask him what medicine he takes. I'll wait."

She dropped the phone on the bed and hurried into the next room. Ransom was shaking from head to foot like a man possessed. One hand pulled futilely at the bedspread, trying to drag it over him. At once Mandy grabbed it and tugged it around him.

"I'll get some more blankets," she told him. His blue eyes looked glazed. "Ransom?"

"Yo." He squeezed the syllable out between his teeth.

"Nate wants to know what kind of medicine you take."

"Chloroquine." A huge, racking shudder shook him.

"Okay. I'll be right back."

It wasn't easy, but he forced himself to keep his attention focused outward. He couldn't leave Mandy unprotected. The worry plagued him, kept him alert long past the point where he would ordinarily have turned inward in his misery. He swallowed three aspirin, no mean feat when he was shaking like San Francisco in 1906. He was conscious of Mandy fussing over him, aware that she felt helpless and frustrated, but hell, there wasn't anything anyone could do.

He heard Nate finally, heard the doctor who wanted to take him to the hospital. "No," he managed to say through chattering teeth. "No. Be ok-k-kay by m-morning."

"I imagine he's been through this often enough to know," said the disembodied voice of the doctor.

"Reckon so," Nate replied, his familiar voice soothing Ransom, who had relied on it often in circumstances that were far more dangerous. "Ransom? Ransom, I'm stationing a deputy here overnight, so don't worry about Mandy. She'll be looked after."

Shaking so hard that he had to keep his teeth clenched, Ransom managed to mutter a slurred, "Thanks."

Secure in the knowledge that Nate would look after Mandy, Ransom let go. The Beast had caught him fully in its grip, and there was nothing for him to do except get through it. Nothing he *could* do except get through it. Closing his eyes, he gave himself up to it.

He had long thought of his malaria as the Beast. It had a tendency to spring on him out of nowhere, almost always when he could least afford it. It snatched him up in its cruel jaws and shook him until he ached miserably from head to toe. Then it took malevolent delight in singeing him with its hot breath, until he felt as if his skin would shrivel up and blacken from the heat.

But worst were the dreams the Beast inflicted. Beyond the rational edges of the mind, incomprehensible horrors lurked. There, lying in wait and ready to spring, were nightmare visions compounded of the jeweled jungles of three continents and the unspeakable realities of international intrigue.

Maybe, he hoped, as another shudder racked him, maybe this time he wouldn't get delirious. Maybe this time the fever wouldn't rise so high that he half lost his mind. It was a vain hope, but he clung to it anyway.

Nate stayed with Ransom while Mandy went downstairs with the doctor. He'd been here himself a time or ten, and he looked down on Ransom with sympathy. "Let's get you out of your boots, old son," he said gently, bending over his friend. "When did you catch this bug, buddy? I thought you got out of Nam clean."

Ransom stiffened and jerked with another shudder, then abruptly relaxed. For a minute he just tried to catch his breath.

"You couldn't have had this all along," Nate remarked, filling the silence the way he often had in the old days, when he and Ransom had faced bad moments. Talk was distracting. "Uncle sure wouldn't have let you go undercover with this little parasite roaming your system." With a powerful tug, he pulled off Ransom's boot.

"In the camp," Ransom said. "I caught it in the camp." Another shivering bout was building. He could feel it deep inside, a kernel of growing tension as his brain decided it needed to bring up his temperature to fight the invasion.

Nate straightened. "Hell, man, did you get any medical attention at all?"

"You're kidding, right?"

Rachel Lee

143

Nate swore savagely. "You always were a mule's butt, son! Why didn't you just come home from Nam and stay put like the rest of us?"

"Like the rest of you?" Ransom gave a ragged laugh. "Right. Like which rest of you? The ones who hide in the mountains and wait for attackers who never come? The ones who sit lost on street corners because nobody wants them?"

A sound caught Nate's attention, and he turned to find Mandy standing in the door, a bottle of pills in one hand, the other hand clapped over her mouth. She stared at Ransom in apparent distress.

"Oh, I don't know," Nate said casually, returning his attention to Ransom. "Like me, I guess. It's possible to fight the good fight just about anywhere. You don't have to hang around in jungles and slave labor camps to find a devil to wrestle with. Hell, buddy, we grow plenty of 'em at home!"

Ransom's grin was little more than bared teeth as another round of tearing shudders grabbed him.

"Get all the blankets you have," Nate told Mandy. Then he returned his attention to Ransom. "Come on, let's get you out of these clothes."

"D-damn you, I d-don't want a nursemaid!"

"Maybe not," Nate said calmly. "I know I never wanted one, either. Tough patooti, pal. When your fever starts rising, we're going to need to cool you down, and it'll be a hell of a lot easier if you're stripped."

"Go home, Tater. Drive your k-kids crazy."

"Fat chance. I've been wanting to get even with you for years. And I'm never one to pass up an opportunity." He looked up with a reassuring smile for Mandy as she entered the room with her arms full of comforters and blankets. Then, with utter disregard for her modesty or Ransom's objections, he stripped Ransom with swift efficiency, leaving him nothing but his black briefs.

Mandy stood on one side of the bed, Nate on the other, as they piled on the blankets. Their eyes met once, sharing mutual horror at Ransom's scars, but neither of them let him know how they reacted to the sight. For an instant, just

an instant, their eyes locked and Mandy saw her own outrage mirrored in Nate's usually calm gaze. Normally the
gentlest of people, she felt capable of murder just then.
Nobody, *nobody,* should ever be treated the way Ransom
apparently had been.

"Go home, Nate," Ransom sighed as the warmth of the
blankets began to relax him. "Go home."

"Yeah, I will. Later." He looked across the bed at Mandy
and smiled reassuringly. "Sure could use a little coffee.
Mind if I make some?"

"I'll make it, Nate." If that was the only useful thing she
could do, then by gosh she would make coffee until it came
out his ears.

Twenty minutes later, just as Mandy was filling a couple
of mugs with coffee, Nate joined her in the kitchen.

"He's being his usual uncooperative self," he remarked
with a half smile as he accepted a mug from her. "Shivering like hell and telling me to drop dead."

Mandy gave him a half smile back but recognized the
male bluster for what it was. "*Should* he be in the hospital,
Nate?"

He leaned back against the counter and shook his head.
"I used to get this regular as clockwork myself, and I always preferred to ride it out in my own bed. It's miserable
as all get-out, but he'll live. The main thing is to keep the
fever down." He looked down at the mug in his hand, hesitating visibly. Then, reluctantly, he added, "He's safer here
than he would be at the hospital. In other ways."

She caught her breath as fear returned. The hairs on the
back of her neck prickled. "Who is it? Do you have any
idea?"

He shook his head. "If I had any idea at all, I'd be
combing this county for lice. That man upstairs saved my
life more than once, and that's only part of it. I intend to
make damn sure no harm comes to him, but I don't have a
clue where to even start looking." He sighed. "Maybe the
arson investigator can come up with something. At this

point, though, there's nothing to be done except keep a sharp eye out."

Shivering against a draft, Mandy rubbed her arms and noticed with shock that it was nearly ten. "Nate! Look at the time! You ought to be home."

"Sorry, doll, you're stuck with me. I told Marge I'd see her when I see her. You can't cope with this alone."

"Of course I can," she said stoutly, although inwardly she wasn't all that confident. What if she couldn't get his fever down? What if he became delirious and she couldn't prevent him from hurting himself? "Besides, you need your sleep. You have a job to do tomorrow, and you can't do it properly if you haven't slept."

"Don't see why not. I have before."

"That doesn't mean you did it properly."

He laughed, his face creasing with genuine humor. "How about a compromise? We'll split it into shifts. I'll promise to call you if I need help with him, if you'll promise to call me."

That was how she came to be lying in her bed across the hall, listening to the deep rumble of Nate's voice as he talked quietly to a restless Ransom. She'd missed a lot of sleep last night and ought to be dead on her feet, but tension infused her with wakefulness. So much had happened in the last few days. Too much to absorb, really. She needed to think about it all, evaluate it, analyze. . . .

Sleep pounced and caught her mid-thought.

"Come on, Bertie. We'll make it."

The sound of Ransom's voice jerked her out of deep, dreamless sleep. She sat up immediately, but needed a couple of moments to remember what was going on. Ransom. Malaria. And Nate was looking after him.

Rubbing her eyes, she glanced at her clock and was astonished to see it was nearly three a.m. Damn Nate, she thought, instantly awake. Shifts, my foot!

She grabbed her robe, jammed her feet into her slippers and hurried across the hall, tying her sash as she went.

In the dim light from a single low-wattage lamp on the dresser, Nate bent over Ransom. The covers had all been cast aside, and Ransom thrashed restlessly, muttering as Nate sponged him with a cloth. Mandy hurried to Nate's side. He glanced at her.

"Honey," he said softly, "he wouldn't want you to see him like this."

"Tough. How high is his fever?"

"Pushing 105, near as I can tell. And this isn't doing much good." He sighed. "Go fill the tub, Mandy. Skin temperature. I've done this a time or two with my kids, and it hasn't failed yet."

"You're going to put him in the tub?"

"That's the idea."

Ransom flung out an arm. "Come on, Bertie, don't quit! Damn it, man . . ." His words trailed off into a mumble.

"Bertie was one of our medics," Nate said. "Got hit in a firefight. Ransom carried him out."

Mandy bit her lip until she tasted blood. "Did . . . did he make it?"

"Bertie? No. He died right after Ransom put him on the Dustoff—the medevac chopper."

Mandy fled. There was no other word to describe her rush down the hall into the bathroom. Filling the tub busied her hands, but it couldn't empty her mind.

She was torn between wanting to comfort, yearning to heal and soothe, and an overwhelming desire to flee before caring cost her any more than it already had. Damn, he looked so vulnerable lying there on the twisted sheets, his scarred body thrashing in the delirium of high fever. So vulnerable and yet so damn strong and powerful that her throat tightened and her breath caught with something she couldn't even name. A felled giant. A fallen warrior. A hawk with a broken wing.

All kinds of crazy similes filled her mind, but they were easier to handle than the idea that Ransom was still so deeply troubled by something that had happened so long ago. Wounds. All kinds of wounds. So many kinds of wounds.

"Mandy?"

She turned swiftly, blinking back tears she only now realized she was weeping. Nate and Ransom were easing through the door, Ransom's arm slung around Nate's neck, his eyes half open as he tried to maintain his grip on consciousness.

"It's ready," she said, bending to turn off the taps.

"Come on, old son," Nate said. "It'll feel like ice. Sound good?"

Ransom was so incredibly beautiful, Mandy thought, as she watched Nate steady him while he stepped into the tub, still wearing his briefs. He might be flushed with fever and barely conscious, but he was still beautiful with a golden sleekness that made her ache.

The sigh that escaped him as he sank into the water was one of pure relief, and the expression on his face was suddenly one of sheer bliss. The tub wasn't really big enough. His knees were bent and rose above the water, which, even when he leaned back, didn't come much above his waist. Scarcely giving it a thought, Mandy reached for the cup she used to rinse her hair. Kneeling, she ladled the lukewarm water over his chest and shoulders.

"I'll get his robe," Nate said. "He'll probably cool down fast now."

She nodded, then remembered. "Nate?"

"Yeah?"

"I don't know if he has a robe. All his clothes are in the two bags down in the kitchen."

"The fire. I forgot."

"John's robe is in the closet at the end of the hall. It'll be a little short, but it'll sure go around." Some part of her was surprised to realize that the thought of Ransom wearing John's robe didn't bother her. Yet just a few short months ago she had gone on a crying jag over that same robe when she had come across it by accident.

"I'll just get a blanket," Nate suggested.

She turned her head and looked up at him, meeting his gaze head on. "It's all right, Nate. Really."

Turning back to Ransom, she resumed her ladling.

"Mandy."

Surprised, she lifted her eyes from his chest and found Ransom staring straight at her. His blue eyes looked a little glazed and sunken, but he saw her. Really saw her.

"How do you feel?" she asked swiftly, touching his cheek with damp fingertips. Still warm, but not burning.

"Like hell." A corner of his mouth hitched upward just a hair. "This is humiliating."

"Screw humiliating," she snapped, not caring if she sounded vulgar. She was too tired to have any patience with macho male hang-ups. "Even Superman has to deal with Kryptonite."

"I probably wouldn't feel so bad if it were Kryptonite that got me. I shouldn't be putting you through this. I should have gone to the hospital."

"Right," she said sourly, dumping more water on the broad chest that she really wanted to nuzzle, wet or not. "Then Nate could have gone crazy trying to protect you from all the people wandering up and down the corridors and pushing into your room demanding blood samples and urine samples and—"

"Okay, okay." He let his eyes close, and his head dropped back against the edge of the tub. "Mandy?" His voice had grown so soft that she had to lean toward him to hear.

"Yes?"

"Mandy, don't be afraid of me. Please don't."

"I'm not afraid of you, Ransom." Her throat tightened around his name, nearly cutting it off. "Not of *you*." Leaning closer, she kissed him lightly on the corner of his mouth.

Behind her, Nate cleared his throat. "Don't mind me," he said, laying his hand heavily on Mandy's shoulder. "Well, old son, have you cooled off enough to let me take your temperature?"

Ransom's eyes fluttered open again, skimming Mandy's face swiftly before they rose to Nate. "I never saw you in the role of nursemaid, Tater."

"That's only because you ain't seen me playing daddy to my girls. Now hold this under your tongue."

Something very like humor glimmered deep in Ransom's eyes as he obediently took the thermometer into his mouth.

Mandy went down to make more coffee while Nate put Ransom into dry underwear and back into bed. From the sounds that trailed down the stairway to her, she thought Ransom sounded almost like himself. When she went back up with her coffee, she managed to persuade Nate to catch some shut-eye on her bed while she kept vigil over Ransom.

"You'll wake me if he gets worse?"

Mandy shoved him across the hall. "Why do you always treat me like I'm some kind of fragile crystal, Nate?"

"Because that's how John always thought of you, swee-tie. As something fine and precious and fragile."

A couple of months ago, she probably would have burst into tears. Tonight she simply shook her head. "I'm about as fragile as a horse, Nate. That ought to be obvious by now. Get some sleep."

Back in Ransom's room, she hesitated beside the bed, and then, driven by needs she was too tired to even question, she lay down beside him and closed her eyes. If he got restless, she would know instantly, she assured herself.

Rolling onto her side, she pressed up against his back and burrowed her nose right into the sheet that covered him. In some way, in deep, seldom-noticed places, she felt her world right itself. It was okay, she thought hazily. He was here, and he would be all right.

No one could touch him or harm him with both her and Nate watching over him. No one.

And for the moment, nothing else mattered.

Chapter 8

She hadn't even closed the curtains last night. That was her first thought when her eyes fluttered open and she discovered that the night's black velvet sky had lightened just enough that she could detect the change despite the dim yellow glow of the lamp on the dresser.

The next thing she realized was that Ransom's arms were wrapped around her and that her back was tucked up against his chest and bent thighs. It was a warmly intimate embrace, and in the unguarded state of just waking, she snuggled back into those arms, moved deeper into his embrace.

He made a soft sound near her ear, a sound that resembled a pleased mumble, and then his hand slid sleepily up from her waist to cup her breast with unmistakable possessiveness.

He had never touched her like that before, and the sharp stab of yearning that pierced her brought her fully awake. This is ridiculous, some part of her mind scolded. The man's out of his mind with fever! Just move his hand away....

But oh, how right it felt! With Ransom it always felt so right, as if she had been created for his mouth, his hands. A tremulous sigh escaped her, and she squeezed her eyes shut, holding herself rigid against a tempest of unfulfilled longings.

She could, with a backward look, measure the barrenness of her life. In retrospect, she guessed she had been as much to blame as her series of foster parents for her sense of alienation. None of them had been bad people, and none of them had intentionally made her feel like an outsider. In fact, considering that she'd felt like an outsider from earliest memory, it was likely that the feeling was something she had been born with—or that had been created with the loss of her birth mother.

Ransom made a soft sound and drew her even more snugly against him, curving his body to a tighter fit against hers. The hand that cupped her breast so possessively tightened a little and stroked softly for a moment before it relaxed.

He was probably having a delightful dream, she thought, holding her breath as awakening desires shimmered throughout her like wisps of magic. How easy it would be to sink into one of her own.

With a sigh, she forced her body to relax and squeezed her eyes shut. For the first time in her life, she felt compelled to stand back and look at herself. Even John hadn't made her take stock the way she so clearly needed to.

No, John had come into her life like a balmy breeze, fitting into almost every nook and cranny so gently and warmly that he was there almost before she knew it. He had made her feel secure and loved, and yet he had never managed to banish her sense of apartness. She had felt as if she were Amanda Tierney playing at being Mrs. John Grant. He'd been a man to grow old with, and yet she had never believed she would grow old with him. She had never felt permanent.

Ransom, on the other hand, made her feel as if she had spent eternity waiting for him. It was odd—disturbing—the way she felt no alienation around him. She knew many people and felt friendly toward some, but no one had ever before made her feel as if she had come home at last.

And that was why she was fighting so hard and feeling so frightened. He would go away. Whether he got killed or not, his life was elsewhere. He was destined to leave her behind, because she would not leave with him. Here, on this ranch, isolated from everyone but a few select friends, she was safe. She had found the castle where she could live out her days and write her books. So what if she refused to face reality? She made her living by creating fantasies for other people to escape into. Beyond her basic requirements, she had no need of reality.

And Ransom was reality. He was a terrifying reality, because he made her every emotion awaken, her every nerve sing. Around him, she could not remain only half alive.

Instinctively, she began to ease away from him, but his hold tightened at once.

"No," he mumbled. "Stay."

She hesitated. He probably didn't even know who she was. Any warm body would do. Again she attempted to ease away.

"Amanda," he muttered. "Don't go. Stay." His arm tightened, and his hand stroked her breast persuasively through her cotton gown. "Please," he mumbled.

So she stayed, her heart swelling painfully with unnamed emotions, her body aching with unfulfilled needs. Eventually, she even dozed.

The next time she awoke, the sky had lightened to lavender and Ransom's fever had broken in a bath of sweat that had soaked both of them and the sheets that were wrapped around him. Instantly concerned that he might take a chill, she started to get up.

"Don't go."

Turning her head, she looked over her shoulder to find Ransom's eyes wide open and very definitely aware.

"You're soaked," she said, ignoring the way her heart started to beat with a heavy rhythm. "I've got to get you some dry sheets before you get chilled."

For a moment his blue gaze searched her face as if seeking something, and then his hold on her relaxed. He let his eyes close, and his head fall back on the pillows. "I've probably ruined your mattress."

Mandy sat up, battling an urge to simply turn and hug him in her relief. "Don't worry about it."

For the briefest moment his eyes opened again and met hers.

"Are you hungry?"

"I'm just tired. I'll be fine, Mandy. Really."

Nate heard her moving around and came to help her change the sheets while Ransom watched listlessly from the rocker in the corner. As soon as they got him back in bed and under the blankets, he fell into a deep sleep.

"He'll be back to normal in a few hours," Nate assured her as they went downstairs together. "He'll wake up as hungry as a hibernating bear, though."

"Are you sure I can't make you breakfast, Nate?"

He dropped a quick kiss on her forehead before he stepped out the back door. "Marge and I always eat breakfast together, sweet face. It's a sacred time. No matter how many things disrupt the rest of the day, we *always* have breakfast together."

Halfway across the yard to his Blazer, he looked back. "You need sleep even worse than I do. Go to bed, Mandy. Charlie Huskins is here, and Micah will take over in an hour or so."

First, however, she took a long, hot shower and slipped into a fresh cotton gown. Before climbing into her own bed, she crossed the hall to check on Ransom and make sure he didn't need anything. Maybe she should have expected it, maybe she was just fooling herself, but she was astonished when he reached out and caught her wrist.

"Lie down with me," he said, and his eyes were both clear and alert. "Lie down with me, Amanda Lynn."

"You need to sleep," she argued, but her limbs went as soft as hot syrup, and she was obeying his demand before the words completely left her mouth. Melting, she climbed under the covers beside him, turning into his arms as he drew her closer. Her head rested on his shoulder, and somehow, as naturally as if it had always been this way, her legs tangled with his.

"Now I can sleep," he said, as if her presence had been all that was lacking before. "Now we can both sleep."

And they both did.

Much later, Ransom looked down at the woman who slept soundly beside him. He could have her, he knew. If he reached out and touched her now, she would turn into him and open like the rose she really was beneath that grim exterior. It would be so simple, he thought as he traced the delicate lines of her face with his eyes. It would be so easy.

And it would ruin everything. She wanted him, she even cared about him, but she had to come to him freely, and he was beginning to despair that she ever would. Poor Amanda Lynn, to be so frightened of what was so right.

Sighing, he lowered his head to the pillow again and closed his eyes. He was still weary from last night's fever, but his strength was returning rapidly.

And maybe it was time he did some thinking of his own. After all, Mandy wasn't the only problem here. She wasn't the one with a murderer on her tail. She had every right to be scared, and he was acting like a numskull, pretending that her fears were phantoms she needed to overcome. No phantom had shot out her windshield or burned down his cabin. No phantom was toying with him, like a cat with a mouse.

And what about the rest of it? What about the past five years? What about his failure to deal with the absolute waste of all he had suffered? Hell, it wasn't as if he had suffered in some great, noble cause. Not one damn thing had been accomplished by his imprisonment except to satisfy a vindictive streak in a woman whose heart evidently had a temperature of absolute zero.

That, he admitted, drawing a deep breath to steady himself against a sudden surge of futile anger, was what really bothered him. If he could have believed that even one little thing had been bettered by his captivity, just one little thing, he could live with the cost. But to pay that price for nothing at all...!

When he came right down to it, he thought grimly as he rode a tide of barely leashed anguish, he could say that about his entire life. All the things that had seemed so important at the time became trivial in retrospect. He had wasted his life, it seemed, risking everything on trivialities.

Well, maybe some of it hadn't been trivial. There had been that terrorist thing in Libya. He'd made an important difference there, had probably saved a life or two. A couple of other times, even in hindsight, his achievements had mattered. But it wasn't a hell of a lot to say for a lifetime.

And it didn't make up for four useless, wasted years in that camp, when nothing at all had been gained.

So who the hell did he think he was, trying to wear down Mandy's defenses and get behind her walls? What did he have to offer her, anyway? A battered, scarred body, a wasted past, and possibly no future at all.

So maybe he'd better get his act together. Maybe he'd better make sure he *had* a future, and then figure out what kind. Only then would it be fair to ask anything at all of Mandy.

Firm in his intention to do the right thing by her, he allowed his fatigue to drag him back into sleep. He had to be rested up by tonight. He had to be ready to deal with this strangely amateurish assassin. With this cat that stalked him in a deadly game.

The best laid schemes . . . The words of the Scottish poet were rolling loosely around inside his head when he struggled awake late in the afternoon. Before he was fully awake, he knew why. Snuggled against him was an enticingly soft morsel of femininity, but he might have been able to resist that. Hell, he had resisted it before. What was harder to resist was the silky thigh that was caught between his legs, pressing intimately against him, making a mockery of the thin barrier of his briefs.

He should be able to move away. That was what he told himself. And told himself yet again. But there was something so exquisite about the warm pressure of her thigh against him, especially for a man who hadn't found release in a woman for nearly five years, that he was paralyzed.

His eyes weren't paralyzed, however, and opening them, he found himself looking straight down the gaping neck of Mandy's cotton nightgown. Deep within, he could see the soft, shadowy cleft between her breasts, and *that* made him aware that he could smell her. God, she smelled good. Warm. Feminine. Sexy.

Damn!

He definitely had to move away. Now. Before he did something dishonorable, such as take advantage of an innocently sleeping woman. Never in his entire life had he done such a thing, and it wasn't that he'd never had the opportunity. It seemed wrong, somehow, to look or touch while she slept, because they weren't lovers. So that made it wrong for him to lie here suspended between heaven and hell by the thigh pressed so intimately against him.

Right.

So move, damn it!

But he didn't move. Instead he lay as helpless as a newborn babe, the breath locked in his throat turning solid while all the air in the universe thickened.

Because *she* moved.

She moved into him, turning closer, snuggling closer, burying her leg even deeper between his, so that he knew with mind-stunning certainty that the soft mound at the juncture of her thighs was pressed snugly against him. Oh yeah!

This was what made it all worthwhile, this sweet, piercing, aching shaft of need that could only be assuaged by another person. By a particular, *special* person. This was no ordinary hunger, no itch to be scratched, no mere accident of hormones. This was the hunger of a warrior for his fairy-tale princess. This was what sent a man out to slay dragons.

But it wasn't his to take.

Mandy stirred again, rubbing drowsily against him like a cat. He had to stop this now, before he lost control and claimed her before she even opened her eyes.

"Mandy. Mandy, wake up." His voice was husky, catching on the breath that wanted to stay locked in his throat. The hammering surf of desire was pounding in his veins again like a force of nature, a force so primal there was no arguing or reasoning with it. He steeled himself to ignore it, steeled himself for her inevitable shock when she awoke enough to realize how intimately she was wrapped around him. Sleep had lowered all the barriers she had tried to erect against him, and she was going to be horrified when she realized it.

"Mandy."

She awoke slowly, stretching and making little noises deep in her throat, reminding him of a kitten. Only a kitten wouldn't have this effect on him. Kittenish or not, Mandy was all woman, and his body recognized it.

"Ransom?"

It was, he admitted reluctantly, priceless to watch her eyes flutter open and grow aware. Precious to watch the color rush into her cheeks like cherry juice when she realized the intimacy of their embrace. Exquisite beyond belief when she recognized his state of arousal and yet didn't yank herself away.

"Ransom?" she said again, this time very tentatively, as if she were afraid to shatter the tenuous moment.

What was she asking him? He didn't know, and suddenly he didn't care. Turning on his side, he pressed his hand against her lower back and pushed her even more intimately into the cradle of his thighs. A groan was torn from him, and his hips, with a will of their own, began a helpless, relentless rocking against her.

He took the time, just enough time, to look down into her startled gaze. As he stared, amazement vanished and her eyes closed. And then, to his stunned wonderment, her mouth curved into a soft smile and her hips rolled responsively against his.

Way back in his mind a warning bell sounded, reminding him to protect her. The condoms he had bought days ago had been moved into the bedside table here when he started watching over her. Not that it really mattered, because if he got this woman pregnant he would bust a gut with sheer happiness. But Mandy probably wouldn't feel so happy, so he forced himself to take a few seconds to dig out the foil package and put it within reach. And then he stripped off his briefs so she wouldn't mistake his intention. He was reaching his point of no return.

Mandy was watching him when he turned back to her. The sheets had been thrown back, and she lay with her nightdress provocatively tangled around her thighs. She was beautiful, he thought. Exquisite. His fairy-tale princess. He should, he thought, offer her a chance to say no, a chance to get up and walk away. But her eyes were soft and hazy, not at all reluctant looking, and his need was strong, so he propped himself on one elbow and said nothing at all.

Her nightgown was made of white cotton eyelet, demure, fresh and clean, yet it gave him tiny, enticing glimpses of the satiny skin beneath. It was, somehow, a perfect nightgown for her and for the moment. It appealed to him in a way that the most provocative satin and lace confections never had. It was...wholesome. Like Mandy. God, how he needed her wholesomeness. Her cleanliness. Her rightness.

Slow. He swore he would go slowly, giving her every bit of pleasure he was capable of. He would worship her and display his reverence for her so that she would never wonder if this was merely a moment of lust. He wanted her to know that it was more, so much more.

Gently, listening to the quickening of her breath, he reached out and swept the hem of her gown upward. Inch by inch he exposed her to his gaze and knew that he had never seen such a beautiful woman. He wished there was some way to tell her that so she would believe it. It wasn't that she was perfect. The pale lines of stretch marks on her tummy took care of that. No, she wasn't perfect, and she was so much more beautiful for being imperfect.

When he tugged the gown over her head, he saw the uncertainty in her gaze.

"Tell me," he said. "Talk to me, Mandy. What worries you? What frightens you?"

His sensitivity tightened her throat. Closing her eyes, she took her courage in her hands. "I want to please you," she whispered. "And I don't know how." A whole flood of insecurities had risen in her, swamping her desires. In her life she had made love with only one man, and one man's measure, so long ago, was hardly enough to reassure her. She was older. She was out of practice. What if...? A whole string of "what ifs" began to form like mocking faces.

The admission tore at him. A woman who had been married, he thought, shouldn't be so lacking in confidence about her skills or attractions as a lover. It was a man's place, most especially a husband's place, to make sure a woman knew her attractiveness and discovered her skills. He felt a spark of anger toward John Grant, but quickly smothered it. It had been four years, after all, and four years was enough to weaken anyone's self-confidence. Truth to tell, his own confidence level wasn't any too high at the moment.

"Princess," he murmured softly, finding first her eyelid and then the lobe of her ear with his kiss, "this old warrior is feeling pretty shaky himself right now. I want this to be so good, so perfect for you—"

Her eyes flew open, and she quickly silenced him by pressing her fingertips against his lips. "I told you, we can shoot for perfect another time."

Behind her fingers he smiled and felt his tensions let go. "That's a two-way street, Amanda Lynn."

Bending, he took her mouth in a kiss that offered no quarter and ran the palm of his hand up her side to her breast. Smooth. Silky. Soft. Warm. Woman. *His woman.*

Ahh.... The sigh was long, heartfelt, and he didn't know if he heard it only in his mind or if he'd really sighed like that, but her hands were touching him, drawing him closer until his hard chest pressed against her soft breasts, until his aching, throbbing manhood was pressed against her yielding heat. This woman's small, soft hands reached for him and drew him closer, and it felt so good, so damn good, to be wanted.

Maybe that was what undid him. With a roar that filled his ears, internal restraints crumbled and long-defended walls crashed. Every last shred of his self-control vaporized in the heat of his hunger.

He took her like the warrior he was. He took her like a soldier who'd been gone too long and had come home at last. All his good intentions blew away in the shock wave. He was man, she was woman, and not one other damn thing mattered.

Mandy felt his control shatter as surely as if shock waves had blasted through the air around her. The firestorm broke over her as he surged into her in a helpless, convulsive plunge, stretching sensitive tissues that hadn't been stretched in years. The pain was a small thing, brief, fleeting, inconsequential beside the need of the man who inflicted it.

She felt the fine tremors of his muscles as he bent over her, ripped by low groans that escaped him with each thrust of his hips. She had thought she knew desire. She had thought she had experienced hunger and need. Now she looked into the tortured face of relentless, driving need and knew that she had never understood what it could be. The thrill of his invasion, the swift, clenching response of her insides to the pleasure of being taken, melted away in a warm compassion, in an overwhelming desire to give what he needed.

This was no soft, sensual claiming. This was raw, vital, a challenge in the face of life, a tearing, throbbing, convulsive ripping of pleasure from the moment. This was as elemental as life and death.

Responding instinctively, she wrapped her legs around his hips to take him deeper, her arms around his shoulders to draw him closer and assure him of his welcome. Closing her eyes, she kissed his cheek and surrendered to his needs as women have always surrendered to their chosen warriors, with tenderness and softness, with welcome and love.

"Mandy, I can't...." The words were little more than a muffled groan.

"Then don't," she said in sudden fierceness, then dug her nails into his shoulders, urging him on.

His back arched suddenly, drawing his head back so sharply that she could see nothing but his throat. His flesh plunged deeper, so deep that she was sure they would fuse permanently. And then, with a groan so low it sounded torn from him, he erupted into her.

Afterward he tried to roll away, but she wrapped her arms around him and held tight, refusing to release him. Her woman's instinct warned that if she let go now, he would never return.

"Mandy..." Again he tried to pull away.

"Hush." She wrapped her legs around him, pinning him to her as best she could. Little by little his body was withdrawing from hers, and she thought how sad it was that the greatest moments of honesty between man and woman had to be so fleeting. And she thought how sad it was that now he would be ashamed because he had lost control.

Lifting one hand from his back, she stroked his hair with all the womanly understanding she felt so full of at this moment. He thought he had become an animal. She thought he had merely responded like a human being. Like a man who had spent too much time in hell, who had been deprived of every bit of life's goodness and rightness and pleasure for too long. But he wouldn't see it that way, because he was a decent man who believed he had just behaved in an indecent, uncivilized manner.

"Nobody," she murmured softly in his ear, "nobody has ever made me feel as desirable, as beautiful and as wanted as you just did. Thank you."

She felt a tremor run through him. Suddenly his face, until this moment turned away from her, turned toward her, nuzzling the side of her neck.

He said, "Yeah?"

She laughed then, a clear, joyous sound, a sound that had been absent from her life for so long. "Yeah," she assured him. "Absolutely yeah."

He stirred again. "Princess, I'm too heavy for you."

She knew it was safe then, for the moment at least, so she let him go. As he rolled onto his side, he took her with him, and then it was he who cradled her.

"I'm sorry," he said gruffly.

"Don't be. I'm not." His arms tightened around her, and she became acutely aware of each and every place his body touched hers. Lifting a hand, she touched his tousled golden hair, his silky golden beard, and smiled when he turned his head to press a gentle kiss on her palm.

"You might be," he said, his voice still gruff. "I clean forgot to protect you."

"It's the wrong time," she assured him swiftly, though she wasn't sure of that at all. The last thing in the world she would be able to endure was having Ransom hang around only because she might be carrying his child. Better that he think there was no possibility. And if she *was* pregnant—well, she would deal with that if it happened. Underneath, though, in the warm soft places of her soul, she knew she wouldn't mind it at all if she had a child. If she had *his* child.

She pressed her face to his chest and inhaled deeply. "You must be starving." She wanted the subject changed *now*. Lying had never been easy for her.

He recognized the change of subject for what it was and wondered if she found the thought of having his child *that* repugnant. The idea pained him. "A little," he admitted, but tugged her even closer. "First, I want to pleasure you."

"No."

The word shocked him. Shocked her, too, he realized as he looked swiftly down at her. "No?"

Color flooded her face. "Uh, not right now, Ransom. Later. You're tired and hungry, and I don't want you to get sick again."

And that was a bold-faced lie, he thought as he let her go and watched her scramble away as if he had suddenly developed the plague. What the hell was wrong with her?

But he kept his mouth shut as she snatched up her nightgown and hurried from the room, promising to have dinner ready in an hour.

He might have thought his behavior had repelled her, had driven her away, except that she had already assured him it hadn't. Closing his eyes, he tested her words in his mind, listened again to her tone as she spoke them. His memory, trained by years of working under conditions where it would have been hazardous to write anything down, reran the conversation verbatim.

No, he hadn't disgusted her. Of that he was sure. Her assurance had been genuine. Then what? What the devil had gotten into her?

She shouldn't have let him get so close to her, Mandy thought as she entered the kitchen later, freshly showered and dressed. Last night's untouched beef sandwiches had congealed on the plates, and beyond the window she saw Micah standing with his head thrown back as he watched the afternoon wane.

Poor guy. She had completely forgotten he was standing guard today. He was probably ready to kill for a cup of coffee.

She called out an invitation to him, and he came readily into the kitchen, waving aside her apology.

"After some of the guard shifts I've pulled," he said, "this one's a vacation."

For Micah, that was a long statement. "I sure appreciate what you're doing."

He shrugged. "Forget it."

She couldn't talk him into staying in the kitchen, though. After the fire at the cabin, nobody was going to relax their guard. He took his coffee outside and resumed his watch, leaving Mandy to face Ransom alone.

Well, she was going to have to face him sometime, but she sure didn't know how she was going to explain her panic in a way that didn't reawaken his self-disgust. How could you possibly explain to someone that you didn't mind playing Lady Bountiful to his needs, but that you were scared to death to let him touch upon your own? Too late, she had discovered her terror of allowing herself to be so vulnerable. Too late, she had realized that with each touch he gave her, she came to depend on him even more.

How could she possibly tell him such things? How could he possibly understand? He was a man, and for men such things were clear cut. For men, sex didn't necessitate emotional involvement. Unhappily, Mandy had just realized that for *her* it did, and that she wasn't prepared to take that step. Might *never* be prepared to take that step. How could she possibly explain?

Ransom appeared for dinner damp from a shower, wearing jeans and a black T-shirt. He looked dangerous, powerful and very masculine. Any lingering frailty from his imprisonment or from last night's attack of malaria wasn't visible. He was beautiful.

In a flash her body betrayed her by reminding her that just a short while ago this man's body had claimed hers. Nerve endings, imprinted like photographic film, tingled with remembered sensations. Standing there, looking at him, she felt again his weight on her, felt again the smooth heat of his skin and the steel of his bunching muscles beneath her hands. Felt again the thrilling shock of his penetration. Shimmering heat engulfed her, turning her legs numb and making her hands shake.

She wanted him. Oh, Lord, she wanted him as she had never, ever wanted anyone or anything. The ache was so deep, so sharp, that it was going to kill her. With terrible certainty, she foresaw the coming anguish.

"Oh, God, Mandy," Ransom said harshly, crossing the kitchen toward her with swift strides. "Mandy, don't look like that!"

The haven of his arms closed around her. He held her, simply held her, while the storm ripped through her.

"It doesn't pay to want anything," she heard herself sob. "If you want things, then someone can take them away from you. If you want things, you can be hurt."

"It seems that way, princess," he murmured. "It sure seems that way sometimes."

"Somebody wants to kill you," she said, as if that were the incontestable proof of her argument.

"It does seem that way."

"Well then!"

"Well then, what?" he demanded, holding her even closer. "Damn it, Mandy, if that's how you feel, maybe you should kill yourself right now. I mean, what's the point of dragging through the next forty or fifty years if you never want anything, never enjoy anything, never *do* anything? I plain don't understand how anybody with your guts can be such a damn mouse!"

"Guts? What guts?" She was sounding more and more hysterical, but she didn't care. "A mouse has more guts than I do!"

"Come off it." His temper was rising. "You had the guts to write a book, didn't you? You had the guts to let somebody else read it, didn't you? In other words, lady, you had the guts to put yourself on the line for something you wanted. And you want to keep writing, don't you? You don't cash in your computer and quit because you're afraid that someday you might not be able to write, do you?"

He slackened his hold on her just a little and drew a deep, steadying breath. "You've got guts, Amanda Lynn. You've got enough guts to go for what you want, enough guts to succeed. You just won't see it. And that makes me so damn mad at you that I could shake you until your teeth rattle."

Abruptly, he let her go and stomped out the kitchen door. Sniffling and wiping at her eyes, Mandy saw him fall into conversation with Micah. *Guts enough to go for what she wanted and guts enough to succeed.* Hah.

Who the hell was he to get mad at her, anyway?

The defender of her castle gates, that was who. The man who had breached her emotional barriers, that was who. The man she wanted with every fiber of her being.

Nate showed up after dinner, while Mandy was washing dishes and Ransom drying, both of them pretending that nothing, absolutely nothing, had happened. Nate seemed to sense some of the tension between them, or so Mandy thought uncomfortably when she caught a curious twitch at the corners of his mouth, as if he were trying very hard not to laugh.

He settled at the table, accepting a cup of coffee but turning down an offer of dessert. "You're looking a hell of a lot better, old son," he told Ransom.

Ransom straddled a chair and faced him, smiling faintly. "You didn't come all the way out here to tell me that."

"Might've come to see with my own eyes," Nate suggested, but the teasing twinkle was gone from his gaze. Noticing its absence, Mandy sat slowly, clutching a dish towel like a lifeline.

Ransom spoke. "It was arson."

Nate nodded. "The investigator called me this afternoon. He found the remnants of a crude timer and some blasting caps, which were used to blow up the propane tank. I'd say they're definitely out for your hide—but you already figured that out."

Ransom didn't even bother to nod. Mandy watched his eyes turn flat, almost blank, and she shivered. There was a stillness to him, a watchful sort of waiting, that she could almost feel. Something in him had shifted.

She found herself thinking that it was as if he had moved to another reality, that although his body remained here, his mind was no longer functioning on the same plane with the rest of them. He had, in the blink of an eye, become a predator. A thrill of fear made her scalp prickle.

"Yeah," he said in a voice gone gritty. "I already figured that out, Nate."

"Well," said Nate, as calmly as if he were discussing the weather, "what the hell do you want to do about it?"

Ransom's blue eyes, hard as glass, fixed on him. "I don't want you to get involved. I don't want anybody else involved in this."

"I figure it's already too late for that." Nate lifted his mug, made a production out of taking a sip.

Mandy looked from one man to the other, sensing some kind of byplay between them that was far deeper than words.

"You've got kids, Nate."

"Sure. I've also got friends, and two of them are in deadly danger. If you think I'm going to stand by and let somebody try to hurt you or Mandy, you've got another think coming. And while we're on the subject, I reckon you should know that Micah feels the same way."

"Been discussing it, have you?" Ransom's eyes remained flat, distant.

Nate hesitated, and for an instant his gaze slipped to Mandy, as if seeking something from her. She stared steadily back.

"Well," said Nate after a moment, "I sent my wife and kids to visit her cousin Lou in Colorado. Marge and Lou hate each other, so I figure nobody in a million years will look for her there. So they're safely out of this. That leaves Mandy. If we can get her out of here—"

"I'm not going," Mandy interrupted, aware of her intention only as she spoke.

Nate and Ransom both ignored her, and Nate continued speaking. "I figure somebody might want you bad enough to use people to get to you."

"That crossed my mind," Ransom admitted.

"Yeah, which is why I sent Marge away. Getting Mandy away might be a little more difficult. Everyone in the county seems to think you two have something going, and everybody knows Mandy. Putting her on a bus won't work."

"I'm not going," Mandy said again. The certainty was like steel in her backbone. However timid and afraid she might be, however frightened of risk and loss, she would not abandon her home, the only home she had ever really known. In fact, she realized with absolute conviction, she would die rather than leave. She pushed her chair back from the table and went to the kitchen door, where she looked out over the twilit yard.

"Mandy," Nate began in the patient tone of one who intended to argue reasonably with someone who was irrational, "you really—"

"No, Nate." She cut him off without apology. "I will not budge. This is my home, and no assassin is going to drive me out of it."

"It's only temporary—"

She turned and faced him. "No, Nate," she said again, calmly. "I won't be driven away, not for a week, not for a minute, not for a second."

Ransom understood at a level so deep it was painful. It was a scar she refused to accept because she knew the wound would never heal. Mandy Grant had lost her last battle and accepted her last wound. She had narrowed her horizons to these thin walls and the roamings of her imagination in a defense against previous wounds that had never healed, and now she wasn't going to sacrifice another square inch of her tiny world.

He wanted to go to her, hold her close, offer her a knight's promises of protection and success, but he had no right to do that. After all, he was the one who had brought this threat to her world; it was because of him that she was at risk. Besides, she wanted nothing from him. She had made that abundantly clear. She had let him spill his seed into her, had opened her arms and legs and taken him into her, had borne his desperation and hunger, and then she had turned from him, unwilling to take even the smallest thing he might have given her.

"She stays." He spoke the words in a voice that was rough with feelings he couldn't express. Feelings she didn't want.

Feelings he couldn't afford to have. For now, for this dangerous time, he could afford nothing but anger. Cold anger. The kind of anger that sat in the belly like an icy lump of lead. The kind that kept his head clear and his attention narrowed.

Mandy looked at him, and once again her scalp prickled. She had written of such things, but never before had she seen a man so furious that there was no room left in him for anything else. Never before had she seen such cold, icy rage.

The Ransom who had wooed her with such gentleness was gone.

Chapter 9

Ransom and Nate sat in the kitchen for a long time, discussing and discarding strategies. Mandy paid them little attention. If there was anything she could do, they would let her know. Until then, she had nothing to offer. Instead she retreated to her study and the world of the book she was working on. It was easy to hide in the cocoon of her imagination.

Eventually she heard them leave the house, the slap of the screen door loud in the stillness of the evening. Later she heard Ransom come back in. She would recognize the sound of his footsteps anywhere, she realized. There was something distinctive about the way he set his feet down, about the slight hesitation in his loose-jointed stride. She heard him prowl the house, heard him moving around in the kitchen, and finally she heard him come into the study behind her. Her shoulders tensed defensively.

He sat in the easy chair, and she could feel his gaze on her as she typed gibberish into her computer and filled the screen with glowing amber symbols that made no more sense than her pounding heart and tightening body.

She felt her awareness of him settle into her abdomen, down low between her legs. It was the first time she had ever felt that kind of awareness, and her fingers fumbled on the keys. All the other feelings in her body seemed to fade away in direct proportion to the awakening sensations down there. The light caress of her jeans when she shifted in her chair was suddenly a pleasurable torment.

"Do you want me to leave?" His question was a quiet growl in the stillness.

She drew a deep breath. "No." Her voice sounded level, but her aroused flesh had begun a slow, steady pulsing that was taking more and more of her attention.

"You could fool me."

She faced him then, intending to— Whatever she had intended, she forgot it when she looked into Ransom's face. The withdrawal to some cold plane that had frightened her earlier was no longer evident. Behind his stony face, in the window of his blue eyes, she saw his pain. Pain she had caused. The pain of rejection.

She drew a sharp breath and closed her eyes against the understanding of what she had done. In an act of unwarranted cruelty she had encouraged him to expose himself, encouraged him to display the ultimate vulnerability, and then she had turned her back on him. He might understand her fears, he might even forgive her for them, but that didn't prevent him from being wounded by what she had done. And she had made it worse, because, while she had run from him like a coward, she had refused to run from the real danger that threatened them all. Despite what she had said earlier, she had acted as if she *was* afraid of him—and only of him.

"Mandy, are you all right?"

The gentle concern she was used to hearing in his voice was conspicuously absent. His tone was matter-of-fact. He asked the question as he might ask it of any stranger.

And that hurt her. Which she deserved, she guessed. Oh, yes, she deserved it. How could she possibly make up for what she had done?

"Mandy?"

She shivered, a huge, ripping shiver that shook her from head to foot. What a fraud she was. She sat here in her carefully orchestrated universe telling herself and the whole world that she was happy with her life, happy with the way things were, that there was nothing she wanted except to be left alone to write her books. Not only did she lack the guts to step outside her ivory tower, she even lacked the guts to admit that she might want to.

"Mandy?"

The indifference had evaporated from his tone. Concern, just a small echo of it, was there now as he reached out and touched her hand.

"Mandy, what's wrong?"

It was that small, fragile hint that he might actually care about her that opened the floodgate and fractured the dam that contained her feelings. A huge sob escaped her, and she reached out blindly, needing his warmth and strength, needing his *reality*, and finally admitting it to herself.

Perhaps the most amazing thing of all was that he gave it to her without a moment's hesitation. He gathered her onto his lap and into his arms, and his hands rubbed her soothingly, gently, while he murmured reassuring nonsense. Incapable of a coherent word, never mind a coherent thought, she pressed her face to his neck and hid within the sanctuary of his arms.

He was, she thought much later, an incredibly generous man. She wasn't at all certain that in his place she could have displayed anything approaching his kindness. She lay quietly against him, her head throbbing, her eyes swollen, her throat raw, her tears dried up. Even then, even knowing the storm had passed, he didn't evict her from his embrace.

"Ransom?" Her voice was a tired croak.

"Hmm?"

"I'm sorry."

A breath escaped him, not quite a sigh. "There's nothing to apologize for, Mandy. It's been hard on you."

How could she explain? For a wordsmith, she was suddenly short of words. "I have plenty to apologize for, and you damn well know it." Scratchy but defiant, her voice grew firmer.

He astonished her then by laughing. It was a quiet, tired sort of laugh, but a laugh all the same. "So okay," he said on a warm chuckle. "Apology accepted."

"You don't even know what I'm apologizing for."

"For this crying jag, I presume."

She sat up straighter on his lap and grabbed his chin, forcing him to look at her. "That's only part of it."

His faint smile vanished completely. "What's the other part?" His gaze was now wary, watchful.

He had a right to be wary of her, she realized with a pang. "I'm sorry for running from you this afternoon."

"Mandy, I—"

She silenced him by placing her fingers over his mouth. "I know you understand. You're a wonderfully understanding man. But that doesn't make what I did right. And it doesn't mean you weren't hurt by it. So I'm sorry. I'm very, very sorry."

For a long moment he was silent and motionless, his eyes holding hers. She returned his measuring look bravely, wondering what it was he saw, and whether he was going to accept her apology. He surprised her by asking a question.

"Why are you telling me this, Mandy?"

"Because...because I want you to know...I realize that what I did was . . . hurtful. That fear doesn't excuse me."

Not a flicker of a muscle betrayed what he might be thinking. "Fear excuses a great deal."

She shook her head. "No. It doesn't excuse a damn thing, and it's time I faced it. Fear is an instinctive thing—any animal can act on it. A human being isn't supposed to respond to every instinct and impulse that way. We're supposed to think, to reason, to use our minds to see beyond such things. I haven't been. I've been...I've been..."

Before she could find an adequately demeaning description for her behavior, Ransom stole her words, her intent and her breath with a devouring, demanding kiss. "Say it, Mandy. Damn it, just this once tell me the truth. Quit thinking, quit analyzing, quit trying to explain things rationally. Just tell me what you *feel. Tell me.*"

She knew what he wanted. She knew because she needed so desperately to hear it from him. "I want you," she admitted hoarsely. "I want *you.*"

He cut her off with another kiss, this one deeper but gentler. "I want you, too, Amanda Lynn. God forgive me, I want you so much...."

Those words tore down the last of her barriers and made a joke of her fears, because, God help her, she needed him the way she needed air to breathe. If she had ever had a choice in this, it had long since been lost. The point of no return had passed unnoticed, fading into the mist.

For a moment, just a brief, almost undetectable moment, they both resisted fate and destiny, they both made one last hopeless and human attempt not to succumb. Caring meant hurting, a lesson they had learned so painfully that it was branded on their very cells. But being human, they were driven by hungers deeper than pain, needs greater than safety.

With a deep sigh, Ransom cupped her cheek in the palm of his hand. Her head was already resting on his shoulder, but at his gentle touch she managed to snuggle even closer. Bending, he pressed his face to her hair and remembered how he had dreamed of holding her just like this during the long, lonely, endless nights of his captivity. It didn't seem odd that he hadn't even met her then, because he had known her in his soul and in his dreams. Later, perhaps, he might be embarrassed by such fancifulness, but at this moment, wrapped in a filigree of feelings that could be described in no other way, he didn't feel foolish at all. He was just grateful he had the opportunity to really hold her, to actually wrap his arms around her and hold her tangible warmth against him. So few dreams ever took substance.

Her fear stood between them, though. Despite her capitulation, he knew she was still afraid. If he said anything to her about his feelings, she would feel he was tempting fate and become even more frightened, so he held his peace and cuddled her close.

There was, too, on his part, an awareness of his own selfishness. He had no right to disturb her hard-won tranquility, to surmount her defenses, not while someone wanted to kill him. Not while he couldn't afford to soften the edge of his anger. Not while he couldn't offer her a future.

Despite feeling selfish, he was unable to draw back from her. It was as if, in some elemental way, he knew that they could have no future together unless she was able to face the present beside him.

To hell with it all, he thought in a sudden, savage burst of feeling. He'd had little enough in his life that had felt as right and as good as this woman's soft warmth curled up on his lap. In fact, there had been *nothing* as right and as good as this. If it made him a selfish bastard to be unable to relinquish these few precious moments, then he was a selfish bastard with no regrets.

As unselfconsciously as a kitten, encouraged by what he had said and the way he held her, Mandy nuzzled Ransom's silky beard and breathed his warm, wonderful scent deep into her lungs. With her head on his chest, the steady beat of his heart filled her ear as she rested against him and his hands roamed gently over her side, her shoulders, her hip. When one of those hands slipped between her legs and squeezed her gently, it seemed a natural extension of the embrace. She shifted, making herself available to him, letting him know that this time she truly welcomed him.

"Can we?" she asked breathlessly. "Is it safe?"

"Shh." He brushed feathery kisses on her eyelids, her cheeks, her lips. "Nate left us guarded tonight. Shh."

Every nagging, pulsing yearning she felt for him settled right between her thighs. For a fleeting moment his hand abandoned her, but only to turn out the light. In the dark, he returned to her, unsnapping a snap, tugging down a zipper, slipping his warm fingers beneath denim and cotton to hot, moist, eager flesh.

"Ransom..." His name was a sighing whisper.

"Shh...shh...just let me," he whispered back. "Let me give this to you, Amanda Lynn. Let me."

She undulated upward against his pleasure-giving hand and let reality slip away. In the dark, in the warm, welcome dark with Ransom so close, nothing else mattered. "Ransom...you..."

"Shh," he murmured soothingly. "Shh... We should have started this way earlier, princess. Slowly. Easily. One long, hot step at a time. I want your pleasure. Every single hot, wet, aching moment of it."

The thrills that ripped through her were generated as much by his huskily whispered words as by his touches. She had never imagined anyone talking this way, speaking so frankly, so passionately.

"Do you like that?" he asked as his fingers glided between her hot satin folds and slipped into her slick depths.

Like it? She had never experienced anything quite like it. She had the brief, hazy thought that John had been a very conservative lover, a tender but unimaginative partner. Until this very moment, she had no idea that she might have missed anything. She opened her mouth, wanting to tell Ransom something of what he made her feel, fearing he might take her silence as rejection.

But he read her silence correctly, and when she opened her mouth he took it with his in a deep, plunging kiss that mimicked the slow, sweet penetration of his fingers. Every blaze of pleasure and excitement he had hitherto ignited in her paled suddenly as his hand and tongue unleashed a conflagration.

She twisted against him, arching upward against his hand with a groan that communicated the intensity of her aching need. His own desires spiraled through him and knotted in his groin. This woman was tinder to his senses even as she was balm to his soul.

They had this little bit of time, just this little window of opportunity, when they could be a man and a woman together. In a couple of hours he was going to have to become an agent again. He was going to have to devote his every attention and effort toward devising a means of drawing the assassin out. But now, for just these few, brief hours while Charlie Huskins and another deputy stood guard, he could forget all that. For just this little bit of time he could claim the colors of his princess to carry into battle with him.

They both moaned when he shifted his hand and dipped even deeper into her receptive, hot depths. Her jeans were a definite hindrance now, and he found himself remembering the full, creamy, pink-tipped breasts that were hidden beneath her blouse. He wanted her naked. Completely naked. He wanted to love her from head to foot so that she would never forget him, would always know that she had belonged to him. So that her every nerve ending would be imprinted with his memory.

He groaned again, this time in a different timbre as he reacted to the most basic of masculine needs: territorialism. Taking his hand from her, ignoring her whimpering protests, he shoved his arm beneath her knees and stood. His strength was suddenly almost superhuman, but he hardly noticed it. He was driven to make this woman his, and the only place to do that completely and securely was in bed. Her bed. It was essential that it be *her* bed. Even as he acted on the imperative, some part of him realized the mystical significance of claiming the princess in her own bower. No other place would make the claiming as complete. No other place would signify her total surrender to him.

He mounted the stairs swiftly, holding Mandy as effortlessly as if she weighed nothing at all. In her room he laid her on the counterpane and stood over her, stripping off his clothes with swift efficiency. There was little light, but even so, he saw her eyes grow wide with knowledge.

And then, depriving him of breath and filling him with fierce triumph, she rose to her knees and began to discard her own clothing. At last. At long last. She was coming to him at last.

His boots delayed him for a few moments, but soon he was free of the final restriction. When he straightened, he found Mandy ahead of him, lying back against the pillows and waiting. He paused, savoring the moment, lingering just a little longer on the brink. And then she lifted her arms toward him.

"Ransom," she sighed yearningly.

His every cell throbbed with the same demand as his loins, but first he had another purpose to accomplish. Instead of sinking into her arms, he knelt beside the bed and touched a finger to her soft lips.

"Shh..." he murmured. "Shh..." Let me worship you, he thought. Let me adore you and cherish you with my mind, my mouth, my hands, my body. Earlier she had met his mindless need with selfless understanding. He needed to show her how much that meant to him. He needed to give her something of what she had given him. And he needed to do it now, because life might deprive him of another chance.

"Ransom?" Her breath caught on his name as his hand swept over her, lightly teasing a nipple, dipping tenderly into her navel, finding its goal at last in the downy thatch at the juncture of her thighs. "Oh..." It was a sigh and a soft whimper as he brought her again, instantly, to a fever pitch.

She should have been embarrassed. Some vestige of her mind was astonished by her wantonness as she lay beneath his hands and let him—no, encouraged him—to touch her in any and every way he cared to. Some part of her wanted to draw back from the totally consuming eroticism of his caresses. Some part of her was afraid to give him the complete capitulation he demanded. She had never, ever, lost herself in the way he was asking of her now, and she was terrified to do so.

He demanded that she drop her deepest, most closely guarded barriers. He demanded... only what he had given her that afternoon in his bed. He demanded that she relinquish her self-control and trust him to carry her through this unscathed and safe. As he had earlier trusted her.

Remembering how he had lost himself in her and how she had intuitively understood how naked and vulnerable he felt, she suddenly understood the true meaning of intimacy. And it was intimacy that Ransom was demanding of her now. Not sex. Not a simple scratching of superficial itches. Not love, not caring, not passion or even need. No, he wanted intimacy, a far more terrible thing, because it ran so deeply and so closely to the most tender and easily damaged parts of a person. Intimacy meant shucking the spiritual skin and leaving every emotional nerve ending open and exposed.

She wondered wildly if she could do it, if she should do it, and then she *was* doing it. Seizing his head, she drew his mouth to hers, claiming him as fiercely as he had claimed her. Her legs parted, opening like a blossom to his deep touches, encouraging him to take more and yet more of her. Let him know, she thought crazily. Let him know how much I want, how much I need, how much he means. Let him know.

And then she gave him the gift of her pleasure. Rising up against his hand, she went to him as he wanted, with her ecstasy offered freely and honestly.

And then, before the pulsing aftershocks had even begun to subside, before she could think about what she was doing and grow embarrassed, she tugged at him, pulling him onto the bed beside her, drawing him over her.

"Now," she said fiercely. "Now!"

He grabbed the foil packet he had thrown on the night table when he discarded his jeans. As soon as Mandy saw it, she snatched it from him. "Let me," she said hoarsely, astonishing herself even as the thought of what she was about to do sent fresh lightning along her nerves. Oh, yes, she wanted to touch him like this, and more. And later, when they were calmer, when the needs had gentled and there was time, she was going to touch him and explore him and learn him.

Straddling her hips, Ransom clenched his jaw and let her do as she wished. No one had ever put a condom on him before, and he found himself suspended between heaven and hell, wondering if he would be able to survive her ministrations. His breath caught as she touched him, and his mind served up a list of all the ways he would *like* her to touch him, stiffening him even more.

"You should have let me go to the doctor," she mumbled thickly, breathlessly, as she rolled the barrier onto him. "You feel so much better naked...."

He also wouldn't have missed this experience for the world. There were no words to describe the fresh flood of passion her gentle touch elicited; there were no words for how it made him feel to watch her touch him with trembling hands, to see her hesitations and her shy delight in what she was doing.

Then, in a single incandescent instant, he claimed her. Buried deep within her, he froze briefly, reluctant to let go of this absolutely perfect moment in time. Around him, he felt her rippling contractions as she responded to the bliss of their union.

Earlier he had taken her as a warrior who had been away too long. Now, with deep, slow thrusts, he took her as a warrior who had come home. He watched her convulse beneath him and around him, watched culmination draw her tight and fling her to the stars. And then he let her watch him, let her see the hunger twist his face, let her hear the groans of driving need that were torn from him.

She felt his climax in her womb. More, she felt it in a deep place that heard what hadn't been said. He had shown her what he could not tell her, what she wasn't willing to hear.

The knight had claimed his princess.

Ransom woke at dawn. Opening his eyes slowly, he saw that the curtains had been drawn back from the window to let in the pink and lavender light. Slowly, cell by cell, he remembered where he was. Facedown in Mandy's narrow bed, he was sprawled widely in a posture more relaxed than any his body had dared adopt since childhood. She had done that to him, he thought hazily. She had unwound him that far.

Almost as soon as he had the thought, he tensed. A movement told him that Mandy was awake, and more, that she was kneeling beside him, looking at him. Oh God! He knew she had seen it before, in bed yesterday and when he'd been so feverish with the malaria. He had the vaguest memory of sitting in her tub while she ladled cool water over him. So she had seen the scars all along his body in the light before. Certainly she had seen his back. She wasn't repulsed.

But every hair on his body stood up with fear. He felt so exposed. He couldn't bear to imagine what she must be thinking, couldn't bear the thought of her seeing his ugliness like this. Even while he knew it wasn't rational, he nonetheless felt ashamed. All the tangled feelings of a victim rose in him, a textbook web of shame and guilt and humiliation. He had to force himself to lie still beneath her eyes, and he did so only because he knew they had to get past this.

His hammering heart forced him to suck in a deep gulp of air, a ragged, tormented sound.

"Shh..." Mandy leaned over him, pressing her palms to his shoulders. She knew. She didn't know how, but she knew, and her heart ached for him, an ache so deep it threatened to destroy her. "Shh..." She leaned closer to kiss the nape of his neck just beneath his shaggy, molten gold hair.

"I was sitting here," she murmured softly. "Just sitting here and admiring you."

"Mandy..." Who the *hell* did she think she was kidding?

"Shush. Let me finish." Her tone sharpened with command, then softened again as her lips found the first scar that slashed across his shoulders. "You're so beautiful, Ransom. So beautiful. I thought so the first time I set eyes on you. Oh, you were too thin and pale, and you looked as if you'd been sick for a long, long time, but there was more

than that. Something so beautiful it shines out of your
eyes."

With each word she kissed yet another scar, working her
way slowly down his back across the tortured map of four
years of his life. He caught his breath and tried to swallow
the lump that was clogging his throat, but his throat just got
tighter and her kisses just kept coming, finding every hurt,
every scar, every damaged part of him.

"The instant I saw you," she murmured huskily, "I knew
you were a warrior. I knew you'd been in battles so terrible
there's no way I can imagine them. I knew..." Her voice
broke and then steadied. "I knew you'd been beaten and
bloodied." She drew a ragged breath and kissed the scars
that marred the backs of his strong, powerful legs. When she
spoke again, her voice was thick with tears. "But I knew you
were still strong. All I had to do was look at you to know
just how valiant and undefeated you are."

He couldn't handle any more of this. She was ripping him
open with tender words and soft caresses. He started to roll
over, unable to speak through his closed throat, but she
stopped him by covering him with her body. Where before
he had been so brutally exposed he could hardly stand it,
now her soft nakedness covered him from shoulder to
calves. Her cheek lay between his shoulder blades, her
stomach pressed softly against his rump, and her thighs lay
gently over his. Reaching up, she laced her fingers through
his.

She wanted to tell him that she would shelter him and
protect him, that she would place herself between him and
the cold harsh world, but she left the foolish words unspoken. At this moment, everything seemed possible, but she
knew that wouldn't last. When faced with hard, harsh reality herself, she was going to dive into the nearest hole and
hide. This was a moment out of time, a fantasy wrested
from the night, and it would evaporate in the light of day.

As the pink light of dawn brightened slowly into gold,
Ransom lay beneath Mandy's protective warmth. He didn't
want to move for fear of shattering the tenuous tenderness

between them. This woman, the woman who covered his exposed pain with her nakedness, this woman was the Amanda Lynn Tierney who wrote fantasies that moved him and touched him. This was the woman who lived only in her fantasies because she was afraid of being hurt.

And damn it, he didn't know how he could possibly prevent that. In her books, good always triumphed over evil, but this wasn't a book. This was real life. When she remembered that, she would run from him again. Needing so much more, he contented himself with tightening his fingers around hers.

"Princess?"

The husky murmur sent shivers of longing pouring through her. "There's a custom," she said, "that when a lady bestows her colors she also has promised her favors."

Her fingers felt so fragile between his that he dared not squeeze any harder. Instead he drew her hand to his mouth and kissed it. He felt another tremor pass through her, and his body responded in kind. Strength flowed through him.

"I thought," he said huskily, running his tongue over one small fingertip, "that a knight had to be victorious before he claimed those favors. It seems to me we got it backward, princess."

She shifted against him in a sinuous, sensuous movement that made him acutely aware of where each and every one of her delectable curves was located.

"Oh, no," she said, her voice suddenly breathy and deep. "We got the colors part backward."

"How so?" Gently, very gently, he bit her fingertip.

Mandy gasped and tried to press even closer. "You've won all your battles, all your victories, already. We can pretend I gave you my colors years ago. I should have."

And probably wouldn't have, he thought, even as he twisted beneath her and brought them, at last, face-to-face and chest-to-chest. Mandy's legs fell between his, and he smiled at the way her eyes darkened when she felt the proof of his arousal.

"Lift up," he said roughly, and positioned her so that she straddled his hips, her most intimate secrets utterly exposed to his marauding hands. He slipped a finger along her moist folds and found the slick nub of her desire. He watched as she arched and whimpered softly at his touch.

"You wouldn't have given me a second look, princess," he told her gruffly. "You would have found me hard and cruel and insensitive. You would have recognized me as a necessary evil, but you wouldn't have wanted me to touch you."

"I would—" Her breath and voice broke as he rubbed her gently.

"You wouldn't," he said flatly. "I was a warrior. I was everything a warrior needs to be. I did everything a warrior needs to do. You'd better understand that before you give me your colors, because I'll do it again if I need to."

He would. She didn't doubt it for a minute. And whatever he said, she had seen the truth in his eyes. A warrior did what he had to. It was *why* he did it that made a difference.

Suddenly, shocking her with his strength, he lifted her until she straddled his shoulders. Then he gave her a kiss so intimate she couldn't believe what her senses were telling her.

"Ransom, no..."

"Mandy, yes," he growled. "I mean to have every one of your favors, princess. Every one. Every way."

She writhed, pinned by his hands, pinned by pleasure so exquisite it was pain. "Ransom...Ransom..." She cried his name as her torment mounted, yet still he kissed her relentlessly, his tongue stripping her of her last inhibitions. Higher and higher he drove her, sending her so far beyond thought that she could only feel.

He felt her break apart. She shattered like crystal reaching its resonant note. He gave himself a moment to taste her pleasure, and then he rolled her over, gathering her close and rocking her until the storm passed.

She wept. Her tears might have frightened him, except that she was also clinging so hard to him that he knew he would have a new set of scars on his shoulders. The pain felt good. Pain was as much a proof of existence as pleasure. Without pain there could be no pleasure. It was the hills and valleys of the emotions that gave life its perspective and its contours. He understood that. She needed to understand it, too, but he didn't know how a lesson like that could be taught. She would have to find the knowledge somewhere within herself.

Before her tears fully ceased, she moved her hands over him, telling him that she was still receptive. He released a breath he hadn't even known he was holding and closed his eyes against the sheer delight of her hands on his flesh. She traced every contour of his hard, powerful chest. When she found the small, hard beads of his nipples, she stroked and licked and nipped until he thought he would go out of his ever-loving mind.

"Mandy..." His voice was a harsh groan of protest, but already she was moving on, sweeping lower in her hungry search, approaching and then skipping away from his manhood in a teasing dance that suspended him between laughter and despair.

And then, stunning him into utter stillness, she reciprocated with her own shy, intimate kiss. He felt her warm, satiny lips and her hot slick tongue on him, and if a squad of commandos had burst through the door right then, he couldn't have twitched a muscle in his own defense.

"Mmm..." she purred as she felt his helpless response. "Mmm."

All that had gone before between them had been shrouded in a dreamy haze, an aura of fantasy that had answered some deep need of their souls. Now, however, that mist was gone. Each sound, each movement, each sensation, took on the hard, distinct edge of reality.

He heard the whisper of his own skin against the sheets as she made him writhe. He had never, ever, let anyone do this to him before, had never, ever, permitted himself to be so vulnerable and defenseless. It didn't matter that he had just done the same thing to her. Adrenaline shot through him as part of him tried to flee, as part of him cried out to escape from this exposure. Hell, yes, he wanted to run. He couldn't bear the thought of a woman, any woman, knowing she had this kind of power over him. He couldn't stand the thought of anyone seeing him helpless like this. Reaching up, he grabbed the headboard, heard himself groan, a sound that rose from the very bottom of his soul. He jerked sharply, and his legs stiffened.

"Ransom . . . ?" A hazy, husky question.

Their eyes met across the expanse of his torso, and what he saw in her soft brown gaze undid the last of him. Closing his eyes, he gave her what he had never given anyone else. "That . . . feels . . . so . . . damn . . . *good!*"

Good didn't even begin to cover it. Ecstasy didn't come close, either. There was something about what was happening that was reaching beyond the physical to the emotional, and it was exhilarating him. Tearing at him. Clawing at him.

And finally, good wasn't enough. Reaching for Mandy with hands that trembled, he tugged her up beside him and tucked her beneath him. "I need you," he muttered roughly. "*Now,* Amanda Lynn. Now!"

In the radiant early morning light, she saw him above her, a golden warrior with eyes the blazing blue of the Wyoming sky. Beautiful. Wild. Powerful.

Unconquered.

Chapter 10

He felt like one great big exposed nerve ending. Standing beneath the shower's heated spray, letting water pummel his face and shoulders, he gave serious thought to just rolling up into a tight ball and pretending he'd never been born.

Men weren't supposed to feel that way, but hell, he'd been on enough battlefields to know that men damn well *did* feel that way, and he was feeling that way right now. Too much, too soon, too fast. In one flaming night of passion, tenderness and soul-on-soul contact, he and Mandy had gotten closer than he'd ever been to another human being.

Well, no, that wasn't exactly true. Back in Nam he'd been that close to Nate and Micah. When you stood eyeball-to-eyeball with the Grim Reaper day after day, with nothing to rely on but your buddies, you damn well got close. You got so you knew another man's smell as well as you knew your own, you knew what he wanted, what he dreamed and what he feared.

But since Nam, Ransom hadn't had anyone to rely on but himself. He'd been a loner. Was still a loner. Even wolves ran in packs, but not Ransom. Last night he'd let Mandy cross the invisible stone wall he kept between himself and the rest of the world. Superficially, he'd seemed no different than anyone else. He let women into his bed, friends into his life, but no one, absolutely no one, got within that invisible wall of stone.

Now someone had, and he felt as if he had been flayed, as if every single inch of his skin had been peeled away. Worse, the only way he could think of to protect himself would hurt Mandy, and he suspected that she felt every bit as skinned this morning as he did. After all, she lived behind some very high walls of her own.

He needed some distance. He needed it savagely. If he didn't get it, he might take it brutally. The thought worried him. He knew himself. Some things were instincts so deep that he acted on them before his mind had a chance to intervene. That was half the point of this shower: to gain time and distance and the chance to think before he acted.

And he sure as hell couldn't spent the rest of the morning hiding in here. Raw as he was, he wasn't sure he even wanted to. The thought of her lying on those rumpled sheets in her narrow bed waiting for him was enough to make being skinned alive seem like a small inconvenience.

Nearly groaning, he turned his face into the spray once more. There was another inconvenience he had been forgetting but couldn't afford to forget any longer: the would-be assassin.

Swearing under his breath, he turned off the water, threw the curtain back and grabbed a towel. He had wasted enough time. In fact, when he thought about it, he couldn't believe how laid-back he'd been about it so far. Mandy had distracted him. Like a witch, she had cast some kind of spell on him, a spell he was so reluctant to break that he was hanging his butt in the breeze just asking somebody to take another shot at it.

Damn!

With the towel wrapped around his hips, he strode down the hall and stepped into her room, words of explanation and excuse already forming in his mind.

She was gone. He stared at the carefully made bed, and then slowly, reluctantly, a smile tugged up the corners of his mouth.

It seemed he wasn't the only one who was panicking.

Mandy heard Ransom's booted feet on the stairs, heard his familiar, faintly hesitant step behind her. She was afraid to face him, she realized. Embarrassment over her actions was only a small part of it. Intellectually she knew that they had done nothing that millions of couples all over the world didn't do nightly. Emotionally, it might take her a little longer to believe it, but that was the least of her problems.

She was afraid that he would expect continued intimacy. She was afraid that he wouldn't let her retreat from the feelings that had overwhelmed her. She needed time. She needed distance. She needed to find her hard-won equilibrium. She needed to reestablish her control over her life.

"Mandy?"

Slowly she turned, her wary gaze rising to his. They stared at one another like ancient antagonists who had met unexpectedly and weren't sure whether to continue an old battle.

"You know," Ransom said abruptly, "I've got the weirdest sensation I've been here before. That I've done this before. Do you suppose we've both been running scared for all eternity?"

Her jaw dropped, but before she could muster any kind of response, he shrugged and a mask dropped over his face. "You crawl into your foxhole, and I'll crawl into mine, princess. It's the safest place to be."

He stomped out of the kitchen, looking both disgruntled and relieved. She should have guessed Ransom was no happier about this than she was. He would be moving on just as soon as he was well again. Just as soon as his convalescent leave was up. Nothing he had said or done suggested that he would do anything else. Surely a man who had been a secret agent his entire adult life needed more excitement than he could find in Conard County.

He might call her princess and say nice things, but when you came right down to it, there was no reason on earth why a man like him should really want a dull brown mouse like her.

The thought hurt, but she refused to consider why. Instead she assured herself that she and Ransom were adults. They were perfectly capable of assuaging their physical needs without becoming tangled in skeins of unwanted feelings. They could, and would, keep a safe emotional distance.

After all, they had both learned their lesson the hard way. Neither one of them was likely to forget it.

The day had turned surprisingly warm, and the sun beat fiercely on Ransom's back as he scraped blistered paint off the side of the barn. He stayed on the side where he could see the house and keep a better eye on Mandy. From here the blackened heap of burnt wood and ash that had been the cabin was invisible. To his left was the corral, where the horses frolicked and grazed by turns. Since the fire, he was loath to keep them in the barn. If the "cat" decided to resume the game, he didn't want the animals to be caught helplessly in the way.

From time to time he dropped the scraper, scoured the sweat off his brow and went to prowl the area, watching for any sign that the person who was stalking him had again come close. When he passed beneath the open window of Mandy's study, he could hear the tap-tap of keys as she wrote, and he could just make out her shadow in the dim interior. She didn't say anything when he looked in on her, and he didn't expect her to.

By now, he figured, she probably despised him. It was a discomforting thought, but one he accepted stoically. If something happened to him, it would be better for her if she hated him.

In fact, in retrospect, he could see that he had been unpardonably arrogant in some respects. He'd had the utter gall to pity her, for one thing, when he was guilty of the same weaknesses. Human weaknesses. She was disinclined to care and he was disinclined to trust, and they were both afraid of the very same thing. It was all very well to philosophize that pain gave life its shape and contrasts, but it was something else entirely to volunteer for another fall down a jagged slope into a spiritual abyss.

Ah, hell, he thought, and wished for a beer. He knew for a fact that there was a cold six-pack in the fridge, but he wasn't going to indulge himself. He couldn't afford to cloud his senses or slow his reaction time, even by the effect of one beer.

He was, he realized, awakening from some kind of daze that had clouded his mind for months. Ever since he had discovered he was safe and protected in the hospital, that he no longer had to fend for himself because others were caring for and protecting him, something inside him had shut down. It was almost as if, in believing that he was safe, he was able to withdraw into some dark, warm internal cave from which he could view everything from a distance. Even the feelings that had been necessary to keep him alive, the anger and the hate, had been shut off behind layers of cotton batting, muffled and nearly silenced.

The return of his anger had been a sign, he realized. The healing hibernation was over. Last night had been part of that awakening. Time and again, during his short stay with Mandy, he had felt himself reaching out, moving out, feeling again. And time and again he had felt himself pull sharply back into the numbness. Last night had stripped away too many layers. There was no way he could crawl back into his cocoon. There was no way he could be numb again.

Instead, he was angry. Instead, his senses were sharpening and clearing as the cobwebs blew away. His foxhole had been filled in behind him, and now there was no choice but to stalk. To hunt. To patiently await the first sign of his quarry.

He was in pain. He was suffering sheer, gut-wrenching, soul-searing, sharp-edged emotional pain. Awareness of what had been done to him twisted like a hot knife inside him. He needed to forget and he couldn't. He needed to forgive, but he wouldn't. The actual physical pain he had endured didn't come close to the psychic pain. And unlike physical pain, psychic pain didn't go away.

Events had driven all thought of the Harvest Dance from Mandy's mind. She was utterly floored several days later when Ransom reminded her it was that night and that she had promised to go with him.

"But . . ." A million objections rose to mind, but not one of them constituted any real excuse other than, "It won't be safe for you."

"I'll be perfectly safe, and so will you."

"But in a crowd—"

"Nate tells me this won't be just any crowd. He says a stranger will stick out like a sore thumb."

"That's true, I guess." The population of the entire county was around 5,500 souls and Nate and his deputies recognized every one of them on sight. Out of those 5,500, less than two hundred usually showed up for the dance. TV, satellite dishes and VCRs made it easier and a lot more pleasant for most folks to stay home.

None of which answered her most important question. "Why do you want to go, Ransom?"

They were eating a lunch of grilled cheese sandwiches and vegetable soup at the long table in the kitchen. He kept his gaze trained on his meal, a custom he had developed since their passion-filled night together. It was a custom that made her long to throw something in order to get his full attention. She refrained, knowing the distance he was keeping was safer for them both.

"I asked you," he answered.

"Well, you can just un-ask me." Her tone took on an uncharacteristic tartness. "I can't imagine why you want to spend an evening dancing with me, much less why you want to spend the evening in a crowd. You're not a crowd type."

"No, I'm not," he agreed. The complete opposite, in fact. "But I *do* want to dance with you." That, too, was a fact, and admitting it to himself was even harder than admitting it to her. He wanted an excuse to hold her again. That would be the safest way to do it, too, because you couldn't make love on a dance floor. You couldn't expose your soul and all your tattered nerve endings. You couldn't make yourself helpless before your own needs. You *could* drive yourself crazy with longing, but he would deal with it.

There was more to it than that, Mandy thought. After the way he had been avoiding intimacy with her—with her co-operation, admittedly—she found it a little difficult to accept that he wanted to go to the Harvest Dance simply to dance with her.

Sighing, she pushed her plate aside and propped her chin on her hand. "Ransom, we really need to talk."

He barely glanced at her. "About what?" He hoped she didn't want to discuss what had happened between them the other night. If he lived to be a hundred and fifty, he didn't think he would ever be able to discuss what had really taken place between them. Some things . . . some things just came too close to the bone, too close to the soul. Too close to private places that weren't meant to be shared.

There had been magic in the air that night, he thought now. Wild magic. Things had happened that could never be explained. Talking about it would simply debase it.

"About what's really going on here," she answered finally. "If somebody is trying to kill you, they're sure going about it in a funny way. Even *I* can see that. It's been days

now since anything at all happened. If somebody really
wants to hurt you . . ."

"Somebody really wants to hurt me," he said flatly. "You
don't shoot out windshields and burn down buildings for a
joke."

"Then . . . you're being toyed with." The feeling was like
cold slime running down her back.

"Looks that way."

"That's . . . that's vicious!"

"So's murder." He looked up finally, and met her worried gaze head-on. "We'll keep you safe, Mandy. Nate and
Micah and I will see to it that nothing happens to you."

"It's not *me* I'm worried about." And she wasn't.
Throughout all of this, she couldn't recall feeling a twinge
of concern for her own safety. "Somebody would have to
hate you an awful lot to do something like that."

Ransom heard the question in the statement but didn't
know exactly how to answer. "I imagine I've made a few
people hate me that way, but it's been so long. . . ." He
shrugged. "Who knows? I'm still trying to figure out who
it might be, especially when I've been gone so long."

"Have you contacted anyone at your agency? Wouldn't
they be able to help?"

Ransom shoved his plate aside. "Let's just say they really don't have anything useful to contribute to this situation."

"Nothing? Nothing at all? What good are they if they
can't do *something* to help you?"

Ransom's eyes were like twin shards of blue ice. "Have
you heard the term 'out in the cold'?"

Mandy drew a sharp breath, and there was a strange
prickling sensation in her scalp. "But you're on convalescent leave. You haven't quit."

He shrugged. "There's really nothing anyone can do,
Mandy. Not a thing. No one has a clue. As far as the agency
is concerned, this appears to be a personal problem of my
own, and there's no evidence to the contrary. I've been in-

active for so long, even *I* find it hard to believe that this has any connection with my work.

"Anyway, regardless of who might be behind this, the agency isn't authorized to provide protection for me, and no one is going to put his career on the line to do it. It's outside their mandate. To put it plainly, they aren't allowed to function actively within the borders of the United States."

"They could ask the FBI—"

"No." Ransom's interruption was short, sharp. "Nobody can do a damn thing that Nate, Micah and I aren't already doing. It's not within the purview of any federal agency."

Mandy drew a deep breath, then another, wrestling with a sense of outrage. This man had worked for that damn agency for years, risking life and limb time and again, and now, when he needed help, he was *out in the cold?*

"Relax, Mandy. This is the way the game is played."

He seemed unperturbed by it, but she found it hard to believe that he could be. Surely he must feel some kind of resentment? If he did, though, she realized slowly, he wasn't going to admit it. This was the way things were done, men didn't grouse about the way things were. Of course not. He'd been playing by these rules for years, and he could hardly criticize them now.

"Surely they owe you something," she argued anyway. "After all you've done—"

"You don't know what I've done," he interrupted with sudden savagery. "Nobody owes me anything. But let me tell you something, Mandy, and remember this well. My list of possible suspects is very short."

"Short?"

"It's limited to the people who know I'm alive. I can rule out my family and Nate and Micah, but I can't rule out anybody else."

It took a moment, but shock trickled through her like ice water. "Your bosses . . ." she whispered in horror.

He didn't even bother to answer. No wonder, she thought. No wonder he wasn't twisting their arms and hollering at them over the phone.

My God.

Minutes ticked away in muffled, appalled silence.

And somehow, she realized abruptly, he had managed to turn the conversation away from her original area of concern: why was it so damn important to him to take her to the dance? Because, regardless of what he said, there was absolutely no way she could believe he merely wanted to dance with her. Heck, in the last three days he hadn't even *touched* her. Not even the most casual of touches. She was, in fact, beginning to feel a little like a pariah.

Which was just as well, she assured herself vigorously. She knew better than to get involved.

Right. That was why she kept catching herself staring at him, filling her eyes with him as if looking might finally satisfy the ache. She noticed everything, from the way his shirts stretched across his powerful shoulders to the way the denim of his new jeans was slowly beginning to mold his shape. She stared at him like a lovesick cow when he was outside and unaware that she was watching. She stored up everything in some hope chest of the mind, a place where she tucked precious memories for later, emptier days. And she was afraid, so very afraid, of that coming emptiness.

Some part of her argued that she should seize every moment now and store up a bundle of good memories against the days ahead. Another, saner part told her to hold herself aloof, because it would hurt less if she refused her feelings the room they needed to grow.

Still another part of her argued that there was no longer any way to avoid the pain. No way at all. Whether he left now, ten days from now, or a hundred years from now, she was going to hurt.

She was, in fact, trying to measure her pain in degrees, to limit her involvement to limit the pain. And wasn't that, she found herself thinking, merely an exercise in futility?

And none of this was getting her any closer to the truth he was withholding. She felt that if he was going to use her, she deserved to understand why. "Why don't you tell me the real reason you're so insistent on this dance, Ransom?"

He stared at her. "Why do you find it so hard to believe that I just want to dance with you?"

"Because you've been avoiding me like the plague since— for the last few days," she amended. She could feel her cheeks growing warm, but she refused to back down. Before their night together, the dance had seemed a gentle, stylized step in a slow courtship. Now it seemed more like a ridiculous pretense. As far as they had gone together, if Ransom really wanted anything further, he wouldn't have to wait to take her to the dance.

He continued to stare steadily at her. "I thought," he said finally, "that you wanted me to avoid you." And he *had* thought so. Her reluctance to get involved was the main impetus behind his own reluctance to trust her. How could you trust someone who might bolt in terror at any moment?

She didn't know how to answer him. Her heart began beating nervously as she wondered what the hell she was doing. She wanted the distance between them, didn't she? If so, why was she trying to provoke him into crossing it?

"The dance," she said finally, her hands clenched into fists on her lap. "What's so important about this damn dance?"

She was acting crazy, he thought, but then, so was he. When the hell had he ever been afraid to take what he wanted? Never. Never! So why the hell was he acting like a nervous virgin around her? "Micah's going to set a trap," he said after a moment. "You and I are going to be very much gone, and Micah and some of the off-duty deputies are going to stake out the house in the hope that the assassin will want to make the most of the opportunity. Everyone in the county knows I asked you to the dance, Mandy. Tom Preston and Marge Tate evidently saw to that."

"So you think someone might try to set another bomb or something?" The skin on her neck crawled at the thought.

"Or something."

Her brown eyes held such sorrowful fear when they rose to his. "They could destroy everything, Ransom. The house, the barn. Everything that means anything to me."

"The point behind the trap is to prevent precisely that," he pointed out. Superficially he was calm and in control, but inwardly the seething volcano was trying to bubble over. He hated to see this woman look so sad and afraid. He hated the thought that he was responsible for those feelings. He hated the fact that those feelings were standing between them. And yet, even if all this trouble went away, what did he have to offer her? What kind of promises could he make her?

She looked around as if seeking some means of escape. He ached for her, wished he could smash something to vent all the feelings that couldn't be unleashed. And then she amazed him.

"I guess I'd better take a backup copy of my book with me tonight. Just in case." Slowly, her eyes came back to him.

"That would be wise." A dozen rash promises sprang to his mind, but he didn't give voice to a single one of them. The longer he lived with the awareness of what he was doing to her, the more determined he became to end it. And he *would* end it. As soon as the assassin was caught.

Until this evening, Ransom had seen Mandy wear only jeans and baggy shirts, except for the prim gray suit she wore to church on Sundays. Tonight she wore a full denim skirt with a flirtatious, lacy red underskirt, and a red silk blouse that instantly reminded him of the creamy curves beneath. In a second passion pushed past his every guard and swamped him. He wanted this quiet, mousy woman with a hunger that defied description.

Only she wasn't a quiet, mousy woman. When she smiled, she glowed with vitality and loveliness. When he made love to her, she blossomed like a rose. For him, she became beautiful. For him, she *was* beautiful.

He knew better. He knew to keep his hands to himself, to keep a proper distance. He knew the dangers of involvement, how quickly the heat between them could burst into conflagration. He knew how he loved to tempt and tease himself by touching her, kissing her, holding her and then pulling away. He knew the spell she cast on him.

All he knew, all his wisdom and caution, failed to stop him. Without a word he reached for her. Leaning back against the kitchen counter, he tugged her into the cleft between his legs until their bodies just barely brushed. Capturing her chin, he turned her face up and looked solemnly down into her wide, nervous brown eyes. Color rose in soft pink profusion to her cheeks.

"You look lovely tonight, Amanda Lynn." His voice was a husky caress. "Lovely enough to be irresistible."

Her breath caught and her pupils dilated. She was close enough to feel his muscular strength, close enough to feel the heat of his response to her. With a sigh that was almost a sob, she leaned into him and drank greedily of his aroma, his power, his warmth. Her hands slipped upward over his chambray-clad chest, testing strength and sinew, coming to rest finally in the golden silk of his hair. She felt the brush of his beard in the split second before his hot mouth settled on hers.

This was where she belonged. Her mind might deny it, but her emotions recognized it. Every cell in her body knew it. Oh God, it felt so good and so right to have his arms close around her, to feel his large hands stroking her back and sides with the intimacy of a lover. How was she ever, ever going to survive without this? Without him?

His tongue found hers in a demanding stroke that said he was out of patience. The touch reached every one of her nerve endings, igniting them, and she responded with an impatience that matched his. In those blinding moments nothing else mattered. Their bodies strained together; their tongues twined and their breaths mingled.

It was Ransom who found the strength to call a halt. He tore his mouth from hers with a deep, heartfelt groan and rested his chin on top of her head. Cradling her with strong hands that were suddenly gentle, he waited for sanity to return to both of them. One way or another, he found himself thinking crazily, this attraction was going to be the death of him. One way or another.

Mandy stepped back suddenly and turned away, thoroughly shaken by the moments just passed. Not because of the passion, but because she felt as if she were being compelled by some force to step outside her emotional fortress. It seemed to be beyond her ability to control, this urge to step into Ransom's embrace. Time and again she threw herself into his arms and gave herself up to him. She had lost control of herself. The realization was as terrifying as anything she had ever known.

The evening star hung bright in the western sky, while the sunset cast a green glow along the horizon.

"It's rare to see a sunset like that," Mandy remarked to Ransom as the pickup rattled along the dirt road.

"Yeah. I've only seen a couple that I can recall."

She was sitting too far away, he thought, conscious of the many reasons why she should. "Can I interest you in stopping at the drive-in for a hamburger before we go on to the dance?"

Mandy was surprised to feel the corners of her mouth lift while a bubble of helium seemed to burst in her stomach. The drive-in for a hamburger. It sounded so...young. So carefree. So like one of the many things she had missed in life. "I'd love to."

Half an hour later they were parked between other dusty pickups at the drive-in, munching burgers and listening to country music on the radio. For a few minutes it was possible to pretend that this was an ordinary date, that she was an ordinary young woman with every right to enjoy herself.

It wasn't an ordinary date, though, and she couldn't forget reality for long. There was a shadow lurking on the edge of this small bubble of happiness. There was always a shadow. She couldn't remember a time in her life when her horizons had seemed completely clear. No, that wasn't true. Briefly, during her marriage, just after she learned she was pregnant, everything had seemed perfect, everything had seemed possible. She had walked around in a haze of sheer joy for weeks.

"That was a heavy sigh," Ransom remarked. He had watched the shadows pass over her face and had a pretty good idea where her thoughts had strayed. She sighed again and looked at him. "Worrying about evil wizards?" he asked.

"I guess. It's hard not to when I think about why you want us away from the house tonight."

He nodded slowly and shoved his trash into the bag. "Yeah. I couldn't pass it up, Mandy. Everybody in the damn county is expecting to see me here, which means either the house is a great target or I am. Either way, something should happen, and we should get to the bottom of this. I want you to promise me one thing, though."

She tilted her head, and he was momentarily distracted by the grace of her slender neck. "Which is?" she prompted.

"Promise you won't step outside the building or wander away from the dance floor on your own."

Cold fingers ran along her spine. It had occurred to her before that she might be perceived as a tool to use against Ransom. He was suggesting nothing she hadn't already thought of, but hearing him allude to it made it seem much more real.

"Okay," she said, hoping he couldn't guess how frightened she suddenly felt. "That's easy enough to promise."

She attempted to joke about it. "So you'll walk me to the ladies' room?"

His mouth quirked. "Sure. And set every tongue in the county wagging." He leaned toward her abruptly and nipped at her earlobe, sending a shiver of pleasure racing through her. "I don't intend to let you out of my sight, Amanda Lynn, and it isn't just because there might be danger."

"No?" Her breath caught on the word, and she felt suddenly as if she were swimming in the blue warmth of his eyes.

"No."

But it was a danger she couldn't afford to forget, she reminded herself a short time later as they drove to the high school gymnasium for the dance. She had suffered losses before in life, and she had no intention of living through them again. Parents, husband and child were all the losses any one person should be expected to endure. Only a complete masochist would set herself up for a second round.

But she could enjoy the passion, couldn't she? If she were very, very careful not to care too much?

All her reservations were soon forgotten in the excitement of the dance. She hadn't come to the Harvest Dance since John's death, and only now did she realize how many people she had lost touch with. Whenever she and Ransom agreed to sit out a dance, she found herself engaged in lively conversation with old friends who seemed to have a lot of news to share after four years. It was almost possible to forget that at every entrance to the room one of Nate's deputies was in evidence. They weren't being obtrusive, but they were there, a reminder she couldn't quite overlook.

But mostly she enjoyed dancing with Ransom. He was a very good dancer, good enough to turn her own relative inexperience into grace. And he held her as if she were precious to him, gently yet firmly. He also turned every dance into an experience so subtly erotic that her flush and breathlessness were only partly from exertion.

"Where did you learn to dance?" she asked him at one point, trying to get her mind off the way his hips kept brushing hers, a light, casual touch that seemed accidental yet occurred in a rhythm that was anything but. Her mind kept replaying the image of him as he had looked in the sunlight on her bed the morning after their lovemaking. So lean and powerful, so golden. So incredibly male and sexy. She got hot flashes just remembering.

"I took lessons years ago when I realized it was a lot less embarrassing to be able to dance than not to be able to. I was pretty surprised to realize that I liked it."

He liked it, all right, and he liked it better with Mandy than he ever had with anyone else. But then, he had never enjoyed sexual teasing the way he seemed to with Mandy, either. He had believed that at his age he pretty well knew himself, but he had learned a few things since finding her, and this was one of them. He enjoyed the teasing, the heightened awareness and the uncertainty about whether anything could come of it. With her, he enjoyed the anticipation as much as he had enjoyed the culmination with other women. He wondered if that would wear off with time, then realized he would never know.

The kindest thing he could do for Amanda Lynn Tierney was clear out of her life, and he couldn't even do that until this matter was settled. His only excuse was a poor one: he had never dreamed that he would bring so much trouble to her castle gate.

"Boy, I'm thirsty," Mandy said suddenly.

The double doors that led to the athletic field were open to the chilly night air, but the gymnasium had grown uncomfortably warm anyway. The floor was crowded with dancers, and it took several minutes for them to reach the bleachers, where Mandy gratefully sat down.

"My feet are killing me," she told Ransom ruefully. "It's probably shameful for a woman to admit it, but I haven't put on a pair of high heels in four years, and these are absolutely killing my feet."

He looked down at those dainty feet in their dainty red shoes with three-inch heels, then raised wickedly sparkling blue eyes. "I can think of a few things that would make those cute little feet feel a whole lot nicer."

Her heart skipped a beat. "I'll just bet you can," she heard herself say. "Are any of them legal?"

A crack of laughter escaped him. "All of them are, but what they lead to may not be. Relax here while I find you something to drink. I'll have Nate's deputies keep an eye on you."

She watched him wend his way around the edge of the dance floor, a broad-shouldered, narrow-hipped man with hair like liquid gold. Her heart skipped another series of beats as she thought about how she had held those hips to hers, how she had kissed and caressed every inch of that magnificent man. She could, she knew, touch him again. If she reached out, he would come to her. If she invited him, he would slide into her bed again and carry her to the mythical places he had showed her once before. He would claim her and make her his. He would sweep her up and carry her away on the whirlwind of his passion.

Oh, yes, and it would be so easy to let him. To ask him. To claim him for her own.

And so dangerous. It would never, never last.

"Is that golden-haired god yours?" asked a bright voice beside her.

Mandy turned, smiling, and found that another woman had joined her on the bench. The woman was blond and absolutely beautiful, Mandy saw, and she felt a twinge of insecurity and jealousy. Suddenly her coach had turned into a pumpkin again. Ransom, she found herself thinking, could never be interested for long in a plain brown mouse when women like this one were interested in him. "He's a friend," she managed to say pleasantly enough.

"Ransom Laird, right?" the blonde inquired, her eyes bright with curiosity.

"Yes." Mandy was tempted to turn away, but she couldn't bring herself to be so rude. There was something about this woman that she instinctively disliked, but she told herself it was merely jealousy that made her feel that way. Somehow, she wasn't quite convinced. "Do I know you? I'm sorry, but I can't place you." Lord, wasn't that catty?

But the blonde didn't take it amiss. "We've never met," she said, still smiling. "I'm visiting my cousin, Bernice Hadley. Do you know the Hadleys?"

"Vaguely," Mandy admitted. Very vaguely. She could recall having met them once.

"That's what Bernice said. You're Mandy Grant, right?" Mandy nodded cautiously.

"Well, Bernice said she thought you might be sweet on this Laird guy, so I thought I'd better check it out first." Her smile broadened. "I'm not going to be here very long, so there's really no point in wrecking your life. Will I wreck your life if I ask him to dance?"

Mandy opened her mouth to say, "Of course not," but what came out was, "Actually, yes." Color rose to her face, so hot that it felt like a sunburn.

The blonde merely laughed. "Okay. No problem." She rose and started to turn away. "Say, do you know why the deputy at the door gave me such a hard time about who I was?"

Mandy shook her head, though she knew perfectly well why this woman had been required to identify herself. Nate had told his deputies to be on the lookout for strangers. "Maybe he was just curious about a pretty woman."

The blonde laughed. "I'd like to think so. Nice talking to you."

Moments later she had completely vanished into the crowd, and try though she might, Mandy couldn't pick her out again.

"Here you go." Ransom sat beside her and handed her a tall paper cup. "Diet cola. Hope that's okay."

"That's perfect." She knew they were serving beer from a keg in paper cups and was surprised Ransom hadn't gotten himself any. He liked beer, though he rarely drank more than a single can at lunchtime.

Of course, she thought suddenly, and the back of her neck prickled. Of course he wasn't drinking. He was on duty, or whatever you called it when you were an agent who was being hunted. He wouldn't want to cloud his senses or slow his reaction time.

"Damn," she whispered.

He looked at her. "Mandy?"

She shrugged. "Nothing."

"Nothing?" His eyes told her that he knew she was lying. "Ready to dance again?"

Mandy shook her head. "No, my feet still hurt. You go ahead and ask someone else if you want."

"Are you kidding?" His voice suddenly took on a husky note, and she found herself drowning in his eyes. "There are no other women here."

Her breathing speeded up. "There's a blonde. Bernice Hadley's cousin."

"A blonde? What blonde? I don't see any." He was teasing; his eyes never wavered from her face.

"She wanted to know if you belonged to me." Why was she telling him this? But the devil was driving her, she realized. She was a moth determined to soar toward the flame.

"And what did you say?" In the depths of his eyes, a smile was beginning to be born, and it was tugging ever so slightly at the corners of his mouth behind his beard.

Nobody but Mandy would even know he was smiling, but she knew, and it practically deprived her of breath. He was so close! She could smell him, his faint masculine aroma, so rich and musky, the shampoo in his hair and beard.

"I said you were a friend."

He placed his right hand over his heart. "I'm wounded."

The devil drove her on. "Then she asked if it would wreck my life if she asked you to dance."

His eyes sparkled. "And you said?"

"I said it would." As soon as the words were out, she wanted to snatch them back. It was such a bald admission, such a bold thing to say. He had, after all, never told her he wanted anything from her but sex. It might anger him that she had said such a thing. It might frighten him away. Men were notoriously scared of emotional involvement. It ought to scare *her* away.

"Did you?" He leaned closer, and his voice dropped until it was an intimate growl. "What do you say we blow this joint?"

She thought it was a great idea.

Yes, take her out of here, Ransom. Go find a quiet place and make love to her. Love her well. Love her completely. You're not going to get many more chances to love her or anyone else.

For now, old friend, I don't think you take my threats seriously enough. Maybe I need to remind you that I mean business. Yes, that might be a good idea. You're just not afraid enough yet, Ransom. Not nearly afraid enough.

Chapter 11

It was almost eleven when they left the dance. The moon had risen high, and stars spangled the dark sky. The Milky Way was a bright band of stardust, and it was possible to understand why the ancients had named it as they had. There was hardly a night sky anywhere to compare with that of Wyoming, Ransom thought as he helped Mandy into the truck. Only the desert had a better view.

He divided his attention equally between the road and the rearview mirror as they pulled out of town, then relaxed a hair when he saw their tail pick them up. Deputy Beaure-gard was doing his duty as planned.

Instead of heading straight home, Ransom pulled over in one of the picnic area turnouts that dotted the banks of Conard Creek and parked in the dark shadows beneath a tree. Without further ado he leaned back into the corner and pulled Mandy against him, so that she rested on his chest, her cheek tucked into the hollow of his shoulder.

Minutes passed in silence while he held her and watched out the back window in the direction of the road. Then, as arranged earlier, Deputy Beauregard, driving a pickup indistinguishable from Mandy's, passed up the road. If an ambush lay ahead, Beauregard and the two deputies in the bed of the pickup would flush it out.

For Mandy, who knew nothing about the second truck, it seemed as if Ransom wanted just to hold her and gently rub her shoulder, but presently he started talking in a quiet, thoughtful voice.

"Once upon a time, I was a kid," he said. "Ages and ages ago, before the dawn of civilization. At least, it seems nearly that long ago. It's almost embarrassing to remember how much planning and maneuvering it took to get hold of my dad's pickup for a date, and then to get the date, and then to get the date to agree to pull over someplace. I actually succeeded once."

Mandy smiled into the dark. "Was it worth it?"

"Naw. I didn't know what the hell to do once we parked. I had some ideas about kissing, but I'd never done it before, and I damn near panicked. I made a stab at it. It embarrasses me to remember how inept I was. It was a good thing Polly Perkins didn't have any more experience than I had. She seemed to think it was okay."

Mandy felt the craziest urge to cry a tear or two for the boy he must have been. Why did innocence always have to die?

"Anyhow," he continued, "I was just thinking how funny it is that you don't fully appreciate some things until you're almost too old for them. Like Polly and me sitting in my dad's '63 Chevy pickup, both of us hotter than Roman candles, because of our ages more than anything, and neither of us knowing worth a damn what to do about it." He laughed softly. "I sure hope Polly found somebody with the answers."

Mandy rubbed her cheek against him. "I'm sure she did."

His palm pressed against the side of her neck, warm against her soft skin. "I sure know what to do about it now, princess. And I'm old enough to appreciate that *who* I do it with matters more than what I do.''

Her heartbeat grew loud in her ears.

"I'm hotter than a Roman candle for you, Amanda Lynn. I'm hot and hard and aching. I don't think I've been this hot or hard since I was sixteen." He caught her hand and drew it down to his groin.

She didn't resist. She stopped breathing, but she had no desire to resist. He was so frank. So honest about it. How could she be any less? She squeezed him and savored the groan that sounded as if it were torn from him. "Here?" she asked unsteadily. "Now?"

"God, Mandy! No, not here. I want you naked. I want you all over me and all around me. I want to be able to get my hands and mouth on every beautiful inch of you." Catching her chin, he turned her mouth up to his and showed her with his tongue just one of the many things he wanted to do with her.

Panting, desperate for air in a universe that had turned to flame, Mandy wrenched her mouth from his. "Let's go," she demanded breathlessly. Was that desperate-sounding voice really her own? She didn't care, and if anything happened to restore her common sense, she would lose her mind.

Ransom squeezed her so hard her ribs ached, and then he let her go so he could start the truck. Once they were back on the road, he tucked her under his arm and drove with one hand on the wheel, the other softly teasing her right breast. Back and forth his fingers brushed across her beaded nipple, and finally, wanting to give him some of his own medicine, Mandy placed her hand provocatively on his thigh. High on his thigh. She heard him catch his breath, felt his muscles flex and tense beneath her palm.

"Ah, lady, lady," he said raggedly. "You better watch that while I'm driving."

It was worse than ever, Mandy thought hazily. Now that she knew what making love with Ransom was like, she wanted him more than ever. Oh God, what was she going to do when he left? How was she ever going to bear the agony?

Almost as if he sensed the premonition of pain that threatened to shatter her mood, Ransom closed his hand fully over her soft breast and gently squeezed, sending another lance of longing straight to the center of her womanhood.

A soft whimper escaped her, and he heard it with such a sense of satisfaction that it defied description. This woman's hunger was more important to him than his own, her pleasure far more gratifying. Making her want him and satisfying her made him feel more like a man than he had ever felt in his life. He wondered how he could ever have mistaken anything else in his life for passion?

Damn! she made him feel alive. Alive in the way he had previously felt only when he was in mortal danger. Anger tried to rise in him, fury at the unfairness of life. Her past and his past were conspiring to deprive him once again. Damn it all to hell, hadn't he paid enough? Lost enough? Suffered enough?

Almost as soon as the angry thoughts burst through his guard, he clamped down on them. It served no useful purpose to think such things. Nothing changed. Life wasn't fair, a reality he had learned in the killing fields at the age of eighteen. Nor was he a whiner. He hated whiners. The anger sat like a cold lump of lead in his stomach, but he was so used to it by now that he hardly noticed it. He simply wouldn't allow it to control his mind or emotions.

Mandy, unaware of the seething fury in the man beside her, snuggled closer to his side and bit her lower lip when his fingers tightened almost painfully on her breast. Such a narrow line between pain and pleasure, she thought mistily. Maybe you couldn't have one without the other. Maybe there had to be pain so you could have pleasure.

She didn't ask any questions, Ransom noted as they pulled off the county road into her long, rutted driveway. He would have asked a million questions by now, but he was a trained agent. He was suspicious down to the last cell in his body. He would have wanted to know if they wouldn't disturb the trap by coming home. He would have demanded to know who would be guarding the house, who would be watching over their safety.

She asked none of those things, and he thanked heaven she was so trusting. He didn't want to tell her that they were still an integral part of the trap, that Micah was out there waiting for the stalker to make a move against them. That they were deliberately making it look as if Ransom were completely exposed. He was glad she didn't ask, because he didn't know if he could tell her a lie, and he knew in his gut that she wouldn't like the truth.

At the back door, he switched off the ignition, and the night was suddenly both silent and still. For a moment neither of them moved, and then Mandy tilted her head up, looking at him.

In the moon's pale, silvery light, his beard and hair were almost argent. She found herself thinking that he looked like a mythical, magical warrior from one of her stories. So magical that she almost feared touching him. Like a unicorn, he might vanish if the enchantment was disturbed.

He was listening intently, she realized, and his eyes were roving restlessly. Awareness trickled through her, driving back the heated feelings that had kept her distracted all the way here. They were in danger, and he hadn't for one moment forgotten it, even though she had.

"Amanda Lynn," he murmured, looking down at her, "I want to bury myself so deep in you that you won't know where you end and I begin."

Her breath caught and shattered in a puff as desire swamped her in waves of hot and cold that left her lightheaded. And then, like a fall into an icy stream, she heard the unspoken *but* in what he had said. He wanted to, but he wasn't going to. Cold swamped her fevered need, freezing it into something close to anger. Pulling away from him, she found the door handle and pressed it.

"Mandy?"

She refused to stop, refused to listen. How dare he treat her as if she were some kind of plaything, a kitten to be stroked into purring surrender and then set aside because it was inconvenient?

"Mandy!" He was trying to keep his voice down so it wouldn't reach beyond the yard, but she was stalking toward the kitchen door in a way that told him only Armageddon would slow her down. Swearing under his breath, he jumped out of the truck and caught up to her just as she reached the door.

"Wait!"

She couldn't have done anything else. He hauled her up against his side and nearly lifted her feet from the floor.

"Damn it, woman," he growled quietly, "you don't make a move without me tonight. Not a move."

And before he let her go beyond the kitchen, he checked out the entire ground floor of the house.

Later she would never be able to remember how they got upstairs, but suddenly they were there, in her room, swathed in the silver moonlight that poured through the sheers. Ransom cradled her cheeks gently in his rough hands and looked down at her with an expression both tender and wondering, an expression that made her throat ache.

This would be the last time, Mandy realized. Something in the way he was holding her and touching her told her that. Grief rose in her, bringing tears to her eyes. This was what she had feared. This was the loss she had dreaded and tried so hard to avoid, and now she found she wouldn't be able to avoid it after all. He was not to be hers, this warrior who had braved her castle walls and walked past all her defenses. He had made himself a place at the hearth of her heart, but he would not stay. Like a true warrior, he was merely pausing to rest between battles.

"Shh," he whispered as he saw the sparkle of an errant tear on her lash. "Shh..." His lips feathered kisses on her face, taking away tears, smoothing over satin flesh.

"Hold me," she begged. "Oh, please hold me...."

"I'll hold you," he promised. "All the night through I'll hold you, Amanda Lynn. No evil wizards, no malevolent spells, no wickedness, will reach you, I swear. I'll keep you safe through the night." *Rash promises,* he thought, when he understood that to ensure her well-being he must leave.

Rash promises, she thought tearily. *Rash promises.* He offered her a night's safety, not understanding that the knowledge of his impending departure brought the malevolence right into the bed between them.

He pulled the pins from her fine brown hair and combed his fingers through it until it settled around her shoulders like a soft cloud. All the while he murmured praise, murmured how she pleased him in every way. The moonlight blurred all the edges, gave an unreal cast to everything, and Ransom hated to draw the curtains. No one could possibly see in, he assured himself with a quick, intent look outside. Not even from the barn roof. Satisfied, he let the curtains be.

Because it was the last time, he undressed her as if it were the first time. Clothes yielded their secrets slowly, a whispering inch at a time, and as each new expanse of skin appeared, he worshiped it with his eyes and his mouth. By the time they stretched out together on her bed, bare skin to bare skin, Mandy was wrapped in a glowing, hazy languor. The dreamlike quality persisted as he trailed kisses over her breasts and thighs, as he touched and stroked and licked her to a fever. And then he brought her to culmination with the gentle, erotic stroking of his fingers. He gave, but he did not take, because he could not afford to lower his guard that much.

Afterward, because he would not take from her, she wept hurt tears, tears of impending grief, tears of unutterable loss. He cradled her tenderly and kissed her damp cheeks, then tightened his jaw against his own pain at having to deny her.

A sound woke Ransom while it was still dark. He roused from sleep with an image in his mind of something heavy falling, and for some reason was convinced that the sound had come from the far side of the barn, in the corral.

Mandy was curled up against him, and he covered her mouth gently with his, rousing her to full awareness without giving her the opportunity to make a betraying sound.

"I heard something from the barn," he whispered when she was fully awake. "I'm going to investigate. You get dressed and stay right here. Promise me you'll stay right here."

The last thing she wanted to do was wait here in the dark all by herself, wondering if Ransom was all right, but she realized that he needed her to make that promise. He would be unable to leave her to investigate unless he was sure she would be safe. In his place, she would want the same thing.

"I promise."

He dressed swiftly in the dark and was creeping from the bedroom before Mandy had even managed to find a pair of jeans. He wished he could be sure she would stay put. It wasn't that he thought anyone would want to harm her, but if she got in the way... If she made an easier target and they thought they could get to him through her...

Hell!

The moon had moved to the west and was hovering high over the mountains, but its light was still bright enough to see what needed seeing. Aware that quick, sudden movements were more apt to attract a watcher's attention, he slipped fluidly and slowly toward the corral, keeping as much as possible to the shadows.

It was cold, he thought with a small portion of his mind. They must have had the first frost, or at least come close to it. Irrelevant bits of information like that kept intruding into his mind, along with the bits that he was interested in, the bits that mattered. He could smell horses, hay, sage, grass, even a whiff of Mandy's marigolds, but he couldn't smell another man. Americans tended to have a distinctly sour odor as a result of the amount of meat they consumed, but there was no such subtle clue in the air, nor could he detect other bodily odors that would betray a watcher's presence.

Ergo, there was no one in the stable yard.

Uneasiness settled across his shoulders like a mantle. He had heard something. He had been in dangerous positions like this too often to believe that he had misinterpreted something in his dream for reality. No, he knew the difference. A sound had awakened him. A real sound.

So he must have misinterpreted the direction from which it came. Turning, he looked back toward the house. Nothing appeared to be amiss there. Besides, he couldn't believe that if he had really heard a noise from the vicinity of the house he would have interpreted it as coming from the corral. He might be rusty, but not that rusty.

No, he thought, looking at the barn, the sound had definitely come from somewhere around here. An owl, perhaps, that had miscalculated and bumped into something? Or maybe some small animal, a raccoon or even a rat.

Somehow he wasn't buying that, either. Each idea he tested didn't feel right, and he knew better than to doubt his instincts.

Every sense straining, he eased around the end of the barn. The horses were quiet, dozing undisturbed. Surely they would have been just a little uneasy if someone were prowling about? Not wanting to disturb them himself, because the noise they would make would cover the sounds he needed to hear, he eased back around the corner and decided to investigate the other end of the barnyard.

Ten minutes later he had explored all the way around the barn and found nothing. Just as he was ready to throw his hands up and conclude that he'd imagined the sound after all, something slammed with a deafening clang into the steel

rain barrel not six feet away from him. Whirling, he saw
water spewing from two sides of the barrel.

He needed no more than that. In an instant he was facedown on the ground and praying like mad that Mandy
wouldn't venture out to see what was going on. Then, with
the icy calm that had saved his neck more than once, he
considered what he now knew: some kind of projectile, most
likely a bullet, had passed through both sides of that steel
barrel as well as through the water it held. He had failed to
hear the telltale report of a gun, or even the soft pop of a
silencer. Heavy caliber, no sound.

That meant sniper fire from a great distance, at least a
half mile, possibly a full mile. That kind of distance told a
tale. Crawling across the hard-packed ground on his belly,
he got close enough to the barrel to see the size of the entry
and exit holes. A .50 caliber round, he would bet, with a
steel jacket. He was also willing to bet the rifle was a Haskins M500, a custom-made beauty that was a favorite of the
Special Forces. It was not a weapon just any Tom, Dick or
Harry could get his hands on.

He had a burning desire just then to call his agency and
see what they would do with that little bit of information.
It was bound to interest the hell out of them, and they might
even be grateful enough to let some information slip to
Ransom, information such as who might be in this area that
he should know about. Unfortunately, he wasn't sure who
he could trust. Maybe Mark . . .

But what interested him more at this point was his enemy's distance. At such a distance, Ransom was safe from
anything except another .50 caliber slug fired from that rifle. He had a feeling that bullet hadn't missed him by
chance. People who knew how to handle sniper rifles were
seldom poor shots, and when all was said and done, that was
a wide miss for a sniper.

Somebody was evidently still toying with him. Unleash-
ing an infuriated growl, he began to crawl back toward the
house. Mandy was probably out of her mind worrying, and

he guessed it was time to bring out some of the arsenal Nate had managed to round up for him. Ransom suspected that Nate's contribution was one of those things the sheriff would prefer not to have anyone know about, so how was he going to explain things to Mandy? Things like a Heckler & Koch MP5K submachine gun, a sweet little number that could easily be hidden under a jacket. Maybe, this once, Mandy was going to have to settle for "None of your business."

He decided not to test his theory that the round had missed him on purpose. Instead he belly-crawled the entire way to the porch, then hunched over as he climbed the steps.

Inside, he straightened and stood at the door overlooking the yard. The sniper couldn't see him there, and he waited a few minutes to see if there would be another shot. He wondered if Micah and the other deputies had gotten wind of any of this and thought it unlikely. The four deputies were scattered to the points of the compass, stationed a couple of hundred yards away from the house and hidden in the terrain, but even so, the sniper was probably so far away that the deputies hadn't detected a thing. Sighing again, wondering what the hell he was going to do now, he locked the door and headed back upstairs.

This was frustrating as hell. Intolerable. This cat and mouse game could go on forever at this rate, and he didn't think his or Mandy's nerves could handle it. There had to be some means of smoking this character out. Maybe he ought to take Mandy away from here. Maybe if they could get this character to follow them, they could get wind of him.

Halfway up the stairs, he hesitated, then turned around, heading back down to the phone in the kitchen. There he dialed an old friend at home.

"Mark? This is King.... Yeah, I know, but I need something, and I figured you might want to trade. Just a small trade." He paused, listening, and then gave a soft laugh. "Well, how's a Haskins M500 with a .50 caliber round strike you?... Just now. Missed me by about six feet, which doesn't make me feel any better." Again he listened. "I know how rare they are. What I want to know is who out here might have one." He laughed. "Yeah, I know it's not much. How soon? Forty minutes? I'll be at this number." He rattled off Mandy's phone number. "Thanks."

He still had a few friends, he thought as he headed back up the stairs. There were still a few people willing to help him under the table.

He stepped into the bedroom, reassuring words already rising to his lips, and looked around.

Mandy was gone.

Micah was stationed in a stand of sage three hundred meters from the barn, about halfway to the county road. Stationed at similar intervals all around the Grant house and barn were three other deputies, all volunteers, all ready to do whatever was necessary to help John Grant's widow.

Mandy, Micah had realized sometime back, was something of a personage in this underpopulated county that, up until John Grant, hadn't lost a law officer in the line of duty since the big flood in '47. John Grant had been well-loved, his loss deeply mourned, and all those feelings had somehow focused on his widow. Consequently, three deputies were giving up an entire night's sleep to watch over her.

Micah was here for Ransom. Ransom had rescued him from a hole in the ground after he had been captured and badly beaten by the Vietcong, then carried him over his back to safety, some forty-five miles through enemy territory. Micah didn't forget even little favors, and often figured he owed Ransom more than life would ever give him a chance to repay.

He heard a clang from the barnyard, clear in the cold night air, and instantly slipped from a state of open awareness to an intense alertness that brought every sound, every shadow, every movement, into crystal clarity.

Minutes dragged by in unbroken silence, and gradually he began to relax into the state of open awareness again, a state where he stilled and listened, simply letting everything wash through him until something caught his attention. A horse had probably bumped up against something. A million things could have made that sound, and he saw nothing suspicious.

And then, close to twenty minutes later, he heard a shout, the sound of a man in mortal pain. He stiffened, thinking it sounded like a bobcat, but not quite. Not quite. He began to creep toward the house, wondering if he would hear it again.

Instead, less than a minute later, he heard a single rifle report on the still, cold air. It was the signal that the trap had been sprung.

Micah found Ransom in the yard, pacing like a caged tiger, rifle in hand. As soon as he saw Micah, Ransom halted and looked at him.

"They got Mandy."

"Well, hell!" Disgusted, Micah looked around and made out Tom Watson and Ed Dewhurst coming in from their posts. That left Charlie Huskins, who had been watching the northwest side of the property, the most rugged terrain. It might take him a few minutes longer to show up.

"I didn't hear or see a damn thing, Micah," Ransom was saying tautly. "I heard something and came out to investigate it. When I'd just about given up, somebody took a potshot at me with a .50 caliber round." He pointed at the rain barrel.

"Hell, I heard the impact of the bullet, but I sure didn't hear a shot." Micah looked at the other two deputies, who also shook their heads. "So the sniper was quite a ways away. Maybe 800 meters or more."

Ransom nodded. "Must've been, if none of you heard anything. Anyhow, they were successful in distracting me. I figure I was away from Mandy for thirty minutes, and I never heard a thing. I should've heard something." He closed his eyes for a moment. "There must be at least two of them. One to fire the rifle from a distance while the other kidnapped Mandy."

"Well, hell," Micah said again.

"I figure they knocked her out," Ransom said. "I smelled something like ether in the bedroom."

"That makes sense, considering you didn't hear anything. Damn it, where's Charlie? He oughta be here. Ed, you know where he's at?"

"Yeah. I'll go check it out, Micah."

"No, wait." Ransom grabbed Ed Dewhurst's arm. "Where was Charlie stationed?"

Micah pointed away to the northwest.

"That's the direction the sniper fire came from," Ransom told him. Little by little, he was piecing things together. Throwing his head back, he stared off toward the northwest, his nostrils flaring like a predator catching wind of its prey. Internally, he was calm. Too calm. It was the calm of a man who knew that everything depended on his ability not to feel anything at all.

"Okay," he said after a moment. "I think it's a foregone conclusion that they want me, not Mandy. Taking her like this is obviously an attempt to draw me out, to get me to come after them. They want to use her against me." He didn't want to think about how. "And that means they're not going to try to make a clean getaway. They want me to find them. Just me."

He looked at Micah. "You do whatever you have to do as a lawman, but you give me a clear field, Micah."

Micah returned the look steadily. "They won't leave the county."

"Fine. I'm going after them. You just keep clear."

"We got a little problem, man. I realize you can't track these bastards until there's enough light, but I can't wait that long to go after Charlie."

Ransom didn't even hesitate. He knew perfectly well that if he and Micah went looking for Charlie Huskins before sunrise, they might mess up tracks that would lead them to Mandy, but he also knew Charlie's life might well depend on immediate medical help. He also knew that if they messed up, whoever had taken Mandy would find a way to leave another trail.

"We'll find Charlie together, Micah."

Micah nodded. "Tom, you go call Nate and tell him what's going down. Me and Ransom here are going for a little hike."

Ransom stopped Tom. "I'm expecting a phone call from a guy called Mark. He'll ask for King. When he does, just say one word—castled."

"Castled?"

"Right. Then he'll give you some information. Probably just a name. Write it down. It may be the name of our kidnapper." Turning, he looked at Micah.

Micah nodded, and without another word the two of them headed out, rifles in hand, to discover what had happened to Charlie Huskins.

Some things were never forgotten, and it sometimes amazed Ransom how fast he could slip back into the habits of the hunter. In an instant it all felt perfectly familiar and natural, and it happened more easily than changing clothes.

Micah was a slightly better tracker and he knew where Charlie was supposed to be, so he led. The ground near the buildings was hard, the vegetation sparse from lack of water. There would be few signs here to guide them.

Bringing up the rear, Ransom took the job of protecting them both while Micah's attention was completely focused on looking for signs. In his hands he held a simple deer rifle, but under his jacket, tucked beneath his arm, was the MP5K submachine gun. Just over twelve inches in length, it was completely hidden. He hoped that when he encountered the kidnappers they would assume his only weapon was the rifle. Certainly they would have no reason to imagine he carried the so-called "room broom" under his arm. Law-abiding citizens didn't have such weapons.

In this direction the terrain roughened rapidly into rocky outcroppings and began to ascend, an early precursor of the mountains to the west. The light was getting worse by the minute, too, as the moon settled in the west and only the very first pale tendrils of dawn stretched over the eastern horizon. It was actually darker now than it had been all night. Depth and perspective were lost. Everything became flat and colorless. If Micah hadn't already had some idea where Charlie should be, there would have been no point in continuing until sunrise. But Micah knew, and he kept moving forward slowly, very slowly, studying every blade of grass and smear of dirt that he could see.

Suddenly Micah held out a hand and squatted. Ransom immediately scanned the area, looking for any sign of danger. When he saw none, he moved closer to Micah.

Low-voiced, he asked, "What is it?"

Micah touched the ground and raised a finger to his nose, sniffing. "Blood."

At once Ransom scanned the area, looking for signs of a scuffle, signs of what might have happened to Charlie. "There," he said suddenly to Micah. "To the left. I'll go."

"No, you cover me. Charlie'll know me. He might not recognize you if he's hurt."

He was hurt all right, Ransom thought as he shadowed Micah. The further they moved into the cleft between two outcroppings, the stronger the smell of blood became. He knew what they were going to find even before Micah swore an oath that Ransom had never heard him use, even under the worst conditions.

"Micah?"

"He's alive. Damn it, Ransom, he's still alive. I can't believe . . ."

Ransom scanned the area, reluctant to take his attention from the clefts and heights that could hide attackers. "Do you need help?"

"No, just keep watching my back. There's only one wound, and the bleeding's pretty much stopped."

Pivoting slowly, Ransom kept watch and tried not to let his fears for Mandy surface. Charlie's injury was a confirmation, a statement that these folks, whoever they were, were willing to kill to achieve their ends. The cat and mouse game was over. Now came the hurting and maybe the killing. Son of a bitch!

Hard, harder than he'd ever had to in his entire life, he clamped down on his feelings. He had never, ever, feared for himself the way he feared for Mandy. Lurking just beyond the barriers that he placed between himself and his feelings was a chaos of pain and fear that would craze him if he let it through. He couldn't afford to let that happen. He couldn't afford to let anything affect the clarity of his mind or the objectivity of his thinking. Drawing a deep breath, he squeezed his eyes shut for a second. Just a second.

"Ransom."

He looked over at Micah. The sky was beginning to lighten at last. In another few minutes the hunt would begin in earnest. "Yeah."

"I've got to carry Charlie back. You go on. I can manage."

Ransom nodded. "First I want you out of this gorge. It's too good a place for an ambush."

He helped steady Micah as the deputy pulled Charlie over his shoulders and straightened to his feet. "Let's go," Micah said.

Ransom grabbed Micah's rifle from the ground and followed him out of the cleft. Only when they reached open ground did he halt. Micah stopped, too, turning to look at him. On his shoulders, Charlie groaned.

"I won't be far behind you," Micah said.

"Don't. Don't follow me. I don't want these people desperate or cornered."

Micah shook his head. "Hey, it's me you're talking to, man. You know better. They'll never know I'm behind you, and now that I'm heading back with Charlie, they'll probably never even look."

"Micah—"

"Forget it, Ransom. You know Nate and me better than that." Shifting Charlie's weight a little, Micah headed back toward the house. In the distance, Ransom could see the dusty beige of Nate's Blazer pulling up at the house, and behind it there was an ambulance.

The eastern sky was pink now. Turning his back on the distant house, Ransom looked up at the rocky terrain.

It was time.

Chapter 12

Several times Mandy had started to rouse, aware that
something was terribly wrong, and then a sweet smelling rag
was clamped over her mouth, sending her back to a dreamless sleep. Somewhere in a dark tunnel that trapped her, she
vomited while a voice cursed savagely and something
clamped her head; then she sank again into the smothering
black velvet.

She heard a bird. It was nearby, bright, cheerful. Hearing it, she felt reassured and let herself drift away again, this
time without the aid of the rag.

What finally dredged her back to the world were thirst
and cold. Blinking, she looked up into the bright blue
Wyoming sky. Early morning, she thought groggily, maybe
nine or ten. What was she doing outside? Sighing, she tried
to turn over into a more comfortable position and realized
that she couldn't move. Not a muscle.

Panic brought her fully awake, and she lifted her head,
trying to see what was wrong. She was tied up. She was

spread-eagled on a rock and tied hand and foot like some kind of offering.

Like a goat set out to attract a lion.

Like bait for a trap.

And no matter where she looked, there wasn't another soul in sight. She would never even know who had done this to her, or what they meant to do to Ransom when he came for her.

Because he would come for her. He was that kind of man, and it didn't matter one whit whether he cared for her or not. Even if she were a total stranger, he would still come for her, because he was one of those damn-fool decent men who would risk everything for a principle. An unbearable pressure gripped her chest as she tried to deny the coming horror.

Oh, God, there had to be something she could do! Nausea welled in her stomach, the aftereffect of whatever drug they had given her. She closed her eyes and tried to calm herself by taking slow, deep breaths. If she vomited while lying on her back like this, she would probably choke. By forcing herself to keep breathing slowly and regularly, she gradually regained her self-control.

And then she cried. There just wasn't any way to stop the tears. They came hot and hard, running down the sides of her head from the corners of her eyes, but not once did she sob aloud. She would not give her captors that satisfaction.

And she struggled. She struggled past the point of reason, hoping she could loosen even one bond. She tugged and pulled at her bindings until her ankles and wrists were raw and sore, and still she pulled, because a single seductive hope kept rearing its head—maybe if she pulled just one more time. Maybe if she yanked just one more time. Maybe with just one more tug she would find freedom. And each time she told herself to stop, that it was obviously hopeless, the hope crept back into her mind until it nagged her into tugging just one more time. Because maybe that one more time would do the trick.

Minutes dragged by, uncounted and countless. Time lost meaning in her endless, unending misery. Whether she wanted to or not, she had time to think about some things, and in the process she made a couple of discoveries that surprised her. She was astonished to discover just how much she loved life, just how much she wanted to live. And she was totally confounded to realize that however much life meant to her, Ransom's life meant even more.

A whole lot more.

Not that he would care, she thought unhappily. If there had ever been even a remote chance that he could come to care for her, she had surely destroyed it with her on-again-off-again craziness.

It suddenly seemed like a good time to make a few resolutions. After all, she would probably be dead before the day was over. This might be her last opportunity ever to promise herself that she would be stronger and braver. It was hard at the moment to try to promise herself that she would try living rather than hiding, because if she could have hidden at the moment, she would have done so in a heartbeat. But she promised herself anyway. If she survived this, she would take a few chances. She would be less of a mouse. She would make love to Ransom until he begged for mercy and then she'd . . .

Oh, hell, she thought as another flood of hot tears blinded her. Who was she kidding? She was never going to get out of this alive. If only there was some way to keep Ransom from sticking his head into the noose along with her!

Ransom moved over the rocky terrain slowly, scanning the area constantly for any sign that could guide him. The past few years seemed to have vanished. He had slipped easily into the intense, single-minded awareness and concentration necessary to the task. He had sunk with hardly a thought into the mind-set of the hunter. Each step he took, he took with thought and deliberation, well aware that he was not only the hunter, but the hunted, as well. A trap lay ahead for him, a trap in which Mandy was also caught. One careless move could be the end for both of them.

Fury carried him tirelessly forward. Some corner of his mind noted that he was in a killing rage, something he had rarely felt. He was not a vengeful man by nature. Vengeance had always struck him as a wasted effort, because it solved nothing. It certainly didn't erase whatever had already happened.

That was just as true now as it had ever been, but now he thirsted for vengeance. He lusted after it. They had taken Mandy. They had scared her and possibly hurt her, and they very likely intended to kill her after they killed him. This time he wanted vengeance. This time, by hell, he would take it.

The enemy had chosen their ground well. This corner of Mandy's ranch was rugged and grew more rugged with each passing yard. Frequent outcroppings made tracking next to impossible. Vegetation was sparse, making it difficult to find signs. With little more than occasional broken blades of grass to guide him, he had to move slowly, and his slowness was to the advantage of the enemy. It also made Ransom even madder with every step, because every minute was another minute of suffering and terror for Mandy.

The thought of what she might be enduring at this very moment clamped around him like a burning vise, squeezing all the anger in the world into a hard knot in Ransom's gut, a knot so hard that it hurt. A knot so small that it became a black hole, sucking everything into it. He could almost hear the whipping, whistling wind in the empty corridors of his mind as anger consumed everything else and left him empty of everything save blood lust.

Once again he saw signs of disturbed ground, and he bent, measuring out a new direction and the passage of time. Before he straightened, he left a signal of his own. Behind him, in the endless trail back to the ranch, were markers that only Micah and Nate would recognize, each one an invisible signpost.

They would come. He never doubted it. He had to trust them to leave him free to act as necessary, trust them to pick up on clues as to his intentions, trust them to be a help, not a hindrance. He couldn't think of two men on earth he would trust more, but Nate was far removed from the realities of this kind of operation, and Micah—well, Micah had been in the Special Forces group in the army until his retirement. At the very least, he was fresher than Nate. But however in or out of practice they were, he had to trust their minds. He had to trust the instinctive understanding that had once been so much a part of them in Southeast Asia. There had been times when he could have sworn that he, Nate and Micah were one mind in three bodies. He spared a hope that that hadn't completely changed.

Pausing, Ransom straightened and looked upward over the rough slope he had been steadily climbing. Turning his head a little, he saw a path through the scrubby pines that clustered ahead of him, leading to the top of the hill he had been climbing for the last several hours. And suddenly he saw the trap.

Hunkering down, he stared up at the bald top of the hill and considered. In his gut he knew Mandy was up there and her captors were waiting for him. Right up there.

All he had to do was figure out how to ransom her. How to exchange himself for her. Otherwise, she would be dead right alongside him.

Motionless, as if carved from stone, he stared upward and pondered. There had to be a way. There was *always* a way.

The path was obvious before him, deceptively clear of obstacles. It was almost as if the forest had opened up for him, like the parting of the Red Sea. The last time he had seen a path like that had been the day he walked away from the prison camp.

And suddenly he was there again. The crisp Wyoming autumn day and pines gave way to steaming heat and thick jungle growth. The path had been before him then, too.

Clear. Unobstructed. He had looked at it and realized it had been there all along. This time there had been a difference.

The difference had been inside him. Before, he had always nurtured a flicker of hope. Before, there had been a spark in him that had wanted to live. Whatever degradation he suffered, whatever dehumanizing torture and humiliation, there had been a part of him, just a small, stubborn flame, that refused to quit. That morning the flame had died. That morning there had been one blow too many. One curse too many. One humiliation too many. He had ceased to care. Death offered his only hope.

So he had looked down that path and taken it, expecting to die.

And now he looked down another path, and once again he ceased to care. Death would be a welcome solution to an awful lot of his problems, and fear of it would not hold him back. If anything happened to Mandy, though, he would cut his own throat without a moment's regret. How could he possibly care what awaited him along that path if walking down it might help Mandy? He had seen the worst. There wasn't a thing anyone could do to him that hadn't been done before. There wasn't a pain or a wound or an abuse he didn't know. There was nothing on God's earth left to frighten him.

Except what might happen to Mandy.

It was that possibility that held him still, that launched his mind into a whirlwind of calculations. Before he could move, he needed to convince himself that he had considered every probability, every potentiality. For himself he would have plunged ahead and trusted his instincts and experience to carry him through whatever was waiting. For himself, he didn't care. For Mandy, he cared more than he had ever cared for anything in his life.

So he would go up there and try to exchange himself for her, and he thought he knew an argument that might be persuasive. Even so, he would be up there, and while he tried to keep the enemy busy talking, he would be able to evalu-

ate the situation, locate the people involved so he could
eliminate them, and try to get Mandy free. And then, if he
survived, he would face the fact that he was the kind of crud
who could bring this sort of trouble to her gates.

Once he had held high ideals; Mandy had come closer
than she probably guessed when she likened him to a knight.
But then, Mandy saw more than she ever let on. She saw
past the webs of illusion to the realities behind, and that was
probably why she was so terrified of her own vulnerability.
Other people sailed through their days viewing everything
through the distorted mirrors of their minds, believing with
blind faith that everything was going to be okay and refusing to consider that it all ended in the grave eventually, anyway. Mandy knew better. She knew that the piper always
had to be paid. She knew that caring meant loss, and loving meant pain, and that each day was a maze of potential
cruelties and suffering.

Could he really blame her for keeping her drawbridges
up? Could he condemn her because she saw the truth and
avoided the rain and the storms, the floods and disasters?
That would be like saying she was crazy because she refused to build her house on the San Andreas Fault. No, he
couldn't condemn her, and that was why he was going to get
the hell out of her life just as soon as he gave her life back
to her.

It was ironic, though, that this woman who refused life
had brought him back to life. Because he had been dead for
a long time. He realized it only in his resurrection, understood that somewhere along the way his ideals had passed
away, his ability to care had atrophied, and that even in his
joy at the prospect of fatherhood he had been little more
than a zombie, a living dead man. His decay had all been
internal, and he had been careful not to let it show. To all
the world he appeared to be the Ransom Laird he had always been. He had thought of his return from captivity as
Lazarus rising from the dead, but now he knew better. He

had been resurrected in Mandy's care, and only because of Mandy.

He swallowed hard as he squatted in the rapidly warming morning light, staring up at the path to life or death, heaven or hell, and he remembered. He remembered how she had taken his shirt from his back and smoothed her palms like healing balm over the ridges of scar tissue. He remembered how his throat had tightened then, too, and how his awakening in those moments had been one of the most painful experiences in his life. He hadn't wanted to feel, but she had made him feel, and it was just like being born. Agonizing.

And losing her would be death, eternity in hell, a cold bleakness forever without end. Amen.

He didn't dare close his eyes now, hardly dared blink, and he couldn't breathe around the lump in his throat. He wanted to scream from the pain of impending loss, but he was the hunter and the hunted, and the hunt was drawing to its inevitable close. Cradling the deer rifle almost casually in one arm, he straightened and stared at the top of the hill.

They were up there, and so was Mandy. He could feel her like a tug under his breastbone, an ache in his heart, a fire in his soul. How could he have been so smug, thinking she needed to understand that you couldn't have pleasure without pain? How could he have thought he knew some mystical secret of life that she failed to perceive?

Damn, she had *known.* She had felt this pain in her chest, this ache in her heart, this fire in her soul, and she had lost John Grant, a loss so great that Ransom was only just now beginning to really understand how she had suffered. Because this was the first time in his life that he had ever loved another person more than himself. He had judged Mandy Grant from ignorance, and he would have squirmed with shame if he hadn't been hurting with the same awful depth that had taught him his lesson. *This,* then, was the price of caring. She had *known.* He had not.

Now that he understood, he knew he would never, ever, ask her to face this pain again.

Never.

* * *

A yellow deerfly, growing energetic in the morning warmth, landed on Mandy's nose. Frantically she wiggled her head, trying to shake the fly away, but the huge, ugly thing clung stubbornly. Sticking out her lower lip, she blew a sharp puff of air upward, and the fly moved on.

Not far, though. This time it settled on her hand, and this time it bit. She jerked at the sharp, stinging bite and wondered almost hysterically if she was going to live long enough to watch her hand swell to twice its normal size. Long enough to cuss because she wouldn't be able to type until the allergic reaction passed.

Long enough. Suddenly there wasn't long enough in the entire universe, in all of eternity. Suddenly she wanted to weep, not for what might never be, but for all she had never let come to be. For all the squandered days and nights, for all the ignored opportunities, for all the friendships never formed, for all the love never shared.

For all the *waste*.

And that was what her entire life had been, she thought desperately now, as her throat ached and a huge weight of grief settled on her chest. She had let reality slip through her fingers in favor of the safety of her dreams and fantasies. Except for the too-brief time with John, she had given nothing of herself to anyone, and that was all that mattered, wasn't it? In the end, an end such as she had come to, when there were no more opportunities of any kind, all that mattered was what she had given, and she had given next to nothing.

She had taken little and given nothing, and nothing, absolutely nothing, had been made better because she had existed.

Lord, she couldn't even lie here and think over all the things she had done, because she had done so little. She might as well never have lived, and that was a hell of a sorry epitaph. Damn, it wasn't even as if she had written a great novel that would move men to tears and laughter in centuries to come. No, she hadn't even achieved that, though she had always longed to. She had just never had the guts to put herself on the line that way—to risk the rejection of something so personal, so much a part of her inner self.

And if... And if she could have just one more chance to do something, to give something, it would be to tell Ransom that she loved him. She had loved him from the moment he had held her beneath the cottonwood and shared her grief. Maybe even from the moment he had tramped up her driveway, appearing like some disreputable golden god. Why had she refused to face it? Why had she run from what had already happened? Damn, couldn't she even face up to what *was?*

Overhead a hawk circled lazily, a black speck in a flawless blue sky, a symbol of utter freedom. Not that she was suited to freedom, she thought sadly as she swallowed more tears. She might as well have spent her life in prison for all the good she had made of her opportunities and freedom.

If... What a vain word. But *if* she could have another chance, she would reach for it all. No matter how frightened she grew, no matter how her knees knocked or her heart quailed, she would risk it. She would love with every ounce of feeling she was capable of. She would give herself, her caring, her time, her concern, to anyone willing to accept it. Maybe... maybe she would even try again to have a child. That thought really made her heart quail. John's death had brought her to her knees, but Mary's loss had filled her with mortal anguish. It was as if she had lost John a second time, and even more completely and totally. With Mary's loss, she had known herself to be truly alone.

A blackbird squawked from a nearby tree, a sound that, at some subliminal level, she recognized as a territorial warning. She was not alone in these woods or on this hilltop. Someone had disturbed that bird. Ransom? Her heart thudded sharply and then began a rapid, heavy pounding. The waiting was almost over. Even the air seemed expectant.

* * *

Micah had long since disappeared into the rugged terrain, but Nate had remained behind. They had both agreed that Nate was too far out of practice and might be a hindrance. So Nate stayed at the house, practically sitting on top of the radio like a hen sitting on her egg, waiting for Micah's call. Around him hovered all of his off-duty deputies and a couple of the on-duty ones, as well. Conard County was a little low on routine law enforcement this morning, but he was damned if he cared. If the voters wanted to get cranky about it, Nate was willing to return to full-time ranching. Hell, he was getting too old for this kind of excitement, anyway. His two best friends in the world were up in those hills somewhere, along with a woman who meant as much to him as any of his daughters, and he'd never felt so damn helpless in all his days.

Glancing around at his men, good men to the last, he wondered vaguely if Micah and Mandy realized how many friends they both had in this county. They were both outsiders, yet both had managed to become an integral part of the fabric of Conard County. Damn it, nothing better happen to them, or Ransom, either. Ransom was another one who would probably fit in around here like a long-lost son, if only he would settle down long enough. Nate swore again, savagely, and a couple of his deputies smothered reluctant smiles.

He wished he had some idea what Ransom was up against. From what Micah had told him, there had to be at least two people out there, one to shoot the sniper rifle and one to kidnap Mandy. That was a minimum, but he doubted there were any more than that. As much as somebody evidently hated Ransom, it didn't seem likely that they would bring half an army to deal with him. No, one person and an accomplice would be about all anybody would want on an operation like this.

But two could be enough. Enough to deal with Ransom if Micah didn't get there in time. Certainly enough to have already hurt Mandy. That thought kept zinging him like a bee's stinger. What if she was already dead? They only needed the possibility that she might be alive to draw Ransom out. They didn't need to *keep* her alive.

He muttered another curse and wished he knew something about whoever was out there. Ransom's friend had called back, but his information had been next to useless, for Nate anyway. Who the hell was *Mantis,* anyhow? The name might tell Ransom something, but to Nate it was meaningless. The guy on the other end of the phone had evidently dragged some information out of Tom, though. Damn, he would have to teach that boy not to spill his guts to everybody who asked. But Tom had told the caller about Mandy's abduction, about Charlie being wounded, about Ransom going off into the hills with nothing but a deer rifle, and Micah going off after him. Hell, what if the caller wasn't a friend? What if Tom had spilled all that stuff to an enemy of Ransom's?

Nate swore yet again and hunted through his glove box for antacids. Too damn old for this, yes sir.

Well, thank God for small favors, he thought suddenly as he heard the familiar sound of a helicopter. He'd sent for the chopper at first light, but there had been some mechanical problem or other. That chopper was the pride of the Conard County Sheriff's Department, a big old army Huey they had refurbished for rescue missions. Aboard her were two of the best emergency medical technicians in the state, and some of the best life-saving equipment made.

The chopper sounded just the same now as its brothers had twenty years ago, Nate thought as he watched the dust-colored chopper settle into the yard. They had called them Dustoffs back then in Nam, the medevac choppers. The sound of those rotors still sent chills dancing along his spine. God, he prayed suddenly, don't let us need the EMTs. Don't let anyone else get hurt.

When the hammering engines were turned off, the side door on the helicopter rolled back, not to disgorge the familiar technicians, but to allow six total strangers to disembark.

"What the hell is going on here?" Nate demanded as two men in dark suits and four men in camouflage approached him. "Where are my paramedics?"

"Sheriff Tate?" said one of the suited men, a tall, thin type with expressionless eyes. "I'm Special Agent Wade Gentry, Central Intelligence Operations. I understand you've got a situation here involving one of our agents."

"Involving *three* of my *friends*," Nate growled. "One of them *used* to be one of your agents, which hasn't seemed to interest anybody very much of late."

Something flickered in Gentry's dark eyes. "It never stopped interesting some of us," he said after a moment. "They've finally untied our hands."

Seconds ticked by in silence before Nate relented with a nod. "Okay. So how did you find out what's going on?"

"A man named Mark, a mutual friend of mine and Ransom," Gentry said. "He phoned me this morning to tell me about a curious call he'd had from Ransom and what he'd learned from one of your deputies."

Nate rubbed his chin. "That was an awful fast flight from D.C."

"I've been in Casper all along, just waiting for the go-ahead. I've been sitting on my hands waiting for the word ever since the windshield in Mrs. Grant's truck was shot out."

Nate stuck his chin out. "Why do I find that hard to believe?"

Gentry shrugged. "Probably because the agency left Ransom thinking nobody gave a damn. But they couldn't promise him assistance until they were sure they could provide it, and they weren't sure. We're not authorized to act within the country, Sheriff. I think you know that."

"I do. So what the hell are you doing here now?"

"There's a little mess we need to clean up. A certain double agent. We've gotten permission. Finally."

"This double agent wouldn't be somebody code-named Mantis, would he?"

Gentry was silent for a moment. "I guess Mark told you that. And I guess he didn't tell you who Mantis is."

"I'm dying to find out."

Gentry sighed. "I'm afraid I can't tell you, Sheriff."

Nate considered several possible reactions to that, most of them enough to get him arrested.

Then Gentry spoke again. "The praying mantis has an interesting peculiarity, Sheriff."

"Yeah?"

"As soon as she's impregnated, the female devours her mate."

Hell, Nate thought, fury twisting through him like a cyclone. Hell. If only there was some way to warn Ransom! "Just what are you planning to do with all this muscle you brought along, Gentry? If you think I'm going to let you go up there and mess things up, you've got another think coming. Ransom was pretty definite about nobody following him."

"I believe one of your deputies went after him," Gentry observed.

Nate sighed and damned Tom yet again. "Micah Parish. He's an exception to a lot of rules. Army Special Operations and a good friend of Ransom. And Ransom didn't even want him. I don't know anything about you, Gentry, or about these guys with you, so don't think I'm going to let you go stomping around out there and possibly cause more trouble. If you doubt me, consider this, I didn't go myself."

Again Gentry was silent for a while. His dark eyes seemed to take Nate's measure, and then they moved to the rugged terrain behind the house. "How long have they been out there, Tate? Four hours? Don't you think by now it's too late to change things? By now he must have found her."

"Maybe."

"And if he has, Mantis is pretty occupied right now."

"Mantis has help. At least one other person, maybe more."

Gentry shook his head. "Just one other person. Mantis prefers working alone."

"Well, thank God for that," Nate said gruffly. "Ransom and Micah won't have any trouble dealing with that. I just hope to God Mandy's okay."

He stared up at the rough, rocky hills and came to a decision. Ransom probably *had* located Mandy by now. "I guess you're right, Gentry. We can't do much to make it worse, not now. Let's go."

It was a little like walking down a tunnel, Ransom thought absently as he climbed toward the hill's bald peak. The rocky shoulder was almost completely free of growth, except for the occasional hardy bush that grew in the dirt the wind had blown into the rocky cracks. On either side rose the tall, proud cones of elderly pines, giving the sense of walls, though they were hardly impenetrable.

It went against his grain to approach so openly like this, but they were waiting for him, and there was no way he could approach that peak completely undetected. No, they would be sure that he had followed their track—there was no other way he could find them—and that made it likely they had watched for him. Trying to conceal himself now would only prolong things.

It was an unaccustomed creepy feeling, though, to walk openly and deliberately into the maw of a trap. There had been a couple of times in his career when he had been in similar situations, but never so completely exposed, never so completely alone. His skin crawled with awareness, and the muscles of his neck and shoulders tightened almost into knots, as if they could harden into a bullet-proof vest. With each step he anticipated an attack, and with each step he was vaguely surprised it didn't come.

He wished he knew who was waiting for him. It was so important to know your opponent, and this time he didn't have even a hazy idea of who he might be up against. That made it harder. It was always much easier when you knew the parameters of a problem. They had taken Mandy to drag him up here, but anyone could have done that. There was nothing revealing in their actions that would tell him what he needed to beware of.

So he walked blindly into the trap, hating it every step of the way. His eyes roved restlessly, seeking any sign; his ears strained for any betraying sound. Any clue would help, but he had none. And for the life of him, he couldn't imagine who might want him dead after all this time? He had crossed all kinds of people over the years, but most of the people in his business saw it as a deadly serious game that was played according to certain rules. Not too many would waste their time coming after him so much later. Most of them realized, as he did, that revenge was wasted effort.

So who the hell was it?

Mandy saw Ransom approach. He was walking toward her as casually as if he were out for a morning stroll. Nothing about him indicated that he felt any tension, that he was aware he was hunted. Nothing except the way his eyes roamed, refusing to settle, even on her.

Her throat tightened until the pain was almost unbearable. Dear God, she loved him, and now he was walking into an obvious trap without a bit of hesitation. Walking with the pride, decision and determination of the warrior he was. Coming to her rescue. Oh God!

Wildly she struggled at her bonds, knowing only that she had to escape so he wouldn't need to come any deeper into the trap.

"Go back," she begged in a tear-thickened voice. "Oh, God, go back!"

But he just kept coming, walking steadily and surely toward whatever awaited him. Tears burned in her eyes, blinding her briefly before she blinked them away. The sun turned his hair to golden fire, and he looked so...so... Oh God, how she loved him!

They had tied her, trussed her like a sacrifice on that boulder, he saw. Rage rose like bile in his throat, scorching him. For this, he would kill. For this, he would take revenge. Whoever had done this to her was going to pay, if he had to reach beyond the grave to do it.

He reached her side and looked down at her. He was beyond speech, and so was she. The table of rock she lay on was at his chest height, and he was able to see with disturbing clarity what her escape attempts had done to her wrists. Without a word, he pulled out his pocketknife and slashed at the first rope. He didn't care if an army surrounded them and pointed their rifles at him, he was going to free her wrists from any more agony.

After he released the first rope, he walked around the boulder, reaching for the second. Just as he touched the blade to the rope, a shot rang out, sending up flakes of granite from the boulder on which Mandy lay. Ransom froze, not moving a muscle except for the fingers of his hand. He tucked the knife into Mandy's hand and closed her fingers over it. A glance at her wet eyes told him she understood.

It also nearly killed him to see the love there. He had done that to her. He had made her care again. He deserved everything that was coming to him and then some. He had breached her castle walls and brought her to this. Yes, he ought to be shot.

"Back away from her, Ransom," came a familiar voice from the trees. "Back away or I'll shoot her right now. I know you, Ransom. You'd rather keep her alive on the off-chance you can rescue her. So drop that rifle and back away."

For an instant he didn't move. He *couldn't* move. Everything inside him froze as a fist of understanding grabbed his stomach and twisted it into a painful knot. And then slowly, very slowly, he dropped the rifle and backed up. If he got far enough away from the rock, maybe he could keep attention away from Mandy so she would have a chance to use the knife.

He backed up another step, then another.

"Hold it right there, Ransom. There are two rifles trained on you right now. One of them's a nice M500, and it's loaded with an explosive round. Your girlfriend will be raw stew."

Ransom held his arms out, away from his body, and turned slowly toward the voice. Tilting his head back, he looked up into the trees. Then, quite calmly, he said, "Hello, Karen. I thought you'd been terminated."

Chapter 13

Mandy stiffened in shock, understanding at once. Ransom's wife. The woman who had betrayed him and sent him into terrible captivity. The woman who had aborted his child. Anger rose in her, anger and pain for Ransom. At that moment, for the first time in her life, she felt honestly capable of murder.

"Not quite dead, darling," came the mocking answer. "It's all your fault that I might well be, though."

"I don't quite see it that way, Karen," Ransom answered while his mind worked frantically, thinking at light speed, considering and rejecting ideas.

"No, of course you don't, darling. But it *was* your fault. All of it. You were a target of opportunity, as they say. If you hadn't pursued me quite so diligently, I wouldn't have been ordered to make use of you. I wouldn't have been ordered to get pregnant. God! The entire idea sickened me. Breeding! Worse, breeding *your* child. You can't conceive how thrilled I was when I learned you couldn't get out of that mission."

"I'm beginning to imagine," Ransom said coldly, turning his head a little so he could see Mandy from the corner of his eye and still keep Karen in sight. A shaft of relief pierced his concentration when he realized that Mandy was cautiously sawing at the rope with the knife he had left in her bound hand. The angle was awkward, and her activity was further limited by the need not to draw attention, but she was working at it. Good girl!

"No, I don't think you *can* imagine!" Karen said bitterly. "You should have died in that labor camp! If you had, everything would have been all right!"

"Why is that?" He was deliberately playing dumb in a bid for time, not that he really knew what the devil he was going to be able to do, but time would at least give him the opportunity to come up with something. He needed Mandy free before he attempted anything, but even more, he needed to know exactly where Karen's accomplice was located. That was now the wild card in the deck. Until he knew where her friend was, he didn't dare do anything.

"Why? *Why?* Did the beatings dull your mind, Ransom?"

"Maybe. It just seems to me that if you could escape the sanction—which you so obviously have—it would have been an even simpler matter to skip the country and start a new life somewhere else. Obviously you have other masters who could help you out." Keep her talking, keep her talking. Restlessly, his eyes scanned the surrounding trees and brush, seeking the other person.

"But I don't. Not anymore, darling, and that's your fault."

"How so?" From the corner of his eye he watched Mandy ease slowly onto her side so she could work at the rope better. He moved again, trying to make it impossible for Karen to watch both him and Mandy at the same time.

"Don't move, Ransom," Karen said sharply. "Your little friend can saw at that rope all she wants. She's not going anywhere alive."

Mandy's hands trembled visibly at that announcement, but she never stopped sawing. It was all she could do at the moment, so she would do it. After she was free there might be an opportunity to do something else, but unless she was free she couldn't do anything at all. And unless she was free, Ransom's options would be seriously limited. Damn, it wouldn't have been any harder to saw through steel!

"Why not let her go?" Ransom asked, keeping his tone carefully neutral as he once again edged away from Mandy. "She can't possibly hurt you now, Karen."

"No, but she can certainly be useful, darling. You're besotted with her. It was written all over your face at the dance last night. And she's besotted with you. She made no secret of the fact."

Mandy's stomach lurched sharply. So Karen had been the woman at the dance! She had actually talked to her!

"So, darling," Karen continued, "she's very useful. She'll do anything to protect you, and I can easily imagine any number of things I could make her do that would drive you utterly crazy."

Now it was Ransom's stomach that lurched, and he had to battle with the horror that rushed through him in sickening waves. He had never imagined such depravity, but he knew Karen was capable of it. Hadn't she condemned him to that prison? If she could do that...

He edged a little farther away from Mandy and scanned the trees, seeking Karen's accomplice. This was not the time to react emotionally, and he clamped down savagely on the feelings Karen was stirring up. At last, he was able to speak coolly.

"I don't see how I can have much to do with your present problems," he said. "If you hadn't betrayed me, everything would have been fine for you. I would have stayed home and raised the child you didn't want, and you could have gone your own way."

"You really are surprisingly obtuse," Karen said sharply. "They had no intention of letting you retire, Ransom. No, they planned to use your child as a hostage to keep you working, but as a double agent.'' She gave a brittle laugh. "Never thought of that, did you? I might almost have enjoyed watching you squirm, but I couldn't stand the thought of having a child. Do you really think I want my body disfigured that way? That I want to go through the positively animal experience of giving birth? No, thank you! I needed to get rid of that child, and they wouldn't let me, so I had to get rid of *you*. Once I was rid of you, the child didn't matter. I didn't have to have it. And having it was the whole problem.''

"And you did get rid of me. That should have been the end of it.''

"Except that you came back, darling. You came back and betrayed me. You not only let *your* masters know that I'd betrayed you, but it became obvious to *my* superiors that I must have been responsible. Once they realized I had defied their orders, they had no further use for me.'' She laughed harshly. "So you see, my darling ex-husband, there's no place on earth for me to hide. But at least I'm going to have the satisfaction of knowing you have paid. And believe me, you *will* pay. Dearly. Starting with that woman.''

The knife at last cut through the rope and Mandy's left wrist was free. Heedless of the danger, she sat up and started working on the ropes confining her ankles. She heard what Karen was threatening and was convinced that her imagination probably couldn't begin to conceive of the horrible things the other woman was dreaming up. Which was just as well, because she really didn't need to be any more frightened than she already was.

And she made up her mind that no matter what Karen threatened, no matter how much they hurt her, she would not do anything they told her to do. No matter what the price, she wouldn't allow herself to be used against Ransom.

"Erik, darling," Karen's voice suddenly sang out, "why don't you enjoy yourself before the bitch gets free?"

Mandy jerked and looked up, her stomach climbing into her throat as she saw a huge, hideous man emerge from the trees. He looked exactly the way Hollywood had always depicted thugs, she thought hysterically. And she knew what he intended to do. It was there in the smile on his lips, the look in his eyes. She bit her lip hard to stifle an instinctive protest and quickly lowered her gaze to the rope she was sawing at. Maybe, just maybe... The hope was vain, but there was no other.

It was precisely the moment Ransom was waiting for. Now he knew where both of them were. Reaching up, he grabbed at his jacket collar as if he were having trouble breathing and managed to rip open all the snaps. Now he could get to the machine gun, but Mandy was between him and Erik. Also, Erik and Karen were so far separated that it would be difficult to get them both fast enough. If Erik reached Mandy and was able to use her as a shield...

"Mandy, lie down. Now!"

She wasn't used to taking orders, and for an instant the command didn't compute. In that instant Erik leapt forward and Karen leveled her gun at Ransom.

Oh God, thought Ransom, it was over. That bastard would get Mandy.

And then, with a bloodcurdling howl that would have pleased his ancestors, Micah hurtled out of the trees toward Karen. At the same instant Mandy came to her senses and lay down flat, giving Ransom a clear shot at Erik. He never hesitated. He whipped out the machine gun and sprayed fully sixty rounds at the huge man. Accuracy didn't matter with this weapon. Mandy closed her eyes, sickened by the sight.

Just before Micah reached her, Karen's gun fired, getting off a well-aimed round at Ransom. The impact of the bullet spun him around and threw him back against the boulder. Mandy heard his grunt as he hit and sat up immediately, just catching sight of him as he sank to the ground. Oh God, he'd been shot! He'd been shot! Grabbing the knife, she sawed frantically at her bonds again, desperate to get to Ransom, while Micah wrestled on the hard ground with Karen.

Suddenly the clearing was filled with a deafening whop-whop sound, and Mandy looked up to see the medevac chopper fly in over the treetops. Oh, thank God, thank God. Sobs began to choke her as she sawed at her bonds. They never would have gotten Ransom down the hill without help. Thank God for Micah. She was going to kiss him until his cheeks turned red.

A cry drew her attention toward Karen just in time to see Micah get his arm under her chin and grab her around the neck. After a few seconds the woman sank quietly to the ground, as limp as an empty rag doll. Micah saw Mandy's horrified gaze.

"I just pinched her carotid artery," he said, bending to handcuff Karen. "She'll wake up in no time. Unfortunately."

"If I had a gun, I'd shoot her," Mandy said hoarsely. "Honest to God, Micah, I'd kill her."

"Yeah, it tempts me, too." He clapped a second set of cuffs around Karen's ankles, then hurried over to Ransom as the chopper settled cautiously on the rocky hilltop.

"How is he?" Mandy demanded, unable to see anything at all except Micah's dark head as he bent over Ransom. Once before she had felt this frightened. She remembered it vividly. She had been standing by John's grave, listening to the minister intone a prayer, and had suddenly realized that she was in labor and it was too soon. She felt just as helpless now. "Micah? Is he—is he—?"

"No. No. He's alive." Slowly he looked up over the edge of the boulder at her. "He's alive, Mandy."

"Is it . . . bad?" She bit her lip until she tasted the coppery tang of blood. She didn't want to hear this. She didn't think she could stand it.

"It's not good."

Nor did it get any better. Her last sight of Ransom was as he was lifted aboard the chopper in a basket stretcher. He was unconscious, and even his lips were white. Mandy couldn't bring herself to glance at the bloody mess that had been his chest.

"He'll get the best medical care available, Mrs. Grant," said a tall, thin man in a dark suit. "I promise you, he'll get the best."

Then he climbed into the helicopter with Ransom, Karen and another man in a suit, and they took off. Mandy was left in the clearing with Nate, Micah and four strangers in camouflage. And the bloody corpse that had been Erik.

"It'll be okay, sweet pea," Nate said to her. "Honey, I swear, he'll make it. That sumbitch will make it or I'll kill him."

She couldn't even cry. For the second time in her life, she hurt too badly to weep. "Where are they taking him?"

"I don't know. I'll find out, but right now, I don't know."

It was as if Ransom had vanished from the face of the earth. He was taken initially to the hospital in Casper, but as soon as his condition was stabilized, he was whisked away on Gentry's orders. Nate tried everything he could think of to discover where he'd been taken, but all trails were dead ends.

"I'm sorry, sweet face," he told Mandy after a week. "We're not going to find him until he wants us to find him."

Mandy regarded him from bleak, dry eyes. "I would just like to know if he's alive."

"Yeah. Me too."

Never before had she felt quite like this, Mandy thought as she moved mechanically through her days. John's loss had been different, a sharper spike of pain that had to be surmounted. This felt . . . endless. As if she had fallen into a pit and was now wandering in darkness over a featureless terrain.

She wrote, but she found little satisfaction in it. A heavy frost killed her marigolds at last, and she cleared the dead plants from the garden, unable to take her usual pleasure in the seasonal task. The freshly turned earth was barren, as barren as her soul.

There was plenty of time for regrets, plenty of time to consider her own foolishness. She had felt Ransom's farewell that last night and had only herself to thank for not having said something, done something, to let him know she wanted him to stay. She couldn't blame anyone else for her craziness, for her inability to reach out, for her emotional cowardice. She felt like that old joke, because she had looked into her mirror and found her own worst enemy: herself.

Autumn deepened, growing colder at night, warming less by day. In the mornings now she needed to break the ice that formed on the watering trough. The horses were welcome work, however. They kept her hands busy and her body tired so the emptiness wasn't quite as noticeable.

It would have been easy, she thought, to fall once again into the belief that if she held herself aloof she couldn't be hurt, but this time she didn't fall back into her familiar patterns. She refused to. This time, she promised herself, whatever happened, she would be a participant, not an unwilling victim.

She began to feel sick in the mornings, and after a couple of weeks she knew why. Hope blossomed, just a frail little tinge of color to her days. Maybe this, at least, would last this time. Maybe, just once in her life, she wouldn't lose. Maybe she could be allowed just one person to care for. Maybe this time her arms wouldn't be left empty, her heart would be filled. Determined, she went to the doctor and began to follow his every instruction.

The days became cold, though snow did not fall, and she spent less and less time outdoors. She liked, though, to stand at the storm door that had replaced the screen door in the kitchen and catch the late afternoon sun. The rays slanted beneath the roof of the narrow porch and poured golden light through the glass, and they felt so warm and bright that it was almost a caress.

She was standing there one afternoon, absorbing the heat and the light, when a shiny red Blazer pulled up into the yard and halted. The sun was behind the driver, concealing his identity in shadow, and all she could see was the outline of a cowboy hat. Nate, she thought, or Micah. One of them must have bought a new car and wanted to show it off. These days she saw Micah quite often. They had become friends.

The driver climbed out and came around the front of the vehicle toward her. Time stood still, and her heart stopped beating. That walk, with its slight hesitation, was as familiar to her as her own face. That shape, a little too lean again, was one her body recognized every line of. His golden beard was a little longer, and when he swept the hat from his head she was shocked to see much more gray among the gold.

Ransom. Her lips formed his name, but no sound emerged. Instinctively, one hand rose to her heart, the other settling protectively over her stomach. He was alive! Her heart began rejoicing, even as her mind issued warnings. He hadn't called, he hadn't written, in all this time. If he wanted her, if he cared for her, surely he would have called? Or written? Dread and joy warred within her.

He opened the storm door, and she stepped back to permit him to enter. Blue eyes, eyes exactly the color of the Conard County sky, searched her face as if he were hungry for the sight of her. But she didn't dare believe that. Not even now, when he stood right before her, did she have the guts to believe in happiness. Not yet.

"I told myself," he said presently, in a voice grown rusty with feelings, "that you were better off without me. I told myself that you were right, if you didn't care you couldn't be hurt. I told myself that I had been unforgivably smug, that I had hurt you by battering at your castle walls, and that if I was half the knight you believed me to be I would walk away before you got hurt any more or any worse. I told myself that I had spent such a short time in your life that you would get over me fast." He drew a long ragged breath. "I told myself I had no right."

Things inside her, old walls, old barriers, old defenses, began crumbling painfully. This was going to hurt like hell, she realized. Regardless of what he said, of what happened next, regardless of the outcome, she was about to shed her protective skin, and it was going to hurt.

"I was sure," he said, "that you wanted me gone. I believed you wanted me to go away before I made you any more vulnerable than I already had. I was convinced you wanted your old life back. And I know I'm not worthy of you."

"Ransom—" The cracks were widening, the dams were crumbling, and she reached out instinctively toward him.

"Shh. Let me finish. I need . . . I need to explain."

Blinking back the threatening tears, she managed a nod.

"I had plenty of time to think about a lot of things while I was stuck in that damn hospital bed. I really got all wound up about what was best for you. And then I realized something else. I realized that I was afraid to trust you. I realized that all the things I was thinking were based on that. It suddenly occurred to me that I had to stop trying to do what was best for you, that I had to trust *you* to know what was best for you. Damn it, am I making any sense?" His eyes scoured her face for understanding.

"I think you're making perfect sense," Mandy answered around the pain in her throat. Why wouldn't he take her into his arms? All she needed, all she wanted, was to be in his arms, to feel his warmth and strength and know that he was still *alive*. Oh, God, why had she needed to come so close to losing him just so she could appreciate him?

"Well," he said after a moment, "that was kind of scary. After...after all that's happened, it isn't the easiest thing for me to trust, I guess."

"I guess," she murmured, understanding.

"So I went off on another tangent, telling myself that you probably hated me by now, because I hadn't even called you."

"Hate isn't what I was feeling." The thought had never occurred to her.

"No?" The question held hope. "Well, I was convinced you couldn't feel anything else. That lasted a few days."

When he remained silent, she prompted him, still seeking the words that would allow her to throw herself into his arms. "And then?"

"And then..." He drew another deep, ragged breath. "And then I realized I can't live without you, that life isn't worth a damn if you aren't there to share it with me, and I said to hell with pride and rationalization and what was best and whether you hate me. I'm here, Amanda Lynn, and I'll be damned if I'll go away again, unless you tell me to. If you tell me to go, I'll go and never come back, but otherwise you're stuck with me."

Stuck with him? As a handyman? As a lover? As a live-in boyfriend? Wild emotions were rising in her, pouring through all the cracks in her defenses, and she had to battle an urge to shake him. She would, she realized with a pang, take whatever he was giving and count herself lucky, but some last vestige of pride and need kept her silent about the baby. He had married once for the sake of a child, and she knew he would do so again. But if it were possible, she wanted him to want her, just her, enough to commit himself. Please, God, I want to have my cake and eat it, too, just once. Just this once, *please.*

And then it struck her that she had to take a step herself. He had spoken of his doubts and reservations, of all the things he feared and worried about, and now it was up to her to reassure him enough to take another step. She *owed* it to him to step toward him just as he was stepping toward her.

"I would *never* ask you to leave," she said hoarsely. "Never."

That word *never* might have been a magic incantation, because suddenly her bleak, gray world blossomed in all the colors of the rainbow; all the sharp edges softened, and pain spun away dizzily as those strong, beloved arms closed around her and lifted her high. Dimly, she realized that he was carrying her upstairs, and her insides clenched pleasurably in anticipation, but mostly she just knew that at long last she had found her place and her identity and her home.

"I love you, Amanda Lynn," he whispered as fiercely as the warrior he was. He lowered her with infinite care to her narrow bed and came down beside her with an expression of wonder in his eyes. "I love you more than life, more than hope. More than I thought it was possible to love."

He didn't wait for an answer, and in truth he hardly needed it. She had told him that she would never ask him to leave, and from this woman that was the most important declaration of all. She had asked him into her castle, past all her moats and drawbridges. She had made a place for him beside her hearth, and she had said she would never ask him to leave.

Gently he kissed away her tears of joy, and gently he claimed her with his body. She wore denim and cotton, but it might have been lace and silk as it whispered away in the waning light. He wore denim and wool, but it might have been shining armor as he cast it impatiently aside. What mattered, the only thing that mattered, was the way their flesh melded, banishing solitude and loneliness, sorrow and yearning. Gently he moved in her, and gently she rose to meet him. Gently. Gently.

"Ah, princess," he whispered, "I've missed you. The light was gone from my soul, and my heart never stopped aching. I felt lost in ways I've never felt before. And all the while I was telling myself to let you go, I was dying because you're part of me. You make me whole."

She wrapped her arms tightly around his broad shoulders and spread her soft palms against the ridged scars on his back. "I love you," she whispered. "I love you. You're my home. My family. You make me belong."

He rose on his elbows and moved harder, his body demanding her response. "You're mine. Mine."

"Yes . . ."

"You'll marry me." He thrust harder.

"Yes." She gasped.

"We'll grow old . . . and gray . . . and . . ." He groaned deeply. "Together. Oh, God, Mandy . . . Mandy . . . Mandy . . ."

They catapulted together beyond thought, soaring upward on wings of passion until they melted in the heat of the sun.

Later, he pulled the comforter over them and tucked her close into the curve of his hard body. "I have to insist on a bigger bed," he told her, a smile evident in the words.

"Of course. King-size." She rubbed her nose against his cheek and inhaled the wonderful scent that clung to his beard. "I thought . . . I thought you were never coming back, that I had driven you away."

"It wasn't exactly that you drove me away, princess. It was that I was suddenly afraid I was pushing you into pain. I began to feel like a man who was pushing somebody out of an airplane without knowing if their parachute was working. I don't know how better to put it. I just suddenly became very aware that I could cause you a great deal of suffering. So I thought it would be best for you if I left."

She tunneled her fingers into the golden hair that covered his newly healed chest. "I sort of felt that way myself. It wasn't easy for me to face the fact that I'd gotten involved in spite of myself."

"And now?" He tilted her face up and tried to read her expression in the dusk. "How do you feel about that now?"

"Glad. Thrilled. Ecstatic." She kissed his neck. "Oh, God, I love you so much, I don't care what it costs." For a long moment she hugged him as tightly as she could. And then she asked the question that had plagued her for weeks. "You haven't told me how badly you were hurt when Karen shot you. And what happened to Karen?"

"Karen's been taken care of," he said grimly. "She was handed over to the opposition, and they're a lot less finicky about how they handle traitors. You don't have to worry about her."

If Ransom felt anything at all about that, she couldn't tell. It was a subject, she decided, that should be buried forever, right now. "And you?" Her hand touched the new, red scar tissue on his side.

"The wound was pretty bad," he admitted. "I'm short a few more parts now."

"What parts?"

"My spleen and a few ribs. They managed to save my whole lung, though."

She shivered and tried not to think how he must have hurt, how close he must have been to death. She might have to face that eventually, but she refused to let it shadow her joy right now.

For his part, Ransom was feeling exposed again, raw and vulnerable, as only Mandy could make him feel. This time, however, he felt no urge to run and hide. This time, as he held her close, that vulnerability seemed a small price to pay for the warmth this woman gave him. Many times, out of necessity, he had trusted others with his life, but never before had he trusted anyone with his heart—not even Karen when she had carried his child. Entrusting his heart to Mandy was suddenly an easy thing to do. She made him feel . . . welcome. Loved. Whole. At peace.

"Mandy? You did say you'd marry me? I didn't dream that?"

She laughed. He had never heard her laugh quite that way before, a joyously free sound. A truly happy unshadowed sound. "You didn't dream it."

"You don't want to sort everything out first?" It suddenly occurred to him that this woman had made a hell of a commitment when she accepted his proposal. She hadn't asked a thing, not where they would live or whether he would continue as an agent. She had given herself without reservation. His throat suddenly tightened, and his eyes burned with a flood tide of feeling for her. "No reservations?" he asked hoarsely. "No doubts?"

"Well..." she said, feeling suddenly more confident and sure of what she was doing than ever before in her life. How could she feel anything else when this golden warrior looked at her as if she were the answer to his every dream and prayer? "There's just one thing you should know first."

"What's that?" The look in her eyes kept him from getting too worried about what she might say. Those eyes weren't about to wound him. No way. They held his with glowing warmth.

Mandy took his hand and guided it down to her stomach, the as-yet flat place where her gift to him was nestled. Feeling suddenly incredibly shy, she leaned up and whispered her news in his ear.

For an instant Ransom didn't move. For just an instant she feared that perhaps he didn't want...

"Really?" The word was husky as it escaped him. "Really?" He pressed his hand more firmly against her satiny abdomen and closed his eyes. "Mandy... Mandy, are you sure? I know how you felt about Mary, how you hurt over losing her, and I wouldn't put you through that again for the world."

"Everything's going to be fine this time," she said bravely. "I want—I want so badly to give you a baby."

He kissed her with every bit of the love he felt for her, but he couldn't quite relax. "It isn't necessary, sweetheart. I'm thrilled with the thought of a baby, but I don't think I could stand to see the light go out of your eyes. I don't think I could stand to see you turn into the Mandy Grant I first met, so sad. Oh God, you were so sad!'' He wrapped her in his arms and squeezed her as close as he could get her. He would do anything, anything, to spare her further sorrow.

''I'm sure,'' she said bravely, hugging him back, sensing his pain and wanting to ease it. ''I want to do this. I *need* to do this. For both of us.''

After a short while he released a reluctant laugh. ''Someday I may figure out how to say no to you. Okay, princess, but this means we aren't going to hang around for a June wedding.''

The smile returned to her eyes and face when she saw the smile in his. ''No? When do you suggest?''

''I figure Friday will do just fine, mostly because I figure I can't swing it any sooner.'' He dropped a kiss on the tip of her nose. ''Of course, if you want a big shindig—''

''No. No. All I want is you. Just you.''

He spent the next hour showing her that he felt exactly the same way. Much, much later, as she was dozing gently beside him, she heard him say, ''If it's a girl, I want to name her Lynn.''

Without opening her eyes, she smiled. ''Okay. And a boy?''

''I'll leave that up to you, Amanda Lynn. Just as long as it's not Ransom.''

That opened her eyes. ''Why? It's a beautiful name!''

''It's a miserable name for a kid. People made jokes and puns out of it all my life. Nope, no Ransom, junior. No kid of mine is going to have to put up with that kind of teasing.''

Hiding a smile, she snuggled closer. ''If you insist. But I wouldn't mind being 'ransomed' again, if you've got a minute or two.''

He groaned. ''Now don't you start it!'' But he rolled her gently onto her back and leaned over her, a glint in his blue eyes. "I'm going to be 'ransoming' you for the rest of your life, princess, and don't you forget it."

Forget it? Not likely! "Then how about starting with a king's ransom?" she purred suggestively. "A princess is surely worth that much."

"She's worth a hell of a lot more, Amanda Lynn," he said, his voice gone completely husky. "One hell of a lot more. And don't you ever forget that, either."

* * * * *

CHEROKEE THUNDER

To Leslie Wainger, with great appreciation.
In order to reach its full potential,
every gem needs a gifted jeweler—
and every book needs a talented editor.

Chapter 1

Damn Texan!

Despite the darkness of the wet, misty afternoon, Deputy Sheriff Micah Parish identified the license plates on the car ahead of him. The damn fool was driving too fast for the road conditions. The driver probably had no idea that the thin layer of moisture on the road could turn to a coating of ice at any moment—and probably would. The first winter storm of the season was marching into Conard County, Wyoming, and conditions had been worsening all afternoon. There wasn't any residual warmth in the ground to keep things thawed, and as soon as the air temperature slipped below freezing, that sheen of water on the pavement was going to freeze into a treacherous glaze.

Damn, he hated this time of year. It seemed like the first time road conditions turned wintry, everyone had to learn all over again how to drive, and half of them decided to relearn the hard way. A night like this usually meant he would be lucky if he had time for dinner, but tonight he was off-duty and on the way home. This year, the first storm would be somebody else's problem.

Except for Texas up there. The car wasn't slowing up any, and Micah could now hear the occasional rattle of freezing rain against his windshield. Muttering a curse, he leaned forward and flipped the switch that turned on the rack of flashers on the roof of his Blazer. Red and blue lights revolved, casting eerie swirls of color over the wet, gray countryside.

He only intended to warn the driver of the worsening conditions and advise caution. He figured he could spend five minutes doing that, his conscience would be soothed, and then he could head home for the steak dinner he had been looking forward to all day.

An instant later, he was wondering if he had caused an accident instead. There was a bright flare of brake lights, and then the car ahead of him went out of control, first fishtailing this way and that, then finally going into a full circular spin. If there was any mercy, it was that the car continued to slow down, finally nosing to a stop into a ditch alongside the road.

Micah was by nature a silent man, but as he eased the Blazer to a careful halt on the grassy shoulder, he muttered a string of curses like beads on a rosary. Even in the rain he could see the gush of steam from beneath the other car's hood, and as he approached, he could smell the distinctive odor of antifreeze overheating on the engine block. The cute white Honda was seriously damaged. He just hoped to hell the occupants were wearing safety harnesses.

Damn, he hated auto accidents. Too often it felt like Vietnam all over again: the torn, dismembered bodies, the stink of blood and the cries of anguish. And all too often there were kids.

This time there weren't any kids. This time there was just the driver, a woman who was sitting upright and clutching the steering wheel in a death grip. She appeared uninjured, but it was impossible to be certain. Reaching out, he threw open the Honda's door and demanded, "Lady, are you okay?"

"Yes." She stared straight ahead, unmoving.

Disturbed, Micah bent and peered in at her, wondering if she had banged her head. She seemed dazed. "Let's get you out of there."

"No, really..." Faith Williams turned automatically to look at him, then gasped. If the seat belt hadn't held her in place, she would have scrambled to the far side of the car in panic.

He was a man, he was a cop, and he was big. That alone was more than enough to awaken her terror, but this man looked hard. Cold. Dangerous. His features were sharply etched—all angles and planes, looking as if they had been shaped in stone—and his eyes, as black as night, held absolutely no warmth. She shrank backward.

He saw her panic and fear, and while it was extreme, it wasn't entirely unexpected. He was a big, powerful man, with a harshly chiseled face, a half-breed who looked like a half-breed, a man who looked wild and dangerous. He even recognized that wearing his black hair to his shoulders didn't do much to make him seem more civilized. But civilization was a veneer Micah Parish wore, not part of his nature. He was perfectly content to have women cross the street to avoid him and even more content to have men think twice about giving him a hard time. It made life easier. Simpler. Micah was a great believer in sticking to basics.

He was, Faith thought as she cowered as far away from him as she could get, a perfect male animal. She didn't think she'd ever seen a man who looked so much like a... like a man. Like a predator. Like a hunter. As wildly, violently beautiful as a wolf. As deadly. And about as trustworthy. He was a man, after all, and she knew everything she ever wanted to know about men. Especially men who wore uniforms.

Micah shifted impatiently, recognizing her fright, understanding it, and feeling absolutely in no mood to deal with it. Dinner was waiting, and it was getting damn cold out here. He was, however, a uniformed deputy, and he couldn't leave a woman all alone in the middle of nowhere to freeze to death. Because she *would* freeze to death. Up this road there was nothing for the next eighty miles except his ranch and the deserted Montrose place. Oh, there were a few other ranches way back off the road, but nothing she could get to on foot. And town lay twenty-seven miles behind them. With the weather turning sour, his was apt to be the last vehicle heading this way before late tomorrow morning.

Touch was supposed to be reassuring, so he touched her shoulder. She flinched away as if his hand were a burning brand. Well, hell, he thought, and stepped back, giving her space. "Lady, your car is dead, and you're going to be just as dead if you don't let me take you to shelter. There's a winter storm on its way in. I guarantee you'll be a frozen corpse before midnight." For a taciturn man that was a long speech, so long it surprised even him. And it was wasted.

People had looked at him in all sorts of ways in his life, most of them with good reason, but he couldn't remember a perfect stranger ever looking at him as if he were the devil incarnate. Reaching up, he pushed back his tan Stetson and settled his fists on his khaki-clad hips. Hell and tarnation. He tried again.

"Lady, I'm a cop. A deputy sheriff. My job is to *help* you. I swear that's all I want to do. Just let me help you so I can get the hell home to my dinner and a warm fire, will you?"

As soon as he spoke, Micah wished he could recall the irritated words. The woman flinched visibly and then reached for the clasp of the seat belt with shaking, awkward hands, as if she couldn't comply swiftly enough.

"I'm . . . I'm sorry," she said weakly. "I'm sorry."

Micah released a relieved breath and stepped back a little more, recognizing that the lady evidently had some kind of problem, but that she was trying to keep a grip on it. So okay. He would stand back if she'd just behave rationally.

Unfortunately, he wasn't able to keep as much distance as they both would have liked. She was dressed for Texas, not Wyoming, and her sedate pumps provided absolutely no traction on the ice that was beginning to glaze everything. When she tried to ease out of the car, her foot slipped and she fell back into the seat.

Micah regarded this development with distaste. "I'm going to have to help you," he said reluctantly. She clearly didn't want to be touched, and he just as definitely didn't want to do any more touching. Cops had hard and fast rules about dealing with solitary females, and every one of them involved avoiding any potential appearance of impropriety. He had broken the first rule when he touched her, and now, fool that he was, he was going to break it again—big time.

A stocking cap completely concealed her hair, but she had wide blue eyes and satiny-looking calves a man would kill to stroke. Nice thighs, too, he realized when she slid forward on the seat and her skirt hiked up. Legs that just went on forever. What the hell was the matter with him, anyway?

He knew all about women. They were turned on by his badge, his gun and his uniform. A cop could get laid any time, anywhere. It was appalling how many women were prepared to trade their bodies to avoid a hundred-dollar traffic ticket. Amazing how many times he had approached a vehicle with his summons book in hand only to find some woman baring her body for his view. Yeah, he knew all about women. They were users, connivers, whores. They weren't in it for the long haul, and they were interested only in what they could get.

He also knew himself. He was a sucker for strays and lost animals. He was a one-finger pushover for anybody in serious need of help. Why did he get the uneasy feeling that this woman was in serious need of help? Why did he suddenly have the gut-sinking certainty that he was in the process of committing a major tactical error? He trusted his instincts. Instincts had kept him alive for better than twenty years in defiance of the odds. This time they were telling him to dump this woman PDQ. This time he had to ignore them.

He tried to steady her on the ice by holding her arm, but she kept slipping away, and he figured he was apt to tear her arm right out of its socket if he kept catching her this way. Without further ado, he scooped her up in his arms and carried her to the Blazer, ignoring her weak protests.

"Shut up," he said finally as he struggled to handle her and open the door at the same time. "Just shut up and hold still."

Those gruff commands would have been enough to stir most women up into a full-scale rebellion. He figured she would call him at least one name and take a halfhearted swing at him. She did neither. Instead, she became instantly very still and very silent, and the fear came back to her face. He ignored it. One way or the other, he was *not* going to get tangled up in this woman's problems, even if he had to pretend he was deaf, dumb and blind for the rest of the night.

He set her on the Blazer's passenger seat and let go of her immediately, then stepped back. "You need anything from the car?"

"M-my suitcases. In the trunk."

No, he told himself, he would *not* ask her what she was so scared of, because she might actually tell him. And if she told him, he would probably feel bound to do something to help her. Didn't he always? It didn't take any effort to remember a half dozen times when he'd felt bound to help someone and then had lived to regret it. It was the story of his life, it seemed.

Opening the Honda's trunk with the keys he had rescued from the ignition, Micah considered giving voice to a few choice words. Damn, it looked as if everything she owned were crammed into this tiny trunk. There was even a coffee maker. Suitcases? Which suitcases? All of them? Smothering a sigh, he started carrying them all to the Blazer.

The roads were treacherous now, and freezing rain mixed with snow had begun to fall. Micah climbed into the warm cab of the Blazer and turned over the ignition. "We're going to my place." He heard her swiftly drawn breath, but ignored it. There really wasn't any other option. He'd spent the last ten minutes, while he carted all her gear, trying to think of one. "It's getting too bad out there to drive back to town, and my place is only a couple more miles up the road."

"What about . . . what about the Montrose ranch? That isn't too much farther, is it?"

"A few miles past mine," he answered, tossing her a curious glance before returning his attention to the road. Surely he would have heard something if the Montrose property had been put up for sale. He was, after all, the likeliest person to want it. He drove slowly, carefully, patiently. On this ice there was no margin for error. "Nobody lives there, though. What do you want with the Montrose place?"

"It's mine now," she said. "Jason Montrose was my father."

In that instant he knew who she was. Faith Montrose. Something wrenched in him, but he forced himself to ignore it. Obviously she didn't remember him, so he could safely pretend not to know her. It had been twenty-five years, after all, and it would be better that way—for both of them.

"Well, you can't go there tonight. I doubt there's enough propane left in the tank to run the heater overnight. You'd freeze. I'll get you there in the morning, and we'll see what needs to be done." He needed his head examined. *We'll* see what needs to be done? Right.

God, she was a babe in the woods, just what he needed for his nearest neighbor. He knew she must be over thirty, and he found himself wondering what kind of life she had led that she didn't know about things like arranging for the power to be turned on, the propane tank to be filled, the pump to be primed. . . . If she had arranged for any of those things to be done, he would have heard about it. No, the Montrose place wasn't ready for occupancy, and wouldn't be for several days at least. Hell. What was he supposed to do with her? Well, when the weather improved he could take her to a motel, he guessed.

At least she wasn't a gabber. She kept perfectly quiet and huddled as close to the door as she could, which caused the shoulder harness to lie right across her throat. He thought of warning her that the seat belt could hurt her throat if they stopped suddenly, but then decided against it. It was none of his business. None of his damn business. As a decent human being, he had to make sure she didn't freeze to death, but he didn't have to do any more than that.

Micah's house was set more than a mile off the county road. At the time he purchased the ranch, there had been a couple of other places in the county he might have bought, but this one had appealed to him because the house was situated among rocky outcrops that gave it a protected feeling. There was only one approach by which a vehicle could arrive, and while that was no longer a necessary consideration in his life, it nonetheless made him more comfortable. The habits of half a lifetime were harder to break than an addiction, and sometimes not worth the trouble. Selecting a defensible location was such a habit. It didn't complicate anything.

Tonight nothing looked appealing, he thought as he jockeyed the Blazer right up to the kitchen door. The outcrops, normally a rainbow of sedimentary colors, were a dismal gray. Even the grass seemed to have become gray under its growing burden of ice, and when he stepped out of the vehicle, ice crystals stung his cheeks. A lousy, miserable, godforsaken night, he thought sourly. He was grateful that he didn't have to be on duty.

He ushered his unwanted guest into the kitchen and paused only long enough to start a pot of coffee. "I've got to check on my animals," he told her. "Make yourself comfortable and have some coffee. When I get back I'll make dinner."

"Deputy?"

Her voice stopped him at the door. Reluctantly, he looked back.

"I didn't get your name," she said, looking like a lost waif in the middle of his large kitchen.

For the first time he realized this woman was tiny. Scarcely an inch or two over five feet. The down jacket she wore nearly swallowed her whole. "Micah," he said after a moment. "I'm Micah Parish."

"I'm Faith Williams," she said politely. "Thank you for rescuing me."

Well, hell, he thought, and crammed his hat tighter on his head. "It's my job," he said shortly, and stepped out into the darkening late afternoon.

Nope. She didn't remember him at all.

It had been many years since Micah had last seen Faith, but he maintained a clear memory of her nonetheless. He'd been a sort of adopted brother to her during her first summer visit to her father. Faith had been six the first time Micah saw her, frightened at being yanked from her Houston home and sent unaccompanied by air to visit a father in Conard County, a father she scarcely remembered. Micah had been eighteen, and to this day he clearly recalled the meeting.

His horse had gone lame in the arroyo that cut between the Wyatt spread and the Montrose ranch where Micah was working for the summer. Micah had been squatting, running his hands expertly up Dutchman's foreleg, when he'd looked up to see a tiny girl with a tear-streaked face and eyes the color of the midsummer sky staring at him. Her hair was long and pale, hanging nearly to her thin little waist, and the hot, dry July breeze blew it across her face like a shimmering veil.

"Are you hurt?" Micah asked instantly, captivated by the eyes, concerned by the tears.

Slowly she shook her head. "No." Her little girl's voice was hardly more than a whisper.

"Are you lost?"

Again she shook her head solemnly.

But Micah knew she was at least four miles from the nearest dwelling, the Montrose house.

Moving slowly so as not to startle her, Micah sat cross-legged on the dirt beside Dutchman.

"Where's your home?" he asked quietly.

"Houston."

He knew then that he was looking at Jason Montrose's daughter. Montrose had made no secret that his girl was coming from Houston to spend the summer with him.

"Where's your daddy?" he asked her.

She shook her head. "I want my mommy." Her lower lip trembled.

Eighteen-year-old boys aren't noted for their sensitivity, but Micah's heart went out to the little girl. "I know," he said.

"Do you have a mommy?"

"She's dead."

Faith's lower lip had trembled even more. "My mommy's in Houston, and I'm going to find her."

Micah wondered what the devil to do now. "It's too far to walk," he told her. "You could walk all summer and still not get to Houston."

"I don't care."

"You'll get cold and hungry, and your mommy and daddy will worry about you. You'll make your mommy cry."

The little face crumpled even more.

"Why don't you let me take you back to your daddy?"

"No!"

Micah sighed and looked down at the dusty clay ground. The little girl stepped closer.

"Are you an Indian?" she asked.

Micah's head shot up, but all he found was honest curiosity. Of course, she was only a child. Moreover, in a spurt of rebellion, he'd let his black hair grow to his shoulders and tied it back with a bandanna around his forehead.

"Half Indian," he answered truthfully. *Half-breed.*

She drew a little closer. "I never saw a real Indian before."

"Well, you have now."

"Can I live with you?"

The question so startled him that he simply stared at her. "What about your daddy?" he asked finally.

"He doesn't care about me. He went away when I was little."

Micah heard the girl's mother in that statement. "Kid, your daddy loves you a whole lot. He told everybody in town how much he loves you and how happy he is you're visiting him. You're gonna make him real sad."

Again the small chin trembled. Micah sighed.

"Tell you what, kid. I'll give you a ride on my horse, and we'll both go back together and talk to your daddy. A real ride on a real Indian horse," he added cajolingly.

It was a long time coming, but finally he got a small nod. Micah lifted her onto his saddle, wrapped her small hands tightly around the pommel, and, with instructions to hang on tight, he walked her and his horse the four miles to the Montrose place.

His welcome by Jason Montrose had been far warmer than a half-breed was accustomed to. And when Micah had knelt in the dust to extract his own promise from Faith that she wouldn't try to run away again, she had insisted that she would stay if he promised to visit her the next day. Looking up at Jason Montrose, expecting the rancher to be annoyed or disapproving, Micah had instead received a nod.

"I second that invitation, Micah," Jason Montrose had said. "You come visit her tomorrow and any other time you feel like it."

Somehow Micah had felt like it quite a bit. He'd been the one to teach Faith how to ride, who'd taught her to swim in the watering hole and how to milk a cow. He was never certain if he was welcomed simply because he made Faith easier for Montrose to handle, but it ceased to matter to him. She was the sister he had never had.

In late August Micah had gone off to the army, and Faith had gone back to Houston. He wrote her a couple of letters from Vietnam and received some crayoned thank you notes in return, but then the horror had gripped him, and he hadn't written anymore.

He'd seen her once again, years later, when he'd passed through Conard County, stopping briefly to visit his buddy

Nate Tate. Faith had been fifteen, and he'd been twenty-seven, a very old twenty-seven. Life's currents had carried him into ever more dangerous occupations. He'd come upon Faith at the swimming hole while he'd been out visiting old haunts. The sound of laughter and splashing, such a clean, wonderful sound, had drawn him. She'd been with a group of kids her own age, all having a good time. Micah had hung back, not wanting to disrupt the fun, and decided not to speak to her. He told himself she probably wouldn't remember him, anyway, and would only think he was some kind of creep.

Turning his horse, he'd ridden steadily away, never once glancing back. Life had taught him that there was no way back. That one brief summer with Jason Montrose and his daughter, that one brief time in his life where he had actually felt that he was part of a real family, was a precious anomaly. He cherished it, but he wasn't foolish enough to believe he could ever recapture it.

And now Faith was here, he thought as he pitchforked fresh straw into a stall. Hell.

He straightened abruptly and leaned the pitchfork against the wall. From his hip pocket he tugged out his wallet and flipped it open. There, facing his driver's license, was a snapshot of six-year-old Faith. Hardened, toughened, callused hands had held that photo countless times over the past twenty-five years. She'd been the family he had never really had. She had been the symbol of all he had fought for. His little sister.

Now the symbol was here, and she was not a symbol anymore but very real and fully grown. And he didn't know what in the hell he was going to do about it.

Micah entered the kitchen with a burst of cold air. Snow sprinkled the shoulders of his jacket. "It's gettin' downright unfriendly out there," he remarked and headed straight for the coffee pot. Moments later he leaned back against the counter and raised a steaming mug to his mouth. He had unzipped his sage-colored winter jacket, revealing the crisp khaki uniform shirt beneath and his shiny silver badge. Almost reluctantly, his eyes strayed toward where she sat at the table.

Her hair, he saw, was just as pale as it had been in childhood, an almost colorless blond, so fine it looked as if it had been spun from sugar. It had been long and straight, but now she wore it in a tousled profusion of curls that fell softly past her shoulders. Touchable hair, the kind a man wanted to run his hands through.

Her face was just as delicately etched, but stronger somehow, firmer looking. And pinched. Life had taught her some hard lessons, he thought, as he deliberately dragged his gaze from her softly pink, gently bowed lips.

And then he saw her stomach. His mug froze in midair, and he frankly stared. She was pregnant. Very definitely pregnant. Five months, he'd guess. Maybe even six. The knowledge had a shocking, unexpected effect on him. It twisted and turned in his gut like a flaming knife, a strong feeling of unholy jealousy. Slowly, he lifted his black-as-night eyes to her small, pale face.

"Miz Williams," he said after a moment, "do you want to tell me what the hell is going on here?"

Her hands closed around the mug of coffee she wasn't drinking, and he didn't miss the tight way she held on to it. This lady, he found himself thinking, was a bundle of very raw nerve endings.

Ten seconds or so passed before she answered him. Her eyes never lifted from her mug. "What do you mean?"

He snorted and took a swig of his coffee. "Pregnant women don't go running off into the back of beyond all by themselves."

She bit her lower lip. "Why not?"

"Why not." He repeated the question without the question mark. Cut it out, Micah, he warned himself. If you don't ask questions, you don't get answers you don't want to hear. You don't get involved. You don't collect another stray. And this woman was giving him plenty of opportunities to avoid involvement. She was backing away as determinedly as he ought to be and wasn't.

"Well," he heard himself saying, "most pregnant women get concerned about things like doctors and someone to call on if they need help. So, is your husband arriving in a day or two?" He'd noted the lack of a wedding ring, but that didn't necessarily mean anything. Besides, on second look he thought he could see a thin line of paler skin on her ring finger. Recent divorce, maybe.

Her color receded even more, making her look ashen. What was with her? he wondered yet again. A casual question shouldn't make her look as if she had just been threatened with a firing squad.

"I don't think—I don't think that's any of your business," she answered in a voice that was thin and strained. She looked at him then, a pathetic attempt at defiance.

"Sure it is," he remarked. "I'm going to be your nearest neighbor. The only neighbor close enough to help out in an emergency. That makes it my business, Miz Williams. Are you going to be alone?"

Her blue eyes wavered and fell, as if she had run out of courage. "Yes."

"Well, hell," he said, and sighed. "What else do I need to know?"

Her eyes snapped back to his face, and she was clearly perplexed. "What else?"

"Yeah, what else? Where's junior's daddy? Does he know about this kid? Is he likely to come along and make trouble? Or did he head for the hills and leave you all alone?"

"It's really not your...not your concern," Faith protested weakly. "I'm not going to bother you. I don't want to bother you with anything."

"I know. But you will." Deciding the air had better be cleared, because maybe then she would see sense and pack up and go back to Texas, he pulled out a chair on the far side of the table and straddled it.

"Look," he said. "The Montrose place is thirty-six miles from the nearest town. The nearest neighbor is me, four and a half miles down the road. Beyond that, better than ten or twelve miles away, are the Lairds and the Wyatts. If you run into anything more severe than a twisted ankle, you're going to be calling on a neighbor for help. That's the way it is in these parts. That's the way it has to be for all of us." He looked at her until she nodded her understanding.

"Now, you're going to stay here with me until we get your power on, your propane delivered and your phone installed. There's no way in hell I'm going to let you stay out there alone with no heat, no water and no phone. You can just plain forget it. Anyhow, I don't think you're stupid enough to try it. So, you're my business. You're my business because I'm going to be the person you turn to when there's any trouble. You're my business because it's my job to protect the welfare of the people in this county, so if you move into this county your welfare is going to be my business. Am I getting through?"

She was gnawing her lip, and she gave only the smallest nod. "I won't be any trouble. I promise. I don't want to make trouble for anyone."

There was something about the way she spoke that made him sigh. It also disturbed some deep, dark place inside him. It sounded wrong, somehow, as if she were afraid. As if it were a world-class crime to disturb someone.

He rubbed his chin and considered starting dinner. After all, he'd said more in the last ten minutes than he'd said in the last week. It wasn't like him to offer opinions on the things people chose to do.

And then, as he studied her bowed head, he realized something so strongly and so forcefully that it never entered his head to question the knowledge. "You're running from someone. Who is it?"

She drew a sharp breath, and her head jerked almost as if she had been struck.

"C'mon, Miz Williams. Who are you running from?"

When she raised her face, he wished he hadn't asked. No one should look as old, as hunted and as terrified as this woman did right now. She released a breath so ragged that it sounded as if it had come from a tattered soul.

"My ex-husband," she said.

Chapter 2

There was a whole lot more Micah needed to know, but he didn't ask. Instead, he showed Faith the spare bedroom upstairs and left her with her suitcases, some fresh towels and the advice to change into something a little warmer before dinner. He himself made a quick change into a well-worn pair of jeans and a red flannel shirt.

Downstairs, he took the time to start a fire in the wood stove that stood in the hallway between the living room and dining room, and then he turned his attention to dinner. The steak, meant for just him, would now have to serve two, but he didn't begrudge her.

The fact that she was fleeing her husband, her *ex*-husband, raised all kinds of questions. From the look on her face, he suspected none of the answers would be pretty. A woman running the way this woman was running was hardly trying to avoid a simple attempt to patch things up.

For a moment, as he stood over the stove, Micah saw her in his mind's eye as she had been so many years ago, the child and the blossoming teenager. She had been full of so much promise, and he had always believed her future would be bright and shining. He had needed to believe it. Now this. What had happened to her?

Well, if it was going to concern him in any way, he figured the answers would fall into his lap with time. They always did. When life set out to drag you into the middle of a mess, it didn't hold anything back.

Of course, he could still hope that she would head back to Texas and make her problems somebody else's concern. Gut instinct said she was staying, though. Right here. Just four miles up the road. Bringing all her problems with her.

And he wasn't going to be able to keep clear, because of the little girl she had once been, and because she was pregnant and alone. Between those three things, Micah figured he was tied into this mess but good. He swore, a single, succinct word that punctured the quiet like a thunderclap.

The blood of shamans ran in the veins of Micah Parish. He could still remember one of the rare occasions in his early childhood when his father, a taciturn, unemotional man, had taken Micah on his knee. Amory Parish had made a stab at being a father from time to time, and on one occasion he had spoken of Micah's mother. She had been a Cherokee medicine woman, the elder Parish had told his young son. Micah's grandfather had also been a medicine man, reputedly one of great power and magic. Amory Parish didn't hold with that kind of nonsense, and he was sure the magic had been a matter of imagination, but he wanted the boy to understand that his Indian ancestors hadn't been scum, no matter what anybody told him.

A boy who was already getting bloody noses from taking exception to being called a dirty Indian, a boy who fed his empty, hungry heart with Arthurian legends and read Sir Walter Scott under his blankets with a flashlight—that boy had treasured that small bit of information about his ancestry. It had made him feel special.

It had also explained his feelings. At least, that was what he called them, those moments of intuition when he seemed almost to step outside time and know, just *know* things he shouldn't be able to. He'd never told anyone about those experiences, and he never would. Even to him they sounded crazy.

Right now, though, his intuition was telling him that he was standing on the edge of a precipice, and that nothing would ever be the same again.

The vegetables and instant mashed potatoes were on the table, and he was taking the steak out of the broiler when Faith returned to the kitchen. She hovered uncertainly in the doorway, as if she feared she were trespassing.

"Pull up a chair," Micah said. "Chow's ready."

"Can I—can I help?"

"Nope. It's all done." He didn't want to look at her, but somehow he couldn't stop himself. He saw the shadow in her blue eyes, a shadow of fear so old she wore it comfortably, unaware that it wasn't natural. He saw, too, an amazing vulnerability. Whatever life had hurled at this woman, she hadn't learned how to protect herself. She hadn't grown calluses or developed a shell. Hell! Somebody ought to tell her that a little emotional armor was a useful thing.

He set the table just like a man, Faith thought as she took her place. Flatware had been dumped beside the plates. A roll of paper towels stood in the center of the table in lieu of napkins. The potatoes had been served in the saucepan, and the broccoli had already been placed on the plates. In spite of herself, she felt the corners of her mouth lift in amusement. She wondered when a woman had last sat at Micah Parish's table.

Micah caught sight of that smile, the faint, tentative shimmer of humor, and he was suddenly aware that Faith was a woman. A warm, sweet-smelling, soft-looking, enticing tidbit of femininity. And despite the swollen curve of her abdomen, plainly evident beneath the soft folds of an oversize blue sweatshirt, she was a sexy tidbit of femininity, too.

Aw, hell. Not that, too!

He turned swiftly away and went to the refrigerator for milk. He would have his nightly beer, but she was going to drink milk. He didn't even bother to ask her. He couldn't have said exactly why, but something in her vulnerability told him this baby was important to her and that she would take every precaution to ensure its well-being.

"Thank you," she said when he placed the tall glass of milk before her. She was touched by his thoughtfulness, and a glimmer of warmth crept into her voice. She looked up, trying to smile. Blue eyes met black, and Texas sank into the dark velvet of a Wyoming night. So deep, she thought. So dark. So mesmerizing. Those eyes were dark pools, beckoning, bottomless. Beyond them, she felt, was something bright and shining, something so bright that it needed to be hidden in those deep, dark pools.

Micah blinked and looked away, uneasily feeling he had looked into the eyes of destiny. Refusing to let the superstitious, fanciful part of his nature get the better of him, he pulled back his chair and sat, giving his attention to his meal.

"That's far too much steak for me," Faith protested when he tried to serve her. "I couldn't possibly—"

"You're eating for two," he interrupted.

"Well, yes," she said uncertainly, "but one of us only weighs a couple of pounds."

Micah's eyes snapped up to hers, and what he saw there had him smiling against his better judgment. It wasn't much of a smile, just a twitch at one corner of his mouth, but Faith saw it, and the great, cold knot of fear in her eased a little more.

He spoke. "But one of you is growing fast."

"Both of us are growing fast," she said ruefully. "But not fast enough to eat all that steak."

The other corner of his mouth reluctantly rose to join the first. As a smile it was small and faint, but it had the most amazing effect on his face, Faith realized with a sense of wonder. Micah Parish no longer looked hard, forbidding or cruel. He passed her the plate holding the steak.

"Cut off whatever you want," he said roughly.

Her hands trembled a little, aware of his eyes on her, and she sliced off about three ounces of the beef. She doubted she was going to be able to swallow even that much if this man kept staring at her this way.

He didn't think that was nearly enough, but he kept quiet about it. He'd already argued too much about something that was none of his business anyhow.

He did, however, cherish a high reverence for life. It seemed a funny thing in a man who had made his living by the sword for so long, or perhaps it was the natural outcome of seeing life valued so cheaply for so long. He held a particular reverence for new life, for the innocent unborn, for the women who carried life in their bellies.

He found himself thinking, as he ate his dinner, that Faith Williams would have been a hell of a lot easier to deal with if she wasn't expecting a baby. A pregnant woman needed someone to look out for her, to look after her, and he had the definite feeling she didn't have a soul in the world.

The first thing he needed to do, he decided reluctantly, was find out something about her husband—what kind of threat he was, and how she was involved. If the man was really a danger to her, he might have some kind of police record, and if he could just get the man's name and the city where he and Faith had been living, he could check it out. But before he invaded her privacy that way, he was going to make one more stab at getting her to tell him herself. Remembering the way she had reacted earlier to his questioning, he didn't think it was going to be easy. After dinner, he told himself.

She wanted to help with the dishes of course. She'd clearly had a very proper upbringing. He wondered, as he passed her a freshly rinsed plate to dry, what she would think of his upbringing. If you could honestly call it an upbringing at all.

His dad had been an Army enlisted man. His mother, a full-blooded Cherokee, had left her husband and eldest child just before Micah's second birthday, taking her newborn second son with her. Micah's father had claimed the division was a fair one, a son to each parent. Micah just plain didn't think about it much at all. He had never seen his mother again and had heard that she'd died within a year.

After that, Micah's upbringing had been catch-as-catch-can, and devil take the hindmost. His father had bounced from one Army post to another, dragging Micah with him and finding a succession of women to look after the boy. None of them had particularly cared for the silent child, and along about the time Micah turned ten, his father stopped trying to pass the women off as housekeepers. Micah had always known better, anyway. His attitude toward women had practically been born in the cradle with him.

He was wiping down the stove when he realized that he had passed the last hour or more in the company of a woman who hadn't talked him to death. In fact, she hadn't seemed to be disturbed by his silence, either. That must be some kind of first.

Turning, he sought her out with his eyes and found her at the kitchen window, looking out at the blowing, whirling snow that was illuminated by the porch light. She had her arms protectively wrapped around her stomach, a pregnant woman's perennial pose.

She seemed to sense his attention and turned her head quickly his way. She made an attempt to smile. "I've never seen a blizzard before," she confessed.

"Never?" He stepped toward her, turning his gaze to the window. Here was his opening. "Whereabouts in Texas are you from?"

"San Antonio."

"I thought you folks got some snow from time to time down there."

"Oh, we do, but nothing like this. Once every few years we'll get a powder, maybe even a couple of inches. But nothing like this." She pointed to the blowing, drifting snow. "How much do you think will fall?"

"The weather report's calling for ten to twelve inches."

She utterly astonished him then by hugging herself and smiling like a delighted child. "Fantastic!"

"Fantastic?" he repeated gruffly, then caught himself. Hell, there was no point ruining her fun by telling her just what kind of extra work a blizzard created for a rancher, or how much fun it was going to be trying to plow out his mile-long driveway. Naw, just let her enjoy it.

But she had heard the implied disagreement in his tone, and right before his astonished eyes, she flinched away from him and shrank into herself. What the hell? And why was she covering her womb as if she expected a blow there? Right there.

"Miz Williams..."

She shrank back even farther, watching him warily as she backed up. "I'm sorry," she said almost blankly. "I'll get out of your way."

"Miz Williams..." She was still backing up, and he saw the danger she was unaware of. Right behind her was a chair, and if she stumbled over it... "Faith, don't move. You're going to—"

The bark in his tone scared her even more, and she took another quick backward step. That did it. Heedless of her fright, Micah leapt forward and grabbed her, catching her just as the back of her leg collided with the chair.

"Damn fool woman," he swore. "If you'd fallen over that chair—"

But she didn't hear what he was saying. She heard his tone, and total panic seized her. Like a wildcat, she fought his hold on her, trying to escape. He felt her panic but didn't dare let her go for fear she would hurt herself trying to scramble away from him. Unable to do anything else, he tightened his hold and took her blows as she flailed wildly at him.

"Miz Williams...Faith...it's okay. I won't hurt you. I swear I won't hurt you...." He murmured as soothingly as he could, using the same tone he used on his frightened or hurt livestock. Again and again she pounded his shoulders and chest with her fists, shoving at him, trying to break his hold. She might be giving him a small bruise or two, but she didn't know a damn thing about protecting herself. Sighing, he braced himself against her hammering and kept murmuring a soothing stream of nonsense, hoping to penetrate her terror with his tone.

Finally he managed to pin her arms to her sides and hold her snugly against him. She wiggled, but she was rapidly tiring.

"You'll hurt the baby," he said. "Shh... It's okay. Shh."

It was exhaustion that quieted her finally, not anything he said or did. She sagged against him, all the fight worn out of her, and her face fell against his hard chest.

"Shh," he whispered. "It's okay. You're safe here, Faith. You're safe."

It was a good thing she didn't look up at his face just then, however, because she would have become terrified all over again. At that moment Micah Parish had a pretty good idea what Faith Williams was fleeing from, and at that moment he was in a mood for murder.

With weary astonishment, Faith felt Micah's grasp on her change. His arms ceased to imprison her, and his hands began to stroke soothingly from her shoulder to her hip, as if he were stroking a kitten. She would never have imagined him to be gentle, but he was gentle right then, touching her with a kindness that made her throat tighten.

He felt the wetness of tears soaking his shirt, and he expelled a breath, letting go of the anger. It wouldn't do a damn bit of good to be angry. Not right now, at any rate. And hell, he didn't want to get all tied up in knots with this woman—or any woman—anyway.

But he sighed again, sensing that the knots were already being tied. Damn, he was a sucker for strays.

Bending, he scooped her up and carried her toward the stairs as if he were carrying a bride over the threshold.

"Easy," he said, when he heard her sharp intake of breath. "Easy. I'm just going to take you to your room. You're tuckered out and need to rest. You have to take care of that baby, Miz Williams."

Upstairs, he shouldered his way into her room and put her down gently on the bed. She stared up at him in the light from the hall, her expression one of wondering disbelief as he pulled the quilts over her.

"You rest a while, Miz Williams. You just rest. If you want to come down again later, you come. I usually like to make some cocoa around bedtime if that interests you."

He paused a moment, then touched her cheek awkwardly. "Was your husband's name Williams, too?"

"Yes." Her voice was nothing but a cracked whisper. "Yes. Frank Williams." She closed her eyes, hoping he would leave it at that.

He didn't, though. "He wouldn't have had any trouble with the law, would he?" A man like that often did, especially if his wife had any spunk at all. And this woman had spunk, all right.

Faith turned her face away. "He's wanted right now," she said wearily. "He escaped from custody three days ago."

Escaped from custody? He was very definitely going to check this out. "Well, don't you worry about him none. If Frank Williams sets foot in Conard County, he'll be dealing with me. Now just you sleep."

He closed the door quietly behind him as he left her.

Back in the kitchen, he pulled the phone off the hook and placed a call to the Conard County Sheriff's Department.

"Fred, it's Micah. Listen, if you're not real busy, I was wondering if you could do me a favor? Yeah, I'd like you to get a hold of the San Antonio police and see if you can get me a rap sheet on a Frank Williams. Might be Francis Williams. I understand he recently escaped from custody, and I have reason to believe he might be headed this way. Thanks, Fred."

After he hung up, he stood looking out at the drifting, blowing snow in the yard off the kitchen, trying to concentrate on the things he needed to do for his animals. He didn't have a whole lot of livestock, a few horses, a few head of cattle, just enough animals to make the place feel like a ranch. Working for the Sheriff's Department, he really didn't have the time to ranch, and he really didn't have the know-how, either, though he supposed he could hire help.

There wasn't any point in it, though, he thought for the umpteenth time. Since youth, he'd wanted to live on a ranch, to have his own spread, to be able to get on a horse and ride until he got tired without leaving his own land. He could do that right now. He'd fulfilled his dream. Building anything bigger, anything more complex, was something a man did when he wanted to leave something to the future. Micah didn't want to do that. Oh, if he had a son or a daughter he probably would, but you couldn't get a kid without a woman, and he'd be damned if he would take any woman into his life. No way.

He knew better. He'd nearly fallen into that trap once, and Micah wasn't a man who ever made a mistake a second time.

Faith cried a little, but tears came easily to her since she'd become pregnant, and they dried just as quickly. She slept for a little while, feeling the day's fatigue deep in her bones.

When she woke, it was nearly ten p.m., and the wind was howling like a banshee around the corners of the house, making the windows rattle and the frame structure creak and groan with each renewed blast. A draft curled across the room and touched her nose with chilly fingers. From downstairs she heard a bang, signifying that Micah Parish was still up and about.

It was lonely in this strange room, and the sounds of the storm were eerie, forlorn. She tried for a while to go back to sleep, but eventually she gave up. At last she sat up and switched on the small lamp on the bedside table. The pink shade cast a warm glow, and Faith wondered if Micah had purchased this house furnished, or if at some time a woman, perhaps a sister, had slept in this room. With all its pink frills, it was certainly not a room Micah would have created, nor was it the kind of room a grown woman would have decorated for herself.

The wind rattled the windows again and howled a desolate note. Sighing, Faith climbed out from under the quilts, deciding that even the company of a man was better than this creepy solitude. At least, the company of a man like Micah.

For a moment, when her feet touched the floor, she paused, remembering. She had acted like a crazy woman, she admitted. He must think she needed to be locked up. Despite that, he'd been incredibly gentle with her. Incredibly caring. The only other man she had ever known to show such kindness to her was the Texas Ranger who had saved her. Garrett Hancock. But Garrett had had a reason for understanding. His sister, he had told her, had once been married to a man like Frank Williams. How was it Micah understood? How was it he was so caring and gentle?

Or was he? *Better than thirty percent of the women in this country are victims of spousal abuse.* Her counselor had told her that shocking statistic. So many! And that meant an awful lot of men were like Frank. An awful lot. And that was why she shouldn't trust Micah Parish, no matter how kind he might seem. He could very well be another of them. Perhaps that was why he lived alone. Perhaps he'd driven a previous wife away.

She shivered as the wind moaned yet again and the draft snaked across the room to wrap her in an icy embrace.

Whatever Micah Parish was or wasn't, she didn't need to worry about it. She had dated Frank for months before they had married, and it wasn't until they'd been married nearly a year that he had hit her for the first time. An abuser seldom showed his colors to strangers. So, for the time being, and as long as she developed no kind of relationship with the man, she was safe.

And all of that was rationalization anyway, she admitted. Micah had somehow managed to make her feel safe when he had held her and endured her blows without retaliating. Something in his voice, in his eyes, in the way he touched her . . . those things made her feel safe.

Or perhaps it was just coming back to Conard County that made her feel safe. After her initial resistance to visiting her father, she had come to treasure her summers here as a hiatus from an increasingly sour mother and a stepfather who preached damnation over the slightest infraction and used his belt as a punctuation mark.

And there had been that Indian boy...Mike, she thought. He was like a soft, warm memory, a feeling more than a visual image. Closing her eyes, she could almost, just barely, recall the incredible security she had felt in her sixth summer, knowing that her father or Mike was watching over her every moment. She had never fallen, slipped or tripped without one of them catching her up in strong, sheltering arms and drying her tears.

But then she had gone home to Texas to find her mother remarried, and Mike had gone to Vietnam and after a couple of letters he had never written again. He must have died, she thought, and felt the dry whisper of an ancient loss. But it was the search for what he had given her that had brought her back to Conard County.

Feeling calmer and more in control, she stood up and tugged her sweatshirt down over her swollen belly. The baby kicked, a soft poke that instantly brought a smile to her lips. She loved being pregnant. She loved the child growing within her. She could hardly wait to hold her son or daughter.

Downstairs, she found Micah in the kitchen, stirring a pot with the promised hot chocolate. He glanced up when she stepped into the room and gave her a nod that said nothing one way or the other.

"It sounds terrible outside," she said shyly, truly seeing him for the first time. He was a man, yes, and a cop besides, but he had carried her upstairs as carefully as a baby and tucked her in with a gentleness that she had never before experienced, not once in her entire life.

Micah turned and looked at her fully. He wondered if she had the vaguest idea how sexy she looked at this very minute, with her hair all tousled from her nap and her cheeks still flushed from sleep. Probably. Women always knew when they looked sexy. It was their stock in trade.

But there was something in her soft blue eyes, a kind of wistfulness that reached him despite his barriers. He was a little astonished to hear himself clear his throat and speak.

"After we have our cocoa, I'll find some boots and warm clothes for you. Anybody who's never been out in a blizzard really shouldn't miss a chance to see what it's like."

Her face lighted. There was really no other way to describe the change in her expression in response to his suggestion. In that instant she seemed to forget whatever was worrying her, terrifying her, driving her.

"Really? We can go out in this? It's not dangerous?"

He felt his mouth trying to frame a smile. He never smiled, but here he was smiling for at least the second time in one day. "Only if we were out in it too long, Miz Williams. We'll only be out a few minutes, just long enough for you to get a taste of what a blizzard is like."

The smile she gave him was warm, genuine. She suspected that he didn't especially want to go out in this, that to him it was nothing but a major inconvenience, yet here he was proposing to take her out just so she could see what it was like. But somehow she felt he wouldn't appreciate an emotional display of gratitude, so she offered him the only other thing she could. "I'd be honored if you would call me Faith, Deputy Parish."

He looked away, giving his attention to the pot he was stirring. Faith waited, wondering if he meant to ignore her, and why he should hesitate over what to call her.

Eventually Micah cleared his throat and spoke gruffly, feeling even as he did that this was another mistake in a day full of mistakes. "You can call me Micah," he told her.

That was not an offer Micah Parish made often, Faith realized. There was something about the rusty way he said it that revealed it was a rare concession.

"Thank you," she said politely.

He made a sound in his throat, sort of a grunt of acknowledgment. "Pull up a chair," he said roughly. "Cocoa's about ready." He glanced at her again and then snapped his gaze back to the saucepan.

"Earlier," he said, and cleared his throat, "earlier, I grabbed you because you were about to fall. I didn't mean to terrify you." That had been troubling him since he'd carried her upstairs, that she still might not understand why he had grabbed her that way. He knew how easily such things could be misunderstood. "The chair was right behind you, and you were backing up. There just wasn't time to be polite about it."

Seated at the table, her hands folded protectively over her stomach, Faith tried to find a way to let him know she understood, and to apologize for her own behavior. The problem was, she didn't see how she could apologize without explaining about Frank, and she didn't want to do that. Talking about it meant thinking about it, and she wasn't prepared to do that, either. Talking and thinking didn't help. Forgetting was the only way she could deal with it.

He was such a large man, she thought as she watched him set the mugs full of steaming cocoa on the table. He tore a paper towel from the roll and folded it awkwardly before he passed it to her. The gesture was touching, somehow, as if he were trying to polish up his world a little to make it more palatable to her.

He should only know, she thought wearily, where she had been. He would hardly worry about whether folding a paper towel would make it a more acceptable napkin.

He sat across from her, and she watched his huge hands cup and lift his mug. Big, capable hands, she thought. She would willingly bet that there was very little this man didn't know how to do with those hands.

And she had to apologize. Now. Before too much time passed.

"I'm sorry," she said abruptly, committed now to saying it.

He looked up sharply, as if he had forgotten she was there. He hadn't. He had, however, grown accustomed to her silence. She was a peaceful presence. "Sorry?"

"Yes. I've been so stupid today. Running my car off the road and putting you to all this trouble... And then the way I acted when—before, when—I can't believe I—I'm just so sorry!"

Well, hell, Micah thought. Maybe he didn't want to see it, and maybe he didn't want to tangle with it, but this woman's face reflected fear, uncertainty and utter misery. Some things a man just couldn't ignore, however much he might want to.

Reaching out, he captured one of her hands in a gentle grip. The gesture was meant to be soothing, but once again he was reminded that for her it was not. She flinched as he reached out, and at his touch she grew perfectly still, perfectly quiet. Kind of like a mouse caught by the eye of a snake. It was a survival kind of stillness, the stillness of the hunted.

Well, hell, he thought again, and let go of her. He damn well better get this woman established at the Montrose place before he got to actually caring what happened to her. He didn't want to think about the kinds of things that could make a woman so scared that she would run this fast and hard with her belly full of baby.

He muttered an oath that caused her to flinch again. Seeing her reaction, he got mad. Not at her, exactly. Maybe at himself a little. Whatever, he was mad.

"Look," he said harshly, "I've never in my life hit a man or a woman who didn't hit me first, and plenty of times I didn't hit back even then. I've got nothing to prove to anyone, least of all that I'm a bigger, tougher, meaner hombre. It's none of my business who made you so skittish, and I'm not asking. Just understand, you have nothing at all to fear from *me.*"

She could almost believe him. She was surprised to realize that she *wanted* to believe him. Intellectually, she understood that not all men were abusive, but emotionally she knew only one thing—that she had once trusted, and her trust had been completely betrayed.

Micah accepted her silence for what it was, and was satisfied. He was, after all, not going to have any more to do with this lady than he absolutely couldn't avoid.

He drained his mug and scraped his chair back from the table. "I'll go see if I can find something for you to wear on your feet in the snow." At the kitchen door he hesitated and looked back. "Faith? Did you bring any winter gear except your coat?"

She shook her head, not looking at him. "I thought I had plenty of time. I didn't expect to come up here so soon."

Or so suddenly, he finished silently. Helter-skelter, harum-scarum, that was how she'd fled from Texas and her ex-husband. Fast. Suddenly. Without warning.

Well, hell.

"Does your ex know about the Montrose place?"

She blanched a little. "I don't think so."

But she was not one hundred percent sure. Great. Saying nothing more, he headed for the back hall closet, where an assortment of winter clothing had collected over the years from previous owners and occupants. He'd considered throwing everything away when he bought the place four years ago, but he couldn't bring himself to be so wasteful. Much of his adult life, as a member of the Army Special Operations branch, he'd lived and worked in underdeveloped countries. The clothes in that closet were by no means worn out, and every time he thought of dumping them, he remembered plenty of people who would have treasured such leavings. As a result, the closet was still full of unused clothes that he had no use for. Periodically he swore he'd give them to the next church rummage sale, and every time he forgot about the stuff until it was too late.

It didn't take him too long to find a lady's pair of blue boots, some bright red mittens, a long, knitted scarf and the stocking cap she'd been wearing when he met her.

"Where did you get these?" Faith asked in amazement as she looked at Micah's offerings. "Do you have a sister or daughter stashed somewhere?"

"Not that I know of. The last owners evidently did, though."

"I wonder why they left this stuff. And my—the bedroom you're letting me use, is obviously a little girl's."

He'd wondered about that himself, a time or two, but he'd never wondered hard enough or long enough to think of asking anyone about it. "I don't know. I heard the last owners had some kind of trouble, but I never poked into it."

Faith looked up at him. "You're not a very curious person."

"Oh, I get curious enough at times," he admitted grudgingly. "But the older I get, the less time I seem to have to waste. I pick and choose what I spend my efforts on these days." Also, he liked to keep life simple, but that was hard to explain to folks. Most people ran around making their lives more complex with every breath they took.

"Come on," he said gruffly. "Pull on the boots. We'll get you your first taste of a real Wyoming blizzard." And maybe it would be enough to send her flying back to gentler climates. A man could always hope for a miracle, not that he ever got one.

Thirty seconds after they stepped out into the kitchen yard, he knew he wasn't going to get his miracle this time, either. Or maybe he *had* gotten a miracle of sorts, because he was damned if he could remember the last time he'd seen anyone light up with sheer joy the way Faith did as she discovered winter. Whatever she had been through, she hadn't lost her capacity to enjoy life, and that understanding made him just a wee bit uncomfortable, because he realized that he had lost his. He couldn't remember the last time he'd been plain glad to be alive. Maybe he had never felt that way.

And surely he had never, at least since earliest childhood, turned his face up the way she did right now to the falling snow. Certainly he had never stuck out his tongue to catch a whirling flake, and he was damn sure he'd never laughed with such glee. She was going to make a good mother, this woman, he thought as he watched her laugh and romp. She hadn't entirely lost the child within her.

Turning, Faith caught sight of Micah watching her as if she were some sort of puzzle to solve. A tan cowboy hat shadowed his eyes from the porch light, but she could almost swear the corners of his mouth had lifted a little. Just a little. As if he wanted to play, too, but had convinced himself he was too old and staid. Too mature and adult.

Before she had time to talk herself out of it, she scooped up a handful of snow and began to pack it. "Is this how you make a snowball?" she asked Micah.

"That's the way," he answered, coming a step closer. "You never made a snowball, even when it snowed in San Antone?"

The wind gusted around the corner of the house, snatching up a cloud of icy snow and flinging it right in Faith's eyes. She jumped backward instinctively and gave a small shriek as the ice crystals blinded her. Immediately, she was steadied by a strong hand on her elbow.

"Are you okay?" Micah asked.

"Just startled." She ought to be afraid, she thought as Micah caught her chin and tilted her face up. She ought to be, but somehow she wasn't. She blinked at the snow on her eyelashes and felt the flakes melting coldly on her cheeks. A soft gasp escaped her, though, when his fingertips fluttered softly against her skin, gently—oh, lord, how gently!— wiping away the dampness.

"There," he said roughly, and stepped back, releasing her immediately. "Are you cold? Do you want to go in?"

"Not yet." She hesitated. "Do you—do you mind?"

"Naw." The blizzard, which until a few minutes ago had been merely an unavoidable inconvenience of another Wyoming winter, had become a wonderland for him. He wasn't sure why, and he refused to analyze it. All he knew was that he was enjoying Faith's enjoyment, and it had been a long time since he had enjoyed much of anything at all.

She was still holding her little snowball, a somewhat rounded, not very ballish ball. She glanced down at it, and then over at him, and in the instant before she hurled the snowball, he saw what was coming in the mischief that lighted her eyes.

"No," he said, and ducked to one side just as she threw. Without a moment's hesitation he scooped up snow in his bare hands and began to pack a considerably more professional piece of cold ammunition. "You asked for it," he said gruffly.

So she had, Faith thought, and reached for more snow. This time she packed it with more confidence, and as a result achieved a much more credible ball. Certain that just one hit from a snowball packed by Micah would damp her enthusiasm, she hurried to get a couple of throws in before he could strike her with a bull's-eye. By the time he finished packing his one very large, very round, very smooth snowball, Faith had hurled three of her own at him and was working on a fourth. She hadn't managed to hit him yet—he was extraordinarily fast on his feet—but she didn't think she really wanted to. What if he got annoyed?

Micah had no intention of hitting her, either, or of even coming close. He was afraid she might slip on the snow and hurt herself. Instead, he kept dodging her rounds and working on his own snowball until it began to seem that he was creating the ultimate weapon.

Faith grew breathless from her exertions and laughter. She couldn't seem to stop laughing. It was exciting and fun to be out here in the dark with the snow blowing and whirling around like fairy dust in the cold wind. For this brief, precious time, she felt young and free and unafraid.

She hit Micah finally, with a big, soft ball that splattered against the middle of his chest. His eyes remained shadowed beneath the brim of his hat, but there was something definitely wicked in the way the corners of his mouth suddenly lifted.

"Now," he said, "it's your turn."

He started toward her, holding his huge snowball out in front of him like a threat.

"You're not going to rub my face in that," Faith said, backing up.

"No. Wouldn't dream of it."

"Why don't you just throw it, then?" She backed up another step, aware of the tension creeping into her. The fun was gone, she realized abruptly. The sight of this huge man bearing down on her was no longer part of a game. It was beginning to feel horrifyingly real, a nightmare revisited. "Micah?"

He was an astute man, highly sensitized to conversational and physical nuances after years in Special Operations and law enforcement. He heard the very faint quaver of doubt enter her tone, felt her sudden tension like a pocket of high voltage electricity in the cold air. At once he halted and dropped the snowball.

"It's all right," he said gruffly. "I was just teasing you." Teasing, for Pete's sake. Micah Parish didn't tease anyone, ever. What the hell was he doing? "Let's go in before you get a chill."

Her fear evaporated the instant he stopped advancing on her, and she felt like a fool. A cruel fool. Words escaped her before she could stop them. "Micah, it's not you."

He looked away a moment before he answered. "I know, Faith. I know. Come on. I'll make some more cocoa."

"What do you know?" she asked, too surprised to move.

"That your husband abused you," he said curtly. "Is that why they put him away?"

Faith shook her head slowly as things inside her began to tremble from unnamed fears and feelings. "Not—not entirely."

"Well, it doesn't matter a whole bucket-load of manure in a barnyard, I reckon." Moving slowly, he reached for her arm. "Come on. Whether you like it or not, you've already been out here too long, and a chill won't do you a damn bit of good."

She let him guide her up the steps and into the enclosed porch, where they could shed their boots before entering the kitchen. He was a caretaker, she thought as he knelt before her and pulled the boots off her feet. Before she even had a chance to set her sock-clad foot down in one of the damp spots, he had slipped her sneaker on and tied it.

"Now the other one," he said.

She shifted her balance and steadied herself with a hand on his shoulder. He didn't even know her from Adam, yet he was taking care of her as attentively as if she were his . . . his wife. The way a wife *should* be cared for, though not the way she had been treated herself, of course.

She could feel the play of his muscles beneath her palm, and she looked down, only to see the curve of her swollen tummy and the top of Micah's head.

In that instant, as if somebody had suddenly cast her backward in time, she was six years old again, and a boy with long black hair was kneeling before her to tie the lace of her shoe.

She caught her breath, but just then Micah looked up at her, an older face. A remote face. A cold, impassive, unapproachable face. This couldn't possibly be Mike from her first summer visit here.

Could it?

"Come on," he said gruffly as he rose to his feet. "You look frozen. Let's get something hot into you."

No, she thought, her heart hammering as she allowed him to tug her gently into the kitchen. That boy was lost to her forever. Even if Micah Parish had once been that boy, he was obviously gone. One look at his face was enough to tell anyone that he had learned life's lessons the hard way.

But she looked at him as he made more cocoa and wondered.

And suddenly she was sure. The boy who had taught her to ride and swim and build forts out of hay bales was standing across the room from her, looking as if life had treated him even worse than it had treated her.

And because he hadn't said anything about knowing her, she kept the knowledge to herself. Maybe he had forgotten her. Maybe he didn't want to admit he knew her. Maybe, if he remembered her at all, he recalled her as the boss's pesky daughter who had tagged after him all the time.

So she kept quiet, drank her cocoa and headed for bed.

And wished until she ached that she could be six years old again.

Chapter 3

Micah stayed up long after Faith excused herself and went to bed. The next two days were his regular days off, so he felt no particular pressure to retire. He would still have to get up at the same time in the morning to tend the animals, but then he could go back to bed if he felt like it.

The blizzard continued to blow and howl around the corners of the house, and periodically the windows rattled from the force of a gust. There would be some fantastic drifts across the road come morning, he thought as he poured himself another hot drink. The plows probably wouldn't reach the end of his driveway before early afternoon.

And that was just fine with him. Apart from his unexpected guest, he wouldn't mind being snowbound a while. A little time cut off from the world was just what he needed after a week like this past one. At least the blizzard would keep Jeff Cumberland's mind off his mutilated cows.

Cattle mutilations occurred from time to time in the area, and after a lot of initial uproar—well before Micah's time as a deputy—people had stopped worrying about UFOs and cultists. Most ranchers still weren't entirely convinced that this was some strange behavior on the part of coyotes, but there was little useful evidence that it was anything else. It was one of those troubling things that people finally learned to live with because they had no other choice.

Micah, who'd seen his first mutilation four years ago during his second day on the job, still found them disturbing. The state lab said the seemingly surgical precision of the wounds was an effect of shrinking flesh around the wounds, and Micah figured they were probably right, but he'd never seen anything quite like it. And he still had trouble believing that a predator would kill a cow and then eat nothing but the tongue and testes or udders.

Two days ago Jeff Cumberland had called the Conard County Sheriff's Office, madder than all get-out. Not one but three of his cattle had been found mutilated in widely separated areas of his ranch. Micah was a highly skilled, experienced tracker, so the Sheriff, Nathan Tate, had asked him to take a look. Micah had looked, had spent the last two days looking, in fact, and had found not one damn thing.

Sitting in his living room now, listening to quiet country-western music on his stereo, he cradled his mug of cocoa on his chest and thought over what he'd seen, and what he hadn't seen.

The weather had been cold and dry for the last month, so the ground had been hard as rock. Micah hadn't expected to find anything as useful as a paw print to identify the predator, but there should have been a sign of some kind. Circling away from the dead animals in an ever widening search, he should have found spoor at least. Something, somewhere, should have betrayed the fact that some hunter had made his meal on that damn cow. There hadn't been a thing. Not a thing. Not around any of the animals. Micah was sure of that. There wasn't even a shadow of a doubt in his mind.

All indicators said those animals had been killed somewhere else and dumped at various places around Jeff's ranch. Micah had heard that claim before, and he had al-

ways been inclined to brush it aside, thinking that most
people could easily miss the slight signs an experienced
tracker would recognize. This time, he was ready to make
the claim himself, because he knew his own skill, and he
knew he hadn't missed anything. There had been nothing to
miss.

And that didn't add up.

Now this blizzard would take care of the whole thing.
They wouldn't be able to look for anything else, and the
state lab was bound to send down the same results when it
finished with the carcasses. Jeff had asked Micah if he was
just wasting time and money sending the carcasses in for
examination, but Micah hadn't been able to answer. Something just didn't feel right. It was itching at the back of his
neck like unfinished business, nagging at the corners of his
mind.

He'd taken a lot of photos of the scene. Most of them
were at the lab being developed, but he had some instant
photos out in the glove box of his Blazer, and for a minute
or two he toyed with the idea of going out to get them. Then
the wind howled again, and he smiled ruefully into his cup.
Nope, it could wait. He'd spent too many years at the mercy
of the elements, and tonight he just wanted to enjoy his
freedom to stay in from the cold.

By 9:30 the next morning, Micah had plowed the full
length of his driveway with the heavy blade attached to the
front of his Blazer. Every year in Conard County, the plows
were attached to the front of the Sheriff's vehicles on Oc-
tober fifteenth. In this isolated area, lives could depend on
a deputy being able to get through on the worst roads. Last
year Nate had raised funds and bought a helicopter for
emergencies, but people still needed to be able to plow.

Snow was still whipping and whirling around and the sky
had a leaden look to it, when he reached the county road
only to discover that, as he'd expected, the county plows
hadn't been through yet. He had hoped they had though, he
thought as he turned the Blazer and headed back toward the

house, largely because he wanted Faith Williams safely ensconced in a motel.

It wasn't that she was a troublesome houseguest. Far from it. He hadn't even seen her this morning, though he had thought he heard her stirring when he came downstairs. No, the trouble was himself. Something about Faith Williams was making him aware of a certain...emptiness in his own life. The existence of holes. Gaps.

He muttered an obscenity and down-shifted as he pulled into the yard near the kitchen door. Turning, he dropped the plow to the ground and cleared the yard between the house and stable.

It was just sex, he told himself. He hadn't gotten laid lately. Not in a long time, as a matter of fact. Not since two years ago when he went to Chicago on vacation to pay a little visit to Billy Bald Eagle. Billy, an old Army buddy, had introduced him to a school teacher who had a thing for Indians. God, how he hated that! Didn't always keep him from taking advantage of it, though. But since he didn't believe in soiling his own nest, he considered the ladies of Conard County to be off-limits, and a man was bound to get a little hungry at times.

He was hungry right now. No use denying it. Sexual irritation was running in his blood, making his nerves acutely sensitive, drawing his attention to things he would ordinarily never notice, like the tight fit of his jeans. Or the way Faith Williams smelled. God, that woman's scent was sheer, distilled *female*. Clean, sweet temptation.

So, no matter how quiet and unobtrusive the lady was, she had to go. Soon. The sooner the better.

Muttering another curse, he parked the Blazer by the door and climbed out. He wanted some coffee, and he couldn't put off going inside a moment longer. There was just so much tending the animals needed, just so much plowing he could do. Damn, he was acting like a foolish kid, hiding out here like this.

The kitchen was filled with the aroma of freshly brewed coffee when he stepped in. Looking around, he saw that his guest had not only made a fresh pot, but she had also cleaned up the kitchen, giving it a sparkle he seldom bothered with. And from the other side of the house he heard his vacuum cleaner growling. Hell's bells! Forgetting his desire for a mug of coffee, he headed for the living room, determined to stop the foolish woman before she hurt herself.

This morning she wore black slacks and a cotton-candy pink maternity top that stopped him dead in the doorway. There was something so softly feminine about that top that he felt like a stranger in his own world. She turned to smile at him, and Micah came face-to-face with all the things he had sacrificed and all the things he had fought his entire life to preserve. She was satin and silk, soft femininity and gentle perfumes, milky skin and blue eyes. He'd seen women like her many times, but always from the far side of a glass barrier he couldn't cross. They weren't meant for him, these gentle creatures, but they embodied all the things he had dedicated his life to protecting. He had lived on the dark underside so that women could be silky and soft and gentle for other men, so they wouldn't have to scramble in the dirt and live in privation and oppression.

It sounded stupid as hell, and he would have gone to the stake before he would ever have admitted it out loud, but somewhere deep inside he had always cherished a kind of icon of womanhood that was in diametric opposition to all the women he had ever known. Inside him, he believed in a woman who wasn't grasping, selfish and cheap. A giving, loving, generous woman. A woman who would bring softness to a life that was all hard edges and jagged peaks.

"Micah?" Faith's smile faded as he stood there and stared at her with an expression that was almost a scowl. Her heart skipped and began to race as she wondered what she had done to anger him.

His scowl deepened. "Leave that vacuum alone, woman. You'll hurt yourself."

"A little vacuuming won't—"

"Damn it, you're pregnant. You shouldn't be doing this kind of work!"

She hadn't been mistreated long enough to become totally crushed. She could still feel defiant, and right now she did. It sparked in her eyes, though she didn't know it, and tightened the soft, lush line of her mouth. Inside her, words struggled to be free, words telling him that she was capable of doing a stupid little job such as vacuuming, that being pregnant didn't turn her into a weakling or an invalid, but she bit the words back. She *had* been mistreated long enough to fear angering a man.

He saw the defiance rise in her, saw her back stiffen and her chin come up, saw the snap of it in her eyes, and he felt the craziest, most contradictory urge to grin. He stifled it. "Go on," he said gruffly. "Spit it out, little lady."

She didn't like the way he called her "little lady." It was derogatory, and she suspected he meant it to be. Again words filled her throat and caught there, unspoken.

He waited a moment, then turned away in utter indifference. If she wouldn't speak up for herself, it wasn't his problem. And he wasn't going to let it become his problem.

Faith watched the big man turn away, and his indifference prodded her more sharply than anything he had said. For too long, nothing she had felt had mattered. Her feelings had been discounted and ignored. She had been made to feel insignificant if the right shirt wasn't ironed or whether dinner wasn't ready exactly on time.

In the past couple of months she had made some headway, with help. The changes were small, but lately, for the first time in her life, she had begun to believe that what she felt *was* important, as important as what anybody else thought or felt. And if her feelings were important, then nobody, *nobody,* had a right to trample on them.

Hardly aware of what she was doing, she charged after Micah into the kitchen and caught up with him just as he was pouring a mug of coffee.

"Just one moment, Deputy Parish," she said. Her voice quavered, and shock at her own temerity tried to silence her. She clasped her hands and felt her heart climb into her throat. Had she lost her mind?

Micah heard her uncertainty, her fright. He turned slowly and leaned back against the counter with his legs casually crossed at the ankles, trying to look as unthreatening as possible for a man of his size and untamed appearance.

"Yes, ma'am?" he asked, keeping his voice quiet.

"I..." Oh, God, she was having a panic attack. There suddenly wasn't enough air in the room, and her heart raced so rapidly that there seemed to be no space between beats. Nonetheless, she forced the words out. "I...don't like the way...you t-talked to me!"

Her words were little more than a ragged gasp, giving him a clear notion of just how much it cost her to speak them. He felt a glimmer of admiration. "Well, I reckon I can understand that," he agreed mildly.

Faith, who had been expecting lightning bolts to strike her dead for her effrontery, felt her mouth fall open. "Y-you can?" she asked in a whisper.

Micah folded his arms across his broad chest, giving her another measure of security. "Sure can," he said. "Would you like some herbal tea? I keep it for a neighbor lady. She's pregnant, too."

Faith edged into the kitchen, stunned by his calm reaction to a situation that for her had held all the potential deadliness of a nuclear bomb. "Which neighbor lady is that?"

"Mandy Laird. She and her husband will be your nearest neighbors on the other side."

"Oh. When is she due?"

"Late May. Tea?"

"Uh, yes. Please." She edged closer, still amazed that nothing bad had happened to her. "Uh, Micah?"

"Yeah?"

"You aren't...you aren't mad at me?"

He turned from filling the tea kettle. "Now why in the hell would I be mad at you?"

"For..." For what? For telling him she didn't like the way he talked to her? That sounded incredibly foolish. She took her courage into her hands once more. "I don't like being called little lady. You're talking down to me as if I were a child, and I am not a child."

He set the kettle on the stove and turned on the gas burner. "Reckon that's a matter of perspective," he said in his slow, deep voice. "I'm forty-three years old, little lady. I've seen things that make grown men weep and sweat with terror. I figure that makes me about as old as Methuselah. However old you are, you're still a far sight younger than me."

There was no way she could retort to that, except possibly to claim that four years of marriage to Frank Williams had made her about as old as Methuselah herself.

She watched him move around the kitchen with athletic grace, taking the box of herbal tea from the cupboard, opening the packet that held the tea bag with hands so big it seemed impossible they could perform such a delicate task. The kettle whistled, and he poured hot water into the cup.

As she accepted the cup from him, Faith looked up into obsidian eyes set in a harsh face. In that instant a trickle of awareness passed through her, a little niggling thing that touched her core with warmth and made her knees feel suddenly weak.

"Easy." He steadied the cup as a tremor passed through her. "Faith? What's wrong?"

Wrong? Only that she was standing closer to a man than she could believe, and doing it of her own free will. Only that some part of her was thinking of that man touching her, *wanting* that man to touch her. God, she knew better! Didn't she? Oh God!

The cup fell from her hand and shattered, splashing hot tea everywhere. Faith's slacks protected her as she turned and ran from the kitchen.

Micah took a quick step after her, then caught himself. Well, hell. She had her problems, which he damn well knew, and he wasn't going to get any more involved than he already was. No way. Uh-uh. No sir.

Yet he took another step after her anyway. Damn, he was a sucker for the wounded of the world. He sure as hell ought to know better by now.

The phone rang, giving him a blessed out. Now he couldn't go after Faith and he didn't have to feel guilty about his reluctance.

"Morning, Micah," said the gravelly voice of Sheriff Nathan Tate. "I just received a rap sheet from San Antonio. You want to tell me why you're so all-fired interested in a guy named Francis Williams? And why he's so important that this rap sheet was hand carried up here by a Texas Ranger?"

Micah's knock on her bedroom door startled Faith. She sat up immediately, unconsciously pulling the pillow over her stomach like protective armor. She wasn't ready to face Micah yet, but it seemed he was going to give her no choice. He probably wanted to demand an explanation for her weird behavior, and he was certainly entitled to one. Or maybe he wanted to yell at her about the broken cup and the mess. Frank would have yelled about it. Frank probably would have hit her two or three times and then stood over her while she cleaned it up. He might even have kicked her while she was on her knees. He'd done that a couple of times. She was always very careful not to break anything when he was around.

"Faith, I need to talk to you," he called through the door.

"I'm sorry about the cup," she said uneasily.

The cup? In the hallway, Micah stared at her door in perplexity. His thoughts had moved far away from the shattered remains of the cup that still rested in the middle of his kitchen floor. "Don't worry about the cup," he said roughly. "The damn cup doesn't matter. Faith, I need to talk to you. Can I come in a minute?"

The fact that he was asking finally penetrated her uneasiness. Frank wouldn't have asked. He would have come through that door all the madder because she had closed it.

"Come in," she said. Nervously, she scooted farther back on the bed and hugged the pillow more tightly.

Micah saw it all, of course, but he had too much on his mind to think about it now. "I just had a call from my boss. Do you know a Texas Ranger named Garrett Hancock?"

Her breath escaped in a whoosh. "Yes. Oh yes! He saved . . . He helped me. Is he hurt? Is something wrong?"

"He's not hurt," Micah hastened to reassure her. "He wants to see you, though. He's here in Wyoming."

"Here? Why?" Her eyes were wide with surprise. And then understanding shook her. "Frank. He's the one who arrested Frank. Oh, my God, he followed Frank up here. . . ."

"No. No." Automatically, he crossed to the bed, intending to reassure her, but when he saw her flinch backward he stopped, remembering that this woman had no reason to trust any man. "He's here because I sent for your husband's rap sheet last night. I wanted to know what you were up against. Anyhow, I guess Hancock thought I might have run across Frank or had dealings of some kind with him."

Her heart had been beating fit to burst, and now it didn't want to slow down. It *couldn't* slow down, not with Micah standing over her, making her wonder what it would be like not to be afraid. Oh God, she was so tired of being afraid!

Moving slowly, very slowly, Micah sat on the edge of the bed and faced her. She watched him with huge eyes and flaring nostrils, with exactly the same kind of wild fear he had seen in a horse's eyes when faced with a rattler. She would bolt if he gave her half a chance.

So he didn't give her a chance. He wasn't sure why he was doing this, but he knew someone had to try to help this woman over her terror, and there didn't seem to be any other volunteers in sight. Knowing this was another deadly mistake in the chain of mistakes he'd been making since he set eyes on her, he reached out and took her trembling shoulders. Then, ignoring her whimpered protest, ignoring her terror, he hauled her up against his chest and wrapped her

in his arms. "It's okay," he said softly. "Just rest against
me. It's okay."

She didn't fight him this time, but whether that was good
or bad he couldn't say. It might be terror keeping her there,
as evidenced by the ripping shudders that tore through her
body, or it might be the early beginnings of trust. He didn't
know, and at this point he really didn't think it mattered. It
was going to take more than one hug to make this woman
trust him or any other man, just like it would take more than
one good woman to change his mind about the whole gen-
der.

He understood the chain reaction of panic, understood
that she would need time to calm down again. Unconscious
of what he was doing, he began to rock her gently, unaware
of making soothing sounds in the back of his throat. In far-
off lands, under conditions that defied description, he had
calmed others this way, hardly even aware of doing it. He
had held terrified children, dying men and injured women,
and he'd done it because it needed doing. The gift of human touch and human warmth was the most priceless gift
in life, and too damn rare, from what he'd seen. As long as
a man had strength in his arms, it was his responsibility to
give that gift wherever it was needed. Micah believed that.
He believed it at a level so deep it wasn't even conscious. He
just acted on it.

Faith's panic receded, quieted by the incredible gentleness of this savage-looking man. With her ear pressed to his
heart and his arms snug around her, she felt safe. The feeling stunned her, and for the longest time she could only lie
against his chest and try to absorb the miracle of feeling safe
for the first time in years.

"Have you seen a doctor about this panic?" Micah asked
eventually, when he realized she was calm and nearly limp
against him.

"My family doctor wanted to give me tranquilizers."

"You're pregnant."

"Exactly. I wouldn't take them, anyway. I don't want to
be doped up." She could hardly believe she was having a

conversation like this with a man. A man who was a cop. Her heart gave a single, uncomfortable lurch and then settled down again. There was no threat in hands and arms so gentle. Not at this moment, at any rate. Surely she could be allowed, for just this little space of time, to seize this feeling and store it up against the future?

Micah cleared his throat. "Sometimes...sometimes when somebody's been through something really bad, professional help can be useful."

She nodded, unconsciously rubbing her cheek against his chest. Micah was conscious of it, though. He was suddenly acutely aware of exactly how many days and nights he had been celibate. His body responded in a healthy fashion to this woman's femaleness, and he clenched his teeth in self-denial. She wasn't his type, he reminded himself. She wasn't looking for a casual, uncomplicated relationship. Hell, she wasn't in the market for *any* kind of relationship.

"I was seeing a psychologist," Faith said after a moment, and moved a little closer, nearly forgetting everything in a growing desire to be just a little nearer to the warmth, the heat, the strength and solidity, of this man who held her with a gentleness she would have sworn no man was capable of.

"Was it helping?"

"A little." She sighed, finding the thud of his heart beneath her to be a wonderful, somehow reassuring, sound. Her hand, with a will all its own, crept around his waist, hugging him back. Just a little. He probably didn't even notice.

But he did, and his throat tightened. He pushed down the feeling. "I don't know if we have anyone nearby who can keep on helping you, Faith."

"It doesn't matter. What it all comes down to in the end is time. I mean, yes, it helped to have someone tell me that it wasn't my fault that Frank beat me. I needed someone to say I had nothing to be ashamed of, that I hadn't done anything wrong. It was nice to hear, Micah, but believing it is something else."

"I know." Yeah, he knew. "What made you come running up here? Why do you think Frank's going to hurt you again?" It seemed to him that if the man had escaped from custody, coming after his wife would be the last thing on his mind. The guy would have to be a real fool to show up the one place where the authorities would be expecting him—wherever Faith was.

"Three—" Her voice cracked, and she started again, growing tense against him. She didn't want to think about this, wanted to dive under the pillow and pretend that none of this had ever happened, but she had an equally strong need to explain to this gentle, savage-looking man just why she was acting in such crazy, inexplicable ways. "Three months ago, while he was out on bail, he came to my apartment. He was mad because I had filed for divorce and he got even angrier when he realized I was pregnant. Why he was mad, I don't know. He was the one who forced himself on me. I shouldn't have told him, but I didn't want him to hurt the baby. I thought it would help keep him out. I tried so hard to keep him out." Her voice had thickened, and her breath started coming in huge sobbing gulps. "When he got in, I tried to get away, but I couldn't. He was so strong...." This time a real sob escaped her, and Micah's arms tightened.

"It's okay, Faith," he said roughly. "It's okay. You're safe here."

She drew another sobbing breath and buried her face against Micah's shoulder. "Garrett Hancock saved me," she said in a choked voice. "Frank was going to kill me. When Frank got out on bail, Garrett was watching him, hoping he might get some more evidence or something. I think...I think maybe Garrett thought I knew more about Frank's doings than I'd said. I don't know. I just know he was there...." Her voice shattered, and she began to weep in earnest.

She regained control swiftly, though. Micah figured she'd had a lot of practice at hiding her feelings.

"Anyway," she said when she again lay quietly against him, "they rescinded Frank's bail because of what he did to me. He's been in the county jail awaiting trial, and as long as he was locked up, I felt... Then he got out. And I wasn't going to wait around to see if he came after me again. I just wasn't going to!"

"No, of course not." Somehow his fingers had worked their way into her long, silky hair, and he massaged the back of her head gently. "Don't you have any family to help you get through this, Faith? Or friends?"

"The friends are all Frank's," she said bitterly. "As for family, they're all dead except my stepsister, and she's in a convent. What's *she* going to do?"

Nothing, he guessed. And there was no way, now, that he would be able to dump her at the Lazy Rest Motel. No way. Hell. He wouldn't sleep for wondering if Frank would manage to find her in such an obvious place.

The baby chose that moment to kick, but instead of simply meeting the soft side of Faith's womb, the little foot met the hard wall of Micah's stomach.

"Well, I'll be . . ." he breathed quietly.

Faith glanced up and caught her breath. His obsidian gaze was fastened to the swell of her abdomen, and there was no mistaking the reverence and awe on his face. For months now she had longed to share this miracle with someone, to share the wonder and excitement of the life growing within her.

"Does it hurt?" Micah asked gruffly.

"No. It's just a little poke." Here was her opportunity to share, and she didn't even think to hesitate. Seizing his hand, she pressed it to her womb, and they both held their breath as they waited. A minute passed, then another, and just as Faith was about to give up, she felt it, the feeling of movement, and then the soft little push from the inside. Right against the palm of Micah's huge hand.

"Well, hell." It was his favorite expression, and it was totally inadequate to the moment. He lifted his eyes to Faith's, and then a small, genuine smile cracked the granite of his features. "Well, hell," he said again, and felt another poke.

Something about the way he was looking at her made her feel as if she had done something totally awesome, though she hadn't done anything spectacular at all. And something about the way he smiled at her made her smile back.

Then, suddenly, as if the unfamiliar feeling of smiles on their faces had jarred them both back to reality, Micah became irritated at himself, and Faith became edgy at being so close to him. An instant later she had slipped away from him and he was already moving toward the door.

"The road should be plowed in a couple of hours," Micah said over his shoulder. "After lunch, we'll go into town to talk to your Texas Ranger."

Boots, Micah thought as he turned the Blazer onto the freshly plowed county road. The woman needed boots. She was wearing the blue boots again, but he was sure they didn't fit properly. She needed boots and mittens and a warmer hat, and snow pants.... She needed a million things, but he would see to the most essential ones before he brought her home tonight. He leaned over and tweaked the heater up a little higher for her benefit, wondering if he had lost his ever-loving mind. It was one thing to rescue someone from imminent danger. It was another to adopt them.

Sitting beside him, Faith tried not to keep looking at him, but he might as well have been a lodestone. Time and time again her gaze was drawn to him, and each time she looked at him she felt a strange, tugging response in her womb.

He was, beyond any doubt, the epitome of masculinity. Even his shoulder-length black hair, with its few betraying threads of gray, did nothing to diminish his powerful male impact. Beneath the brim of his Stetson he wore mirrored, aviator-style sunglasses that seemed to complement the harshly chiseled planes of his face. He looked as forbidding as the snow-drifted, barren countryside outside the car.

She wondered what had made him so hard. That hardness was a veneer, she thought, because she had seen something of the man beneath, a man who opened his house and his arms to a frightened stray, and who offered his protection for no better reason than that it was needed.

Biting her lower lip, she looked away and wished she had the courage to question him a little bit. What had happened to him in the twenty-five years since she had last seen him? Why had the quiet, gentle youth she remembered turned into such a hard, guarded man?

He turned his head toward her and caught her staring at him. She felt color rise hotly into her cheeks as she stared at her own distorted reflection in the mirrored lenses.

"You look like a curious kitten," he said in a deep, rumbly voice. "What are you wondering about?"

Suddenly she was wondering about a whole pack of things, and none of them had to do with the facts of his past. The question had held a sensual undertone, and as inexperienced as she was, Faith nevertheless picked up on it. Surely she had misunderstood? This man couldn't possibly find her sexually attractive! Not when she was misshapen with almost six months of pregnancy!

He had returned his attention to the road almost as soon as he spoke, leaving her to wonder why the thought that this man might find her attractive didn't terrify her. And leaving her to conclude that he couldn't possibly find her attractive, anyway, so her terror, or lack of it, was irrelevant.

She stole another glance his way and again felt the impact of their differences. He was all male, and she was a woman who understood better than many the threat of a man's greater size and strength. This man surely outweighed her by a good hundred pounds, and he towered over her by more than a foot. He was considerably older than she, vastly more experienced. And he was solid. She felt that about him, just as she felt he was utterly self-contained. He needed nothing and no one, yet anyone who needed him would not be disappointed. He was a rock to lean on.

Dear Lord, how she wanted to lean! For so long she had been alone with her demons and her terrors, without any-

one to turn to for even a shred of comfort or support. The
strength of her need gave her breath a ragged sound as she
quickly turned her head and looked out the window. It
wouldn't be fair to Micah to lean on him, of course. And it
wouldn't be good for her, either. She had a child to think of,
a child who was going to need a strong mother who had
found direction in her life.

She needed to get her act together during the next several
months, and letting someone else handle her problems
wasn't the way to achieve that. It was time for Faith Montrose Williams to finish growing up.

There was bitterness in the thought, because she had been
raised to be a wife, to make a home for a man who would
deal with all the realities while she created a haven for him.
Nobody had bothered to suggest to her that she might have
to be self-supporting, or that a child might depend on her
meager, uneducated abilities. Nobody had ever warned her
that being a wife might be a nightmare, that the man who
was supposed to care for her might routinely beat her bloody
and then try to kill her. Nobody had ever warned her that a
man might be so jealous of his own carelessly planted seed
growing in her belly that he would kick her in the womb.

God, she felt so betrayed! She could still hear her own
mother's voice telling her not to let anyone know she was
smart, because boys didn't like brainy girls. She could still
hear the naggings that she had to be sexy, but not bright,
that she had to make a man feel important, even at the cost
of her own intelligence and pride. She had to be a reflection
of a man's whims. Her own needs and wishes were to take
second place. A good wife was one who kept her man
happy, whatever it took. Yes, she could hear it all, and in
retrospect she could see how she had been betrayed. She had
never been asked what she liked or wanted, had only been
told over and over again what appealed to men. It didn't
take a genius to see the implication that was never stated:
that *she* didn't matter.

And when her husband was unhappy and hit her, it was
her fault, of course. If she had kept him happy, he wouldn't

have hit her. If she hadn't served chicken, he wouldn't have hit her. If she hadn't fallen asleep before he got home, he wouldn't have hit her. If she hadn't spoken pleasantly to that nice clerk at the store, he wouldn't have hit her. If she had known how to be a woman, how to be a wife, he wouldn't have hit her. It was all her fault, because if she had mastered a woman's role, which was to please a man, her man wouldn't have been so unhappy with her. Each blow, each curse, had labeled her a failure as a woman. And each blow, each curse, each criticism, had made her feel more guilty, more ashamed, more deserving of the violence he showered on her.

"But it wasn't my fault!"

"Faith?"

She had been so caught up in her thoughts, in her anger and grief, that she only now realized she was crying again, and that she must have spoken at least some of her thoughts out loud, because Micah had pulled to a stop.

"Faith?"

She refused to look at him as humiliation began a slow burn in the pit of her stomach, right next to the rage that never faded, the icy, cold knot of anger that never eased. "Sorry," she said thickly. "I cry a lot since I got pregnant."

"You need to cry," he said roughly. "Here." He handed her a wad of tissues and then shifted into gear again. Least said, soonest mended. It was time to quit getting in deeper.

Thankful he didn't question her, Faith wiped her eyes and sniffled her tears away. God, she was so tired of it all—tired of being afraid, of feeling sad, tired of being tired of everything.

By the time Micah pulled up in front of the Sheriff's office, she once again had a grip on her feelings.

The office was right on the main street of Conard City, in the shadow of the courthouse. Most of the town looked to be of recent vintage, but the courthouse had been constructed by someone with a yen for Victorian style Gothic architecture, and the result produced a rather pleasant feeling of age and charm. The Sheriff's office was in a corner storefront overlooking the courthouse lawn and most of the town's businesses. On this cold, snowy afternoon, there were few people about, giving the town an almost deserted air.

Inside, Micah guided Faith through the front office with a nod for Charlie Huskins, who had just returned to duty after being wounded two months earlier during a kidnapping attempt. It was the most excitement Conard County had seen in years, but Micah had the uneasy feeling they were about to have a lot more excitement.

"How're you feeling, Charlie?" Micah asked.

"Great. Just great." Charlie's smile was broad and warm. He figured he owed Micah his life, because Micah was the one who had found him and carried him out of the rugged terrain where he had been shot. "Nate and the Ranger are waiting for you in Nate's office."

Micah nodded and touched the small of Faith's back gently. "Through there," he said, nodding toward Nate's door.

Faith tensed, every instinct telling her to turn around and walk out. It was cowardly, she knew, but it seemed as if Frank were going to haunt her forever, as if she would never be able to escape from all the fallout. If it was a bad dream, she wished it would all just go away. But of course it wouldn't.

Because his life had so often depended on it, Micah had become an astute judge of men. He approved of Garrett Hancock the instant he clapped eyes on him, and after a moment Hancock evidently came to a similar conclusion about Micah.

Sheriff Nathan Tate was an old army buddy of Micah's. They had served together in Vietnam long ago and kept in touch over the years. Four years ago, when Micah had retired from the army, he had stopped in Conard City to say hello to Nate and accepted a position as a deputy. He had never regretted his decision.

Except possibly right now, Micah thought grimly as they all settled into chairs around Nate's desk. Things here were getting out of hand. What had started out as a neighborly hand to a stranded motorist looked like it was about to get messy and complicated.

"Are you doing all right, Faith?" Garrett Hancock wanted to know. He looked, Micah thought, like a successful Texas oilman in his neatly tailored gray suit and lizard skin cowboy boots. When he moved, the badge pinned to his shirt became visible. "You weren't hurt when your car went off the road?"

"No, I'm fine, Garrett." And relieved that Micah had evidently explained her present circumstances. "Deputy Parish has been very kind."

Garrett nodded to Micah, as if he considered Micah's help to Faith to be a personal favor. "You took off like lightning, Faith. Nobody knew where you'd got to, and I was more than a little worried."

"I didn't want to hang around when I heard Frank had escaped." All her attention focused on the Ranger. "Is he coming this way, Garrett? Is that why you came all the way up here?"

Garrett smiled crookedly and shook his head. "I came flying up here because late last night the San Antonio police got a request for Frank's rap sheet from the Conard County Sheriff's Office and I thought Frank might be here. Now that I know *you're* here, I consider it a definite possibility that he might show up in the area." He looked at Nate and Micah.

"So let's have the story," Nate said. "I take a personal interest in the doings in my county."

"Francis Avery Williams," Garrett said, "is a former San Antonio police officer. He's charged with a whole range of felonies, some of them federal. It appears he's been the kingpin of a large drug smuggling operation, that he was operating several houses of prostitution, and that he had his fingers in a fencing operation. He's also wanted for the attempted murder of his wife, and I would personally like to wrap my hands around his throat." He smiled without humor.

"He's been responsible for shepherding drug shipments up from the border, and we've begun to suspect that he has some major organized crime connections, though we still haven't put together all the pieces on that. It appears that Williams isn't a cop who went bad but a criminal who became a cop to get on the inside track. Nor was he the only cop involved in the drug trafficking. We expect to make another ten or fifteen arrests very shortly."

"No small-time operator, then," Nate remarked.

"Far from it. All the alarms went off when we got your fax last night, because we've long suspected he had at least one out-of-state connection, but we haven't been able to put our finger on where." He turned to Faith. "Does Frank know about your father's ranch?"

Faith's hands were knotted so tightly into fists that her short nails dug into her palms. "I don't know," she said tautly. "I didn't think so, but I'm not completely sure." It was the nightmare again, she thought despairingly. Questions about Frank coming at her from every angle, no one ever able to believe how very little she knew about the man she had lived with for four years. An endless, awful nightmare, until she wished she could just throw back her head and howl.

And suddenly, unexpectedly, into her unending nightmare, came a gentle, reassuring, strong touch. Micah, inwardly cursing his own weakness, reached out and closed his large hand on her small, soft shoulder. That touch was like a beacon in the night, telling her that even if she couldn't escape the nightmare, she wasn't alone in it.

"Is there a possibility he could have known?" Garrett asked.

Faith tried to think, but somehow her mind kept veering to the large hand on her shoulder, toward the man who had touched her womb with such reverence only a couple of hours ago. And why, she wondered raggedly, did they keep questioning her as if she had done something wrong? She wasn't the criminal, but Micah was the only one who seemed to understand that.

Something inside her snapped like a string stretched too tightly. "I don't know," she managed to whisper, and then, in a single, swift movement, heedless of what Garrett or Nathan Tate might think of her, she swung around in her chair and buried her face tightly against Micah's powerful shoulder.

Well, hell, he thought. But the surge of protectiveness that rose in him was fierce, and his arms closed around her, supporting her, sustaining her.

Slowly he lifted his head and looked straight at Garrett. "That's enough, Hancock. She's not the criminal here. I'm not letting you or anyone else badger her."

Well, hell, Micah thought, looking into Nate's face and seeing a reflection of his own surprise. That sure tore it. He was a one-finger pushover for anybody in trouble. Yep, he sure was.

Chapter 4

It was bad enough to announce to the Ranger and his own boss that his objectivity was shot to hell. But not as bad as putting his arms around this woman and letting *her* know that she could count on him to place himself between her and any threat.

That counted as sheer stupidity on his part. He'd been around the block enough times to know that there were women who wouldn't hesitate to use that kind of knowledge to take advantage of a man and tie him up in so many knots that he'd never get the kinks out. What did he know about Faith Williams except that as a six-year-old she'd stolen his heart? Twenty-five years had passed since then, and she could be any kind of person now. God, at his age he shouldn't be a sucker for icy blond hair and sad blue eyes.

The sheriff opened the door of his office and called out to Charlie Huskins. "Charlie, you take Mrs. Williams into that empty office across the way and see that she gets a hot cup of that herbal tea I keep around here for Mandy Laird."

Faith sat up reluctantly, hating to leave the security of Micah's embrace, but aware that she was being pointedly dismissed. She hesitated, looking deep into Micah's dark eyes and registering his complex tangle of feelings. "I'm sorry, Deputy," she said unsteadily.

Rising, she lifted her chin and looked straight at Nate, realizing that, from Micah's point of view, he was the important person in the room. The sheriff must be wondering what had gotten into Micah to defend a woman who was supposedly a stranger. From the outside Micah's actions would certainly appear unprofessional, and Faith felt a need to defend him against that presumption. "Deputy Parish and I were acquainted many years ago, Sheriff. In fact, he was like a brother to me the first summer I spent up here with my father. He naturally feels protective."

So she remembered him after all, Micah realized with unexpected pleasure. He didn't want her defending him, but on the other hand, it said something about her that she wanted to. Maybe Faith still had some of that little girl in her, after all. Not that it was going to make any difference. His mystical, superstitious side kept trying to tell him that these events were destined, that there wasn't a damn thing to do but plunge ahead and hang on for the ride. It was difficult for a man with the blood of shamans strong in his veins to believe he had found Faith by accident on the road yesterday.

When the door closed behind Faith, Nate sank into his chair and regarded Micah across the scarred desktop. "You know better than that, you crusty old Injun."

One corner of Micah's mouth took a short, upward hike. Nate had been teasing him that way since their days in the jewel green jungles of Southeast Asia. "Reckon so," he agreed.

"She wouldn't be the towheaded tyke in your wallet, would she?"

Micah gave a short, silent nod of confirmation. The hell of living in Conard County with friends like Nate Tate and Ransom Laird, who went all the way back to the Stone Age with him, was that they knew things like that about him.

They knew what he carried in his wallet; they knew what made him sweat and what made him scream.

"Well, that explains it," Nate allowed. He'd known about the picture, but this was the first time he'd ever connected it with Jason Montrose's daughter who, as a summer visitor nearly twenty years his junior, had seldom crossed his path. "I just about forgot you worked out there that summer. So, what do you think about this, old son?"

Micah spared the Ranger a glance. Garrett Hancock, surprisingly, didn't seem disturbed by these developments. "I think," Micah said after a moment, "that she's been mistreated something fierce. That she's scared to death, that she came here to try to find some kind of safety and security for herself and her child. You Rangers have a different idea?"

Garrett's lips tightened for a moment: "We just can't afford to take chances, Parish. The woman was married to Frank Williams for four years. It's entirely possible that she may have had some idea of his activities. She may know things she doesn't realize she knows. We can't afford to overlook that possibility."

"Badgering her isn't going to get anything out of her," Micah said flatly. "She panics the minute a man gets on her case over anything. Hell, she panicked last night when I said something sarcastic. That man must've been all over her all the time."

"He was rough on her," Garrett agreed. "You might be interested to know that on two occasions she called the police for help. The first time, when they arrived and found out that Williams was a cop, they walked away. An hour later a neighbor brought her to the hospital with a broken arm, two black eyes and a lacerated scalp. She claimed to have fallen down the stairs."

Micah swore savagely, and even Nate looked a little stunned.

"The next time, the cops didn't even bother to answer the call," Garrett said. "Faith wound up in the hospital that night, too. She never called the police again. Not even the night he tried to kill her by stabbing her. By the time I broke down the door, he'd inflicted a couple of pretty deep wounds."

Garrett sighed and eyed Micah grimly. "Personally, Parish, I don't think she knows a thing about what Williams was up to. Unfortunately, mine isn't the only opinion that matters. And I'm worried that Williams will come after her. After what I saw that night three months ago, I don't think the man will quit. He wants her dead."

"Why?" So much for his notion that Williams would have the sense to stay away from the one place he would be looked for.

"Why?" Garrett shrugged. "The psychologist who interviewed Williams said it's simply so nobody else can have her."

So nobody else can have her. Micah ran that assessment around and around in his head as he drove himself and Faith back to his ranch. Before leaving Conard City, he had taken her to Freitag's Mercantile and gotten her properly garbed for the weather. Then he'd stopped by Bayard's Garage and told them where her Honda could be found. Dirk Bayard promised to dig it out and call with an estimate in the next day or so.

When Faith quietly protested that Micah had better things to do with his time and she would take care of things herself, he simply looked at her with his black-as-night eyes and didn't say a word. Faith subsided immediately.

There had been a few more stops, first at the rural electric co-op office, where she paid the required deposit and arranged for her power to be connected. Then came the telephone office, where the procedure was repeated, and the propane company, who promised to check out her gas appliances when they filled the tank.

And everywhere they went, people treated Faith like family. Warm smiles met her, people promised to look after her needs immediately, and she was made to feel as if she had always lived here.

Inevitably, she turned sideways on the seat and watched Micah as he drove. He had said nothing one way or the other about her claim that they were old friends from her childhood, and she wondered if he remembered, or if he thought she was making it up.

"You're looking curious again," he growled when they were a few miles out of town. "Go ahead and ask. I don't promise to answer."

The mirrored sunglasses swung around toward her, and Faith caught her breath, thinking what a male archetype he was: huge, dark, his black hair flowing warriorlike to his shoulders. He wore snug denim that sculpted powerful thighs and embraced his masculinity with a boldness that made Faith's mouth turn suddenly dry. His shearling jacket hung open, revealing that even when he sat his stomach was so hard that not an inch of flesh bulged over his belt.

Faith licked dry lips, and Micah turned his attention back to the road. "Well?" he asked. He was afraid that if she licked her lips again he was going to forget all his good sense and lick them for her.

"Do you . . ." she licked her lips again. "Do you remember that summer you taught me to ride?"

He didn't even hesitate. "Yeah, I remember. I remember finding you out in that arroyo at the boundary and wondering if a fairy had suddenly popped up from the dust. You sure were the tiniest little thing. Still are, I reckon." He sent a brief glance her way. "I thought you didn't remember me."

"I didn't, at first. It was when you helped me with my shoes last night that I suddenly remembered a time when you tied my tennis shoe for me. It's funny," she admitted, looking away for fear she would betray her wealth of emotion, "I remember calling you Mike, but other than that, I remember you only as a feeling."

Micah didn't reply immediately, and Faith listened to the engine's grumble with a heart that tapped time in an uncomfortable rhythm. Had she embarrassed him somehow with that admission? Perhaps. As a rule, any discussion of feelings had men hunting for a six-pack and a ride to the nearest fishing hole.

Just as she concluded that Micah meant to say nothing more to her, he spoke, his deep voice like the rumble of distant thunder. "A feeling? You mean you don't remember that you used to think I was the 'bestest Indian' in the whole world?"

An embarrassed little laugh escaped her even as she felt a quiver of pleasure that he was unexpectedly teasing her. To look at him, a woman would never imagine Micah Parish as a tease. "I really said that to you? How did you ever stand me?"

"It wasn't too hard. You were such a little mite, and so serious all the time." He had spent a ridiculous amount of time trying to think up ways to make her laugh, too, but he left that unsaid. The boy he had been then was so far removed from the man he was now that it was like looking back on a stranger.

He did admit one thing, though, because it reminded him of something he could never afford to forget. "You were the first person who ever called me an Indian as if it were something to be proud of."

Faith turned immediately on the seat and looked at him, a frown creasing her brow. Micah showed her only his profile, a strong, stony profile. "I guess you've faced a lot of prejudice."

He gave a small negative shake of his head. "Not since I reached full size and joined the army."

No, Faith thought. Few people would want to tangle with someone Micah's size, especially someone who looked as if he could handle himself with deadly ease in any kind of situation. For the first time in months—maybe years—she felt interested in someone else and wondered how to ask for more information. "Were you...did you stay in the army very long?" That seemed a safe enough question.

"Twenty-one years."

"That's a long time."

"Sure seemed like it sometimes." He braked and turned slowly onto the county road leading to his ranch. The sun had begun to melt the snow from the plowed pavement in a few spots, but in others the slush was treacherous. It gave him an excuse to stay quiet for a minute or two. All this talking was unusual for him, yet he kept feeling compelled to do it. Something about Faith wound his vocal cords up like a toy motorboat.

"Did you ever marry?"

The question caught Micah sideways, because he was expecting her to continue with questions about the army. Before he had a chance to choose his words with his usual care, he answered her. "Came pretty close once." Well, hell, he thought, tightening his grip on the steering wheel. Now she was going to want to know what happened. Women always did, and he had no one but himself to blame for what was coming. Damn it, what was wrong with him today?

"What happened?"

There was, buried deep within him, an old festering anger. In childhood he had learned that to be a half-breed was to be the lowest of all the races of humanity. Neither Anglo nor Indian, wanted by no one, belonging nowhere. The young child had hurt, but hurt toughens and hardens. In the place of pain he had cultivated anger, and in the place of caring he had grown calluses.

His saving grace had been his ideals, unwittingly planted in his soul by the books he had read to fill his empty days. Mythical and historical tales had filled his mind with great deeds and high ideals. Nurtured in the stony soil of anger, he had developed a strong sense of the importance of honor, loyalty and duty. He had discovered compassion for those who were weaker, and reverence for life.

But the anger remained, festering, and sometimes the poison spilled out. Now, on the snowy country road, with signs of yet another storm building in the west, he slammed on the brakes and brought them to a rough halt.

Turning, he stared at Faith from behind the mirrored lenses. "What is it with women?" he asked her, his voice a quiet whip crack in the truck cab. "I never met a woman who didn't want to poke her nose into places it didn't belong."

Faith instinctively shrank back against the door, seeking to place more distance between them. Micah's hands remained on the steering wheel, gripping it tightly, giving her no cause to think he might strike, but she was afraid anyway. Conditioning like hers was not easily overcome. "I'm sorry," she said faintly. "It's none of my business."

"No. It isn't." But he didn't release the brake. Instead he turned his head, staring straight ahead. "I was just back from my first tour in Vietnam," he said after a moment, telling her and wondering why he was doing it, but doing it anyway. "She was the prettiest thing I'd seen since—in a long time. She wore my engagement ring for a week. Just long enough to make her father good and mad. I didn't measure up to a Mercedes and her allowance."

Shrugging, he started driving again.

"You mean she dumped you because her father threatened to cut her off?" Faith couldn't imagine it.

"Yep." He wanted this subject closed *now*. He was afraid the poison would spill out if he tried to tell anyone all the other things he had learned from Dawn Dedrick. Things like it was okay to take a savage into your bed and show him off like a pet jungle cat, but a half-breed sure as hell wasn't good enough to marry.

In retrospect, Micah often wondered why that had come as such a shock to him. It wasn't as if he hadn't long since realized that half-breed was about the dirtiest word in the language.

"Micah?" Faith spoke tentatively. "I'm sorry I made you mad."

He sighed. Two more days, he reminded himself. He just had to hang on for two more days, then she would be at her own place and he could get back to normal.

He wasn't too worried about Frank Williams. Since the man had never been to the Montrose ranch, according to Faith, he wasn't going to be able to find it without asking for directions. In a place as underpopulated as Conard County, it was the easiest thing in the world to alert people to be on the lookout for someone asking for the Montrose place. Here, the frontier mentality prevailed. People as isolated as they were knew how much they depended on their neighbors, and they considered it their duty to look after one another. It was one of the reasons Micah stayed here. Some of the citizens of Conard County would never accept him, but enough of them treated him decently to make the place feel like home.

And the land. He loved the land. He felt a mystical connection with it and cherished the way it weathered the seasons, always changing yet continually unchanged. Sometimes he wondered if the connection he felt sprang from all the years he had spent being bounced around from army post to army post. The land was so enduring, while he himself had always felt so transient. Perhaps he felt a part of the land because he felt a part of so little else.

Turning into his driveway, he felt a sense of belonging that helped satisfy needs he had never really analyzed. When you lived your life on a knife-edge, as he had for so many years while in the Special Forces, you didn't have a whole lot of opportunity to philosophize, or very much inclination to do so.

People assumed—and Micah was content to let them—that the Special Forces spent all their time training for eventualities that had rarely occurred since Vietnam. In truth, Micah had been an active operative, had parachuted into deserts and jungles and frigid tundras, and had collected military intelligence from within the borders of many unfriendly nations. In the dead of night he had jumped from cargo planes with orders to gather certain kinds of intelligence and no way home except through his own skills and daring.

And when he walked out from behind supposedly impenetrable borders, when he set foot once again on free soil, he had neither the time nor the inclination to ponder life's mysteries. Instead, he would drink a couple of beers and get laid, not necessarily in that order, and then begin planning the next mission. And in between missions, there was always the training, the endless training, that kept a man honed to his uttermost limits. Self-indulgence had no room among the Special Forces.

This ranch was, in fact, the only real indulgence of his life. Here he had the space he had always craved, the absolute physical solitude to match his emotional isolation. He was a solitary, self-contained man.

So what the hell was he doing with this woman?

"Conard County, Conard City, Conard Creek," Faith remarked as they neared the house. "I always meant to ask Dad if there are any Conards left in Conard County."

In spite of himself, Micah chuckled quietly. "There's one. Emmaline Conard, generally known as Miss Emma, runs the Conard County Library."

Faith felt her own mouth curving into an unexpected smile. "She's ninety and never married, right?"

"Nope. She's about your age, and never likely to marry."

"Why not?"

Micah braked near the kitchen door and switched off the ignition. The sudden quiet seemed almost loud. "Well, it was back before my time, but I've heard rumors about a traveling man who neglected to mention he was married. What I know for sure is that any man who's ever been bold enough to show any personal interest beyond a question about the Dewey decimal system has been run off in no uncertain terms. Nobody bothers to ask anymore."

"That's sad."

Micah paused, his door open and one booted foot on the ground. "Is it? I would have expected you to feel she's better off avoiding men."

Faith averted her face, feeling inexplicably, ridiculously, near tears again. "Not all men are like Frank," she whispered huskily.

He almost didn't hear her. It was a whisper so soft and so eloquent of unshed tears that he felt suddenly transported back in time to the child who had missed her mother and the half-breed Indian boy who had tried so hard to make the pain easier for her.

He'd had no right then to dry her tears, and he had even less right to do so now, but that didn't stop him.

With a muttered oath, he climbed out of the Blazer and came around to Faith's side. He yanked the door open, and before she could move a muscle, he scooped her off the seat and carried her into the house. Almost six months pregnant and she hardly weighed more than an eiderdown pillow. She needed to eat more. She needed to take better care of herself.

She needed to be taken care of.

It wasn't like him to act without a clear plan of action, but on more than one occasion in the past twenty-four hours, Faith had provoked him into instinctive reactions that came from the gut. This was one of them. He had no idea why he had picked her up, no idea what he intended to do with her as he carried her into the house.

In fact, he realized with a sudden pang of uncharacteristic trepidation, the only thing he was certain of was how right she felt in his arms, how right it seemed to carry her into his house, how right it was to have her arms around his neck and her sweet breath warm on his cheek.

"Micah..."

"Hush." He spoke softly, almost gently, as he kicked the kitchen door closed behind them and headed for the stairs. Distance. He had to keep his distance, but he was failing abysmally at that, and had been ever since the instant he set eyes on her. He'd never been able to keep any distance from her, not even when she'd been only six years old and knee-high to a mushroom.

Solitude. He needed it, craved it, hungered for it. He was his own best friend, and the only person in the world he truly trusted, other than Nate Tate and Ransom Laird. He was complete unto himself and seldom regretted it.

And he was shaman. Over the years, over the miles, that fact had come to take on a wealth of meaning through experience. He saw what others failed to, felt the threads of reality as a tangible thing. In his blood he sensed the currents of life in ways beyond the ordinary. A sixth sense set him apart, guided him and goaded him.

His army comrades had said that Micah Parish could track a ghost across water. They had claimed he had eyes in the back of his head. They had said he could hear sounds in the silence before they were made. They had not nicknamed him Chief or Geronimo, or even Breed, as they often did with other Native Americans. No. They had called him *Brujo*. Sorcerer.

But being a shaman wasn't helping him right now. It wasn't making a bit of difference to the fact that something inside him was cracking wide open and letting need pour through. The solitary man suddenly didn't want to be solitary. The self-sufficient man was suddenly insufficient.

It was time to get his distance back.

Strangely unafraid, Faith clung to Micah's powerful shoulders as he carried her up the stairs. His expression was grim, controlled, his eyes like a dark fire.

For years now Faith had resented her own diminutive size, believing that people would have been far less likely to shove her around if she hadn't been so small. Micah made her feel that smallness acutely, but in a different, provocative way. He made her feel fragile but protected, small but cherished. He made her feel that his great size was not a threat but a shield.

He shouldered his way into her room and gently laid her on the bed. Then, standing over her, he drew a deep breath and closed his eyes. After a moment, he spoke.

"You take a nap. It's been a long day. I need to go out for a while."

Her voice stopped him at the door. "Will you be gone long?"

The question held undertones he didn't want to deal with. "A while," was all he said. "I'll be out a while."

He didn't go far. He didn't even take the Blazer. Instead, he stomped out into the cold yard, and around the rear side of the barn, then climbed a narrow trail in the rock face that stood guarding his buildings. It was a long, taxing climb, worse in the snowy, slippery conditions. No novice could have made it, but Micah took it steadily, with only a slight deepening of his breathing. In places he needed to go nearly hand over hand, but he never paused. Frigid meltwater soaked his knees, but he scarcely felt the chill of it.

At the top, nearly knee-deep in last night's snowfall, he stopped to look down at his house and barn.

It looked just the way he had dreamed it for years. In the growing twilight, with the snow all around, it looked exactly like the place he had envisioned for so many years in so many alien lands. Even the white smoke curling up from the chimney was a part of the dream. In his gut, in his shaman's soul, he understood that nothing happened, absolutely nothing, unless first it was dreamed.

Throwing back his head, he drew a deep lungful of the cold, clean air. A fresh storm was marching in from the west, as yet a low line of clouds scarcely higher than the mountains in the distance. It would soon be dark, and he debated for a moment whether to return immediately along the treacherous path he had just climbed or to take the longer, safer way around. Tilting his head a little, he judged the encroaching night. It would have to be the longer way.

Turning, he headed away from the setting sun and the approaching storm. With each step, his control settled more firmly into place, and the silence and solitude returned to his soul. This was how he was meant to be, he thought, as night gathered softly around him. Alone in the cold, surrounded by the vast barrenness of the Wyoming winter. One with the wilderness.

Dreamless.

Half an hour later, Micah had just reached his driveway again and was striding toward the pinpoints of light that came from the house. He was cold, his jeans were soaked from the knees down, but the discomfort scarcely penetrated his awareness. Hard, mindless exercise was a focus that lifted consciousness out of its ordinary rut to an altered state. Discomfort and pain ceased to have any meaning, and all the garbage was cleared from his mind.

He felt the vehicle before he heard it. The vibration came up from the frozen ground, muffled a little by the soles of his boots, but alerting him nonetheless. He paused, and shortly he was able to make out the distant rumble of the approaching vehicle.

What now? he wondered, just as the flare of headlights swung toward him into his driveway. Standing back to the side of the drive, one foot braced in the mound of snow he had earlier plowed out of the way, he waited for the visitor's arrival.

A minute later a familiar black Suburban pulled up beside him. The window rolled down, and Gage Dalton leaned out. As usual, he sported a couple of days' growth of dark stubble on his cheeks, a marked contrast to the premature silver of his hair.

"Howdy, Micah."

"Gage." Micah nodded. "What brings you out this way?"

"Jeff Cumberland's got two more mutilated cattle."

"Well, hell," Micah sighed. It never rained but it poured. "How fresh are they?"

"Fresh enough. Since last night's snowfall."

"I suppose the ground's all trampled up now."

"Nope. That's why I came to get you. Nate's ordered up some floodlights, and they're hoping you'll take a look before it gets all messed up. Near as I can tell, these two weren't far apart, and both were spotted this afternoon by Cumberland's foreman. His horse's tracks are the only ones in sight."

Without another word Micah walked around to the passenger side and climbed in. "I need to go up to the house and change first. I'm soaked to the skin."

"Right."

Gage shifted into gear and accelerated smoothly. In the dim light from the dashboard, a jagged scar was visible on

his cheek. The gossips of Conard County speculated end-
lessly about it and other rumored scars, but then, Gage
Dalton was the kind of man who, scarred or not, would have
been the subject of avid gossip. Mystery cloaked him. The
story of those scars was a tale Gage had never told anyone
in the county, but Micah suspected they had something to
do with the background that had made Nate hire Gage as a
part-time investigator.

"I hear Jason Montrose's daughter is staying with you,"
Gage remarked.

"Just until her power's on. What are folks saying?"

"Just that her ex might be looking for her with trouble in
mind."

"She's had a bad time of it," Micah said.

"So I hear. By now I reckon most everyone is keeping an
eye out for strangers. After what happened to Mandy and
Ransom Laird, you hardly have to convince people that
trouble can come to Conard County. Everyone I talked to
today seems eager enough to help out. If Frank Williams
sets foot in the county, we'll hear about it."

Micah pretty much figured they would, too. He just
hoped they'd hear in enough time.

"I sure don't think anybody's going to get directions to
the Montrose ranch from anyone in this county," Gage remarked as he pulled to a stop beside Micah's Blazer.

"Come on in for some coffee while I change," Micah
suggested. Gage needed no more urging. It had been a long,
cold day.

Faith was in the kitchen when they entered, in the middle
of frying the pork chops she had found thawing in Micah's
refrigerator. At first she had hesitated about making herself so at home in his kitchen, and then she had decided that
whenever he came back in from the cold he was going to
want a meal.

That was *something* she could do, she thought with a
twinge of bitterness. She could prepare a good, nutritious
meal. She could keep a spotless house, get ink stains out of

uniform shirts and iron a perfect set of military creases. Some résumé.

Micah paused just inside the door, taking in the incredibly domestic scene in his kitchen. Complete, he realized with a sense of shock, down to the frilly pink apron Faith wore over the swelling mound of her belly. In that instant, an instant during which time seemed to abruptly halt, he realized that he had dreamed this, too—in unguarded moments. Hell!

"Faith, this is Gage Dalton. He and I need to go out to the Bar C ranch on business as soon as I change."

"Ma'am." Gage tugged off his black Stetson, revealing silvery hair, startling in a man who appeared to be only in his mid to late thirties. His eyes were a stormy gray-green, like the sky before a squall. Faith dragged her gaze away from his disfigured cheek, thinking he must have been as handsome as sin before he got hurt.

"I offered Gage some coffee...." Micah's voice trailed off. He felt awkward in his own kitchen, he realized. Awkward telling her that he'd offered Gage coffee, as if he should have cleared it with her first. Man, he was losing his mind!

"I just made a fresh pot," Faith hastened to say. "Should I pour you some, too, Micah?"

"Yeah. I'll be back in a minute." He left without a backward glance, glad to escape the sensation that reality had just shifted course in some way, and that nothing was at all the way he'd thought.

Faith set two mugs on the table and filled them, signaling Gage to take a seat. "Are you a deputy, too?" she asked him. He wasn't wearing a uniform, but he'd apparently come on official business.

"Not exactly. I work on a part-time basis for the sheriff as an investigator, but I don't do any of the daily law enforcement stuff."

"Has there been trouble out at the Bar C?" She cast her mind back to the summers she had spent here as a child, trying to recall the Bar C. "That's the Cumberland ranch, isn't it?"

"Just a couple of cattle mutilations," Gage answered. "We're hoping Micah can pick up some kind of sign as to what did it. Sure would be nice to put the mystery to rest."

"I've read about those," Faith said, turning the chops. "Don't some people think aliens do it?"

"There was a whole uproar about it maybe fifteen years back. Some folks claimed it was devil worshippers, others thought aliens must be taking samples of some kind. The state lab insists that it's just normal predator activity."

"What do you think?"

Gage gave her a slow smile. "Well, ma'am, it might be aliens, but I sure think they'd want samples of something besides cattle."

Faith laughed. "That's a good point. But if it's wolves or coyotes or whatever, why do they take only a few parts?"

Gage shrugged. "If it was easy to explain, people wouldn't be talking about aliens."

Micah heard the laughter as he came back down the stairs dressed in a freshly pressed uniform. The sound was so out of place in this silent, empty house that he paused to listen to it—and to battle an unreasoning surge of jealousy that it was Gage who had first drawn that sound from her. Ridiculous, he told himself, squatting by the wood stove to ensure that the fire would keep Faith warm until he returned. Childish.

Convinced that he had sternly squashed the ignoble portion of his nature, and that the fire would keep the house warm for hours yet, he returned to the kitchen.

Faith turned toward him immediately with a welcoming smile that tightened when she saw his uniform and the gun belt hanging low on his hips. It wasn't exactly the same utility belt that her husband had worn, with all its little pouches, but it was close enough to stir the memories.

Somehow she had forgotten her instinctive tension around the police, but now it returned in an uncomfortable rush.

But this is Micah, she told herself. *Micah.* Micah who had soothed her tears and put bandages on her small cuts when she had been a child. Micah who had treated her so gently since he helped her from her car yesterday. Micah who had shared her awe at the baby's movements. There was absolutely no reason to be afraid of him.

But she was tense anyhow, and her eyes followed him almost warily as he crossed the room and reached for the mug of coffee she had poured for him. Such a big man, she thought, towering over her by much more than a foot. Such a strong, powerful man.

He glanced over at her. "Are those chops burning?" The question was mild, non-accusatory, but Faith jumped.

"Oh!" She turned swiftly and found the chops had almost passed the point of being edible. "Oh!" Quickly, she forked them out of the pan onto a plate with trembling hands. "I'm sorry! Oh, I'm so sorry."

For a long moment there wasn't a sound behind her in the kitchen; then Micah said, "I'll follow you in my car in just a minute or two, Gage."

"Sure." A chair scraped, and booted feet clomped across the floor. Seconds later the door closed behind Gage.

Faith clung to the counter, her back to Micah, trembling so hard it was visible. He was going to hit her. That was why he told Gage to go ahead. Frank always hit her when she screwed up like this. He wouldn't care that the meat would only be just a little dry, that it wasn't ruined at all. He would hit her. Instinctively, she tucked her chin down to her chest and drew her shoulders up. Tensed in expectation, she awaited the inevitable blows.

"Faith." Micah's tone was soft, gentle, a coaxing murmur. He stepped toward her.

"I'm sorry," she whispered. "I don't know how it happened. Really...I shouldn't...I...I'm sorry! I'm such a screwup!"

Huge hands, hands that could have snapped a man's arm in two as if it were a dry matchstick, huge, powerful, dark-skinned hands, closed with ineffable gentleness on her small, trembling shoulders.

"It's all right, Faith," he murmured. "It's all right. Really. No one's going to hurt you. No one's mad at you. You're not a screwup. Hush . . . just hush . . ."

Ignoring the resistance in every muscle of her body, he gently but firmly turned her around and then wrapped her snugly in his powerful arms. With her head buried against his breastbone and his arms holding her close, she no longer feared that he was going to hit her. After a moment, a long, seemingly interminable moment, she sagged against him.

"That's better," he murmured, stroking her riotous blond curls. "That's better. I promise you, Faith, I will never, ever hit you. Never. And as long as I'm anywhere in sight, no one else will ever hit you, either. I swear it."

A shudder passed through her, and then she leaned even closer against him, telling him silently that, for the moment at least, she believed him.

"I wish I could stay," he said, keeping his voice pitched soothingly, "but Nate needs me out at the Bar C. I'll probably be gone for a few hours, but I sure would like one of those chops when I come back."

"I . . . I ruined them. . . ."

"No. No. They're not ruined. Nothing's ruined." Except him. His objectivity and his distance were shot to hell. His fingers were combing through hair that had the texture of silk and lightly brushing against a neck that felt like warm satin. Womanly aromas filled his nose along with the homey ones of cooked food, and Micah Parish was wondering why he couldn't have some of those things he had spent his whole life fighting to protect.

The foot of an unborn child kicked him gently, a soft reminder that time was an endless flow and it was a man's purpose to pass his seed to the future. A man was driven to it, and right now he wanted like hell to mate. The urge was rising in him, fed by soft femininity, by full breasts pressing against him, and even by the swelling womb of a woman who was fulfilling her God-given purpose by bearing life.

Life was that simple, really, but people turned it into a complex maze of pitfalls. It was the pitfalls that made Micah step back and turn for the door.

"I'll be back in a couple of hours," he said over his shoulder. "If you need anything, call the Lairds. The number is by the phone."

Shaking, shaken, Faith watched him go.

Chapter 5

The remote corner of Jeff Cumberland's Bar C Ranch
looked like a scene lifted from a movie. Dark storm clouds,
limned in silver by a crescent moon, were beginning to scud
across the star-strewn sky. Floodlights on tall tripods had
been set up at both mutilation sites, a jarring eruption of
modernity into the timeless winter landscape.

Micah understood the politics of being sheriff—as an
elected official, Nate had to keep the voters reasonably
happy—but he wished to hell that this time Nate had spared
the overkill. Sure, Jeff was upset. That was natural. Cattle
weren't exactly cheap commodities, and Jeff's herd was
more valuable than most, since he ran a prize-winning
breeding program, but it wouldn't help Jeff or anybody else
if all the evidence was destroyed in an attempt to look as if
the sheriff were doing his job.

"I know, I know," Nate said to Micah as the latter
slogged up to him. The vehicles had been kept at a good
distance, and there was a deputy to warn all comers to keep
to the already trampled ground. "Fred and I were the only
ones to approach the carcasses, and we never got closer than

fifteen feet." He handed Micah a hand-held floodlight. "You won't find diddly."

Nate was a good tracker, too. Maybe a little rusty, but good, so Micah figured there was no point in looking for anything obvious. If the mutilators had slipped, it would be in some barely detectable way.

"This is an awful lot of mutilations in a small area," Gage said as Micah and Nate joined him at the edge of the circle of light.

"Yeah." Nate's agreement was sour. A couple of these a year could be ignored. Five in three days was the kind of thing that could raise a lynch mob in quiet Conard County—if the folks found a target.

Squatting, Micah sifted fresh snow through his fingers. It wasn't dry enough to have blown away all signs of who- ever might have been here, or to have blown off the dead animal. That meant the steer that lay in the middle of the circle of light had been dropped there since the snowfall. Or just as it was ending. Otherwise, the carcass would have been drifted over by snow.

There were no tracks in the fresh snow, and Micah was already reaching some hair-raising conclusions by the time he squatted beside the carcass. The tongue was gone; he saw that immediately. The eyes had been left alone, though, and they were a delicacy most predators didn't pass up. The genitals were also gone, another typical sign, and the exci- sion was typically neat, looking as if the cuts must have been made with a knife. The day had been dry and cold, but cold enough to shrink the wounded flesh so much?

Micah had never been squeamish, but he really didn't care for this part of his job, he thought as he moved the steer's limbs and examined the wounds. Ah, this one had been disemboweled, too. That was new. He sat back on his haunches thoughtfully and studied the animal.

A while later he moved around to the other side and studied the animal from that angle, too. Not much blood at all, but that was usual for these kills. Nothing new. Except that if the animal had died here, its body heat would have melted the snow around and beneath it.

He signalled Nate and Fred to come over and help him lift the carcass a little. He didn't particularly want to move a ton of dead beef, but he needed to see just how far the animal had melted itself into the snow. If it had died here, there should be a layer of ice beneath it.

There wasn't.

"Well, hell," he said to no one in particular. "Where's Jeff?"

"Right here," Cumberland answered from behind one of the floodlamps. "You want me to come over?"

"Yeah. There's no sign to disturb. I want you to see this, though. You, too, Gage," he added to the investigator.

Both men joined him, Nate and Fred beside the dead steer.

"If this animal died here," Micah said flatly, "its body heat would have melted the snow, and then, as it cooled, the meltwater would have refrozen. I figure a ton of beef should have melted its way right through the snow to the ground. It didn't. See that? The snow is compressed from the weight, but it didn't thaw and refreeze."

Jeff Cumberland swore. He didn't need a diagram.

"Let's go look at the other one," Micah said, straightening. "I reckon we'll find the same thing, though."

Once again he checked very carefully for any kind of sign in the snow, and once again he reached the same conclusion.

"These cattle were dropped here," he said flatly. "Right now, I'd bet somebody brought them out here on a helicopter, already mutilated, and shoved them out."

The five men looked at one another, none of them voicing the obvious question: Why?

"I think," Nate said roughly, "that we'd all better keep our mouths shut about this for the time being. For now we'll say it's a typical mutilation." He looked at Cumberland. "Jeff?"

"Yeah. Fine." The rancher looked angry, but more, he looked disturbed. The most obvious conclusion, one that went as unspoken as the obvious question, was that someone was out to give Cumberland a hard time. None of the men gathered around the carcass had any idea why that should be. Cumberland was both well liked and well respected.

Nate turned to Micah. "Thanks for coming out here. Sorry I interrupted your break. Take Friday off, too, if you want. Mrs. Williams might need some help getting settled."

"She might. Thanks." With a nod, Micah turned to walk away. Gage moved alongside him. Neither of them said anything until they reached their vehicles, when Micah turned to the other man.

"You have some connections at the state lab, don't you?"

Gage nodded. "You need me to call in a favor?"

"I'd sure appreciate it if they'd put the Bar C cattle on the top of their priority list. These aren't the usual mutilations. Any of 'em, not just the one that was disemboweled."

"I'll call them in the morning," Gage promised.

"Thanks." Micah swung up into the driver's seat and shoved his key into the ignition. Now to go home and find out if Faith had recovered from her earlier fright.

Damn! Imagine a man hitting a woman like that. The memory of how she had hunched up and waited for the blows made him ache, and it made him mad. Nobody—man, woman or child—should ever have to feel like that.

The back porch light was on to guide him, and the dim light over the sink was on, too, but Faith had evidently gone to bed. He was relieved. Things were churning in him, things that weren't pretty or very nice. Needs, savage from long denial, kept trying to rear their heads, and he just didn't feel like wrestling with even the least provocation right now.

His dinner sat on the counter next to the microwave. It was wrapped in plastic, ready to be heated. The thoughtfulness touched him. Not once in forty-three years had anyone left a meal out for him.

While he heated the meal, he removed his gun belt, then unbuttoned his shirt and pulled out the tails, making himself reasonably comfortable. He knew he'd made a mistake when he heard Faith's soft "Oh!" behind him.

"I didn't hear you come in," she said. "I must have been dozing."

He hesitated a moment, then shrugged inwardly and turned to face her. A man's partially bared chest hardly constituted indecent exposure, and surely she had seen chests before.

But never one like his, Faith thought, staring in spite of herself. Never one so smooth, so muscled, so free of hair, with such a warm, coppery tone. Never one that tapered down to a belly so flat that every ridge of muscle showed. She suddenly didn't find it at all incredible that she should want to reach out and touch him. It somehow seemed like the most normal thing in the world to yearn to press her palms to that warm, smooth skin.

Micah saw her breasts rise with a sudden, deep breath, saw her pupils dilate, but he couldn't tell whether it was fear or arousal that caused her reaction. Probably fear, he thought, and reached instantly to button his shirt. He turned to face the microwave.

"Thanks for leaving dinner out for me," he said.

"You're welcome." Frank had never once said thank you for anything, least of all something as small as leaving out a plate of food for him. She edged closer, recognizing yet again that this man was not like Frank. Not like Frank at all. The idea of a man so utterly different from her ex-husband drew her like a warm fire on a cold night. Fantasies cherished in childhood surged to the forefront of her mind, reminding her that once she had believed in a good and gentle man, a man whose touches would be welcome, whose caresses would be pleasurable. Her life so far had made a mockery of those dreams, but perhaps Micah . . .

"I thought you were asleep," he said gruffly. "I figured you'd gone to bed."

"I...I waited up," she said, gathering her courage in both hands and taking a step toward him. She had promised herself that she was going to stop acting like a mouse, and while she might periodically backslide, as she had earlier, she was still resolved to show some courage. "I wanted to apologize."

He turned and stared at her, his black-as-midnight eyes steady but unrevealing. "What for?"

"For acting like such a ditz. I'm sure I embarrassed you, and Gage must have thought he'd walked into a madhouse."

Micah muttered a word Faith was not accustomed to hearing. Shocked, she blinked and felt a blush rise to her face. "I'm not very good at that, either," she said in a breathless rush.

He stared at her hard, doubting his ears, and what he saw made a chuckle rise in him. It didn't quite escape—his laughter rarely did—but it curved the corners of his mouth upward into an unmistakable smile. Faith, he realized, was bravely trying to make a joke. It was there in the tentative sparkle in her eyes, the hopeful set of her mouth. She was trying to step aside from her anxiety and act normally. She was trying to bridge the gap her fear kept opening between them. The smile he gave her now brought an answering smile to her lips and lightened the shadows in her blue eyes.

There was so much courage and trust inherent in that small attempt to reach out to him that emotion momentarily tightened his throat. "Come here, woman," he said roughly, and opened his arms to her.

She hesitated, as he had known she would, but not long enough for him to regret his impulsive invitation, not long enough for him to rescind it. And suddenly she was there in his embrace, willingly and freely this time, offering him a trust so great that it pierced his solitary soul.

Yielding a long, deep sigh, as if everything in him had awaited this very moment, he closed his eyes and bowed his head until his face was buried in the soft, silky curls atop her head.

"I've been worrying about you all evening," he said reluctantly, his voice hardly more than a rough murmur. "I hated to leave you alone when you were so upset."

"I'm used to being alone, and I'm used to being upset, Micah." What she wasn't used to was being utterly comfortable and content in a man's embrace.

The microwave pinged, and Micah released her, thinking that he'd damn well better be careful about taking Faith into his arms, because he could easily grow accustomed to the comfortable way she fit there. Accustomed? Hell, he could get addicted!

She had set his place at the table earlier, so she couldn't do even that much to help as he sat down to his dinner. With a casual movement of his hand, he invited her to join him at the table, so she poured herself a glass of milk and sat across from him.

"Were you able to find out what happened to the cows?" she asked.

Micah gave a small, negative shake of his head. "Just a mess of things that don't add up." He didn't want to discuss it right now. He had told Nate and Jeff all he knew, and they were the only ones who really needed to know. Until he heard something from the state lab, he had nothing to add that wouldn't be pure speculation, and he wasn't the speculating type. He had been trained as a fighter, as a killer, as a commando, and as an intelligence gatherer. He dealt in facts, in the way things really were, and he tried never to pass beyond theory into speculation.

But inside, where no one else could see, ancient instincts were telling him that things were not as they seemed. What met the eye was sometimes an illusion. Troubled, he stabbed his fork into a chop and then, suddenly, looked up and caught Faith staring at him.

"Do I amuse you?" he asked. She watched him a lot, he thought. Closely. Frequently. It might be from fear or uncertainty, it might be something else altogether. Whatever, he chose his words to anger her, hoping that if he pushed her past caution she might bring some of her fears out where he could deal with them.

Instead of getting angry or withdrawing, she shocked him. "You fascinate me," she admitted, coloring brightly.

His black eyes imprisoned her. "How so?"

"You seem . . . so sure of yourself. So strong. So independent. I was wondering what it must feel like not to be afraid of every little thing."

He finished his second pork chop and started on his third before he replied. By then Faith had concluded that she had sounded foolish to him. After all, he feared nothing and probably couldn't imagine why she was such a quivering coward about everything. And then he spoke, his voice like deep, dark velvet.

"Fear is a survival instinct," he said slowly. "Everyone feels it. That's why most people don't stick their hands into the flame on the stove."

He made it sound so simple, so natural, yet she knew that the fears she felt were not natural.

"The circumstances that threaten us determine our fears," he continued just as slowly, his voice flowing like a lazy summer river. "When our circumstances change, gradually our fears change, too." He turned his head and met her gaze squarely. "Yours are changing already, Faith."

They were, she realized. Just a little. "What are you afraid of?" She had no business asking, but she needed to hear this strong, self-contained man admit to just one thing that frightened him, even if it was of no consequence. It would make him seem more human, more approachable. Closer to her.

It was his turn to astonish her, to shock her, and he did it as if compelled, revealing something he had never told anyone else in the world. "I'm afraid of being buried alive."

Speechless, she stared at him, her blue eyes huge. Micah looked down at his plate and sighed. That had sure as hell torn it, he thought grimly. Now would come the questions, and he had no one but himself to blame. She would ask, and he would have to decide whether to answer or to be flat-out rude. He wasn't afraid to be rude, but he didn't want to treat Faith that way. She deserved something better than that.

So he didn't wait for her to speak. Shoving his plate to one side, he rose. "Let's go sit in the living room," he said harshly. If he had to bare his soul even this little bit, he was going to do it comfortably, with a cup of hot coffee in his hands in an environment as far as he could get from the nightmare that still haunted him.

He sat on one corner of the couch and felt momentarily surprised when Faith sat at the other end instead of taking the safer position on the easy chair. Her chin was lifted in a way that told him it had been a conscious decision, another act of defiance in the face of her conditioned terrors.

The lamplight was a warm, golden glow. Wind rattled at the window panes and gave him an excuse to postpone the explanation.

"Another storm is hitting tonight," he told Faith. "I radioed the office a little while ago, and they told me about it. We don't usually get this much snow around here."

"Really? Why not?" Somehow she had thought of this place as being deeply buried in snow most of the time.

"We're in the rain shadow of the mountains. Most of the snow and rain falls up there, which is why we have so few trees around here. Last night we got half the normal snow-fall for an entire winter."

"What about tonight?"

"Just a couple of inches, but the way the wind is blowing, it'll probably drift up real good." It always drifted deeply around his house and barn, which, along with the rocky terrain that provided protection, created a wind-break where snow caught. It created a lot of extra work, but Micah had never been afraid of hard work.

And the question was still hanging between them. He could see it in her eyes, could almost hear it on her lips. Well, he could have kept it light. He could have said he was terrified of snakes, or getting old. No one had forced him to say something so obviously real. No one had dragged him over the line from sociable chitchat to stark honesty. Now, however, feeling compelled to finish it, he didn't know how to begin.

Faith settled it. Astonishing him with her perception, she spoke softly into a silence that had grown far too long. "What happened, Micah?"

He wasn't a man who ever flinched from the tough things in life. When he set out to do something, he did it. He had decided to tell her, and he didn't attempt to make light of it or minimize it. He didn't shrug it away. He handed the truth to her without varnish, evasions or omissions.

"Back during the Vietnam conflict, I was wounded and taken prisoner by the VC. The Vietcong. We called them Victor Charlie, or just Charlie." He watched her, waiting for withdrawal or denial, but she only nodded acceptance and understanding.

"They held me for about seventy-six hours," he said, revealing that he had counted every single one of those hours. Every one of those minutes. "In a hole in the ground. It was so narrow I couldn't sit. I had to stand. Most of the time they kept the top of the hole covered so that no light at all got in. There was just me, the dark and the bugs." He heard Faith's soft murmur but ignored it. "Anyhow, from time to time, when they got to feeling really nasty, they shoveled dirt in on me."

"Oh, my God..." It was a whisper. He looked at her, saw the horror. Now he did shrug.

"It kind of stayed with me," he said.

"How...how did you escape?"

"A good buddy of mine, Ransom Laird. You'll meet him before long, since he's your neighbor. He came back after the firefight to find my body and take care of it. He's that kind of guy. When he didn't find me, he realized I was still alive, so he came looking for me. By the time he got me out of that hole I was so weak from infection and dehydration that he had to carry me over his shoulders. To this day, I don't know how he managed it."

She broke free then. She broke out of the prison of terror that had been hammered into her by blows and words. She overcame a hurdle so high that only minutes before it had appeared insurmountable. Caring carried her over it effortlessly.

Without a thought, without room for fright, driven by a need to comfort, she moved down the couch and threw her arms around Micah. Pressing her face into the curve between his warm neck and his shoulder, she leaned into him, chest to chest. She didn't say anything. Silently she clung to him, holding him fiercely, telling him with her arms what she could not find words for.

Amazement held him still for a moment, but then he closed his powerful arms around her and felt her sigh as he hugged her close. It felt as good to her as it did to him, he realized as he sensed the whisper of her sigh against his neck. She wanted him to hold her. God!

His thoughts strayed, and he let them. The nightmare of being buried alive barely touched him anymore, only haunting him on rare occasions. It seemed far away right now. Other things seemed far more important, like this woman's warmth and femininity, her enticing fragrance, her gentle weight on his chest. He needed her to touch him, needed it ferociously, both as a man and as Micah Parish.

It was easy for him to care, but hard for him to need. He had discovered a long time ago that as long as he needed nothing, he could not be hurt. His strength and his solitude resulted directly from that understanding. He could love, but he refused to need to be loved.

But right now, with this soft, warm woman curled up against him, he felt those needs, and for this moment, he didn't batter them down. He ran his hands along her back, feeling the graceful, smooth line of her, the delicacy of the skin and muscle over her ribs. So small, dainty and fragile. There was something about that fragility and her inherent vulnerability that drew him, mesmerized him, made him hungry.

She needed his protection. She needed his strength and his care. And for Micah, the need to be needed was the biggest need of all.

His shaman's blood rose powerfully in him then, battering back thought, reason and caution. For just this sweet, short time, he chose to simply be. To feel. To drift in the current that claimed him.

Lifting Faith, he turned her and settled her onto his lap so that her shoulders were cradled in his arm. With his other hand he captured her small chin and turned her face up to his. For long moments he studied her, hunting for any sign of fear or reluctance. What he saw, all he saw, was a shimmering, scarcely born hope.

Releasing a breath he hadn't been aware of holding, he bent his head and lightly, softly, caressed her lips with his own. To his absolute wonder and amazement, he felt her respond shyly. Hesitantly. As if not quite certain of what he wanted or whether she could provide it.

Micah was a man of wide experience. Sweet and slow, hot and savage, these were matters of mood for him. His only stricture on sexual intimacy was that it be mutually consenting. Mutually pleasurable.

In Faith's tentative response to his kiss he felt a hopeful ambivalence. He thought of pulling back, but then her hand slipped upward from his shoulder and her fingers slid into his hair. Gently, almost unconsciously, she pressed him closer.

A ragged sigh escaped him, and he moved his lips just a little harder against hers, demanding nothing, simply asking for whatever she chose to give him. Until he was sure she knew she had nothing at all to fear from him, he would press her for nothing. Every move would be of her choosing.

But she was not yet drawing any lines. Her other hand found his cheek, her soft, warm palm coming to rest gently against the jaw muscles that moved slowly as he kissed her. Micah wasn't accustomed to gentle touches. Even when making slow, sweet love, women tended not to be gentle with him. No one thought he would break; no one thought he wanted it or needed it.

He had not known until this very moment just how much he craved it. How much he needed someone to care about him in a way that made her treat him gently.

Shaken to his roots, he took his mouth from Faith's and pressed her face to his shoulder. No more, he thought. No more. This woman had a power in her, a power to touch him in places he had never, ever let anyone touch him. She had the power to strip his solitude from him. She was dangerous.

"Micah?"

Reaching up, she touched his face again with the same gentleness, a touch that implored him to look at her. Helpless against such a plea, he looked down. Her eyes were wide. They were also hurt and embarrassed. Hell, he hadn't meant to hurt her!

"Faith, I . . ." I what? he wondered. What could he possibly say?

"You don't have to explain," she said quickly, her color rising. "I know I'm not very good at sex, and being so pregnant I'm not even—"

He covered her mouth with his fingers, silencing her quickly. "You don't know what you're talking about."

He felt her lips part beneath his fingers, felt her draw a breath to speak, and realized that this woman was losing her fear of him. Here she was, lying across his lap, her hip pressing against him intimately enough that she surely must realize he was aroused, and yet she was preparing to argue with him. That understanding made him want to laugh. Instead, he smiled.

"Hush," he said. "You're playing with fire."

No, she hadn't realized how aroused he was. That became apparent to him when she went suddenly very still and her gaze strayed downward. And then a delightful pink tide rose into her cheeks. *Now* she knew he was aroused.

"Oh," she said. A small, quiet sound.

He waited for her to grow frightened, anticipated a wild attempt to get off his lap. Instead she simply lay there. After a second or two she stole a glance upward from the corner of her eye.

"A woman is beautiful in all her seasons, Faith." He thought it a simple truth, but she saw it differently. His hand still cupped her chin, his forearm resting innocently between her breasts. She caught that hand and moved it to her stomach. Moments later he felt her child move.

"I've been feeling fat and ugly and very much alone, Micah Parish," she said softly. "You've made me feel beautiful and safe." A small smile curved her lips, and a little sparkle came to her eyes. "But I'm still fat. I'd like to relieve you of my crushing weight and spare you any more discomfort, but I'm afraid I'm stuck. I can't do sit-ups anymore."

She might feel fat, but as far as he was concerned, she didn't weigh anything at all. He lifted her easily and set her on the couch beside him. It would have been wiser to preserve a distance, but when she displayed no desire to move away, he gave in to his own desire to wrap his arm around her shoulders and hold her against his side. Seemingly content, she rested her cheek against his shoulder.

Presently he spoke, addressing a very different subject. "Are you sure you want to move out to that ranch all by yourself?"

"Yes." She tilted her head, trying to see his expression, but saw only the underside of a very strong chin.

"I wish you'd think about it some more," he rumbled. "If anything happens, it'll take time for help to reach you. There won't be another soul for miles—unless you arrange for some kind of live-in companion."

"Don't worry about it, Micah. Believe me, I'll be safer out there all by myself than I have been at any time in the last four years."

"You haven't been pregnant before."

"What difference does that make? At this point there's absolutely no reason to believe I won't finish my normal term without any complications. Believe it or not, I was in a lot more danger driving Loop 410 in San Antonio."

A faint smile lifted the corners of his mouth. She was right about that, but he wasn't suggesting she go back to San Antonio. It was clear after his talk with Garrett Hancock earlier today that moving back there would be a big mistake. Garrett was concerned not only about Frank himself, but about Frank's cohorts. Some of them might think Faith could testify against them.

"Why are you so determined?" he asked finally.

"It's something I have to do, Micah." She leaned forward and looked directly at him. "I've been dependent and helpless for too long. If I'm ever going to be a good mother, I need to be able to stand on my own two feet. I need to be able to take care of *myself* first."

He couldn't argue logically against that. He could only point out alternatives. "You don't have to be utterly alone to learn independence, Moonbeam."

The nickname he had given her that long-ago summer slipped out before he even knew he'd remembered it, and the sound of it brought a surprisingly delighted smile to Faith's face. "I'd forgotten you called me that," she said clapping her hands. "I'd forgotten! I loved it, Micah."

He reached out and caught a handful of her soft, silky curls. "It still looks like moonbeams," he said gruffly. "I've been all over the world, but I've never seen hair quite this color anywhere else." And only then did he realize he had even been looking.

Moonbeam. Well, hell.

Faith had gone up to bed, and Micah sat alone in his living room with the company of another mug of coffee and Lee Greenwood singing he was proud to be an American. Then Lee started singing about taking his baby on a morning ride, and Micah changed tapes.

Moonbeam. The long-forgotten nickname should have awakened countless memories of Faith as a child, should have made it possible for Micah to reestablish his emotional distance. Instead, in that flash of time when he had spoken it, it had taken on an entirely new quality. A sensual quality. This woman was moonbeams and lace, satin and silk, soft murmurs and gentle heat. She was a promise of all the soft, warm, womanly things that he had never had in his life.

She had none of the brassiness or confidence of today's working woman. And he guessed she was going to have to develop some if she was to stand on her own two feet in today's world, even in Conard County. Damn shame.

Micah was no male chauvinist. He didn't feel women were less capable or less intelligent than men. He simply felt they were different, with every right to that difference. Their bodies were designed to nurture life, and men's bodies were designed to protect life, and he just plain didn't understand why so many people had a problem with that. There were many modern arenas where men and women were equally competent, and he was perfectly willing to acknowledge that. Why those arenas become a battleground where men and women tried to deny their respective differences or to lord it over one another was something he plain didn't understand, and didn't want to.

What he did understand was that in his personal life he was old-fashioned. He wanted a woman who wasn't afraid to be a woman. A woman who didn't feel threatened by his masculinity. A woman who could accept his size and strength and his role as protector. A woman who wouldn't need to diminish him in order to strengthen herself. A woman who wouldn't feel diminished by him.

A woman who would realize that he needed gentleness, too.

He muttered an oath and headed for the kitchen to refill his mug. He hadn't let himself think about these things for a long time. Ages ago, when he had been a young man, he'd pondered things like this during long, solitary nights in hostile lands. Then he had realized that solitude was his fortress, that he could be whole unto himself.

He *was* whole unto himself. And he wasn't going to let a few restless yearnings change that. No way.

Micah Parish didn't need anyone or anything. Not even the gentle touch of a moonbeam.

Chapter 6

The next morning, Micah was called in to work. Jed Barlowe, the county drunk, had gotten a little disorderly. He had, in fact, taken over the bell tower at Good Shepherd Church and was firing potshots at passersby.

"You'll be careful?"

Faith's words caused Micah to pause as he fastened his body armor over a T-shirt. Once again he had thought her safely in bed, and once again he had been wrong. She moved with amazing silence on her very light feet. He turned to find her in the open door of his bedroom.

"Careful of what?" he asked casually.

"I'm not a fool, Micah Parish," she said sharply. "I was married to a policeman long enough to realize y'all don't wear those damn vests unless somebody is shooting."

"We're supposed to wear them whenever we're on duty, Faith."

"I know that. I also know none of you do, except maybe rookies. What's going on?"

With a sigh, he fastened the last tape and reached for his uniform shirt. Well, hell, he thought, and here he'd been thinking it might be nice to have a woman around. This one in particular. But now she was staring at him in that way a man recognized in his gut, that I'm-not-going-to-give-an-inch-so-you'd-better-just-tell-me look. The one that said she was prepared to be a royal pain in the butt.

"Jed Barlowe's up in a church belfry," he said finally. "He's drunk, and he's got his peashooter, and we just need to keep people off the streets until he passes out or runs out of liquor, whichever comes first. No big deal."

She edged farther into the room, watching as he buttoned the neatly pressed shirt. The vest beneath added just enough bulk to make the shirt snug around his middle.

"You're not going to try any fancy SWAT moves, are you?"

Micah looked at her. "Honey, Conard County doesn't have a SWAT team."

"It has you."

She was genuinely concerned. He wasn't accustomed to seeing that look on anyone's face, in anyone's eyes. And being unaccustomed, he had no defenses against it. "Don't worry. I didn't survive twenty-one years in the Special Forces just so a drunk could shoot me. I'll be home for dinner. Will you be okay?"

"I'll be fine." She wasn't going to let him change the subject that easily. "It's your day off. Why couldn't they handle this without you?"

He reached for the button of his pants and hesitated, looking at Faith. Seeing she had absolutely no intention of budging, and that she didn't seem at all concerned that he was about to unbutton his pants so he could tuck his shirt in, he went right ahead and did it. She never batted an eye.

"They need all the help they can get," he said, answering her question. "Nate can't call everybody off patrol and leave the whole county unprotected because Jed Barlowe got a wild hair."

He faced the mirror over his dresser and turned up the collar of his shirt. Faith continued to watch as he drew on a dark green tie and knotted it. Then he picked up his badge, a shiny silver star, and leaned forward to see better as he pinned it on.

"Here, let me," Faith said. Along with ironing military creases, she was a whiz at pinning on badges and collar insignia. The layer of armor prevented the contact from becoming in any way intimate, but her hands trembled nonetheless. With each passing hour, her desire to touch this man grew. How could she possibly explain the wild urge she had to touch his strength, to see if she could make him tremble, too?

He saw her hands tremble and misunderstood. He thought of the courage it must take for her to come this close and offer to help him with a task she must have performed often for the man who had mistreated her. Looking down, he could see only her soft curls and her shaking hands, and he needed to see more.

"Faith, look at me."

Slowly, she tilted her head up and looked straight at him. He looked so magnificent, she thought. So untamed. "Take care, Micah," she whispered. "Take care."

Then, before she could betray any more, she turned and walked from the room.

"Nobody knows what the hell got into him," Nate told Micah when the latter arrived at Good Shepherd Church, a medium-sized white clapboard structure near the center of town. "Reverend Fromberg was out here shoveling snow for half an hour at least before Jed started shouting obscenities from the belfry. He didn't see Jed get past him into the church this morning, so he must have been in there last night when Fromberg locked up. Probably passed out," Nate added with disgust.

Micah nodded, but his attention was centered on the church and possible means of access. They were all standing well back, behind barricades and a row of sheriff's vehicles. All the occupants had been removed from the surrounding houses and businesses and were awaiting the outcome in the high school gymnasium.

Maude Bleaker, whose diner was directly across the street from the church, and whose usual breakfast business had been interrupted because of this incident, shouldered her way up to Nate, ignoring the deputy who tried to hold her back.

"Nathan Tate," she said angrily, "you've got to stop this now! That man's been nothing but trouble in this county since he had his first taste of his daddy's home brew. I don't think a soul would shed a tear if that man were shot right now."

"Maude, Maude," said the gently chiding voice of Reverend Fromberg, "that's a harsh, unforgiving attitude."

"I know it, Reverend, but that man is beyond forgiveness. He's been vulgar and troublesome all his life, and now he's threatening the good folks of this town." She turned her anger back at the sheriff. "We've all been hearing what a great marksman this Cherokee deputy of yours is! Let him prove it!"

"That'll be enough, Maude," said Nate. He knew Micah's hide was thick, but his own wasn't. Nothing got Nate's dander up faster than the feeling that one of his friends was being attacked. He turned away from Maude and looked at Micah, whose face was chiseled granite behind his mirrored glasses. "What do you think?"

"If somebody can keep him distracted for thirty seconds, I can reach the building. After that, it'll be a snap. Hell, Nate, the man's drunk out of his mind."

"If it's that easy, I'll have one of the other deputies do it. You're on break." Nate didn't for a minute believe it would be easy, which was why he'd sent for Micah in the first place. It just stuck in his craw to hear Micah speak as if it were a piece of cake.

Micah swung his head around and looked down at Nate. "It's that easy for someone with my training. I'm the only one who's trained. I'll do it."

While Jed Barlowe shot another couple of wild rounds at the sheriff's vehicles and missed by a country mile, Micah went into the diner, ignoring Maude as if she were invisible, and pulled on winter camouflage over his clothes.

"What weapon do you want?" Nate asked him.

"Just my side arm and knife. He's so drunk I can probably take him down without using any weapon if you can just keep him occupied with what's going on outside."

Nate half smiled. "Maybe I'll have Maude holler at him through the megaphone. That ought to rile him good." Across the room, Maude gave a snort.

"Yeah." Bending, Micah checked the knife he always kept holstered in his boot. "Okay, I'm ready. I'll circle around through the alley and come up behind the church. I'll radio just as soon as I'm in position, and then you start the diversion. I'll have to maintain silence after that so he doesn't hear me. Give me at least thirty seconds to cross the open ground, just to be safe."

"You'll get it," Nate promised.

Maude Bleaker, watching this exchange, had grown mercifully silent. As Micah brushed past her toward the diner's rear door, she reached out and stopped him. Slowly he turned his head and looked down at her. He disliked being distracted at a time like this, but his expression revealed nothing.

Maude spoke. "I didn't mean anything by what I said out there, Deputy. I was just mad."

He regarded her stonily for a moment, then gave a brief nod. "Forget it, Miz Bleaker. I have." He'd long ago become deaf to such inferences.

"The name's Maude, Micah Parish," she hollered after him. "Don't be forgetting *that*."

An invisible smile tugged at the corner of his mouth as he stepped out into the snowy alley. Maude Bleaker was a longstanding believer in lawmen who shot first and worried about it later. She had also said something nasty to everyone in the county at one time or another. All things considered, he had come off lightly.

He paused, drawing a couple of deep breaths, shifting his mental focus to an almost tunnel-like awareness of the task at hand. Last night's snowfall had drifted deep in the alley. Someone had started plowing it out and then stopped, probably because of the excitement Jed Barlowe was stirring up.

At places the snow reached nearly to his hips, but Micah slogged through it as if it weren't there. Ten minutes later he stood in the alley by the corner of Houlihan's Hardware and reached for the microphone attached to the collar of his camouflage. "I'm in place," he told Nate quietly.

He could see the steeple clearly from here, and just as clearly he could see Jed Barlowe. Jed was leaning against the rail that ringed the cupola where the bell hung just beneath the spire. His attention was fixed on the crowd of cars and deputies in front of the diner, and Micah could see only the back of his head as he leaned out and shouted something.

Now! Micah thought, and darted across the open ground toward the back side of the church. Distantly he heard the report of a .357 Magnum, and registered that Jed was shooting again. He was damn glad the man hadn't brought anything more heavy-duty on his little spree. He would be a hell of a lot more dangerous with a high-powered rifle of the kind a lot of locals kept for hunting predators.

Take care, Micah. The memory of Faith's parting words joined the swarm of impressions he was drinking in with every sense. The snow beneath his boots made a dry crunch that muffled his running steps. The cold air knifed his lungs and made his earlobes ache. Every sense was fine-tuned to hypersensitivity.

He was one with the wind as he ran.

And then he was there, flattened up against the back door of the church, which, naturally, was locked. Breathing slightly more deeply than usual, he pulled up the hem of the camouflage jacket and felt around for the key Reverend Fromberg had given to Nate. When his fingers closed around it, he spared a backward glance at the wide expanse he had just crossed. His footprints were there, a beacon for anyone who cared to look. He was counting on Jed being too drunk to notice.

Inside, the church was dimly lit and warm. The day's gray light poured through stained glass, creating crazed patterns of jewel-like colors across the floor and pews. The bell tower acted as an amplifier, funneling Jed's curses and shouts down into the nave as Micah stripped off the camouflage and his combat boots. He tucked the boot knife into his belt, next to his holster.

On silent, bare feet, he climbed the tower, stepping close to the wall to avoid causing a stair to creak.

You'll be careful?

Faith's question whispered through his mind. No woman had ever asked that of him. No woman had ever given enough of a damn to ask that of him. It made him uneasy. He shoved the whisper of her concern away, having no time to deal with it right now. Later...later he would think about all the ramifications in that one little request. About the tie that it implied.

Jed had stopped shooting, but he was still shouting some creative obscenities down at the deputies below. When Micah neared the top of the stairs, he found the trap door open. Edging up another step with caution, he found Jed with his back to the trap door. The drunk was hollering something about Nate's ancestors.

Now!

Just as his upper body emerged through the trap door, Jed swung around drunkenly. Micah froze as the business end of the pistol centered dead on him.

"Damn half-breed," Jed mumbled. "What the hell...?"

"Put it down, Jed," Micah said in a tone that had been unhesitatingly obeyed by men under extreme conditions. "Put it down before somebody gets hurt."

"Yeah," Jed said, and staggered to one side. His hand instinctively tightened on the pistol and squeezed the trigger.

Micah took the shot dead center on his vest. It jarred him a little, but some instinct made him grab the sides of the trap door before he fell down the stairs. Pain blossomed in his chest, momentarily threatening his consciousness, but he

gritted his teeth and battered down the blackness by sheer
force of will.

"Holy..." Jed gaped, the pistol slipping from his hands
as Micah thrust himself up into the belfry. "Hey, man, I
didn't mean to—"

"Maybe not," Micah said through gritted teeth, as he
kicked the pistol away. "Maybe not. And maybe you better
get facedown fast, Barlowe, before I think about the fact
that you could have killed me."

The sun had come out from behind the overcast clouds
around noon, and toward three it had sunk low enough in
the western sky to slant golden light across the soft, white
snow dunes. Fascinated, Faith watched the light change. She
hadn't realized that plain white snow contained so many
colors, from dusky blue shadows to sparkles of red.

Earlier she had run across Micah's clothes hamper and
had been glad to busy herself washing his clothes. Now she
set up the ironing board facing the kitchen windows and
ironed his uniforms while she kept an eye on the stew she
was simmering for dinner.

And for just a few moments, while no one was watching
or judging her backbone, she admitted to herself that this
was the kind of labor she loved. She enjoyed cooking and
cleaning and washing and ironing; and all she had ever
wanted out of life was a home of her own, a good husband
to look after, and a house full of children. She had never felt
any burning desire to build bridges or make money or go to
the moon. What she wanted was a family. Her own family.

But that was not to be. Now she had to find strength and
purpose so that she could give her baby all that it deserved.
The trust fund her father had left her would maintain the
ranch and pay the most essential bills, but she would have
to earn anything extra herself. She wondered if Micah might
want to hire her as a housekeeper.

The sight of a shiny red Blazer pulling up in the kitchen
yard startled her out of her thoughts. While she wondered
if she should pretend no one was home, she watched a man

climb out and walk around to the passenger side. As he turned, the light caught his face, and she was able to see that he had a full golden beard.

Faith instinctively backed up from the window—she had little cause to trust men—but then stopped as she watched the man help a woman out of the car. He bent, laughing, and brushed a kiss on the woman's cheek before they both turned toward the house. That gesture reassured Faith as nothing else could have. There was no hesitation when she went through the mudroom to open the door.

The golden-haired man smiled at her from the bottom step. "You must be Faith Williams. I'm Ransom Laird, and this is my wife, Mandy."

This was the man who had rescued Micah from the VC. Faith felt her face break into a wide, welcoming smile. "Please come in. I just made coffee and was about to make some tea."

When everyone had settled around the table, and Mandy and Faith had shared a few laughing remarks about the joys and discomforts of pregnancy, Ransom turned to Faith.

"I hate to be the heavy here, but Micah asked us to come over and tell you he's going to be a little late. He's not hurt," he hastened to add as Faith drew a sharp breath. "Well, bruised a little, but not hurt."

"He was shot, wasn't he?" Faith felt everything inside her grow terribly still, and hardly felt Mandy reach over to take her hand. No, she thought. No. Not Micah!

"He's all right, Faith," Mandy said, squeezing the other woman's hand. "Honestly. I talked to him myself. They think he's got a cracked rib. Painful but not serious."

"Then why isn't he here now?"

Ransom answered her. "Because he neglected to tell anyone that when Jed Barlowe accidentally discharged his weapon, the bullet hit him. Micah thought he was okay except for some bruising, thanks to his vest, but later, when the adrenaline wore off, he realized it was a little more than that. Anyhow, they only just X-rayed him, and I guess they're wrapping his ribs right now. They're going to hold him for a couple of hours to make sure there are no internal injuries, then he'll come home. But he's fine, Faith. Really.''

It was dark when Ransom and Mandy, assured repeatedly by Faith that she was quite all right by herself, took their leave. She wondered, as she stirred the stew one more time, what Micah had told the Lairds about her. They had seemed to think she would be upset and worried, which indicated they thought she had some kind of long-standing relationship with Micah. She felt as if she did, she realized. She felt as if she had always known him, and yet in many ways she had just met him.

Closing her eyes, she could imagine him coming through the door, his Stetson cocked low over his eyes, his shoulder-length black hair tousled from the wind outside. She could imagine those dark eyes settling on her in that measuring way they had, revealing nothing, yet missing nothing.

And when she held her breath, she could remember the touch of his lips on hers just last night. Her experience of men wasn't wide—her stepfather had made certain of that—but she knew the kisses she had received from Micah were special. He had made her feel that if she just entrusted herself to him, he would show her delights beyond imagining. The kind of things a young girl had fantasized before her rude awakening in marriage. The kind of things she still fantasized about in unguarded moments.

She shivered a little, realizing that she hadn't felt trapped or threatened when he wrapped his arms around her. No, she had felt good. Treasured. As if a previously unperceived yearning had been suddenly answered.

By the time Micah was released from the hospital, he was feeling like a caged lion. He had stayed only as long as he had because he wasn't stupid, and he recognized the potential danger of internal injuries. That hadn't kept him from chewing on the bit, though. He hated to be confined in any way.

The night was clear and cold, the waning crescent moon little more than a silver arc in the sky. When he parked the

Blazer by the back door, he waited a couple of minutes in the dark, listening to the silence of the vast open spaces around him. There was no sound save the sigh of the wind, a lonesome, lonely sound.

It suited him to a T.

Inside, though, someone was waiting for him, and he felt a little guilty. He'd gone out of here this morning like some kind of macho fool, promising the little woman he'd be home from war in time for dinner. Dinner hour was long past, and when he'd checked with Ransom just before leaving the hospital, Mandy had taken the phone to give him an earful about how worried Faith was.

Well, hell. The woman had been in his life for a mere forty-eight hours. Surely it was too soon for her to be getting all wound up about his health? But then, he admitted reluctantly, time was no measure of feelings. He'd seen the concern in her eyes that morning, and he knew damn well that if their positions had been reversed, he would have been concerned for her. It was no big deal, just ordinary human caring.

He grunted as he climbed out of the Blazer. His ribs were just bruised, but they hurt like hell whenever he bent wrong. The tape helped, but only time would heal him.

Once again his dinner awaited him beneath plastic wrap on the counter beside the microwave. This time, however, Faith didn't make an appearance, for which he was perversely grateful. He'd had enough fussing today to last him a lifetime. After eating a huge bowl of her stew, he switched out the light and headed upstairs, thinking that the years eventually caught up with a man, whether he wanted to admit it or not. He was plumb tired tonight.

He got his shirt off with only a few muffled groans, but when he sat down to take off his boots, he knew he was in trouble. There was no way he could bend far enough to reach the laces. He tried, but pain brought a cold sweat to his forehead. Well, he could sleep with his boots on. It wouldn't be the first time he'd done it. Damn, he hated that.

It was the grungiest feeling in the world to sleep with your boots on.

A soft tap on the door alerted him to the fact that Faith must have overheard some of his grunts.

"Micah? Micah, are you all right?"

"I'm fine, Moonbeam. Just fine . . ."

She wasn't buying his assurances without seeing for herself. The door to his room opened slowly, with almost visible uncertainty. She peeked around the edge until she found him sitting in the straight-backed chair beside his bed.

"I heard you groan," she said tentatively. "Do you need help?"

Well, hell, he thought, she was already here, and it *would* be nice to sleep with his boots off. "I can't quite reach my boot laces," he admitted.

"Oh, they've got you all taped up!" she exclaimed softly as she came into the room. All her hesitation had vanished with his request for her help. The white tape wrapped him mummylike from his small coppery nipples to below the waistline of his pants. "Can you breathe?"

"That doesn't seem to be a problem." Damn, he thought, not wanting to notice, but noticing anyway, that she looked adorable in a pink chenille robe and fuzzy pink slippers. Her hair was a wildly tossed mass of fairy curls, and one of her rosy cheeks bore a crease from her pillow. "Sorry I woke you," he said.

"Don't worry about it." Trying not to stare, she knelt before him and fumbled at his boot laces. His chest was magnificent, though, and her gaze kept straying upward as she wondered if that skin was as smooth and warm as it looked. She loved the warm tone of it. And those arms! She had never dreamed that real men had arms like that, so muscular and powerful.

Micah saw her straying gaze, caught a glimpse of her yearning, and felt the immediate response of his body. No, he told himself. No. He wanted no woman in his life, and this particular woman was not meant for casual relationships.

Besides, he had put the ladies of Conard County off-limits with good reason. It was hard enough to face old flames day after day, but even worse when the whole county gossiped about it and shared in all the juicy details. He reckoned that the aftermath of a failed love affair in Conard County must feel something like reading about yourself in the supermarket tabloids. Just look at poor Miss Emma, who probably still heard about her traveling man more than a decade later.

Faith's hands fumbled at his laces, but she finally managed to loosen them enough that he could kick the boots off. "Thanks," he said roughly.

Still kneeling before him, she tilted back her head and smiled up at him. "You promised you'd be home for dinner, Micah."

He didn't want to, but he felt himself smiling back. Just a small upward lift of the corners of his mouth, but he knew she saw it when her eyes began to sparkle. "So I did," he agreed. "Guess I should apologize."

"Apologize?" She shook her head. "I don't want an apology."

Before he was foolish enough to ask what she wanted, she started to stand, and he reached out to steady her. And suddenly she was standing right before him, between his legs, his hands on her hips, her gently swollen womb right in front of his eyes. Almost as if he couldn't help himself, he leaned forward and pressed his cheek to her. He felt a small soft kick, and a rusty chuckle escaped him.

"She's driving me crazy tonight," Faith confided impulsively. "Kicking and turning so much I feel like I'm on a roller coaster."

"She?"

"She. I'm sure it's a girl."

Micah felt another poke. And at almost precisely the same instant Faith's soft warm hand slipped into his hair and pressed him even closer.

"Micah?" Her voice was little more than a shivery whisper.

"Hmm?"

"Thank you for letting me share this with you. I've wanted so badly to share this. I never dreamed how hard it could be to be pregnant and not have anyone to share it with." Looking down at her hand against his dark head, she had the craziest feeling that he was like a wild thing, consenting to be touched only briefly, that at any moment he would rear up and disappear. The thought brought a deep pang.

The tendrils drawing them together were invisible, but he could feel them in the air around them. Reluctant to lose the warmth and closeness, yet needing to preserve his solitude, he pulled back, lifting his cheek from her womb. Her fingers trailed slowly down from his hair to his shoulder as he straightened.

Two things hit him simultaneously, shaking him: her warm fingers were touching the bare skin of his shoulder, and her breasts were now right at eye level. The belt of her bathrobe rode up over her tummy and just under her breasts, accentuating their fullness.

"Faith..." He had no idea what he was going to say, and speech became impossible when her palm settled on his shoulder. It had been too damn long.

She edged closer to him, as if she missed the warmth of his cheek against her. Tilting his head back farther, he looked up and wished he knew what she was thinking. It was a totally uncharacteristic wish in a man who cherished his solitude and wanted to share it with no one. He couldn't remember the last time he had given a damn what anybody was thinking.

Her gaze, he realized, was locked on her hand resting on his shoulder. Turning his head, he could see her milky skin against the duskier color of his own, the long strands of his dark hair trailing across her pale fingers. The contrast was an erotic jolt that zapped straight to his groin.

"Micah?" Faith's voice was now barely a whisper, a shaky whisper at that. "Micah, I feel ... funny...." Shaky. Hot. Cold. Paralyzed.

At once his powerful arms wrapped around her, and the next thing she knew, she was perched on his thigh, her side pressed to his chest.

"What's wrong?" he asked. "Do you feel sick? Does something hurt?" But even as the questions sprang to his lips, a look at her told him that she wasn't sick at all. Her hand remained on his shoulder, and now she moved it. Slowly. Testingly. Her eyes still focused on his shoulder.

"You feel...so warm," she whispered shakily. "So nice. Micah, I..."

She couldn't seem to complete the thought, but he really didn't need her to. He could feel it in the unsure, restless movement of her hand against him, could see it in the way she licked her lips and stared at him in fascination.

The same fascination was blooming in him. For two days now he had been fascinated by the warm, living satin of this woman's skin, by the tousled curls that looked as if they had been spun from moonlight. Her fragrance had been a continuing temptation, her soft woman's body a lure he had struggled to resist.

Now she was perched on his knee, so close he could hear the whisper of her soft, short breaths and feel the radiance of her body warmth like a welcoming aura. Closing his eyes against the visual temptation she presented, he struggled to find his famed self-control, a control so strong and unbreachable that some of his comrades had nicknamed him the Robot. This small, slight woman did what no threat had ever been able to: she made a joke of it.

And her small, soft hand continued to knead his shoulder. In that single touch there was a world of yearning and a wealth of uncertainty. He opened his dark eyes again and turned her face toward him. "Look at me, Faith," he said hoarsely. "Look at me."

Slowly, almost dazedly, her blue eyes lifted to his. Her pupils were dilated, her lips parted, her cheeks flushed. And damn it, she was confused. The woman didn't even know what was happening to her! How the hell was that possible?

"Micah?" A mere breath. A mere puff of sound. As if in the mindless grip of hypnotic suggestion, she leaned toward him.

His control might be disintegrating into dry dust around him, but part of his mind was still analyzing, thinking, concluding. Right now it was concluding that Faith's former husband had abused her in another way, that Frank had taken his sexual satisfaction from her without concern for hers. If she had ever experienced even the earliest twinges of arousal, it wouldn't have been long before carelessness and lack of affection would have smothered them.

Now she was sitting on his knee and experiencing for the first time feelings she couldn't name and impulses she didn't understand. If he exercised his own control right now and set her aside—surely the only wise thing to do—he would wound her again. She might never again let these feelings surface, might never again dare to touch a man. He might well put the seal on what Frank had done.

Well, hell!

Yet he hesitated, wondering if he had enough control to carry her any further without giving in completely himself. It was a question he had never needed to ask himself before, and it set him back on his heels. But he couldn't leave her like this, with her barely born feelings crushed under a ruthless dismissal—or even a kind one.

Trapped. It was a feeling he hated, even when it came about through his own scruples. He was feeling trapped right now, and it gave him the edge over his shattering control. Feeling again firmly in the driver's seat, he drew Faith closer and urged her head to his shoulder.

"Hush, Moonbeam," he said, his voice as dark as the night. "Just lean against me and close your eyes."

Ignoring the temptation of her belt, he brought his hand to her cheek, where he felt the smooth warmth that had so enticed him. She was so small, so soft, so delicate, and she woke the tenderness he kept buried in his soul. He touched her now with that tenderness, tracing the curve of her jaw until she shifted restlessly and her head unconsciously turned into his touch, seeking more.

He caught his breath, then steadied himself. Her trust, he realized uneasily, was penetrating barriers that had never before been pierced. How could she trust him so readily, so easily, after what she had been through? Was this leftover conditioning from that long-ago summer when he had watched over her?

But what did it matter? She was leaning into him, trusting him, receptive to him, and he wanted her more than he had ever wanted anyone or anything. She was a song in his blood, like his Cherokee ancestry. She was a hope he had never allowed himself and a dream he had hardly dared to have. For just these few brief minutes he was going to sacrifice caution and succumb to feeling.

Catching her beneath the chin, he turned her face up and settled his mouth over hers. There wasn't an ounce of resistance in her. She opened for him like a blooming rose, inviting his invasion and possession. Starved to learn her taste, he plunged his tongue into her.

Warm, sweet, eager. She welcomed him as if she had been waiting forever, and her tongue shyly imitated his movements. He teased her gently, taking care not to frighten or overpower her, making sure she never felt trapped. Gently he held her, and tenderly he kissed her, slipping his tongue playfully along hers, careful not to let eroticism grow beyond friendliness.

And then he forgot why he was being careful, because she turned into him and lifted her arms snugly around his broad, bare shoulders. God, how he *needed* to be held! The thought slipped past his guard and bounced around in his mind like a pinball, zinging here and there and leaving everything changed in its wake. The man who needed nothing suddenly needed her until he ached with it, until his throat tightened and his diaphragm froze on an unborn sob of longing. Gasping, he lifted his head and battled his own weakness.

Micah Parish had just faced his own loneliness.

"Oh, Micah." Faith's whisper was shaken as she pressed her face into the curve of his neck and inhaled the wonderful scent that was peculiarly his. "Oh, Micah..." she sighed again. At the worst possible time in her life, it suddenly appeared that fairy tales weren't lies. She hardly knew how to cope with the shock of this unexpected yearning. For months now she had been imagining a life that would be free of men. Completely. For months she had been building a castle in the air where she could be safe because she would be beyond reach. Now this. Now the terrifying, wonderful, awesome possibility that a man could actually make her want and need, that he could actually bring her pleasure and a sense of security. Why now, when she least needed another complication?

In her sigh he heard none of her reluctance. What he heard was her yearning, and since it exactly matched his own, he tipped her face up again and claimed her mouth. This time he kissed her with unabashed eroticism, his thrusting tongue telling her exactly what he wanted to do with her.

When her head fell back against his shoulder in complete surrender, he knew a warrior's fierce triumph at sweet victory. Sucking her lower lip between his teeth, he growled softly and felt for the tie of her robe. A tug released it, and his hand, with unerring instinct, found its way inside, searched out a path past buttons and fuzzy flannel, and then surrounded its objective, a warm, full, firm breast.

"Oh!" The sound escaped Faith on a sharply drawn breath. "Micah..."

Their eyes met, his dark and deep, glowing like black fire, hers blue, bright, slumberous with awakening passion. Her lips were swollen and wet from his kisses, parted to accommodate the rapid breathing that pressed her breast rhythmically into his grasp.

"Did he ever touch you like this?" Micah demanded suddenly, angry at himself for handling her this way, furious at Frank Williams for abusing her. "Did he ever make you feel this way? Did he ever, just once, make you feel *good?*"

Faith shook her head slowly, just once. Then she ripped the breath from him by the simple act of turning to press herself hard against his hand, by the simple, broken statement, "Never. Oh, Micah...I never...ever..."

The brutality she had lived with had never been clearer to him. In that instant he found his sagging control and battered down the wrath that could do no good. Had there been a way, he would have erased from her memory all the bad things, but there was no way. All he could do was show her that it didn't have to be bad. That a man could give her good things. She deserved to know that.

Gently, as if unwrapping the most priceless piece of porcelain, he brushed back the front of her nightgown and bared her breast to his gaze. She had the finest, palest skin, with a delicate tracery of blue veins that only heightened his awareness of her incredible fragility.

Tucking the fabric under her breast, he lifted her nipple to his mouth. He heard her gasp at the first touch of his tongue, and then she grew completely still, holding her breath in anticipation. He had heard that a pregnant woman's breasts became terribly sensitive, so he took exquisite care.

Her nipple had already begun to swell, but he lapped gently at it with his tongue, listening to her soft gasps, until the nubbin was hard. Then he took her into his mouth to suck her gently and listened with deep pleasure to her muted groan.

"Micah..." His name was little more than a moan that trailed away, but there was no mistaking her reaction when her hands found his head and held him close and tight. Her fingers tunneled into his hair and hung on tensely.

"This is how it should be, Moonbeam," he muttered roughly against her soft, satin skin. Lifting his head, he looked down at her dazed expression, at her soft breast, at the hard peak of her reddened nipple. She was beautiful. Exquisite. He wanted her naked; he wanted her garbed in nothing but her God-given beauty. He wanted to hold her swollen belly in his hands and press kisses there to let her know she wasn't at all fat or ugly, but was perfect in her pregnancy.

And then he saw the scars.

Chapter 7

He didn't like this. He didn't like this at all. Pausing after he shoved another of Faith's suitcases into the rear of the Blazer, Micah took a moment to stare out across dazzling snow at an equally dazzling blue sky.

She wasn't anywhere near as sure now that Frank knew nothing about her ranch. When he had questioned her closely this morning, she admitted that she might have mentioned the place to Frank. Maybe she had mentioned it several times. But Frank, she insisted, had never been interested in the ranch.

That was the giveaway, Micah thought now. Frank had never been interested. How could she know that if she had never discussed it with him? What it came down to was that Faith desperately needed to believe that Frank would never even think of looking for her there, so her mind had played little games with the facts and nearly convinced her that he didn't know about it.

Micah figured that if Frank really wanted to get Faith, he would remember the Montrose ranch fast enough when he discovered she had left San Antonio. Finding it wouldn't be easy, with everybody in Conard County alerted to a dangerous stranger looking for the Montrose place, but it wouldn't be impossible.

So he had tried to persuade Faith to stay with him until Frank was apprehended. That was when he discovered that although she might be small and fragile, she could be as cussedly stubborn as an army mule. Somehow, at some point, the woman's mind had diddled with reality and convinced her that she would be safe at the ranch. Micah had tried every argument his agile mind could manufacture, but Faith had refused to budge an inch. In her mind, her father's home was an unbreachable fortress, a sanctuary no evil could penetrate.

Damn it, he should have made love to her last night. Hadn't he read somewhere that lovemaking released that bonding hormone, whatever it was? He'd had the perfect chance to make her want to stay, and he'd blown it because he got mad about her scars.

Aw, hell! Turning, he stomped back into the house for another load. It would have been unscrupulous to take advantage of her that way, he told himself. He would never have been able to forgive himself. She probably never would have forgiven him. She wasn't a casual type.

The phone started ringing the instant he set foot on the porch. He stamped his feet twice to knock the snow off and then stepped inside to answer it.

"Parish."

"Micah, it's Dirk Bayard. About the white Honda you had me tow in?"

"Right. How bad is it?"

"I can have it running by noon if you want. It just needs a new radiator. I won't be able to fix the body damage until next week, though, but it can be driven until I get the new grill in."

"Go ahead. The lady needs a car."

She needed more than a car, he thought irritably. More than the pickup truck he'd been planning to lend her when she wouldn't even allow him to use the lack of car as a reason for her to stay with him. She could use a new brain, one that thought clearly.

Talk about getting a wild hair.

He hated the feeling that it was at least partly his fault she was in such an all-fired rush to get out of here. When he'd seen those fresh red scars where her husband had stabbed her, he'd gotten furious. Blind angry. And Micah Parish in a rage was a scary thing. A terrifying thing. He'd been told so often that he never let his temper get out of hand.

But it had almost gotten out of hand last night.

He could hardly blame her for wanting to get out of his house as fast as possible. He hadn't hurt her or anything, but if his temper was terrifying to other men, then it must be even more so to a woman who was accustomed to being battered by a man when he got even a little bit annoyed.

Inside Micah, the full-fledged fury of a thunderstorm existed. When he became truly angry, the air seemed to snap with energy around him, and it was almost possible to feel the lightning. There were times when he even fancied that he could feel the atmosphere warp around him as if bent by incredible force.

No, he could hardly blame Faith for wanting to get away from him. How was she to know that such force and strength could be harmless, that he would never hurt a hair on her head, no matter how furious he became? He was willing to bet that Frank Williams had promised her more than once that he would never strike her again.

Picking up the box that contained her meager supply of kitchen utensils, Micah stomped out of the kitchen and into the bright, cold day. The propane truck and the phone installer were supposed to arrive at her place at ten, and time was getting short if they were going to be there to greet them.

"Micah?" Faith's light voice called him from the porch. "Gage is on the phone."

Well, hell, what now? He shoved the box into the back of the Blazer and strode back to the kitchen. This morning Faith wore jeans and a fuzzy lavender sweater. She had a liking for soft colors and fuzzy fabrics, and Micah was discovering that he did, too. And he had never guessed that they made jeans for pregnant women.

Why the hell hadn't he just loved her silly last night?

He picked up the phone. "Morning, Gage."

"Morning. I thought you'd want to know that a buddy of mine up at the state lab says they should be faxing the results of their examination of Jeff's cattle late this afternoon, around four. He hinted that things weren't adding up."

"Thanks, Gage. I'll come in this afternoon."

"How are the ribs?"

"Okay." He'd had to wear cowboy boots so he could use the bootjack to remove them later. They weren't half as stable as his preferred combat boots, but there weren't any laces to fiddle with, and as long as he didn't have to do any running or cover rugged terrain, they would do. At least they made it possible for him to get by without help.

Bending to pick up Faith's boxes and suitcases hurt, too, but it was only a brief, sharp pain that let up as soon as he straightened. He could endure that quick jab without much trouble, and he sure as hell wasn't going to let Faith heft this stuff.

When he hung up, he turned to find her watching him with concern in her blue eyes. "I'm fine," he said gruffly.

Her brief nod was more of an acknowledgment than an agreement. It occurred to him that if he claimed he needed her help, she would stay to look after him. But that would be dishonesty, and he wasn't dishonest. Nor did he want any dishonesty in his relationship with her, wherever it led.

"Why don't you rest a moment and have some coffee?" she suggested.

It would, he realized abruptly, be all too easy to get addicted to her concern. It wasn't that he wanted to be fussed over, or that nobody would care if he dropped dead. He had friends, good friends, who would grieve at his death. But never in his life had he had someone who cared about him in the small ways—the ways that mattered.

He glanced at his watch and figured they could spare a few minutes. Maybe if he took another stab at it, he could get her to give up this craziness.

This time, though, instead of telling her all the reasons why she shouldn't go, he simply asked her to stay.

Her hands tightened around her mug of herbal tea, and she regarded him solemnly. "I have to go, Micah. I have to stand on my own two feet just once in my life."

"Before you got married—"

"Before I got married I lived at home with my mother and her husband. I've never once been truly independent."

He thought about that a moment and inevitably wondered how it had come about. These days most kids flew the nest just as soon as they had the opportunity.

"My mother was sick," Faith said after a moment. "Someone had to look after her, and I don't regret it, but I missed the experience of being on my own. I think if I'd had that experience, I never would have stayed with Frank for so long. I keep thinking that if I had known I could manage by myself, I wouldn't have been so afraid."

She made a small sound, something like a sad little laugh. "It's pathetic, isn't it? Spineless."

"I'm sure there was more to it than that." As a cop, he knew a little something about the spiral of domestic violence, and as a Green Beret he knew something about psychological warfare. "You love someone, so you forgive them. Make excuses for them. And you think you must be somehow at fault, so you feel guilty. And finally you feel so worthless, so totally like a failure, that you believe you deserve the abuse."

She looked at him wonderingly. "You really do understand."

"Hell, yes. It's Basic Brainwashing Technique 101. From childhood we're conditioned to believe that if we're bad we'll be punished and if we're good we'll be rewarded. Religions are built on the concept, and most children are raised with it. It's straightforward operant conditioning, and it doesn't even have to work at a conscious level."

He reached across the table and touched her hand. "Unfortunately, cause and effect don't have to be apparent. If the effect is bad, the cause is assumed. That's what happened to you, plain and simple. People don't find it easy to believe that bad things just happen, that there doesn't have to be any direct cause when they become the victims of violence. Invariably, the first assumption they make is that they did something to bring it on themselves."

Faith nodded, a suspicious shine in her eyes. This was more than she had hoped for, she realized suddenly. That anyone other than another abused wife would understand. That a man could actually understand what had happened. It had all been explained to her, of course, when she went for counseling. She had desperately needed to know how she had let herself come to that, and she had been told pretty much what Micah had just told her. But somehow, hearing it from him validated it in a way that her psychologist's explanation had never done.

And the most comforting realization, the one that warmed her, was that he didn't think she was weird or sick or crazy. He thought there was nothing wrong with her, that she had simply been an ordinary woman caught up in things she didn't have the means to battle.

She watched him glance at his watch yet again and then rise to carry his cup to the sink. He was a genuinely unique man, she thought. Hard in ways that would make him a truly formidable enemy, yet surprisingly compassionate.

He faced her, leaning back against the counter, resting the heels of his hands on the edge. "Are you sure you won't reconsider?"

He would make it so easy to stay, she thought. Micah Parish was a caretaker, and he would take care of her so well that she would probably never notice a lack in her own fortitude and independence. But that wouldn't be fair to either of them.

"I have to," she said again, and rose to carry her own cup to the sink.

He was big, he was a cop, and he was a man, but she felt perfectly safe approaching him. Just three days ago she would have found it impossible even to think of doing such a thing, yet here she was doing it. He had an untamed appearance that probably frightened many people, and there was a hardness to his features that could be intimidating, but she knew she could walk right up to him in perfect safety. If he lifted a hand to her it would be only to comfort or to bring her pleasure.

Reaching out, he caught the back of her neck in one of his large hands and drew her close. When she stood against him, her face pressed to his chest, he closed his arms around her and felt her wrap hers around his waist. "If you need anything at all, you just call me, Moonbeam. Don't ever hesitate to call me."

They arrived at her ranch in time to meet the woman from the telephone company. After the phone was installed and working, the propane tank was filled and all the appliances checked out, they headed into town to get Faith's car from Dirk Bayard's shop. From there, Faith went grocery shopping and Micah went over to the sheriff's office.

He still didn't like it, but he was beginning to accept the fact that he couldn't stop her. He could, however, make sure that the patrolling deputy in the area checked on her at least once during his shift. Most of them, being the westerners they were, would probably check on her even more often than that.

"Well, well, well," said Velma Jansen, the department's dispatcher as Micah came through the door. "It's the famous deputy himself. How are the ribs, big boy?"

Velma was sixty, scrawny, leathery and as tough as a marine drill instructor. She had a shamelessly big mouth, a heart that was even bigger, and she mothered the deputies until they begged for mercy.

"Prime, Velma," Micah joked back. "They're prime."

"There's a club for cops like you, you know," Velma said. "You big, tough macho types who are idiotic enough to let someone else get off the first shot. You can only join if your life is saved by your body armor. Big honor, right?''

"Ignore her, Micah," Charlie Huskins advised from the duty desk. "She's been holding body armor checks all day. Nobody gets out that door without proving they're wearing it."

Micah had no difficulty whatsoever imagining the scene this morning as the day shift tried to get out that door and were confronted by a determined Velma, all four-foot-ten of her. He wondered if she poked their ribs to check or made them take their shirts off. It was almost enough to make him grin.

He held his hands up in the universal sign of surrender. "I'm not on duty, Velma."

"Nate was hoping you'd come in," Velma said. "He had to go over to the high school, but he'll be back shortly."

"Trouble?" Micah asked.

"Oh, no," she hastened to assure him. "Nate and Marge had to talk to the guidance counselor. One of their daughters is having trouble in algebra or something."

Charlie spoke up. "He wants to ask you again about pressing charges against Jed Barlowe."

"Jed didn't mean to shoot me," Micah said flatly. "The man's a fool, but he isn't a murderer."

"Then you're a fool, too, Micah Parish," Velma snapped. "The man's a danger, whether he means to be or not."

"We can charge him with drunk and disorderly," Micah said patiently. "We can charge him with public endangerment, illegal discharge of a firearm, and a whole bunch of other stuff, but I'll be damned if I'll press an attempted murder charge."

"See, Velma?" Charlie said. "I told you Micah's as honest as the day is long."

"It'll be small comfort if Jed Barlowe gets drunk again and shoots somebody."

"I don't think Jed will be out on the streets for a long time as it is," Micah said.

An hour later he was telling the same thing to Nate, only Nate was a lot quicker to agree than Velma. "I just needed to be sure, old son," Nate told him. "The county D.A. wants to make some headlines, and I need to be able to assure him you weren't just confused yesterday. Consider it finished."

Micah started to rise, but Nate waved him back. "Gage said the state lab is going to be faxing down the results of the necropsies on those cattle of Cumberland's."

Micah nodded again. "He called me this morning. That's part of the reason I stopped in."

"Good. Now, what's happening with Faith Williams?"

"She's moving out to the Montrose ranch today."

"Damn. You couldn't stop her?"

"Short of committing a felony?" Micah shook his head. "She's stubborn."

"Then she ought to fit right in with a neighbor lady I can think of." Nate sighed and shuffled the stack of waiting paperwork. "What is it with these women, Micah? They sail along like a ship before the wind, and then all of a sudden, at some little provocation, you find they've tossed the anchor overboard and ain't going nowhere, nohow. They're all scared and frightened and then, bam! They've got a backbone made of unbending steel. And always at the wrong time."

"Trouble with Marge?"

Nate glanced up wryly. "Does it show? Never mind. Faith Williams is a bigger problem. I don't cotton to the idea of a pregnant woman out that far all by herself. Not in my county. Short of condemning the property, I don't guess there's much to be done except to alert the patrols to keep a close eye on her. Damn it," he said in annoyance, "doesn't she understand how fast a body can get into serious trouble?"

"She's never been alone before." Micah stretched out his long legs. "I asked Mandy and Ransom to keep an eye on her, too."

"Maybe Mandy can talk some sense into her."

Micah's face remained expressionless. "Mandy Laird? The woman who said no mad arsonist was going to drive her from her home? The woman who was planning to conduct her own solitary pregnancy at a ranch every bit as far out as the Montrose place?"

Nate suddenly laughed. "That's what I mean about women!" A moment later, all vestige of humor had vanished from his face. "I have a bad feeling about this, Micah. A bad feeling."

Micah nodded. "Tell you one thing, Nate. At the first sign of trouble of any kind, I'll carry that woman out of there bodily."

"You do that, son. You do that."

"Well, hell." Micah's comment pretty much said it for all of them as they pored over the necropsy report. He'd been hoping for something, anything, to add to the not-quite-right feeling he had about the mutilations. All the lab had come up with, however, was a more detailed description of what he already knew.

They were Cumberland's cattle, all right, but Micah had already judged that by the apparent age of the brand mark. Cause of death for both was exsanguination, followed by excision of the tongue and genitals. He'd already figured that from the lack of blood around the wounds or at the scene. Detritus from around the animals' hooves was awaiting further analysis.

"Sure to be good old Wyoming clay," Nate said sourly.

"Aw, be optimistic, Nate," Gage said. "Maybe they'll find the seed of a plant that grows only in the desert or something."

Nate looked hard at him and then gave a short laugh. "Maybe you Feds are used to that kind of break, but out here in the boonies, all we get are a slap, a lick and a prayer."

Micah looked at Gage. A Fed? Past or present? But before he could pursue that intriguing line of questioning, Nate was moving on.

"The guys at the lab are good," Nate said. "I shouldn't put them down. They try. They just don't have all the facilities and experience bigger localities have." He turned to Micah. "Head out, scout. I don't expect to see you in here again before Monday, and then you'll take the desk."

"I'm fine—"

Nate silenced him with a gesture. "You know as well as I do that an instant of instinctive hesitation could cost you your life. As long as those ribs hurt at all, you get easy duty. End of discussion."

Micah had taken orders for too many years to argue now. Outside, he pulled on his Stetson and his mirrored sunglasses despite the waning afternoon light and peered down the length of the street toward the supermarket. Faith's Honda was gone, so she must have headed back to her ranch. He decided to follow and make sure she hadn't run into any trouble.

Fifteen miles later, at the turn onto County Road 118, he was berating himself for being a fool. If the woman was bound and determined to live all alone in the middle of the godforsaken reaches of Conard County, then why the hell did he care? She could have stayed in San Antonio where, despite her protests, there were surely people who cared about her. Hell, that Ranger, Garrett Hancock, probably would have hovered over her like a protective hen. There were hospitals nearby, emergency medical services within minutes, plenty of police protection....

Scotch that thought. The woman didn't want police protection. Didn't believe in it. Didn't trust it.

With reason.

And because of that, she was hiding out in the middle of nowhere, and Micah Parish, who wanted no part of such doings, couldn't put her troubles from his mind.

"Well, hell," he growled into the silence. He should have loved her senseless last night. It would have been easy enough to do, considering that she had never before enjoyed sex. He should have loved her until she was incapable of arguing with him about a thing. Then he should have made her agree not to go haring off anywhere until Frank was caught and the baby was born. At least then he could have kept a close eye on her, and Frank would never think of looking for her at Micah's place.

But he'd gotten mad. And she had looked at his furious expression and grown frightened. He couldn't blame her for that. Not at all. But when he watched her shrink back from him, he had grown even madder and simply carried her to her room, leaving her alone in the dark on her bed. Then he had gone outside and run out to the county road and back. In his bare feet. It had been just about enough to cool him off.

Not that he would ever be entirely cool when he thought of those stab wounds. If he ever managed to get his hands on Frank Williams, he vowed he would teach the man the meaning of fear. The kind of fear Frank had taught his wife. The kind of fear no human being should ever have to experience.

His hands tightened on the steering wheel, and he pressed down a little on the accelerator.

Of course, it was a damn lucky thing he *hadn't* made love to Faith last night. There was no place in his world for a woman, and Faith was the kind of woman who would expect to become part of a man's world if that man wanted to become part of her body.

She was not, he thought, like most women. He had lived among enough cultures to understand that between most men and women, a relationship was a simple social and economic transaction. In return for his protection and support, a woman gave a man access to her body and sons to look after him in old age. It was straightforward, elemental, necessary to the survival of the species.

But human beings were capable of more dimensions than those necessary to survival. If they weren't, he wouldn't feel the forces of nature like a rush of wind in his head. He wouldn't feel the passage of the seasons like a hymn in his blood. He wouldn't be able to imagine a bond between people that transcended time and space.

And he wouldn't now be feeling loneliness like a requiem in his soul.

Faith, bless her, had hit him right between the eyes with that one. In all his life—at least, all his *adult* life—he had never been lonely. Solitude and loneliness were not the same thing. Far from it. And he prized his solitude, but how could a man remain solitary if he started to feel lonely?

He didn't want to feel lonely, and he suspected if he ever broke down far enough to make love to Faith, he would spend the rest of his days feeling lonely. Of course, he could ask her to stay, but that came right back to the central problem: he didn't want a woman in his life. He didn't want anyone in his life except a couple of good friends who knew how to keep their distance. Distance was meaningless to women. They invaded a man's space and took up residence. They certainly couldn't conceive of spending weeks in silence and separation.

So he didn't want to get involved, and it was a damn good thing he hadn't loved her senseless after all.

But his body ached, his loins yearned, and his solitude felt suddenly empty. And it was possible, in that empty aching, to wonder why he had always lacked the very things that most men took as their due. Was it something in him? Was it something about his heritage, his sixth sense, his way of thinking?

It was him, of course. He needed a mate who could enter his solitude without destroying it. Such a paradox was impossible. No mere mortal could do such a thing.

Faith heard the Blazer pull up to the house and never doubted it was another deputy coming to check on her. She had arrived home at three-thirty that afternoon, and almost the instant she started unloading the car, a Conard County Sheriff's car had pulled up and Deputy Ted Waring had insisted on helping. When all the groceries were inside, he accepted her offer of a mug of coffee and advised her that she could expect a deputy to stop by a couple of times a day.

"That's an awful lot of interest in a single citizen," Faith had remarked. She wasn't sure she wanted such a close association with cops, although Micah had gone a long way toward easing her mind on that score—at least with regard to the Conard County Sheriff's Office. It had been a shock to realize, when she saw Deputy Waring, that she no longer felt fear when she saw the tan Blazer and the khaki uniform. Micah had gotten her past that in just a couple of days.

"Sheriff Tate takes a personal interest in everyone in the county, Mrs. Williams," Deputy Waring had told her. "Some folks need more looking after than others is all."

Before he left, he had given her another advisory. "Hal Wyatt owns the spread just west of you. Some of his best heifers wandered through a break in the fence sometime in the last couple of days, and he's had some cowboys out looking for them. If you happen to see some men on horseback, don't worry about it."

Now another Blazer was pulling up as night settled over the land. This time, though, it was Micah who climbed out.

There was no mistaking the bubble of joy she felt when she saw him. It had been years, absolutely years, since she had experienced the champagne of sheer happiness, yet here she was, feeling it now. Right now. Because of this man with his dangerous, hard face, his wild aura, his exotic eyes. This man who looked as if he could snap her in two with his bare hands and whose innate gentleness made her breath catch.

And without a single thought for self-preservation, without a backward glance at the years of terror and pain that had been inflicted on her, she let Micah see that joy. She flung open the door with a huge, welcoming smile, and before he quite knew what had hit him, she was in his arms.

The winter chill clung to him, and he smelled crisply of the cold and himself. His shearling jacket was stiff against her cheek, his leather-gloved hands icy against her back, but his lips were hot when they found hers in instinctive response to her welcome.

This, he thought, was what it felt like to come home.

He was a wayfarer. He had traveled beneath the suns of alien lands most of his life. As an adult he had risked his neck more times than he could count to preserve the ideals of the country that had deprived his mother's people of everything. Ideals that far exceeded the grasp of most ordinary men. Micah believed in those ideals. The American Dream to Micah was the Human Dream and the birthright of all men. That belief had carried him into dangerous situations with nothing but his wits to protect him. He had won medals, had a drawerful of such mementos, enough "fruit salad" to throw him off balance if he wore it.

But never, ever, had he been welcomed home.

Her mouth was hot, wet, eager beneath his. In this kiss she was a full-fledged participant, and equal partner in the dizzying thrust and counterthrust of tongues that spoke in ways clearer than words.

Then suddenly, as if they both simultaneously realized that they weren't ready for the implications inherent in their actions, they broke apart.

Micah listened to the sound of his ragged breathing, knowing that he'd just had another unwanted revelation. He listened to the ragged sound of her breathing and knew that she wasn't ready for any of this. So much for his famed control.

"How are you making out?" he asked roughly, to fill the silence before it grew uncomfortable. He needed to wall off that kiss into a compartment of its own, to prevent any discussion of it or apology for it.

She astonished him with something that sounded like a very genuine laugh. "I've been on my own for precisely five hours, Micah. I haven't had any time to make out well or poorly."

He glanced down at her and liked what he saw. The pinched look that had been so evident when he first found her on the road had magically been erased. Her hair, that mass of silvery blond fairy curls, was wildly tousled around her face, and her lips looked soundly kissed.

"Coffee?" The pot she had made earlier for Ted Waring was still warm on the hot plate, and she poured a healthy mugful for Micah. "Actually, I've begun to consider some of the logistics of living here. It suddenly occurred to me that I'll need my own snowplow."

"Don't worry about it. I'll plow your drive if it needs doing."

"I couldn't ask—"

"I didn't hear you ask."

Jason Montrose had died before Micah returned to Conard County, and this house had been built maybe fifteen years ago after the original ranch house burned to the ground. It was a single story building, unlike most in the area, built of brick. Micah looked around him, noting again the relatively new appliances, the gleaming no-wax floor. He would bet that Jason had done all this with his daughter in mind.

"Mind if I look around?" he asked Faith. Earlier, he had looked over the barn and surrounding terrain and learned the layout of the house, but he wanted to check out the house again. Years of training compelled him, just in case. *In case?* God, he hoped his sixth sense wasn't involved in the urge.

The house had been surprisingly dust-free, surprisingly well kept, when she had arrived. She had expected to find dust inches thick and all kinds of spider webs, even evidence of mice. Instead, she had found a dwelling that looked as if it had been vacated only months before, not years. Oh, there had been dust and some evidence of spiders, but nothing like what she had expected.

Walking through it with Micah now, pointing out things, her instinct was to be glad he hadn't caught her with the place in a mess. She took pride in her housekeeping, and even though she had barely arrived, it would have embarrassed her to have to show a filthy house.

But even as she was chatting pleasantly about what a nice house it was, unease was nibbling at the edges of her comfort. She kept getting the most unsettling feeling that the residents of the house had walked out only moments before and might return at any time. That was ridiculous, she told herself. Silly. No one had ever lived here but her father, and he had died five years ago.

Micah never entered a room without learning all the exits and entrances within seconds. It was an old habit, another one of those that was just too much trouble to break. He also liked to know whether the windows were locked and how well. Faith watched him check out every room with an intensity that finally silenced her, an intensity even greater than he had showed that morning. In the end, she just let him do his thing.

"Jason really did a fine job," he remarked when they returned to the kitchen. "Even after all this time there isn't the slightest draft around any of the windows or doors. Wish my place was half as airtight."

They settled at the table as they had done on other nights in his kitchen, him with his coffee and her with her tea.

"I hated it when Dad's old house burned down," Faith remarked. "It was years before this place felt at all like home to me." But it was only now, as she sat there with Micah, that she realized it was going to feel lonely and empty beyond belief when he left tonight. It wouldn't be the same as her apartment in San Antonio, where she could hear other people any time of the day or night. Here, there wouldn't even be a passing car to hear once Micah left.

"Where did you grow up?" she asked Micah. "Not around here."

"No. My dad was army, and I grew up all over the world. By the time I graduated from high school I'd lived in twenty-seven different places in eight different countries."

"That must have been hard on you and your mother."

"My mother left when I was two."

"That must have made it even harder on you." She could tell he wasn't keen on this subject, but she was full of questions, and as long as he didn't get angry, she wanted to ask them.

He studied her impassively, his harsh, dark features and black eyes revealing nothing. She wanted to know, and he was a little surprised to realize that he wanted to tell her some of it.

"I don't remember my mother at all. Somewhere I've got a picture of her, but it never meant much to me. She was a Cherokee medicine woman, or so my father told me once. They met when he was posted to Oklahoma, and I guess it must have happened fast, because he was only stationed there for three months. I suspect leaving must have been a real wrench for her. After a couple of years she bailed out and took my younger brother with her. Almost a year later my father said she had died."

"Do you know her family?"

Micah shook his head. "No. I don't know a thing about them, except that her father was also a medicine man. My father either never knew about them or forgot it all by the time I got big enough to ask."

"But what about your brother?"

"Gideon stayed with her relatives, I suppose. I don't really know. My father only mentioned him once or twice while I was growing up and—" He broke off and shrugged. "He's never been real to me, Faith. I never knew him. By the time I got around to being a little curious about him, my father had died."

Faith had the worst urge to reach out and touch him, but she suspected he would reject any gesture of sympathy. "So you don't really have any family, or any Cherokee roots."

One corner of his mouth lifted a hair. "Isn't this the great melting pot? I've melted, Faith. True blue American mongrel."

"Except that I imagine there've been a lot of people who didn't see it that way."

"Well, I do find it kind of ironic that my Cherokee ancestry seems a bigger cause for interest than my European ancestry. We all go back to Eve, don't we?"

Faith smiled. "So I would have said. I think it's a shame, though, that you don't know much about your mother."

"How much does anyone really know about a parent?"

"Very little, I guess." She rose and put the kettle on. "I sometimes think I ought to do something to make sure I leave some kind of legacy for my baby in case something happens to me. I've just never been able to imagine what that could be."

Micah studied her almost solemnly as she moved around the kitchen. He was still following her with those dark-as-midnight eyes when she returned to her seat across from him. "My mother left me a name," he said after a moment. "I think it's the best legacy she could possibly have given me, because I was able to carry it with me everywhere, and no one could ever take it from me. Not even her."

"You mean the name Micah?" Faith's eyes were wide, interested, and she leaned a little toward him. "It's a beautiful name."

He shook his head. "No, I mean the name *she* gave me. My father said she gave it to me as soon as I was born and made him write it down so it wouldn't be forgotten. She called me Speaks with Voice of Thunder." He had never told that to a living soul. Never.

"Oh, that's beautiful," Faith murmured. "Oh, Micah, that's beautiful. And it's so perfect for you! I could almost believe that she was able to see you full-grown...."

Micah looked away. "Maybe she did. I don't know. I never told anyone about it before."

"I won't tell a soul," Faith promised. "Not a soul."

Why the hell was he telling her all this? he wondered, and slowly brought his gaze back to her. This woman kept unlocking the private places inside him. One at a time, little by little, she opened the doors. Like a moonbeam, she slipped into the darkest corners.

A mortar round exploded deafeningly, and dirt flew everywhere.

Micah jerked awake, instinct and training both keeping him utterly still as another hollow crash resounded through the darkness.

Thunder. Lightning flashed brilliantly, blinding in its intensity. Damn, he'd heard of it, but he hadn't quite believed it. A winter thunderstorm.

He sat up and swallowed a groan as his ribs protested. Well, that sure explained the dream, he thought as another crash of thunder ripped through the night. It had been years since he had dreamed of being in a heavy firefight. Years.

The digital clock beside his bed said it was shortly after two. His body said he was through sleeping for now. He threw back the covers and swung his feet to the floor. The linoleum was icy, and he once again promised himself he was going to rip it up. The bare wood wouldn't be quite so cold. Or maybe he would put down rugs. Faith would probably prefer rugs.

The thought jarred him as much as the imagined mortar attack had. Muttering a choice word, he rose and began yanking on his clothes. Who the hell cared what Faith would like? They lived in their own homes, in their separate worlds, and he must be losing his mind.

He considered going downstairs barefoot, but once again his training intervened. A man wasn't prepared to deal with much without his boots on. Moving cautiously, he managed to get some socks on with only minor discomfort and only a couple of four-letter words.

Downstairs, he started a pot of coffee and then stepped outside. The air was cold and would probably grow much colder by morning, if the storm was any indicator. The advancing cold front would have to be strong to generate this kind of weather.

Thunder rolled hollowly again, and lightning flashed, burning an afterimage of his barn onto his retinas. Incredible. He hoped Faith was sleeping through this. He couldn't imagine that she would feel very comfortable with this kind of violence all around her the very first night she spent alone in her new home.

But he relished it. He reveled in the way the cutting wind snatched at his hair and whipped it around him, the way his ears burned from the cold, the way the air crackled with the charge of the storm. Each and every sensation was a keen affirmation of life. With his head thrown back and the wind grabbing at him, he felt so vigorously alive that he could almost sense the rush of blood in his veins.

Alone and alive, a solitary shaman without a people, without a real home—it was his way. *Brujo.*

Into the silence and solitude, into the stormy night, borne on the breath of the wind, unease came. At first he thought it was just the storm's restlessness, but before long he knew. Something was wrong.

When the feeling wouldn't abate, he turned to go back into the house, thinking that he would get a heavier jacket and check out the animals. He had scarcely taken a step into the kitchen when the phone rang shrilly. He reached for it immediately, sure it must be the office needing him for some emergency as a result of the storm.

Instead it was Faith.

"Help me," she sobbed. "Oh, God, help me! He's going to kill me!"

Lightning flared across the sky, and with a click, the line went dead.

Chapter 8

With Micah's phone dead, he couldn't call for backup. The storm's electrical activity cut up his radio transmission badly, and he wasn't at all sure that Ed Dewhurst was able to make heads or tails of what he tried to tell him.

He didn't wait for confirmation, though. He shouted into the microphone as he roared down his driveway and skidded around the turn onto the county road. The Blazer fishtailed wildly for a moment and then straightened out. There were enough dry patches on the pavement to make it possible to speed up.

His shotgun, fully loaded, was upright in the dash rack. Beside him on the seat was his holstered .45. In the glove box was a 9mm Browning with a full clip. A damned arsenal, he thought, and it wouldn't do him a bit of good if that creep used Faith as a hostage.

The Blazer seemed to be moving in molasses, though in fact he covered the four miles of county road between his place and hers in just about five minutes. Five minutes was a long time. Five minutes was long enough to stab a person thirty or forty times. Five minutes was long enough to suffocate a person. It was enough time to die a dozen times over. And he still had to get up her driveway.

Through a blast of static he heard Ed again, and this time it sounded as if Ed had gotten the most essential bits of information. He said he was on his way.

Faith's house was completely dark. Not even the porch light punctuated the stormy night. Nor was any vehicle other than hers apparent. Of course, Frank could have hidden an armored troop carrier behind the barn, or even inside it. And although the wind had been blowing, there were still too many tire tracks in the snow to be able to tell at a glance if someone besides Faith had come but not gone.

It was every cop's nightmare, entering a dark house with no idea how much danger waited inside. Micah left his shotgun locked to the dash, deciding the 9mm Browning would be of more use in close quarters where accuracy might well be essential. He tucked his knife into his belt, where he could have instant, unfettered access to it. In his left hand he carried his aluminum, eight-cell flashlight, turned off but ready, with the butt on his shoulder and the bulb pointed downward. As such, it was a good defensive weapon.

Thunder rolled again, and lightning flickered psychedelically. The storm was moving off, softening its fury.

He listened at the door but could hear nothing from within. It did nothing for his state of mind, however, to find the door unlocked. A twist of the knob opened it, and he stood on the threshold of the pitch dark kitchen, listening intently.

He smelled ozone on the cold air, and then on the warmer interior air he scented the musty odor of a long-empty house, the faint lingering fragrance of coffee, and the even fainter perfume of Faith's presence.

He eased inside and closed the door behind him, shutting out any extraneous sounds from the storm. A *plink* came from the vicinity of the sink—a dripping faucet. The refrigerator clicked to life and hummed. There was no one else in this room. His nose was certain of that.

He flicked on the flashlight and pointed it into all the dark corners, driving back the shadows. Nothing appeared to be disturbed. He moved on to the living room and again found nothing and no one.

Frank must have found Faith asleep in bed. Micah's stomach tightened at the thought. Half-prayers mixed with curses flitted around the edges of his mind as he forced himself to concentrate on what needed doing right now. She could be dead already. Or Frank could be holding her in one of the bedrooms with a hand over her mouth and a gun at her head, or a knife at her throat. He had to find her. Now. Every second might be critical.

The first two bedrooms were also empty, as was the bathroom. That left Faith's bedroom, the one she had pointed out earlier as the room that had been hers when she visited her father. A violated sanctuary, he thought, and eased the door open quietly, carefully.

Again he hesitated on the threshold, every sense straining to detect motion, sound, smell. Here Faith's fragrance was stronger, along with the sharper tang of terror. She was in here; he was certain of it. He was also equally certain that no one else was. Had Frank fled already?

"Faith?" He switched on his flashlight again and scanned the room. "Faith?" At least he couldn't smell any blood. Still, there were a lot of ways to kill without spilling blood. "Faith?"

A small rustle, barely a whisper of sound, like the brush of fabric against skin, drew him to her closed closet. Steeling himself against whatever he might find, he reached for the closet door.

"Faith, it's Micah," he said, and flung the door open.

In the brilliant light of his flashlight, he saw her. She was huddled in a small ball in the far back corner, half buried in clothes and shoes. Her blue eyes were wild with terror, and her face was as white as the driven snow.

At that same moment he heard the growl of a powerful engine approaching and knew that Ed Dewhurst had arrived. Reaching up, he keyed the microphone that was clipped to his shoulder.

"Ed?"

"None other. I'm pulling up right behind your unit. Where are you?"

"Back bedroom, west side. The house appears to be clear, but I haven't checked the basement yet. The woman appears to be unhurt but terrified. Stay where you are while I ask her a few questions."

"Will do."

Micah squatted, taking care to keep the bedroom door in full view. "Faith?" He spoke gently, as he would to a terrified child who didn't know him. "Faith, where's Frank?"

She blinked then, repeatedly. And the terror faded from her face to be replaced by confusion. "Micah?" Her voice was a small, shaky whisper. "Micah?"

"It's me, Moonbeam." He realized suddenly that he was behind the flashlight and that she couldn't see him at all. At once he pointed it away from her. "Where's Frank? Where did he go?"

"Frank?" She blinked again, and then her hand flew to her mouth. "Oh, God, I heard something. The storm . . . it was like that night . . . and then I thought . . ."

Micah leaned forward, touching her arm gently, beginning to understand. "Was Frank here, Faith? Did you see him?"

Slowly, she shook her head. "No. I didn't see him. I heard . . . the storm . . . ." Confused, she fell silent and shook her head again.

Micah keyed his microphone. "Ed? I think it was just a flashback set off by the storm, but come in and check out the basement, will you? The stairs are behind the door to the right as you come into the kitchen."

"Consider it done. Micah? You want me to call off the mob?"

"Yeah. I don't think we need anybody else."

He rose and hunted up the light switch. As soon as the overhead fixture came on, Faith relaxed visibly.

"It's all right?" she said, looking at him with so much trust that Micah felt something inside him twist. How could she look at any man with that much trust, he wondered, let alone one as hard as he was?

"It's all right, Moonbeam," he said gruffly. "You're coming with me."

Bending, he helped her from the closet and then held her close, letting relief and gratitude wash over him. Later he could ask her what had happened, but right now all that mattered was that she was safe, that Frank hadn't harmed her.

"You're sure you're okay?" he asked her. "Frank wasn't here?"

"No. No." A ripping shudder passed through her, and she pressed closer. "I was so scared. Oh, Micah, I was so scared!"

"Shh. You're coming home with me, baby. I'll keep you safe."

For once she didn't argue.

Ed Dewhurst appeared in the doorway. "All clear," he said.

"Thanks, Ed. I'll finish up here."

"I'll wait until you get outside, then. Just to be sure."

It was 2:30 in the morning, Faith was pale and shivering, and Micah could see no point in lingering. "Grab whatever you need for tonight," he told her. "We'll come back in the morning to get the rest of your things."

It was then that she showed a spark of spirit. "But..."

"Screw it," Micah said bluntly. "You can argue yourself blue in the face, woman, but this time you'll lose."

She tilted her head back and peered up at him. In the depths of her blue eyes he could see the moment she realized he wasn't going to be budged. Moments later she was stuffing a change of clothing into an overnight bag. When she wanted to dress, Micah nixed the idea.

"Just pull on your parka and boots over your night-gown," he told her. "We're going straight home, and you're going straight to bed."

He warmed up the cab of the Blazer before he would let her leave the house, and then he insisted on carrying her across the snow so the hem of her gown wouldn't get wet.

Once again he made her feel cherished and opened a deep wound she was only just beginning to acknowledge. This, she thought, was how she had once believed that men cared for women. And although other women claimed they didn't want this kind of caring, Faith admitted she had always wanted it. Independence was a nice thing to have, but there were times when nothing would do but to have someone take care of you. Not all the time, just sometimes, like now, when the small act of carrying her to an already warmed car made her feel infinitely precious.

But Micah was not like other men, she thought as they drove back to his ranch. Not at all like other men. Twenty-five years ago he had been special, and today he was even more so, as if life had honed him until only the good things remained.

Closing her eyes, she rested her head against the seat back and tried not to think about what had happened tonight. Micah had told the other deputy it was a flashback, and she guessed it must have been. A particularly loud crack of thunder had cast her suddenly back into her apartment in San Antonio. Until the moment she recognized Micah behind his flashlight, she'd been huddled in terror awaiting the next blow of the knife, hearing Frank's threats in her head.

Bitch! I'll cut that baby out of you!

Shivering even in the warmth of the Blazer's interior, Faith opened her eyes to drive the memories back into the dark places where they belonged. The storm was nearly over now, little more than an occasional distant growl and flash.

"I'm sorry I dragged you out in the middle of the night," Faith said. "I seem to remember calling you. I must have."

"You did, but I was awake." He glanced her way, his face shadowed eerily in the poor light of the dashboard instruments. "I'm glad you called me. I'd hate to think of you huddled in that closet all night."

"But it's so. . . stupid. Embarrassing."

"No." Without hesitation, he reached out and covered her restless hand with one of his. She immediately returned his grip, tightly. "I've had a few flashbacks. There's nothing stupid about them. And they're only embarrassing in retrospect. When you're having one, it's as real as today. More real. I'm glad you called me." He said it again, with even more emphasis. Then he remembered the unlocked door he had found. "Faith, did you lock your door before you went to bed last night?"

Several moments passed before she answered uncertainly. "I'm not sure. I don't remember. Why?"

"Not important." But it *was* important, and he would have felt a whole lot better if she could have remembered.

The night had begun to turn truly bitter. When he climbed out of the car in his own yard, the wind that nipped his ears had knife-like icy fangs. He carried Faith once again, setting her on her own feet only when they were safely in his kitchen.

"You don't weigh more than two feathers," he remarked as he helped her struggle to get out of her coat. "Are you sure you're eating enough?"

"I've never been very big."

"Do you want some cocoa?" She looked like she needed a little time to wind down. Her eyes were too bright, her cheeks were still too pale. Her hands moved restlessly, plucking at her white flannel gown nervously. Maybe she needed to do a little talking, too.

"I'd love some."

Micah nodded and turned to the stove. "Did you bring a robe?"

"I forgot." She sat at the table and propped her chin on her hands. "I'm warm enough. It's okay."

"We'll get it in the morning, along with the rest of your stuff." He mixed cocoa powder and sugar in a pot with a small amount of water and turned on the stove.

"Micah, really, I—"

He interrupted abruptly, without apology as he poured milk into the saucepan. "Stuff it, Moonbeam. Enough is enough. There's no way on God's earth I'm going to let you stay out there alone until your ex is safely back behind bars.'' He muttered a word that brought a flood tide of color to her cheeks, then turned around to glare at her. ''I was a fool to let you get away this morning. Damn it, woman, there's a point past which independence becomes sheer stupidity and cussedness.''

''Cussedness?'' She blinked. ''Plenty of people have thought I was stupid,'' Frank and her stepfather, to name two, ''but nobody's ever accused me of obstinacy.''

''Well, I am and you are.'' Suddenly he leaned forward and peered at her. ''Are you laughing?''

A surprising smile curved her mouth. ''Well, yes. I kind of like the idea of being obstinate. I've been such a doormat all my life.''

He was trying to adjust to this unexpected side of her when just as suddenly as it had come, her humor fled. She hunched visibly in her chair and wrapped her arms around herself. ''It was so scary, Micah,'' she said quietly. ''I was so terrified. Frank wants to kill this baby.''

''The *baby?* Why the hell does he want to kill the baby?'' Some things were beyond the comprehension of a normal mind.

''Because it's *his*. He told me that I was his and the baby was his, and he could do anything he wanted to us. He was mad because I tried to get away from him, and because I was taking the baby.'' She shrugged one shoulder. ''I don't know. He was mad that I got pregnant, too, even though it was his fault for not waiting until I—'' she broke off and then continued. ''If I'd ever been able to figure out what it was that made him so angry, maybe I would have been able to keep from making him so mad.''

''Don't. Don't even think like that, Faith. It'll drive you crazy. Men like that don't need a reason, and they use anything for an excuse. If it wasn't one thing, he would have found another.''

She looked up at him. ''I know, but...''

"But you're human, and you keep trying to understand it. You never will, though. All the reasons and all the excuses don't add up to understanding. There's just something seriously wrong with the man."

And standing here, thinking about it, made him furious. How could any man want to kill his own seed? How could any man want to hurt the woman who nourished it?

It was a stupid question. He'd been around the block more than a few times, and he knew what people were capable of. It might violate his every sense of rightness and offend his every feeling of decency, but somewhere there was somebody capable of doing almost anything.

Frank Williams didn't want anyone else to have his wife, including his child. He probably felt jealous of the baby that occupied her body. The child was a trespasser, an interloper. An invader.

"Well, hell." He was hardly aware of speaking aloud, but he *was* aware of the rage that churned inside him. His protective instincts were aroused like never before, and his innards weren't likely to quiet down until he was sure that Faith and her child were safe from that scum.

"Micah?"

Hearing her uncertainty, he focused his dark gaze on her and saw that he was frightening her. It must be there, plain on his face again, he thought. All the rage he was feeling, all the desire to smash something in order to make her safe. And it was scaring her.

"I'd never hurt you," he said flatly. "Never. But damn it, Faith, I'm human, and sometimes I'm going to get mad. Right now I'm so mad at Frank I'd like to bash his face in. And I'm not going to apologize for the feeling, so either go to your room or get used to it."

Scowling, he turned his back to her and stirred the cocoa. The milk was beginning to steam. Ready enough. He turned off the gas.

"Micah."

It was a good thing she spoke before she touched him, because he was wound tighter than a spring, and he didn't like to be touched without warning. He always needed the time to stifle his defensive reactions, to steel himself for the invasion of his personal space. She gave him the time. Barely. His muscles turned to iron beneath her fingers.

"I know you wouldn't hurt me," she said.

Slowly, battling the dregs of his earlier tension over her safety, battling the upsurge of a different kind of tension because of her proximity, he turned his head and looked down at her. The absolute truth in her expression ripped a hole in his heart.

This woman had far more courage than she knew, he realized. More than he had guessed. Not only had she struck off into the unknown by herself, but now she stood firm in the face of an anger that had made some of the world's toughest men uneasy. More, she had the guts to trust him when she had no reason to trust any man.

Turning toward her, he wrapped his powerful arms around her and drew her close to his chest. "I'll take care of you, Faith. I swear that man won't get near you." Holding this woman, he realized uneasily, was getting to be as natural as breathing. "Now, how about that cocoa?"

Faith went to bed a short while later, but Micah stayed downstairs, hoping to shake the restlessness that plagued him. Tonight's activities had roused primitive feelings of all kinds, from the violent to the sexual. He didn't have any problem with his primitive side. It was part of him, like his face or his hands, and he accepted it as a facet of his nature. Sometimes it was useful. Sometimes, like tonight, it was troublesome. And when it was troublesome, he felt restless and caged and aware that with just the smallest provocation he might try to break out.

Another long, cold run would probably help, but he didn't want to leave Faith alone. He had a strong feeling that her night wasn't over, that the fallout from the flashback hadn't really hit her yet. She couldn't possibly shelve all the feelings the nightmare had reawakened without some difficulty. At this moment Frank's vicious assault on her was as fresh as if it had happened a few short hours ago, not three months.

She was probably, he thought, lying awake in her bed, staring at the ceiling with her heart pounding and her mouth dry, trying to tell herself to calm down. Exhaustion would carry her off eventually, but for now she had to deal with it all over again. Mostly she had to deal with the immediacy of the feelings. Because of the flashback, the muffling effect of time had vanished.

Thinking about that only made him more restless. He needed to do something, and there wasn't a damn thing he could do. Every instinct and urge told him to throw something, break something, bash something—preferably Frank Williams. Every cell in his body demanded that he *fix* things. And he couldn't. Lacking a target or any kind of outlet, he paced like a wild thing caged.

An hour later—longer?—he paused at the foot of the stairs for the umpteenth time and ground his teeth. This wasn't helping a thing. Not a thing. He would go up and check on her. If she was asleep, he would go out to the barn and clean stalls. If she wasn't asleep . . . if she wasn't asleep, maybe he could comfort her.

His boots rang loudly on the wood stairs. He hadn't carpeted them and probably never would. Another one of those defensive habits, not to muffle any sources of noise that could provide a warning. Right now, though, he cursed the racket and tried to tiptoe, not wanting to disturb Faith if she was sleeping.

She wasn't asleep. When he gently pushed her door open, he found her sitting upright in the middle of her bed with every light in the room blazing brightly.

"I can't sleep," she said unsteadily. "I keep remembering. . . ."

He hesitated, unsure what to do.

"Don't leave me alone," she whispered. "Please don't leave me alone."

That much he could do. When he held out his hand to her, she scrambled from the bed and flew to him. His large hand swallowed hers whole, and the bones of her small fingers felt incredibly fragile. He wondered if he would live to regret this night, but that didn't keep him from guiding her to his room and motioning her into his bed.

She was getting into every corner of his life and soul, he thought as he used the bootjack to yank off his boots. Now, for the rest of his solitary days, he would be able to imagine her as she was right now, sitting propped against a pillow in his huge bed, with the colorful Hudson Bay blanket pulled to her chin. In the warm cascade of light from the small lamp on the table beside her, her pale hair was a wild halo, her blue eyes nearly swallowing her face as she waited. Trusting. That was what was really killing him. All that trust he wasn't sure he deserved, not when his body kept trying to remind him that she was a woman and he was a man.

Some remnant of wisdom kept him from removing any more clothing except his belt. For comfort he unbuttoned his shirt cuffs, but then, fully clothed, he stretched out beside her on top of the blanket. He hadn't lost it all—yet.

When he opened his arms, she turned into them without hesitation, finding a comfortable spot on his shoulder to rest her head. The bedside light remained on.

"Talk," he said. "It helps."

"Nobody wants to hear this stuff."

"Well, I don't want to hear it, either. But it needs telling, and I'll listen." His tone was gruff, but his hand was infinitely gentle as it found its way into her soft-as-silk-and-moonbeams hair.

"Nobody ever listened before," she said in a voice tight with choked feelings that ranged from bitterness to anger. "I tried to tell my stepfather, and he told me Frank beat me for my own good. It was a man's duty, he said."

Micah swore under his breath. "I'm listening, honey. I'm listening. It's a man's duty to protect those who are weaker, not punch them around. Your stepfather was wrong, baby. Dead wrong." God, he hated to think how that had undermined her attempts to find help. "The cops didn't help you, either, did they?"

"No. I thought they would have to, but...but..." The breath she drew was almost a sob. "They've got some kind of code about getting each other into trouble...."

He hugged her closer and dropped a kiss on her temple. "I know. That kind of thing happens when you don't know who's going to be guarding your back. It doesn't make it right. Every one of them who failed to help you deserves to be horsewhipped."

"I just...couldn't believe it when they walked away." Her voice was thick with the tears that still hadn't begun to roll down her cheeks. She needed to cry, he thought. She really needed to let it all out. "I felt so alone. So alone!"

He held her and rocked her gently and waited for the tears that never came. She fell asleep eventually, curled against him, and he continued to hold her.

He wondered what she would think if he told her how much he wanted her and decided she would probably be horrified and frightened. She had no cause to expect anything good from a man.

And then he remembered how just last night she had responded to his kiss and his touch. If he hadn't seen those scars, they would have made love right then. He was certain of it.

But no, he told himself. It would be wrong. He didn't want to get involved, and she was too emotionally fragile to handle an uninvolved relationship. Or any kind of relationship. He had to give her time and space to heal. And maybe, in giving her the time and space, he could get over this incredible urge to make her his.

He'd never felt like this before, he realized uneasily. He had never wanted anyone or anything quite this badly. And he had never gotten this degree of satisfaction from holding any other woman, from comforting any other woman. It was as if Faith were attached to his heart by an invisible string, and her every feeling was transmitted to him somehow, tugging and pulling on his own feelings.

They *both* needed time and space.

* * *

A sunbeam woke her in the morning. Blinking awake, she stared at dancing dust motes that sparkled against the incredibly clear blue backdrop of the winter sky. For an instant she felt like a child again, waking to the excitement and promise of a spanking new day. A sense of wonderful contentment remained with her even when she realized that she wasn't a child anymore, and that she was waking up in Micah's bed. Or maybe it remained *because* she was waking in his bed.

Her flashback last night had freshened all her fears, but sleep had once more muffled them with distance and time. What remained fresh in the morning light was all that Micah had done last night. He had come racing at her call, ready to protect and rescue her. He had drawn her out of her terror and comforted her. Then he had taken her home with him and held her through the night.

She didn't think her own mother would have done half as much for her as Micah had done since her car ran off the road.

And now she was lying in his amazingly comfortable bed beneath warm blankets with a sense of well-being she knew she owed directly to him. He had made her feel as if she mattered, a feeling that had been sadly lacking in her life.

Her baby stirred, giving a series of rapid little kicks and pushes right across the front of her womb. She's turning over, Faith thought, and smiled in pleasure at the life growing within her.

"Morning, sleepyhead."

Micah's deep voice drew her gaze to the door. He stood on the threshold, dressed in jeans and a red and black flannel shirt, and in his hands he held a tray.

"Breakfast in bed for the lady," he said, coming toward her.

"Oh, Micah," she murmured as he set the tray on the bedside table. "You shouldn't have gone to so much trouble."

"No trouble. You had a rough night, and you could stand a little pampering. Hell, you could stand a lot of pampering." And he had never in his life wanted to pamper anyone. He piled the pillows behind her, then drew up the chair beside the bed so he could help her.

"Face it, Moonbeam," he told her with a definite twinkle in his midnight eyes, "your lap is gone for the duration. You'll just have to borrow mine." With that, he picked up the tray and balanced it on his knees so she could reach it.

"It's a cold, beautiful day out there," he told her. He'd brought a mug of coffee for himself and sipped it while she ate. "When you get dressed, we'll go back for your stuff. I don't want any arguments about it, either."

"But it isn't right, Micah. I don't want to put you to so much trouble!"

"No trouble. Hell, woman, you're less trouble than a mouse in the house by far. And a mouse never cooked me dinner."

Her shy blue eyes lifted to his. "You like that?"

"I should have said so. Yeah, I like it. After living alone most of my life, it's really a luxury to come home and find a meal waiting for me. You're a good cook, too, so I'd consider it a fair trade, if you need to do something to keep from feeling like you're imposing." He'd figured that out about her. Her drive for independence needed to be assuaged, so he would assuage it.

"I also noticed," he added, "that you did my laundry and ironing. Now, I have to draw the line at that. That's too much bending and lifting, and too much time on your feet. If you try to do it again, I'll feel bound to take my clothes to the cleaners in town to keep you from doing it."

She peered at him, gauging his seriousness. He meant it. "Okay, I won't touch your laundry. But, Micah, women all over the world work in the fields and . . ."

"I know all about the rest of the world. I also know about the infant mortality rate. No heavy work or I'll take you with me wherever I go. No scrubbing floors. No laundry and ironing. I'll concede on the vacuum cleaner, but not another thing.''

Impossibly, Faith felt the corners of her mouth lifting in an irrepressible smile. Even when he was being domineering, Micah made her feel good.

That smile was nearly Micah's undoing. He was putting on a good show of being a friendly, thoughtful guy this morning, but every cell in his body was remembering that he had held this woman's sleeping body for hours last night, and that he had suffered for it.

Oh yes, he had suffered. Throbbed. Ached. Hungered. *Hell.* He felt like the wolf in Red Riding Hood. Deceptive. Underhanded. Conniving. Reprehensible. This woman was beginning to trust him, and he was sitting here with a wolf's smile on his pretend-sheep's face while wanting to fall on her and bury his body so deeply in her that they would both forget they had ever been alone.

God! And he had the nerve to think Frank Williams was a crud! This woman had more than enough to deal with. She didn't need some oversize half-breed savage slavering after her....

The thought drew him up short and opened a surprising window in his mind. *Slavering? Half-breed savage?* The words that Dawn Dedrick's rejection had branded on his soul. Was he actually applying them to himself? Was he actually assuming that Faith would apply them to him?

How many times had he heard those words in his mind and then walked away before some woman could actually say them? Why had he always assumed she would? Why had he never lingered to find out that she might not?

Because women didn't stay. Had never stayed. Not his mother, not all his father's ''housekeepers'' and ''friends.''

Good God, did he really think this way?

''Micah?''

He had turned to stare out the window as veils of self-delusion were stripped away. He suddenly felt oddly naked and raw. He had thought he knew himself. A man who spent so much time alone felt comfortable even with the dusty places in his soul. Except that there had been corners and rooms he hadn't even known existed until this very moment.

"Micah?"

He turned slowly and looked at her. Moonbeam. Fairy princess. The icon he had cherished in his shaman's heart through all the dry and empty years. But she was no icon, no fairy princess, no moonbeam. She was a woman who had suffered and was now locked in the prison of her fears, just as he was.

She was a woman whose gentleness somehow touched him in places that no one else had touched. He didn't know if that was good, or if he liked it, but like a wolf drawn by the brilliance of fire, he just kept circling closer anyway.

What he wanted right now, this very minute, was to lie down beside Faith and hold her close. What he wanted was to kiss her softly, gently, repeatedly. He wanted to learn her shape, her hills and hollows, with his huge hands, hands he would make as gentle as a man could. He wanted, touch by touch, kiss by kiss, to draw her into his world, into his passion, into his need.

She was through eating. He gripped the tray and stood. "Get ready. We need to get your stuff."

Faith watched him walk from the room and wondered what she had done to bring that desolate look to his dark eyes.

The day was extraordinarily cold and bright, and the glare of sunlight off the snow was almost painful to her eyes. Micah disappeared behind his mirrored glasses, and Faith thought she might be wise to get a pair of her own.

Once again she watched him as he drove and wondered at his self-containment. She envied his apparent self-sufficiency and wished she could emulate it. She couldn't, though. There was a part of her, she realized, that would always feel empty unless she could share it. There was a part of her that needed to love, and while she might never have the husband she dreamed of, she would now have at least a child to love. Maybe that would be enough. It had better be. Her need to love and be loved had made her vulnerable before, and she didn't want to risk that again.

Micah drove slowly along the county road, taking time to enjoy the pristine beauty of the winter day. There would be plenty of other days like this before spring thawed Conard County, but familiarity would jade the eye and deprive the view of its breathtaking quality. That was one thing twenty years with the army had taught him: to take time to appreciate beauty wherever he could find it.

"Look!" He braked gently and pointed off to the right. "A jackrabbit."

Faith looked but couldn't see it until it took flight across the rugged snow-covered ground. She was still smiling delightedly when the rabbit had disappeared and she turned back to Micah. "I'd forgotten," she said. "I'd forgotten how beautiful it is here."

As he turned into her driveway he braked suddenly, bringing them to a halt at an angle across the road. He recognized both his tire tracks and Ed's from last night. All the department's Blazers used exactly the same heavy-treaded, studded snow tires. Overlaying his tracks, however, was a fresher set from a smaller, lighter vehicle.

It might be nothing. It certainly looked as if the smaller vehicle had come back out. He hesitated another moment, then pulled the Blazer to one side of Faith's driveway.

"Micah? What's wrong?"

He glanced at her, but his mirrored glasses completely hid his thoughts from her. "Not a thing," he said. "I just want to check something out."

Probably a neighbor, he told himself, but couldn't remember any of the local people owning small vehicles. People who lived on the ranches hereabouts needed full-size trucks and four-wheel drive. Some of them owned Lincolns or Cadillacs, but none of them would have made tire tracks this size. This looked like the imprint from a Japanese car or truck. It could have been somebody from town, but...

He climbed out of the Blazer anyway and squatted by the tracks ignoring the fierce ache of his ribs. From his pocket he pulled a notebook and made a swift sketch of the tread marks. They were recent. One set considerably more recent than the other, hardly melted yet in the morning sun. Walking a little farther up, he looked for some flaw that would make this set of tires stand out from any other, but he didn't see one. There were a whole lot better substances for taking an impression than snow, unfortunately.

And it probably didn't matter, he told himself as he returned to the Blazer. No reason it should.

"Is something wrong?" Faith asked again when he slid into the vehicle beside her.

"Not a thing. I was just curious about those tire tracks. They're fresh this morning, and I don't recognize the tread. That's all."

"Do you always devote so much attention to things like that?"

He turned his head and looked straight at her. Tan Stetson, long black hair, mirrored lenses. Just the look of him was enough to jam her heart into high gear. So male. So virile. And for the first time in a long while, that recognition didn't strike her as a threat.

He spoke, his voice a deep, smooth sound. "For twenty-one years I couldn't afford to ignore things like that. Not ever. It's become a habit."

Her car was still parked where she had left it yesterday, apparently untouched and undisturbed. Faith reached for the door handle as soon as Micah brought the Blazer to a halt, but he reached out and restrained her.

"You wait here," he said. "I want to check things out first."

"Why?" She was beginning to get irritated by his caution and felt she at least deserved to know why he was acting this way.

"Why?" He gave her a faint smile. "Because I'm a cop, lady. It's what I do."

He unnerved her even more by removing the shotgun from the clamp on the dashboard. "You ever fired one of these things?"

"When I was a kid," she admitted reluctantly. "Dad taught me."

"Good. I'm sure you won't need it, but do me a favor and hang on to it anyway. It's loaded and ready. I'll leave the engine running, but I want you to lock the door after me. Got it?"

She nodded slowly, understanding that something had disturbed him. Micah Parish wasn't a man who tiptoed through life, and if he was taking this many precautions, he had a reason. Without another question or any objections, she handed him her house key.

"Lock it," he said as he climbed out, and he waited to make sure she did. When she pressed down the button on his side, she heard all the other locks click with a solid thunk.

He gave her a thumbs-up and then turned toward the house. She noticed that he pulled his jacket back away from his gun, and that he unsnapped the holster. And to think she hadn't even noticed he was carrying his weapon when they left his house!

He would have checked the yard for footprints, but so many servicemen had come and gone that the ground was thoroughly trampled. At the door, Micah tested the knob and found it locked, but loose. Ed had locked up last night, right? Chances were a neighbor or even a salesman had stopped and left upon finding no one at home. But Micah didn't take chances. When he opened the door, he was standing to one side so he wouldn't be silhouetted against the brilliant day, an easy target for anyone inside.

Then, moving swiftly, he removed his sunglasses, stepped inside and closed the door. The glasses had kept him from adapting to the brilliant outside light, so he was able to see quite clearly. The kitchen was just as he remembered it from last night, and the refrigerator hummed exactly the same note. The hot water heater gurgled quietly and then fell silent.

There was a new odor in the house. A sour smell. An unwashed body smell. Someone *had* gotten inside.

Micah pulled his gun and cursed his cowboy boots as he tried to move quietly across the kitchen. The odor was absent when he opened the basement door and peered down the stairs, so the intruder had not gone down there. Instead, he followed the odor into the living room. There was a framed photograph lay facedown on the coffee table in a spray of shattered glass. Nothing else, not even the TV, had been touched.

Touching nothing, he moved on, certain now that someone had deliberately come to terrorize Faith.

Neither of the spare bedrooms had been touched, but in the doorway of Faith's bedroom he froze and stared in total disbelief. He'd seen a lot of terrible things in his life, but nothing had ever quite affected him as much as the destruction of Faith's room did. It wasn't the mess. It wasn't the holes punched in the wall, or even the word scrawled in red lipstick over the headboard.

It was the way her clothes had been slashed. Each and every single item had been pulled from the closet and methodically shredded.

Chapter 9

The sun had gone down more than an hour ago. Faith stood at the kitchen window of the Laird house and peered out into the night, wishing with all her might that Micah would come for her and take her home with him.

He was looking for Frank. So was every available lawman in Conard County. From time to time Ransom Laird called the sheriff's office and asked for the latest developments, and each time Nate Tate told him they were still chasing leads. Frank had been seen at Maude's diner, Nate had said. Just yesterday. Maude hadn't thought much of it because he hadn't asked any questions. He'd been a stranger, though, so she'd remembered him well enough to recognize a mug shot.

Micah had left Faith in the care of Ransom and Mandy, telling her that Ransom would give her the best protection available, but that since Frank would never look for her there, it was just an added precaution.

Faith understood his motive and was grateful for his care and the care of the Lairds, but the day had been an incredible strain. Trying to be polite and pleasant for hours when worry was stretching her nerves to breaking was almost more than she could stand. Mandy clearly didn't expect her to make the effort, but Faith had been raised to believe that no situation excused discourtesy.

Closing her eyes, she vividly remembered the look on Micah's face when he had come out of her house that morning. He had been furious, so angry that his face had turned as hard and cold as stone. Micah didn't get angry the way most people did, Faith realized. He didn't shout or yell or throw things. He grew quiet. Cold as glacial waters. Silent and still. It was scary. The air around him seemed to crackle with power, and she got the feeling that if he let go, nothing on earth would stop him. Faith had seen him that way twice now, and both times she had had the wild fancy that he might reach out and grab handfuls of energy from the very air like a sorcerer.

Despite that, she couldn't wait to see him again. Couldn't wait for him to show up and take her away with him. If she had half a brain, surely she would feel safer here with Mandy and Ransom. But even though the Lairds made her feel welcome and safe, they didn't make her feel as safe as Micah did.

"Faith?" Mandy spoke from behind her. "Shouldn't you put your feet up or something?"

Faith turned, managing a smile. "Probably. I'm too tense to sit, though."

"I can imagine. At least join me at the table for a cup of tea. I hate herbal tea, you know. And I'm still not convinced caffeine is bad for the baby."

Faith nodded. "But you don't want to take a chance."

Mandy wrinkled her nose. "Exactly. I've never been much of a risk taker." She put the kettle on the stove.

Just then Faith heard the roar of an approaching engine. "That's Micah." She turned and all but pressed her nose to the glass in her eagerness.

Ransom was suddenly beside her, his hair and beard looking like polished brass. "Let me make sure first, Faith."

He was holding a shotgun, and he urged her gently back from the window.

It was Micah. He came onto the porch and into the kitchen looking weary and a little frustrated. Without a word, he held out one arm to Faith. When she came to him, he hugged her to his side. Even through her sweater she could feel the outdoor cold that clung to him. "You okay?" he asked roughly.

"I'm fine, Micah. I'm fine. Frank?"

"Not yet. But if a termite sneezes in the county tonight we'll hear about it. The man can't make a move, Faith. Not a move. We'll get him."

"Coffee, Micah?" Mandy asked.

"No thanks, Mandy. I just want to sack out so I can get on this first thing." He looked down at Faith. "You want to come with me?"

"Of course!" She was astonished that he needed to ask. "I'll get my jacket."

He watched as she hurried to the living room, and he managed to ignore the significant looks exchanged by Ransom and Mandy. Let 'em speculate, he thought. He was taking care of Faith because somebody had to, and he didn't see any army of volunteers lined up. That was all. And this damn sexual attraction he was feeling would just have to burn out with time. It was that simple, and he would be damned if he was going to complicate his perfectly simple life by letting things go any further than they already had.

He was still telling himself that when they were closed up in the cab of the Blazer and driving down the county road, Faith's tempting feminine scent wafting all around him, carried on the blast from the heater. He had never in his life known a woman who smelled so damn good. Afterward, he thought of that drive as twelve miles of sheer hell.

"Sheriff Tate said Frank was seen at Maude's diner," Faith said. "Is that in town?"

"Yeah. Right across from Good Shepherd Church and two blocks from Main Street. Not too many tourists find it."

Faith turned a little on the seat. "You think he knows the area?"

"Maybe. Maybe not. Hard to say." Hard to think when his body had decided that his self-imposed celibacy ought to end *right now*. Even his brain was trying to join the mutiny by throwing up erotic images faster than he could erase them. "He's been seen a few other places in the last day or so, too. Scranton's Service Station. The drugstore. He's not staying at any motel or rooming house, though." It really bothered him to think that if the storm hadn't scared Faith last night she would have been at that house when Frank arrived. That he probably would have shredded her with the knife, just as he had shredded her clothes out of thwarted rage. "Nate has a couple of deputies watching your house tonight, in case he goes back."

"God, Micah, doesn't it ever end?" What had she ever done to Frank except try to love him? Why couldn't he just leave her alone? It was over. *Over.*

Micah reached across the seat, found one of her hands and squeezed it gently. "We'll get him. If he stays in Conard County, we'll get him."

"And if he doesn't stay?"

How the hell could he answer that? "Faith, I'll make you a promise right now, on my honor as a man. I'll keep you safe, regardless of what it takes. I promise you that."

It was a rash promise, but he was fully prepared to keep it. He had been trained to hunt men across continents, and after twenty-five years of risking his neck for faceless principles, he wouldn't hesitate to risk it and everything else for someone he cared about.

But Faith astonished him. Before the sound of his words had even begun to fade, she turned toward him. "No, Micah. Don't make promises like that. I'd never be able to live with myself if anything bad happened to you."

Well, hell, he thought. He had every intention of keeping his promise, whether she wanted him to or not, but it moved him that she was concerned for him.

He felt a gentle touch on the back of the hand that clasped hers and glanced down to see her other hand caressing him, stroking him gently, softly, in the way no one else had ever touched him. As if he were precious.

God, how the hell was he going to withstand all this temptation? Not only did she manage to make him hornier than he had felt in years, but she was driving him crazy with the need for her gentleness, of all things!

That touch pierced him in other ways, too. It said so much that she wanted to touch him that way, that she felt safe to do so, free to do so. It made him want to touch her back, made him want to encourage her to touch him in other ways, other places.

Micah looked so tired, Faith thought as he helped her down from the Blazer and into the house. He looked as if he had missed too much sleep last night, as if he had been hurting all day—and he probably had been, from his bruised ribs. And after saying he just wanted to sack out, the first thing he did once they were inside, even before he took off his jacket, was to start a fresh pot of coffee.

As soon as the pot was bubbling, he turned toward the table, shucking his jacket with movements that seemed a little stiff.

"You're sore," Faith remarked.

His dark eyes snapped to her face and then drifted away. "A little. The second day is always the worst."

"Do you want me to take care of the animals for you?"

He hung his jacket over the back of a chair and looked at her, wondering which one of them was losing their marbles. She couldn't seriously be proposing to perform that kind of heavy work in her condition? He opened his mouth to argue with her, question her, scold her and then snapped it shut. It didn't matter, and he only wanted to fight with her to get his mind off the impossible ache in his loins.

He answered her question curtly. "I took care of the chores before I came over to get you." Because he had needed to work off a huge quantity of steam. Because he hadn't wanted her to be alone for even the short time it took him to look after his livestock.

She edged closer. "Won't that coffee keep you awake?"

"Moonbeam, *nothing* can keep me awake when I decide to sleep. I learned a long time ago to sleep anywhere, any time, under any conditions."

She watched him settle in a chair and lean forward, resting his elbows on the table while he massaged the back of his neck with his fingers. He must have refused Mandy's offer of coffee because he didn't feel like socializing, she thought, because he clearly didn't want to get to bed all that fast. It was, in fact, still early. *She* certainly didn't feel like going to bed.

Instead, she had the worst urge to reach out and touch him. She would have liked to rub his neck for him, to feel again the wonderful warmth of his smooth skin. She would have liked to sit on his lap as she had the other night and feel safe as only Micah had ever made her feel. His embrace had been engraved in her memory during childhood, she thought. Closing her eyes, she could still remember how warm and secure she had always felt when Micah snatched her out of harm's way.

That feeling had lingered into adulthood, and after the past few days, she didn't think it was misplaced. With Micah she was safe, and that understanding unleashed a whole flood of yearnings.

But he was tired and sore, and she was still a little afraid of how such feelings could enslave her, so she redirected her attention.

"Are you hungry, Micah? I could fix you something."

He looked up slowly, and just as slowly shook his head. "Honey, what I'm hungry for, you aren't serving."

"Oh." And then understanding struck. "Oh!" She could feel her cheeks burn.

He'd said it because he expected the truth to send her scurrying off to her bedroom. The blunt admission of his desire was a far cry from what happened when he kissed her and held her, and in the absence of seductive heat, he really thought she would run, which would be best for both of them.

But she didn't. Instead, she stood there staring at him with wide, startled blue eyes that were framed by a profusely blushing face and riotous pale curls. She looked, he thought inanely, like an alarmed Dresden doll, all pink and white porcelain. Fragile. Sexy. Damn!

"I . . . see," she said uncertainly. Breathlessly. Her hands curled into tight little fists at her sides.

"I doubt you do," he said drily. If she did, she would certainly be running. And sparing him this draining exercise of willpower that was rapidly disappearing.

"No, I . . . do see," she insisted in that same breathless voice. "Don't you . . . have a lady friend?"

He was stunned by that question and what it revealed. She was talking of physical needs that could be assuaged by any body, and while there were times when a man could and would settle for precisely that, it wasn't the kind of thing a gently reared woman should consider to be the norm. Unless someone had . . . "Did your husband keep a lady friend?" he asked harshly.

Her color heightened even more painfully, and she clasped her hands over her swollen womb, twisting her fingers tightly. She looked down. "Of course. I couldn't . . . I wasn't . . . he said . . ."

For a long moment Micah didn't move. He didn't even breathe. The coffeemaker burbled and popped and then finished brewing in a hiss of steam. He hardly noticed, though five minutes ago he would have said he'd kill for a cup of coffee. Right now he *could* kill, but not for anything so measly as a cup of coffee.

He couldn't leave her like this, he realized. The understanding sounded in him like the clear note of a crystal bell, whole and irresistible. He couldn't leave her with such a low opinion of her attractions.

The air became thick with portent. He could feel it, registering it in the depths of his shaman's soul. A cusp had been reached, a critical point of decision. There would be no going back from this moment. Whatever he did now, he would have to live with it forever.

Faith stood there before him, eyes down, hands knotted, and he could feel her painful vulnerability. She had, he understood, revealed something to him that she had never revealed before. She had exposed what she believed to be her deepest flaw. She had laid her soul naked before him, and that certainly must mean she trusted him not to wound her further. It must mean, too, that she was reaching out in hope of a healing touch.

And why did the gods give power to a shaman if not to heal the hurts of others?

The chair scraped on the tile as he stood up. He waited, and after a bit Faith found the courage to look at him again. She was so small, he thought, so tiny. How could anyone find it in him to mistreat her?

"I've got," he said slowly, "a burning in my soul, a crying need for a woman's gentle touch. *Your* touch. And I can tell you right now, Moonbeam, that nobody else will do."

She caught her breath and bit her lower lip. Her eyes remained fixed on his face, her expression mirroring a mixture of hope and terror. "I'm . . . I'll disappoint you!"

The words burst from her in a rush, and they were all he needed to hear. They conveyed her consent as well as her deepest fear, and her consent swept away the last barrier, the last defense, the last objection.

"Aw, Moonbeam," he said huskily, "you couldn't begin to disappoint me."

Ignoring her protests that he would hurt himself, ignoring the ache of his bruised ribs, he lifted her into his arms and carried her up to his room. When he reached his bed he lowered her feet to the floor and drew her comfortingly against his chest.

"I want you," he said in a rough whisper. "God, woman, you've been driving me out of my mind. The way you smell, the way you look, the way you touch me sometimes..." He unleashed a ragged breath. "I promise I won't hurt you. I promise I won't do anything you don't want me to. I know

I'm big and scary, I know I look mean, but honest to God, Moonbeam, I'd never hurt you.''

"I know." Her whisper was broken, a tattered breath. "Oh, Micah, I know." Slowly she tilted her head up and looked at him. "I trust you." She did. Oh, God, she did! Her heart hammered wildly, and she knew he must see that she was trembling, but as terrified as she was, she trusted him. It would be enough, she thought, to give him what he needed from her, such a little thing compared to all he had done for her. It would be enough, and if along the way she rediscovered the warmth and tingles that he had given her before, she would feel blessed, because she had never felt such things before. She would believe, just a little, that perhaps someday she could be a normal woman.

He bent and pressed a soft kiss on her forehead. "I'll be careful of the baby, too."

He stepped back and reached for the hem of her sweater, lifting it slowly. She battled an urge to stop him, not because she feared what he was about to do, but because she was suddenly conscious of all her flaws. Her pregnant belly was certainly no sensual inducement, and the red scars from the stab wounds were ugly in the extreme. But Micah knew they were there, knew she was pregnant. Hiding herself would be futile, because he already knew.

"I wish . . ." The words escaped her on a sigh.

"What do you wish, Moonbeam?" he prompted quietly when he had cast the sweater aside. She stood before him in a lacy white bra and her maternity jeans, an incredibly arousing sight. His body began to throb in earnest.

"I wish I were beautiful for you," she said truthfully. "Not all fat and—"

He silenced her with a finger across her soft lips. "I told you before, a woman is beautiful in all her seasons. Carrying a child enhances your loveliness, Faith."

"But it's not even your child!" And with a sudden, sharp pang, she wished it were.

He hooked his thumbs in the elastic waistband of her jeans and gently pulled them down, until the entire smooth swell of her abdomen was visible. He pressed both warm palms against her, as if cradling her womb, and smiled when he felt the faint stirrings of the child within her.

He looked straight into her eyes, a look meant to give weight to his words. "When I spill my seed in you, this child becomes mine, Faith. I mean it."

Before she could absorb his words or even react to his enigmatic statement, he released the clasp of her bra and her breasts fell free. The lacy scrap flew across the room to join her sweater, and then, while she was still drawing a quick breath, he lowered her to the bed and was tugging her boots off, then her jeans.

"Tonight," he said, "I expect nothing from you except your permission to touch you. I don't want you to do anything unless the urge takes you. I don't want you to feel that you have to do anything at all except close your eyes and experience what I want to give you."

"But you—"

"Shh. I want you to pretend that this is the first time ever, that you know nothing at all about any of this. Forget what you think you know, Faith. This is *our* first time."

Totally naked now, she lay on his bed and looked up at him. He had turned on the bedside lamp, but even in its warm glow he looked dark, huge, mysterious. Forbidding. And lying there nude, when she should have felt utterly self-conscious, she was conscious only of him, of his power, of his innate majesty. Of his virility. Suddenly, more than anything in the world, she wanted to see him as naked as she was. Unclothed, in his natural state, he would be magnificent.

Inside her, cold places began to heat, and deep in her center a strange unfolding began to happen. She was unfurling for him, softening, opening.

His dark gaze raked her from head to toe, but instead of embarrassing her, it heated her more. "Truly beautiful," he said quietly, and meant it. From the crown of her head to her impossibly dainty feet, she was exquisitely formed, and her pregnancy merely added to her womanly ripeness. She was a woman meant for a man's hand, a man's *gentle* hand. She was meant to be a vessel of love and life. She was meant to be the hearth around which a man could center his entire existence. She needed to be cherished and protected, and in return she would give him meaning, purpose and her loving, gentle care.

His chest squeezed with yearnings he had long buried and refused to face. Ignoring them even now, he turned his attention to her and to her needs. She was meant to be cherished, but she had been abused. Kneeling beside the bed, he bent over her and pressed a soft, warm kiss to each of the scars Frank had dealt her. There were nearly a dozen, some clearly superficial, others clearly worse. As his lips found each one, he heard her draw a quick breath and felt her heart leap.

"How can you trust me?" he asked, resting his cheek against her womb. His voice was rusty with feelings he tried to hold in check.

"How can I not?" she asked softly. He had cared for her tenderly since the instant he'd found her. Reaching out, she touched his head with her hands, caressing his smooth cheek, slipping her fingers into his long, soft hair. She gave him the gentleness he craved in the deepest places of his soul, and she did it without even knowing he needed it. She did it because it was hers to give, and it was what she gave best.

He felt that gentleness and squeezed his eyes shut, swallowing hard against the sudden locking of his throat. It had been a long day, he told himself. He was tired and worn. His ribs had ached like hell every single minute, and no matter how fiercely he'd concentrated on the job, Faith had been at the back of his mind. All day long he had worried about her, worried that she was worrying, worried that she was frightened. Hoping to God nobody told her what that man had done to her clothes.

Now she was here, trusting him when she had no reason to trust, lying naked and warm in his bed, waiting for him to do what men did to women, expecting it to be whatever she had experienced with Frank. Expecting the worst but ready to give it to him because it was what he needed.

Damn it, he didn't want it unless she wanted it, too!

And it was up to him to make sure she did.

Straightening, he pulled the blanket over her and then rose to his feet. "Do you want the light on or off?" he asked, waiting.

She swallowed but met his dark gaze bravely. "I want to see you." Her words were a tight whisper, barely audible, but he heard them and smiled. It was a warm, genuine smile, unlike him, yet somehow very like him. It was a part of him he seldom shared, and Faith hugged the knowledge to her heart.

He moved around the room casually, as if he were preparing for bed on any normal night. She had half feared he would stand over the bed and disrobe, making her absorb it all at once, but he didn't. First he shrugged out of his shirt, balled it up and threw it in the hamper beside his dresser. Standing there, with his back to Faith, he removed his watch and emptied his pockets, taking his time about it.

It gave her time, too. Time to soak in the glistening breadth of his shoulders, the rippling muscles in his upper back. Time to notice the old, puckered scar in his right shoulder. A bullet wound?

Then he strode to the bootjack, giving her a chance to admire his chest once again, above his taped ribs. To think that she had never seen a man so beautiful, or dreamed that one could be.

He was tall, muscled, broad-shouldered, narrow flanked, copper-skinned. He reached for his belt buckle, neither facing her nor turning away. She held her breath as he popped the buttons and yanked the zipper. The sounds were loud in a silence that seemed to have grown thick, as if the air were turning into molasses. He dropped his jeans and gave a grunt as he bent to free his ankles.

"Damn ribs," he muttered, and kicked the jeans aside. His legs were smooth, free of coarse hair. Smooth, sleek, powerfully muscled, the same gleaming, dusky tone as the rest of him.

He faced her then, a pair of plain white briefs the last barrier between them. Faith's hands knotted into the sheets, and she licked her dry lips, waiting, wondering, hoping, dreading. Nothing, she reminded herself, ever lives up to its billing. Reality never measures up to hopes and dreams.

But that didn't keep her from hoping and dreaming.

When she didn't shrink, cower or protest, Micah knew she meant to stay. With one quick movement, he skimmed his briefs off and slipped under the blanket beside her.

"Come here, Moonbeam," he said gruffly, and tugged her into his arms, tucking her snugly against his powerful body. So small, he thought again. So fragile. A careless touch could shatter her.

How good it felt to hold her! Without the barriers of clothing, her skin was like warm silk against him. She made his heart feel full, made his arms feel full, filled holes he hadn't even known were there.

She reached up and touched his cheek, and when he looked down into her blue eyes, he knew this embrace pleased her as much as it pleased him.

"You don't have a beard," she murmured, stroking his cheek.

"Nope. A convenient gift from my mother's people."

"I like the way you feel. So smooth and warm."

"I like the way you feel, too. Like satin. Like silk." Like all the forbidden things, all the things he'd denied himself and had been denied. Her womanly perfume filled his nose, her softness pressed him and made promises to him, and her lips beckoned him. Bending his head, he kissed her. At any moment, he thought, tenderness was going to incinerate in the inferno of passion.

But he wanted to hang on to the tenderness for a while longer. He'd known so little of it in his life, and this woman so easily gave it and evoked it in him. Letting it swell in him now, he kissed her gently, exploring the heated depths of her

mouth with a coaxing tongue until she softened even more
against him and answered in kind.

And then his hands began to roam, palms warm and
rough against her as he quested over her hills and hollows.
He sought to awaken in her the same hungers he was feeling, longed to bring her to the fulfillment he expected to
find.

One of his huge hands swallowed her breast, stroking it
gently, kneading it until it became an aching mound. When
he felt her hands in his hair, tugging his mouth toward her,
he knew fierce triumph. It was there, the need, the hunger,
the human yearning for love and its release. It hadn't been
thoroughly battered from her. Sliding down on the bed, he
took her nipple into his mouth and sucked. Each pull of his
mouth drew an echoing throb from his loins.

"Oh, Micah . . . Micah . . ."

Her broken sigh filled him with deepening heat and satisfaction. In a moment of honesty so stark it shook him, he
faced his need and acknowledged the barrenness of his shaman's soul. For a young man, a good cause was enough, but
he was no longer young. He needed more, so much more.

Shivering with feelings she had never felt before, Faith
pressed his head closer and gave herself up to the inner
storm. Something primitive and earthy was rising in her,
something wild and free and never before unfettered. She
wanted . . . she wanted . . . oh God, how she wanted! She
wanted the fulfillment of dreams that life had never granted;
she wanted the touches and caresses that she had once
dreamed would bring pleasure but had only brought a cold
ache and sense of self-disgust. She wanted the rightness that
had always been denied her.

She reached out in need and found warm, smooth skin,
the resilience of flesh and blood. When she touched him,
when her hands began to stroke his shoulders and back, to
knead his hard muscles and tug him yet closer, he shud-
dered, and a deep groan escaped him.

"I'm sorry," she said swiftly, instinctively, as fear
swamped her burgeoning hunger. "I'm sorry." Frank had

called her a whore when she had touched him, and then, when she had done nothing, he had called her frigid. She was no good at this. No good at all. Everything she did was wrong.

She tried to twist away, but Micah caught her and tucked her face into his shoulder. "Shh," he said. "Hush, Moonbeam. It's okay. I'm sorry I scared you. It just felt so good when you touched me."

Shock turned her instantly rigid. It had felt good? He had liked it? "Good?" she repeated numbly, lifting her head so she could see him.

"Good," he repeated softly, holding her gaze steadily. This night, he thought, was going to demand a frankness and honesty from him that he had never before given anyone. The women he had shared this with in the past had all been experienced enough to interpret a shudder, a groan or a caught breath. He had never before needed to talk about what was happening, how he was feeling.

His arms were around her, holding her close. Now, while her eyes were still locked on his, he brought his hand around and began to fondle her breast. Her blue eyes darkened at once, and her lids drooped. She caught her breath.

"Do you like this?" he asked, his voice a deep, quiet rumble.

"Y-yes." The word emerged on a hiss of breath.

Her nipple swiftly beaded, and he plucked gently at it. "And that?"

"Yes . . ."

"You liked it when I sucked on you."

She wanted to close her eyes in embarrassment, but somehow she couldn't. Somehow, as if he possessed a sorcerer's power to bend her to his will, her eyes remained opened and locked on his. She could sink into the dark depths of his eyes, she thought hazily, dimly aware that her hips had begun a gentle, helpless rocking. She wanted to sink into him. "I liked it," she admitted huskily.

"I'm no different than you," he said quietly. "I like to be touched. And when I groan, it means I like it a whole hell of a lot. You go ahead and touch me however you want, whenever you want, and don't worry about it. You couldn't hurt me if you tried."

But before she could test his assertion, his mouth had fastened to her nipple, and his hand had swept down to touch her between her legs. She was instantly caught on the arc of a welder's torch that seemed to burn from breast to belly. Her every nerve turned into a ribbon of silken fire, and her mind gave up any attempt to think. No one had ever made her feel like this before. No one.

He felt her surrender to the heat, felt her melt as his fingers stroked her dewy core. There was a time to take things slow, but he knew with deep certainty that this was not it. She was riding a crest of feelings she didn't understand, and at any moment they might well frighten her into awareness and reluctance. At any moment he might do something that jarred her with remembrances. He needed to move swiftly and bring her through to the other side before some self-protective instinct pulled her back from the precipice.

Her legs parted readily for him, and he settled between them on his haunches. Gently, he reached out and touched her soft, velvety folds with his fingers, watching her every nuance of expression, listening closely to the tempo of her breathing.

"Micah. Oh, Micah." His name passed her lips as a breathless whimper, and her hips rolled upward toward him. Her eyes were scrunched closed, but that was fine with him. Somehow he felt that right now was not the best time for her to see him hovering over her, a large, cruel-looking man with a fully aroused body. Right now she needed to find what was inside her.

He slid forward a little and lifted her hips onto his knees, her heels onto his shoulders. Her eyelids fluttered, but when he stroked her slick folds a little harder, she groaned and lifted toward him. Leaning forward, he pressed himself into her.

She caught her breath, then shivered, as she felt him enter her. A deep, clenching thrill seized her, and she wondered vaguely why she had never before realized how good it could feel to be stretched and filled by a man's desire. Deeper he pressed into her, pushing her legs up toward her head, but not too much. Dimly she realized that he had put them in a position where he could not possibly place his weight on her, where she could at any time thrust him back with a shove of her legs. He was making sure he did not hurt her.

Her eyes flew open then and looked into the fierce face of a half-breed warrior, a man who, despite his own needs, was placing her comfort and safety above all else. His face was a grimace of passion, and his restraint was testing him sorely as he eased slowly into her hot depths.

And then the wildness in her broke free.

Passion thrummed in her blood, and instinct took precedence over thought. She needed him. She needed his deepest possession. She needed him to fill her, take her, claim her, empty his seed into her. Separating her legs, she dropped her heels to the mattress and opened herself fully to his hunger.

"Deeper," she said hoarsely. "I need to feel all of you."

His eyes widened a little before narrowing again with desire. She locked her legs around his waist and pulled him closer. He leaned over her, on his hands and knees now, and sank slowly into her with a groan that rose from the soles of his feet. Hot. Wet. Slick. Her silken depths surrounded him.

"Micah!" She sounded frightened, but he understood. She needed more. She needed pressure he wasn't providing. She was afraid she would hang in this exquisite limbo between heaven and hell forever. He wanted to promise her he wouldn't leave her there like that, but his voice was gone, his larynx incapable of anything but the deepest groans of pleasure.

Slowly, cautiously, he stretched out over her, pushing his knees back little by little until his manhood was buried in her to the hilt. Still, he kept his weight from her womb, though he wanted like mad to feel her beneath him from shoulder to knee.

He moved. Gently but firmly, he pulled back a little and then thrust into her all the way. In. Out. In. The pressure building in her center was intense, causing her to arch against him in irresistible need. All of him. She needed all of him. Again and again and again.

"Micah!" A gasp made of yearning and fear.

"Easy, honey. Easy." He forced the words out and shifted onto his left elbow, keeping his weight off her as he slipped his right hand between them. His ribs objected, but he damned them and kept on. His touch affected her like an electric shock. Her eyes grew huge, and she bucked once, wildly.

"Micah?" Now she sounded desperate.

"Let go, baby. Let . . . go."

Her legs tightened around him, drawing him deeper than he would have believed possible, making him feel surrounded by her slick heat. Her heels dug into his buttocks, and within her he felt a wild, uncertain fluttering of muscles.

And then she rose one last time against him and the rippling contraction gripped them both, hurling them over the cliff edge to completion.

She didn't seem to want to let him go, so he eased away and then pulled her half onto him. Someday, he thought, he would feel her completely under him, breast to breast and belly to belly. Someday, when there wasn't a baby to consider, he would show her just where passion could lead. Someday.

She stirred, her curls tickling his smooth chest. "I never dreamed it could be like that," she murmured.

He smoothed her hair with a gentle hand. "Not bad, huh?"

"Not bad?" She repeated the words uncertainly, fearfully, and then lifted her head. When she saw the glint in his dark eyes, she smiled. "Micah Parish, you're teasing me!"

"Could be." He ran his thumb along her lower lip, realizing with something like amazement that he wanted her again. Right now. This woman had an incredible effect on him. First she broke down a few barriers that hadn't been breached in years, if ever, and then she turned him into the hormonal equivalent of a sixteen-year-old. Dangerous stuff. Dangerous lady. "I'm starving," he announced. "I just remembered I haven't eaten since breakfast."

"I'll make you—"

"No. You'll stay right here. I'll bring you something to eat. And tea. Or would you rather have milk?"

Downstairs in the kitchen, he pulled out sandwich fixings, intending to create a masterpiece that might tempt Faith's appetite. No way did that woman eat enough.

He froze suddenly, mayonnaise jar in one hand, mustard in the other. Well, he'd sure as hell done it now. He'd taken the woman into his bed, and since she was going to be his next-door neighbor, he'd as good as taken her into his life. Of course, she'd already been there, but not this way.

Well, hell. Didn't he know better? Hadn't he learned long ago that women were scheming connivers who—

Abruptly, he silenced himself midthought. What he'd learned about women in the past didn't apply to Faith, and he damn well knew it. It was because she was so different that she had slipped past all his defenses to end up where she was at this moment.

Still, this was not one of his brighter moves. Nope. The last thing he was interested in was a long-term relationship, and Faith wasn't made for any other kind. Stupid. Sheer, utter, incredible stupidity on his part.

And yet... Yet he was going to go back up there, feed her, and then love her with every bit of patience, caring and passion he could find in himself. He was going to love her until she never again was able to hang her head in humiliation because she believed she wasn't what a man wanted or needed. Until she never again thought herself lacking.

It sounded pretty, too, this noble desire to make her feel better about herself. The truth was, he wanted her like hell on fire. Again. And again. And yet again.

He wanted to do with her all the things he'd set aside because he had first needed to sweep her over the fortress wall of her fear. He wanted to spend hours learning every inch of her. He wanted to prop himself over her in the lamplight, touch her softly from chin to toe and discover every little place that could cause her breath to catch. He wanted to learn every one of her textures and temperatures and tastes.

And then he wanted her to learn him the same way. He paused in the act of spreading mayonnaise and closed his eyes against the swift shaft of need that stabbed him. He hadn't wanted a woman to touch him like that in so long that he couldn't remember ever having wanted it. That kind of touching was a drawbridge flung over an emotional moat. Dangerous. More than sexually seductive, it would be emotionally seductive.

It required no great leap of his imagination to know how it would feel to have her gentle fingers running all over him like that. He wanted it so badly that his mouth turned dry and his hands shook.

They hadn't yet begun, he realized. A blistering word escaped him as he faced what was happening. The two of them hadn't even begun.

And it was already too late to stop.

Chapter 10

Before going downstairs Micah had given Faith one of his flannel shirts to wear. He knew she would still feel miserably self-conscious with him for a little while, and he wanted to spare her as much discomfort as he possibly could.

He found her wearing the blue shirt, buttoned right up to her chin, although it didn't achieve quite the closed up effect she wanted, since her neck was a great deal slenderer than his sixteen-and-a-half inches. The collar sagged, revealing an enticing amount of creamy skin.

Funny, he thought as he set the tray on the bedside table, he'd never thought about skin color before, but he was thinking about hers, and he had to admit the sight of his darker skin against the paler canvas of hers was arousing to him. But then, everything about the two of them together was proving to be arousing.

Wearing only his jeans, he sat on the edge of the bed beside her and pretended he didn't notice her trepidation. Second thoughts. Hell, there were always second thoughts. He was having them, and so was she. Naturally. But just as naturally, he didn't want either one of them to do too much thinking before morning. That would be time enough to retrieve his solitude and distance and give her back hers. For now they had this one night, and they would be fools not to seize it.

Leaning forward, he damned his usual reserve and kissed her warmly on the lips. For this little while he could step out from behind his walls and give her the cherishing she needed. He could open up enough to let her know she was special to him.

His kiss was like the answer to a prayer. "Oh, Micah," she whispered brokenly against the astonishingly soft heat of his lips. She had watched him come into the room moments ago and felt again the impact of his raw masculinity, the burst of fright at his size and strength, at the harshness of his face. Her heart had started hammering, and her insides had quailed, unsure what to expect now that he had gotten what he wanted from her.

And he gave her this, this incredible, surprising tenderness, the amazing softness of a mouth that looked unyielding, the awesome gentleness of hands that surely could crumble stone.

"Oh, Micah," she breathed again, shakily, and lifted her hands until she could tunnel her fingers into the wild silk of his hair and feel the strength of the bone beneath. And after years of silence about her own feelings, she couldn't hold back the words another minute.

"You're so beautiful," she said brokenly, holding him closer, afraid he would vanish in a wisp of smoke like the magical creature he surely was. "So beautiful. Like the hawks in the sky, or the wolves on the tundra."

She heard him swallow and felt his hands knot on the pillow beside her head. He lifted his head enough so that their eyes could meet, midsummer blue and midnight black. Once again she felt that behind those dark pupils was hidden a light too bright for mortal eyes.

"Moonbeam," he said roughly. "All gossamer and silk. Too fine, too precious. You're going to blow away in the next blizzard if you don't eat something."

He shattered the moment as effectively as he might have shattered a brick with the blade of his hand. Her eyes darkened with hurt, and she looked away. In that instant he would have snatched back the words if he could have, but it was too late. She had opened something painful in him, and he had reacted instinctively. Now it was too late.

But deep inside, despite the hurt, Faith understood. She needed to draw some deep breaths and blink fiercely until she found her control, but she understood, and understanding kept the wound from becoming too deep.

Outside the wind kicked up, rattling window glass, causing the old house to groan. Inside, they ate their sandwiches by warm lamplight and gradually the instinctive distance he had thrust between them evaporated.

Micah spoke casually to her of his years in the army, confining himself to tales that would make her smile, and coaxed her into speaking of her summers in Conard County with her father. Clearly, whatever good Faith knew of men had come primarily from Jason Montrose. She spoke of him with evident love.

"I miss him," she admitted to Micah. "It's been more than five years, and I still miss him."

When he was convinced she wouldn't eat another mouthful, he carried the tray back downstairs. Faith took the opportunity to go to the bathroom and wash up a little. She considered getting her nightgown from her own room but decided that Micah's shirt felt better somehow. Comforting. And then she began to wonder nervously if Micah expected her to sleep in her own bed or stay with him.

Uncertainty swamped her and she hesitated, finally leaving the bathroom to hover doubtfully in the door of his bedroom. He was already there, standing at the window, the curtain pulled back in one hand as he stared out into the night.

So beautiful, she thought again, wondering why that word had disturbed him. Her palms itched to touch him, to feel again his hot, smooth skin, his bunching muscles like resilient steel as he hovered over her. Other more intimate places were already yearning to know his possession yet again. She would never, she thought fearfully, get enough of what he had given her tonight, not if he gave it to her all day, every day, for the rest of her life.

And she didn't even know if he'd had his fill of her and wished her gone.

He turned suddenly, a sleek, supple movement, and saw her in the doorway. His shirt practically swallowed her whole, the tails reaching to her knees. He smiled.

The smile brought her farther into the room, though she moved hesitantly. He smiled so rarely, she thought, and even more rarely did he smile with his eyes. His dark eyes were smiling now. At her.

"That shirt never looked that sexy on me," he said, his voice as deep and dark as the night outside.

Sexy? The word caused her heart to leap. He thought her sexy? She thought of herself as pale and colorless, as exciting as white rice.

"You're going to get a chill, standing barefoot on this cold floor," he said, as he walked over and picked her up in a swift easy movement, then tucked her into his bed.

That answered one question, she thought with a relief so strong that she trembled from it. He hadn't had his fill of her. Not yet.

He plumped the pillows behind her so that she could lean back comfortably, and then he sat beside her on the edge of the bed, facing her.

"How do you feel?" he asked. "Seriously."

She searched his dark eyes and saw that he wasn't kidding. He was genuinely concerned. "I feel fine," she told him. "Wonderful, actually."

"Nothing hurts? Nothing aches? Nothing is cramping?"

She shook her head, understanding the direction of his concern, and was so touched by it that her throat tightened. "It's perfectly safe for pregnant women to have sex, you know. Unless there's some kind of problem, and I don't have any problems."

Have sex? Had she actually used that term? That troubled him in ways he didn't want to analyze. Not right now. Not when his distance was vanishing in the smoke of re-igniting passions. Instead he leaned over her, propping himself on his elbows and catching her head between his huge hands.

"Sex," he said gruffly, as he gently ran his thumbs along her cheekbones, "has always been something I've had whenever I needed it, like taking a shower or eating a meal." He watched the color heighten in her face, watched her lips part as she caught her breath in growing awareness. "Making love," he continued just as roughly, "is something I may have done a half dozen times in my whole life. What I'm doing with you, Moonbeam, is making love."

He kissed her then, gently, intent on taking each step slowly, savoring each touch until they both went half mad from need. His lips molded hers, sucking, tugging, sensitizing, and then his tongue slipped into her mouth, playing a surprisingly erotic game of tag with hers.

All the while his mouth seduced her, his hands worked the buttons of the shirt she wore, and the next thing she knew she was bared from shoulder to thigh, and he was looking down at her, drinking in every detail with his dark eyes. Before she could react, he bent and kissed the mound of her belly. Then, taking care to miss nothing, his hands began to travel everywhere his eyes had already been.

"Shh," he said softly when she opened her mouth and stirred as if she might stop him. "Shh... You remind me of a rosebud, all soft and satiny, with so many dark, fragrant secrets hidden in your folds." His fingertip slipped into some of those folds, and he watched himself touch her with unabashed pleasure. "So perfect. So hot. So sweet. And right here is this secret little button...."

She gasped and arched, and she saw him smile in the instant before he bent and took her breast into his mouth. His hands went everywhere, traveling gently but missing nothing, until she felt as if she were lying in the center of a silken whirlwind. He was showing her all the secrets of her body, secrets she had never imagined existed. How could she have suspected that the back of her knee could be so sensitive, or that strong hands kneading the arches of her small feet could feel so exquisite?

How could she have dreamed that she could need to touch him back, that discovering him could become an irresistible drive?

When she plucked at the button of his jeans, Micah didn't hesitate. He rose and stood right beside her, letting her see what he had earlier barely let her glimpse. This time he yanked the zipper and dropped his jeans and there were no briefs beneath to maintain his modesty. Not that he was feeling any. The touch of her gaze on his loins affected him almost as strongly as a physical caress.

Kicking his jeans away, he faced her and waited, letting her look as she would. He knew how much he liked to look at her, how much he enjoyed the sight of her feminine attributes. He wouldn't deprive her of the same enjoyment, if she felt it.

She did. He was absolutely perfect, and the sight of him heightened her excitement. When she held out her arms he lay beside her on the bed, and when she pushed him gently onto his back he complied, watching her from heavily lidded dark eyes.

She reached out and then hesitated, glancing up at him.

"Whatever you like," he said huskily. "I'm hungry for your touch, Faith."

The words unlocked something inside her, and she reached out eagerly. It was like stroking a great big mountain cat, she thought, all smooth, sleek and wild. His muscles bunched beneath her caresses, almost as if they were reaching out for more, and little by little she grew bolder, especially when he growled and purred just like a sunning lion.

"Here," he said on a husky breath, and drew her hand toward his nipple. "Just like I do to you."

Understanding streaked through her like wildfire, and she took full advantage of realizing that he liked what she liked.

He jerked sharply when her tongue touched him, and groaned deeply when she nibbled at him.

When her hand began wandering lower, he encouraged her with husky, hoarse mutters of "Yes, yes..." and he tightened like a tightly strung bow when at last her hand found him.

"Oh, Moonbeam..." he groaned, and she knew how much she had pleased him. And pleasing him, she realized, was at least as erotic as anything he did to her, and far more satisfying.

Suddenly he caught her beneath her arms and lifted her so that she straddled him. Startled, she looked down into his sleepy, sexy, dark eyes and saw the upward lift of the corners of his mouth.

"Like this," he said. "You're in charge."

The possibilities were already occurring to her, but she felt so exposed like this. Smiling even more broadly, he reached out and cupped her breasts, swallowing them in his huge hands. Pleasure zig-zagged through her like an electric current, from his touch to her center.

"Like this," Micah said again, his voice deep. "I want to see you. I want to watch you. I don't want to have to worry about you. I'm so big, Moonbeam...."

His hand left her breast, found her moist heat and touched her persuasively. She lifted herself and allowed him to guide her with his amazingly gentle hands. Moments later she was drawing a long, shattered breath and throwing her head back as he filled her. So deep. So hard. So big. So satisfying.

He was right. This way she didn't have to worry, either, and she could control every sensation. He held her hips, moving her gently until she seized the rhythm and began to rock against him in a way that made him moan and made the tightening coil in her grow tighter.

"Like that," Micah mumbled. "Yeah, like that...come on, baby...reach for it...."

More. Harder. Deeper. Closer. Oh! Oh... She shattered in a shower of sparks and collapsed.

* * *

His breathing was as ragged as hers, his chest as slick with sweat, when she returned to herself. She lay on his chest, their bodies still joined. He had his arms around her and was holding her close. She couldn't remember anyone ever having held her like this, as if he simply didn't want to let go.

"Beautiful Moonbeam," he whispered, and buried his fingers in her hair to cup the back of her head and keep her close. For now he was past worrying about anything. It was enough to hold her, to keep her close, to know that later, when the urge rose again, he would be able to reach for her and know the miracle of her loving again.

He ran his hand down her back, savoring the feel of her skin, the fragility of her structure. So perfect, so tiny, and she had come to *his* bed, had trusted him enough to be vulnerable, had wanted him enough to reach for him. There was a miracle in that, never mind the explosive satisfaction she had given him.

Tomorrow, he told himself, would be soon enough to face the emptiness she would leave behind her in his life. For now, he didn't want to waste a minute of heaven.

"I'm crushing you," she mumbled.

"Faith, you're no heavier than the damn blanket."

Her head popped up, and to his amazement she was grinning. "Since when does a blanket weigh a hundred and fifteen pounds?"

"You weigh that much? I don't believe it."

"I weigh that much now."

He ran his hand down over her smooth flank. "I'm relieved to hear it. I was sure you didn't weigh anywhere near enough. You look like you'd blow away in a strong wind."

Giving up what was apparently going to be an unequal battle, she dropped her head to his shoulder. Her knees were supporting her so that she didn't squash her stomach, and for the moment she really wasn't any more eager to give up this intimacy than Micah evidently was. She liked the way he was stroking her back and bottom, as if the feel of her pleased him. He made her feel as if Faith Montrose Williams were enough for him all by herself, as if she didn't lack a thing he wanted or needed. The feeling was priceless.

Later he pulled the blanket over them, turned out the light and tucked them together like spoons. His arm cradled her, and beneath it he felt the stirrings of the life she carried. In the dark he smiled and spread his hand over her, to better feel the baby.

"Sleep," he said quietly to both of them. "Sleep."

Faith slept, knowing that she and her child were safe in the magic circle of strong arms.

During the night Micah woke. As always, he was instantly alert, instantly clearheaded. He was lying on his back now, and Faith was tucked against his side, her head on his shoulder. The whisper of her warm breath on his skin was a caress. Reaching out with his senses, he felt the air, searched the house, checking internally and externally for the cause of his waking.

A gust of wind rattled the window, and the house seemed to shake, but that was natural. Minutes ticked by in silence as he listened and waited, but finally he relaxed. Everything was as it should be, at least here within his walls. Faith must have moved or made a sound. He was not accustomed to sharing his bed with a woman. In fact, not once in his entire life had he actually spent the night with any woman other than Faith, or slept with her and held her while she slept.

He liked it. Or rather, he amended honestly, he liked having Faith here like this. He quite frankly couldn't imagine doing this with anyone else.

Closing his eyes, he gave himself up to the rare pleasure, keeping one corner of his mind attentive to anything unusual, but allowing the rest of himself to wallow in the warmth and closeness he felt right now.

He lay there feeling the darkness as if it were tangible. For years the night had been as much his fortress as his solitude was. Much of what he had done in Special Operations had been accomplished under the sheltering cloak of night. It had given him his greatest freedom of action, his greatest safety.

Now, with Faith lying beside him, the night was taking on an entirely different character, bringing back the magical sense of wonder and awe that he had felt as a youth when he stood beneath the stars and felt as if he could fall upward into the vastness of the Milky Way.

He remembered that boy with sudden vividness, almost as if he had been cast back to that moment in time. Micah Parish had once been eighteen and had stood beneath the diamond-studded black velvet of the Wyoming night sky, aching for things never known and lost, aching with homesickness for a home that had never been his. He had wondered and yearned and felt the ineffable sorrow of grieving for something he couldn't remember.

His throat tightened in remembrance, then tightened even more when he realized that Faith's hands were moving with gentle purpose. He opened his mouth to speak her name, to verify that she was awake, but he swallowed the sound. Determining whether she was sleeping or not didn't matter as much as not frightening her. Let her touch him as she would.

He was emotionally raw right now, emotionally vulnerable. He wasn't sure why, but for once he didn't fight it. For once he felt it was all right to let the floodtide of feeling wash over him, to give himself up, to trust.

Her hand stroked him as if she wanted to learn his every plane and angle, as if she wanted to memorize a tactile map of his contours. And she touched him gently, so gently, as if she found him precious. His throat tightened up again, and when he swallowed, the sound was loud in the quiet room.

"Micah?"

She *was* awake. Her hands moved boldly lower. He liked that boldness, liked that she felt comfortable enough with him to be bold. "Hmm?"

"Do you mind?" Her voice was a shy whisper.

"Hell no, Moonbeam," he said gruffly. "Seems like I've been aching my whole life for a woman to touch me like you do."

Her hand stopped, and he could feel her shift until she was looking up at him. Once again the night protected him from exposure. She couldn't read a thing, and he knew it.

"How do I touch you, Micah?"

"Like you care." The words were out before he'd made a conscious decision to speak them. Stark, truthful, they seemed to hang in the air. They could become a weapon, or they could become a foundation. Life had taught him that women used that kind of confession as a weapon, which was why he never shared his innermost self with anyone. He didn't know why he'd felt compelled to do so now, but he would have to live with the results, whatever they were. Unconsciously, he tensed.

"Oh, Micah..." The words escaped her in a shattered whisper. "Oh, Micah... I *do* care."

She turned into him, throwing her arms around him in an attempt to offer him the same sense of security and warmth his embrace gave her.

Her hand began to wander again, lovingly, no longer shy or hesitant, but simply gentle and tender. He liked it, and now she knew it. He remained wary—she could feel it, almost as if he were resisting the very silken bonds he craved—but he remained still beneath her hands, though from time to time a rumble of pleasure rose in him.

This, Faith thought, must be what it was like to pet a grizzly bear. Even as she took pleasure in touching him, pleasure in his pleasure, she couldn't quite forget that he was a man, that he was big, and that he was dangerous. A grizzly could break a horse's neck with one snap of its powerful jaws. Micah Parish could probably break a man in two with his hands. She couldn't quite forget that, even as she held her grizzly enthralled with the gentle stroking of her hand, even as she reminded herself that he had always treated her with the utmost gentleness.

Her soft touches were reaching him in ways he had never been reached before. Sunlight seemed to be flooding into dark, dusty places as she made him feel treasured and precious. No one had ever made him feel treasured before. No one.

But gradually the tenor of her touches changed. He felt her growing need as acutely as he felt his own. Pressing her gently back, he sent his mouth foraging where before he had sent his hands. He felt the ripples of shock shake her as he claimed her with his tongue, but he felt, too, the ripples of profound pleasure. She cried out, and he felt fiercely triumphant when he heard the sound. She was so quiet, so inhibited, so repressed. He wanted her open, free, confident, able to shout out her pleasure or her pain.

The lash of his tongue drove her higher and higher. The sounds that escaped her became almost frantic mewls as she clutched at the bedsheets and writhed in the grip of his hands and mouth. "Beautiful..." she thought she heard him say once, and then fulfillment lifted her on its crest and flung her high, so high, beyond thought to pure feeling.

The ringing of the bedside telephone awoke Micah to the clear light of a winter day. Grabbing the receiver from the cradle, he dragged it to his ear.

"Parish," he said.

"Well, old son," said the gravelly voice of Nate Tate, "we caught the sumbitch just fifteen minutes ago."

Micah sat bolt upright. "You did? Where? What happened?"

"He walked bold as you please into Maude's this morning and ordered breakfast. Maude obliged him and then slipped out back to call us. He's being booked right now. I called the Texas Department of Public Safety, and I guess they're going to ask for extradition, so maybe we can get the bastard out of the county by the end of the week.

"Regardless, you tell Faith Williams that he stays behind bars until his extradition, so she doesn't have to worry about him anymore."

After he hung up, Micah turned and found Faith watching him with wide, hopeful eyes. She had pushed herself up a little against the pillows, but the blanket was drawn snugly to her chin, concealing her nudity. For some reason that almost made him smile.

"Frank's in the slammer, Faith."

She drew a deep breath and squeezed her eyes shut. "Oh, thank God," she whispered.

"Nate said to tell you he'll stay behind bars until he's extradited to Texas, so you don't have to be afraid of him anymore."

She opened her eyes, and two big tears appeared on her lower lashes. "Oh, Micah." Suddenly she forgot modesty and flung her arms around his neck, squealing with delight and relief. "Oh, Micah! I'm so relieved!"

He held her, listening to her mixed laughter and tears, and wondered why he couldn't shake the chill grip of premonition. Somehow, he thought uneasily, he knew this wasn't over, they weren't finished with the mess yet.

"I want to celebrate," Faith said suddenly, leaning back to beam up at him from a tear-streaked face. "Oh, please, I haven't celebrated anything in years...."

"Sure," he said swiftly. "What kind of celebration do you want? A party? I bet I could get a crowd together for—"

She reached up, silencing him with her fingers. It said a lot that she dared to do that. "I don't want a crowd," she said huskily. "I just want to celebrate with you."

Micah had celebrated many times in his life, almost invariably with a group of his comrades-in-arms. They had celebrated successful missions, their marriages, even the births of their children. Never, though, had anyone wanted to celebrate with just him. As if only he could add to the joy by sharing it. As if he were truly special. As if he were the only one who mattered.

"Sure," he said, putting a tight rein on strangely active emotions. "That sounds great to me. What do you have in mind?"

Suddenly she bit her lower lip and flushed a little. "I guess I sound awful."

"Awful? Why?"

"It's terrible to feel so jubilant because somebody's been sent to jail."

His face softened a little, and he reached out to touch her halo of pale hair. "Faith, after what that man did to you, I wouldn't think you were awful if you wanted to go to the jailhouse and poke sticks through the bars at him."

She glanced up at him from the corner of her eye. "You wouldn't? Really?"

"I wouldn't. Really. I definitely think a celebration's in order. Champagne is out of the question, but maybe we can drive over to Laramie for the day and find something to do."

"Wonderful! But I need to go home and get something decent to wear. I only brought one change of clothes."

Well, hell, Micah thought. He hated to do this, but he didn't see any way around it. Why did he have to be the one to inflict Frank's final blow?

He settled back against the pillows, tugging her down with him so that he could hug her and see her at the same time. Her expression was expectant, smiling, still flushed with the joy of her fresh liberation from terror. Hell!

"Faith, I'm afraid you don't have any clothes at home anymore. Frank ruined them."

The joy faded, to be replaced by the all-too-familiar pinched look of fear. "Ruined them?" she repeated hesitantly. "All my maternity clothes? Not that there were very many. It seemed silly to spend a lot of money on clothes I'd only wear for a few...*all* my clothes?" She bit her lip and blinked hard. "What did he do? Burn them? He did that once before and made me wear the same clothes for a... Did he burn them?"

He looked away and wished she hadn't asked that. He really wished she hadn't asked that. He'd been planning to get over there and clean up the mess before she saw it. Why couldn't she be satisfied with knowing the clothes were ruined? Why did she have to know exactly how? Why couldn't he simply lie about it? Because he had never in his life consciously lied about anything. Because she didn't deserve to be treated like a child, however much he might want to protect her.

He tightened his arm around her and felt her child stir against his hip. The incredible, wonderful miracle of life. Why did folks always have to muck it up somehow? "He cut your clothes up pretty bad," Micah said finally, avoiding the word *slashed*, even though it had been the first to spring to mind when he saw the destruction. "Anyhow," he added, trying to move past the matter quickly, "I'll wash out your things this morning, and maybe we can find a place at the mall in Laramie to get you some new clothes."

Slowly he turned his head again to look down at her and found she was lying stiff and still, worrying her lower lip with her teeth, her eyes tightly closed.

"Aw, babe," he said huskily, suddenly feeling totally helpless. A moment ago she had been so jubilant, and now she was lost and afraid all over again. He wanted so badly to make it all go away, but he couldn't.

"M-Micah?" Her eyes popped open suddenly, wide, luminous with tears she kept blinking back.

"Yes, Moonbeam?" He shoveled his hand into her hair and tried to soothe her by gently stroking his fingers against her scalp.

"I don't think it's e-ever going to g-go away completely. Not ever."

"It will. Believe me, it will. You should be feeling a whole lot better already, with the man in prison."

"I thought I was safe last time he was in jail!"

There wasn't any way he could argue with that. "I know," he said finally. "I know."

Her hands tightened on his shoulders, and he responded by tightening his arms around her. "At least," he said after a moment, "at least right now we know where he is. At least, right now, you don't have to be afraid."

She pressed her face hard into the hollow of his broad shoulder, and he felt her tears scald his skin. Too much, he thought. She had been through just too damn much. Even her moment of joy was shadowed. How could one slender, fragile woman withstand so much? How could she just keep taking blow after blow?

"I'm sorry," she said brokenly. "I'm sorry. I never cry. . . ."

"Damn it, woman, don't you dare apologize to me for crying!" Great, now he was losing his patience. Torn by her pain, he was blowing his cool. Wonderful. Next thing he knew, Faith would be cowering from *him*. But somehow he just couldn't shut up. "You've been through more than anybody should have to endure. You've survived, and you've come through strong, whether you know it or not. If you need to cry a little—well, hell, woman, people have murdered for less! What's a couple of tears?"

Instead of shrinking from him, she burrowed even closer, and he held her for a long, long time. It would be all right, he told himself grimly. Somehow, by God, he would make it all right.

Chapter 11

Washing Faith's clothes had been quite an experience, Micah thought in bemusement hours later as he sat in the concourse of the mall and watched her hunt through the clothing racks in the store facing him. He'd insisted on doing the washing himself while she sat at his table wrapped in the Hudson Bay blanket and drinking tea. He hadn't bargained on the tininess of the articles. He was accustomed to doing his own laundry, which was full of large, sturdy items. He hadn't been prepared for the fragile wisps of her lace panties and bra, or how small even her maternity sweater was. Awe and sensual pleasure were not two feelings he expected to experience at the washing machine.

Watching her now, he suspected she was on a tight budget. He would have liked to help her out, would have loved to buy her every pretty thing she saw. And he could afford to, because he'd always been thrifty with his earnings and had invested wisely over the years. He could buy her those things without blinking, but he wasn't sure how she would take it.

Damn her independence, he thought with something between affectionate amusement and frustration. She reminded him of a feisty kitten, all sharp little claws and
determination. He admired her for it, but she kept frustrating his protective instincts. And around her, his protective
instincts rose sky high. Frank might have battered her, Micah thought now, but he sure as hell hadn't killed her spirit.
She would be all right. He didn't know if his nerves would
survive her recovery, though.

She was hesitating over a cardigan sweater, he saw, a
gentle lavender color that would suit her perfectly. Probably too expensive, he thought, watching her return it to the
rack. The reluctance in her movement brought him to his
feet and into the store.

"I liked that sweater," he told her as he came up beside
her. He saw the look on the saleswoman's face, and it would
have taken a moron not to know what she was thinking of
the big bad Indian hovering over the tiny Dresden doll. He
recognized the look but ignored it, as he'd been ignoring
such things all his life.

"It's nice, but really, Micah, it's too expensive, and I
don't need it," Faith said. "I'm buying that blue one."

"Lavender's your color, though."

She looked up at him and smiled, a glow in her eyes that
plucked utterly new feelings out of his soul. "You think
so?"

"I know so. Let me get it for you. Call it an early Christmas present."

"But..."

He shook his head slowly and smiled at her. "If you don't
let me get it for you now, I'll just have to come back on my
next day off to buy it. What a waste of a trip."

The saleswoman waited on him as if he were a conta-
gious disease. He hardly noticed. Some things mattered and
some things didn't, and this saleswoman was definitely in
the latter category.

Later, though, as he helped Faith carry her purchases out to the Blazer, she remarked, "I wonder what got into that salesclerk. She was so friendly at first."

Micah opened the back of the Blazer and dumped his bundles inside. Then he turned and took Faith's from her, tossing them in after.

"I guess," he said slowly as he locked the tailgate with his key, "she doesn't like Indians."

Faith drew a sharp breath. For a moment he hesitated, not wanting to see whatever was written on her face, uncertain of what he might find. At last, though, he turned his head. Slowly. And looked down into a pair of very blue, very indignant, very pained eyes.

"You get this all the time, don't you?" she asked.

He tilted his head a little, not quite a nod, not quite a shrug or a dismissal. Just an acknowledgment.

"Doesn't it make you mad, Micah?"

"Not since I was a kid."

"But..." She trailed off, uncertain how to express herself.

"Moonbeam, getting angry doesn't do a damn bit of good. It doesn't fix a thing, it doesn't change a single mind. All it does is eat a hole in my stomach. Now, if you don't mind being stared at because you're hanging around with a big, ugly Indian, let's go find a place to eat."

He guessed she didn't mind, because when they entered a restaurant fifteen minutes later, her arm was tucked securely through his, and her head was held high in an unmistakable challenge. Micah smiled inwardly and ached a little as he realized that this small, frightened woman was teaching him what it meant to be cherished.

He'd been in this particular restaurant on several occasions with Nate Tate when they'd come into Laramie on business, and he already knew he wouldn't encounter any trouble from the staff. He'd chosen it specifically for that reason, because he wanted Faith to eat a good meal, not spend all her time being indignant about the way somebody spoke to him.

The menu was a good one, full of the plain, hearty foods he preferred. The waitress was a friendly redhead who remembered him from other visits, and gradually he saw Faith begin to relax again.

"Don't be defensive for me, Faith," he told her. "It really doesn't bother me, and you're beating your brains out against a brick wall if you try to argue with bigotry."

"It has to bother you, Micah," she argued. "It *has* to."

"It did, once upon a time. Not any more. Moonbeam, listen. I've lived all over the world, thanks to Uncle Sam, and I can tell you one thing for sure—damn near *everybody* is bigoted about *somebody*.

"In the army I got quite an education in psychological warfare, and some of it was like having a light come on in my head. One of our instructors explained bigotry as a leftover genetic component of the race from the days of tribalism, when there were just two groups of people, us and them. Fear of outsiders still operates at an instinctive level."

He smiled up at the waitress as she placed their plates in front of them and then resumed his discourse. "In my case, it's even worse because chances are the people who see me today were hearing from granny, or great-granny, how she lived in terror of losing her scalp. After I got to thinking about it like that, it stopped bothering me." And he was running on like motor mouth again. He'd been doing that a lot since Faith arrived. Falling silent, he watched her slice into her steak. "*Your* scalp," he heard himself say suddenly, "sure would have been a prize."

She looked up, startled, and then laughed. God, how he loved to hear her laugh. And it struck him suddenly that right now, at this moment, she was no longer afraid of him, that she was willing, like a tigress, to take on the world to protect *him*.

Well, hell. He didn't like the feeling. It made his throat tighten, for one thing, and it made other things inside him feel . . . different. Damn, he thought longingly, what had happened to his distance? What had happened to that carefully maintained space between him and the rest of the world?

He had the worst urge to get out of there, to go back to his ranch and run barefoot in the icy snow, to run naked in the cold until the soft, warm feelings were frozen out of him.

Coward. He was a damn coward. He could handle this. Hell, he'd handled far worse than a crazy desire to let a woman curl up in all the empty corners of his life. It was just a temporary aberration, he told himself. She had her life, and he had his, and now that Frank Williams was caught, they would both go their separate ways again. After all, no Dresden doll, no vision of moonbeams and gossamer, would settle for a hardened, used-up half-breed. Just as soon as she realized she was safe, just as soon as she understood that she no longer needed protection, she would gladly give him back his distance.

He had planned on suggesting a movie, but Faith was looking tired by the time they finished dinner. Neither of them had slept much last night, and Faith was pregnant besides. As soon as he paid the bill, he bundled her into the car and turned them back toward Conard County.

When Faith yawned for the second time, he coaxed her into stretching out on the seat and resting her head on his thigh. She fell asleep in moments, and he was alone again in the dark, with nothing ahead of him but a long gray ribbon of empty road.

Faith awoke in a state of total terror. Strong hands gripped her and were lifting her in the darkness, like the night that . . . the night that . . .

She screamed.

"It's okay, Moonbeam. It's okay. Shush, honey. Easy. . ."

Micah. Oh, God, it was Micah. Drawing deep gulps of blessed air, she turned into him, let him lift her from the car and carry her toward the house. "I'm sorry," she whispered raggedly. "I'm sorry."

"Forget it. You've been through hell, woman. It takes time to get over it. That's all. Just time and patience."

He would know, Faith thought suddenly as he climbed the steps. He knew what it was like, didn't he? He'd been nearly buried alive, tormented while he was helpless, tormented for days by men who must have seemed demented.

He knew.

Releasing the last of her terror with a shuddering sigh, she turned her face into the fragrant warmth of his neck. They passed through the darkened kitchen and started climbing the stairs.

"You know what I wish?" she whispered. "I wish I could have been there for you the way you've been here for me."

He didn't answer immediately, just continued climbing steadily while she soaked up his heat and listened to the thud of his steadily beating heart. Even that heartbeat was a strong, contained sound, she thought dreamily. It was with gladness that she realized he had carried her into his room, not hers.

Micah lowered her onto his bed and pulled her boots off. They fell with a thud to the floor, and then he reached out to turn on the lamp, to drive the night away.

"I'll go down and get your clothes," he said. "Want anything else?"

She shook her head, studying him from strangely solemn eyes.

He gave her a brief nod and headed out of the room. At the door, though, he hesitated, then said over his shoulder, "You were there for me, Moonbeam. You were there."

Leaving her feeling utterly confused behind him, he stomped down the stairs and decided that finally, after years of suspecting it, he was at last utterly losing his mind. Why had he ever admitted such a thing? It was crazy. Totally crazy!

But as he stomped down those stairs through his dark house and out into the cold winter night, he remembered being twenty years old. He remembered being in excruciating pain and in a state of terror so total it defied description. He remembered standing in that hole in the darkness, expecting to die at any moment, knowing that at any time the trap door above his head might open to unleash another hail of dirt and offal onto his head. He remembered thinking that if he accomplished nothing else, he wanted to die unbroken.

Pressing his palms against the tailgate of the Blazer, he locked his elbows and leaned against the vehicle, head down. She'd been there. Her little girl's voice had called him out of that hole and tugged him back to Conard County. Memories of that summer, memories of teaching Faith to ride and swim, to throw a lasso and catch a fish, had kept him sane. He had, quite simply, closed his eyes to what was really happening and relived the best summer of his life.

It had been the best summer of his life because of Faith. Without her, he would have been just another inexperienced, underpaid cowpoke on the Montrose ranch. Instead, she had drawn him to her father's attention, had drawn him into an almost-family. Jason Montrose had treated him like a son, and Faith Montrose had treated him like an adored older brother, and for ten short weeks Micah Parish had known what it meant to belong.

He hadn't been able to keep his emotional distance from that little girl, so what in hell had made him think he could keep his distance from the woman she'd become? She had grown up, she had changed, she was in no way like the child he remembered, but she still had the power to fascinate him, although the fascination was of an utterly different character now.

An utterly different character, he thought again, and straightened. It was cold out here, a cold that was making him feel lonely, and if he had an ounce of the sense he had always believed he owned, he would be inside thawing his soul against Faith's warmth. Whatever distance he'd had was shot, whatever solitude he'd once preserved had vanished, and he might as well just take pleasure in whatever good came his way. There would always be time later to deal with the inevitable pain.

* * *

The shower was running when Micah returned upstairs. He would like to shower with her, he thought as he set the bags containing her clothes to one side. He would like to get under that hot spray, soap her all over, then have her soap him. He didn't have the slightest difficulty imagining just how she would feel, all shivery and slick against him.

Whoa!

No way. That kind of thing would be dangerous as hell when she was so pregnant.

He smiled slowly, realizing that it had been years since he had felt as playful as he did at this moment. And if he felt playful, why not play?

Faith turned beneath the shower spray and squeaked when she saw Micah watching her. He'd pulled the curtain back a little at the other end of the tub, and just his head and one gleaming shoulder were visible as he leaned in and watched her with the strangest smile on his face.

"Sorry," he said. "I didn't mean to startle you."

She gave an unsteady little laugh. "I just didn't expect to see anyone. . . ."

"Why not? Did you think I could resist a chance to see all this beauty?" His smile broadened.

"I'm not beautiful."

"Maybe not to someone else, but to me, you are most definitely beautiful. Exquisite. A fairy tale princess."

Another protest died on her lips as he stuck his arm into the enclosure with her and reached out to touch one of her nipples ever so lightly with the tip of his index finger. At once both her nipples rose and swelled in response.

Impossibly, his voice seemed to have dropped another octave when he spoke, sounding now as deep as a distant rumble of thunder. "Perfect," he said. "Absolutely perfect." His finger trailed down to trace a circle on her belly. "A fertility goddess." Slowly, he raised his gaze to her face. "Do you suppose you might be about ready to get out of there?"

She supposed she was about ready to collapse. She had known terror could make her knees weak, but she had never guessed desire could do it, too. Micah steadied her as she stepped over the edge of the tub onto the mat, then toweled her dry with exquisite care.

He was wearing only his jeans now, and Faith leaned over him, gripping the smooth strength of his broad shoulders for support. This, she thought as he lifted her foot and dried it with breath-stealing gentleness, was the way it should be between a man and a woman. She felt safe, cared for, eager. She felt free to bend over and kiss the top of his dark head, felt free to smile when she heard his breath catch at the gesture.

He dropped the towel and closed his brawny arms around her waist, shutting his eyes and pressing his cheek to her for a long moment in a sweet, sweet hug.

And then, lifting his head, he blew a raspberry on her belly.

Faith shrieked.

Micah laughed out loud for the first time in more years than he could remember, then scooped Faith up to carry her laughing and squirming into the bedroom. He laid her on cool sheets and then lay down beside her, intent on keeping her laughing.

But Faith had other ideas, and when she tugged the snap of his jeans open, his breath left him in a rush, and he forgot all about teasing her and tickling her gently, about blowing raspberries on her tummy and all the other ideas he had for making her giggle.

Propped on his side on one elbow, he froze in agonizing anticipation and watched as she pulled his zipper down and then reached inside to touch him. Other women had done that over the years. Other women had touched him with practiced hands and knowing fingers, but no one, no one at all, had touched him as Faith did.

Her hands trembled, fine little tremors he could feel, and that electrified him. What electrified him even more was knowing she found this difficult but wanted to do it anyway, for him. And for herself.

"Tell me," she murmured, her breath catching. "Tell me if I do something wrong."

"You don't do anything wrong. Not ever."

She turned her head and looked straight at him, and the vulnerability he saw in her eyes ripped a Wyoming-sized crater in his heart.

"I like the way you touch me," he told her, things inside him aching, crashing, shifting, in the emotional earthquake she had set off. "I like it, Moonbeam. God help me, I *love* it. Don't stop."

Was that really him saying those things? He'd never... But now he was, and he meant them, and to hell with what it might cost. He needed whatever touches she wanted to give him, and he didn't want her to stop because she didn't realize how much he wanted it.

"Help me," she whispered breathlessly, tugging at the denim of his jeans.

He lifted his hips and pushed his jeans down, helping her to wrestle them off his legs. When she began running her hands ever so slowly up his legs in teasing sweeps that came closer and closer to his sex, he decided he must have died and gone to heaven.

Along about the time she reached his upper thighs, she looked up at him, and something in her expression reached out to touch his soul. Then, before he could do more than register the impact, her mouth found him. *Hot, sweet, wild.*

A deep, wrenching groan escaped him, and along with it went the civilized veneer he wore. The touch of her lips and tongue turned him into man elemental, unleashed the raging fires he kept carefully banked, and set Micah Parish free of a lifetime of carefully accumulated control.

He wanted. He needed. Nothing else mattered but his needs and this woman. He forgot all his hard-learned emotional lessons. He forgot all the walls and barriers he had built. He forgot the myth he had tried to live up to. He forgot everything except that never, not once, in his entire life had he received what he needed from a woman.

With another groan, he drew Faith up over him and covered her hungry mouth with his. His woman. *His woman.* Possessiveness rose in him savagely, stronger than thought, a deep-running instinct. He needed to love her so well that she would give herself totally. Completely. Forsaking all others.

He needed a woman who was his, just his. He needed his mate, the mate he'd never had. The mate he had foolishly thought himself quite happy without—until Faith. She was reaching him at a level so elemental, so basic, that he could almost feel the connection of his soul to hers. If she left him—oh God, if she left him . . .

He couldn't even bear to think of it.

He swept her beneath him, taking care not to burden her with his weight. Possessiveness made him protective. She was his to care for, to shelter, to cherish, to love. He would place himself between her and every danger or fear. He would ensure that with him she was always safe. He would give her nothing but joy and comfort.

"Micah . . . oh, Micah . . . oh!"

He plundered her gently with his mouth, transforming his need to keep her into sensual, silken bonds that would make her want him more. He would make her his by giving her what no one else ever had. It was that simple. A man didn't hold a woman by making her his slave, his toy, or his victim. He didn't hold her through terror, or fear, or superior strength. A man kept his mate by making her want to stay. A man kept his mate by pleasing her.

He brought her close to the edge by gently sucking her breasts. It took nothing else to bring her to writhing impatience, but he gave her more anyway. By the time he joined himself to her with a slow, deep, gentle thrust, she was gasping his name on every breath and begging him to please, *please,* love her now.

And somewhere, in the grip of his powerful need, he made the mistake of declaring his possession.

"You're mine," he said raggedly as he pumped into her, his body nearly convulsing with each lunge. "You're mine, Moonbeam." He wanted her to know he wanted her that much, forever, if she would just have him.

She heard something else entirely.

When Micah's alarm went off at six, he was alone in bed. He could smell coffee, though, and guessed that Faith, bless her, had awakened early and decided to make him breakfast before he went to work.

Smiling, he rose to the new day with more eagerness than he had felt in years. Today, he thought as he gave himself a sponge bath, he was going to ask Dr. MacArdle to take him out of this damn tape. Surely they had something removable he could wear so he could shower. He suspected the doctor had taped him up only to keep him from taking the stuff off. That would be like MacArdle, all right.

Still smiling, he dressed in a fresh uniform, strapped on his holster and gun, grabbed his Stetson, and headed downstairs to give his woman the good morning kiss she deserved.

On the threshold of the kitchen, he froze. Faith was sitting at the table, fully clothed, rigidly upright, her hands tightly folded. Beside her sat her suitcase and the bags of clothing.

"Moonbeam?" His voice cracked almost imperceptibly on the pet name he had given her. He really didn't need an answer. He knew a woman who was leaving when he saw one.

"I-I'd really appreciate it if you'd take me home this morning, Micah," Faith said, her voice wobbly.

He didn't move a muscle. In an instant he became cold granite, head to foot. "Why?" he said.

"Well, F-Frank's in jail, so I'm safe now, and... and I r-really need to be independent. I-I told you, Micah. I have to stand on my own two feet!"

She was afraid of him. He could see it. Damn it, she was afraid of him! Why? *Why?*

Still he didn't move, didn't even blink. He stared at her, facing a loneliness he knew was going to damn him for the rest of his days. She had shattered everything that held that loneliness at bay, had disintegrated his distance and torn away his solitude, and now she was going to abandon him. And it was his own fault, because he knew better than to trust a woman.

"Tell me the truth, Faith," he said flatly. "Just tell me the truth."

Slowly she lifted her head, until she was looking straight at him. He saw the fear in her blue eyes, saw the tears she was fighting, saw the courage that sustained her despite everything.

"I don't belong to you," she said tensely. "My baby doesn't belong to you." She closed her eyes suddenly, hearing Frank in her head, seeing once again the evil gleam of the knife in his hand. *You're mine, Faith. That kid's mine. I'll do anything I want with either one of you.* And just as clearly, she heard Micah telling her that when he spilled his seed in her, the baby became his. Telling her last night that she was his. *Mine.* God, how she hated and feared the sound of that word! Her eyes flew open. "I'm not yours," she said again, almost desperately. "I'm not anyone's!"

Every single feeling inside Micah shut down. Of course she wasn't his, he thought distantly. Why the hell had he ever thought she might want to be a half-breed's woman? Ignoring her as if she had ceased to exist, he poured himself a cup of coffee and a bowl of cold cereal. He ate standing at the counter, his back to her, unwilling to see her fear, her tears, her anguish. Unwilling to feel anything ever again. Damn, he'd known better.

When he finished, he rinsed his bowl in the sink and then turned, lifting the suitcase and bags without glancing at her. "Let's go," he said harshly. At the door he paused a moment to grab his uniform parka and throw it over his shoulder, but he didn't put it on. He needed the cold. He needed the kind of cold that would numb him all the way to his soul, but for now he would have to settle for Wyoming's November ice.

He didn't speak to her again until they reached her house. He felt her looking at him repeatedly, but he ignored her. He wasn't going to give her an opportunity to try to smooth over her rejection of him, nor was he going to listen to her plead for his understanding, the way women often did after they shafted a man. She had said all that needed saying, he figured, and he wasn't going to give her a chance to drive the knife any deeper.

When he parked at her door, he told her to stay put. "I'm going to clean up the mess Frank left before you go in there," he said roughly.

"Micah, I can—"

He rounded sharply on her. "No."

She shrank back against the door, but he was damned if he cared anymore. Leaving her outside in the locked vehicle, he made his way to her room and began gathering up all the shreds of slashed clothing. He was not a vindictive or vengeful man, and his only thought was that no one, absolutely no one, should ever be faced with evidence of such hate being directed toward them.

He found a large trash bag in the kitchen and filled it with the scraps of cloth. Then he found a rag and some pine cleaner and went to scrub away the threats and filthy words that had been scrawled in lipstick across the wall above her bed. Nobody should have to see that kind of thing. Nobody.

"Okay," he said to her twenty minutes later. He helped her down from the Blazer, escorted her into the house, then carried in her bags. Without looking at her, he checked the phone to be sure it was working, then picked up the bag of scraps. He would burn them at home; he sure wasn't going to chance Faith looking in there and seeing what Frank had done.

At the door, he stopped and spoke over his shoulder. "You can still call me if you need anything," he said gruffly. "That's what neighbors are for."

Outside he tossed the bag into the back of his vehicle and paused a moment to draw a couple of deep breaths of cold air. Nothing had changed, he told himself. He had only thought it might, but it hadn't, so everything was just the way it had always been.

Except that now he knew what it felt like to have his heart torn out by the roots.

Chapter 12

"Jeez, Micah," Charlie Huskins said to him as he entered the office, "you look awful. Are you okay?"

Before he could dismiss Charlie's concern with a remark
about a sick animal keeping him up all night, Nate butted
in.

"Get your backside over to Doc MacArdle and have him
look at those ribs."

Micah turned right around and marched back out the
door without argument. He'd been planning to see the doctor anyway, and it saved making excuses to conceal the
truth. And what had happened to his poker face, anyway?
He was usually unreadable, but this morning he must be an
open book.

The doctor's office was in his home on Front Street, a
prosperous avenue of elderly, elegant homes that housed
Conard City's higher social classes. Dr. MacArdle wasn't
back from morning rounds yet, but the nurse, Joanne, took
one look at Micah and put him right in the examining room,
assuring him it wouldn't be long.

Yep, he must look like hell. Curious, he walked over to the small mirror that hung over a sink and peered at himself. He didn't think he looked any different.

Shrugging inwardly, he wandered over to the window and stared out at the cold, gray day. There wasn't a speck of color left in the world, he thought. Not a one. The trees were barren, the snow dingy, the sky overcast.

"Howdy, Micah." Ben MacArdle stepped briskly into the room, carrying a clipboard and wearing the knee-length white coat that was his habit. The coat was beginning to get a little snug around his middle since he'd married last spring.

"Morning, Ben. I was hoping you could get this tape off me."

"I figured you'd be about ready to rip it off yourself by now." Ben glanced up with a smile. "Come on, take off your shirt. Nate's worried about you."

"He is? What'd he do, call you at the hospital?"

"He called Joanne. Said you looked like a vampire who'd missed his last meal."

"Well, hell."

"You look a little drawn, all right."

"I'm just tired, that's all." He *was* tired, he thought as he hung his crisply pressed shirt—Faith's doing—on the hook and turned back to the doctor. Tired in a bone-deep, soul-deep way he had seldom felt before.

Removing the tape wasn't a difficult task, requiring only that Ben clip away at it with scissors, since a layer of cotton batting lay between the tape and his skin.

"Will you look at that?" Ben said with a whistle as he pulled the tape away. "All the colors of the rainbow and a few I don't think I ever saw before."

Micah looked down at the bruise that covered his entire left side from nipple to waist. Experimentally, he poked at it with a finger. "Not tender."

"Bet this is, though," Ben said, and pressed on a bruised rib. Micah drew a sharp breath. "Thought so. Take a deep, slow breath."

Micah emerged twenty minutes later with an elastic bandage around his middle that he could remove when he wished, and a clean bill of health. Ben had offered the opinion that it wouldn't hurt Micah to take a few more days off, Micah had made a few noncommittal sounds, and Ben had thrown up his hands.

Nate was waiting when Micah returned to the office. "Ben said you could use some more time off."

Micah stared stonily back. "Not today," was all he said.

Nate studied him a moment. "Okay. Not today."

"Frank Williams is in the tank?"

Nate nodded. "His extradition hearing is Wednesday. Garrett Hancock is flying up tomorrow, and he has every intention of taking Williams back to Texas with him."

"Won't be soon enough for me."

"How's Faith doing?"

"She moved back to her own place this morning." Micah turned toward the stairway that led upstairs to the jail. "I think I'll go take a look at the guy. If I ever run into him, I want to know who he is."

Conard County didn't have much need for a jail and boasted only six cells in an armored room on the second floor of the building. A deputy sat guard around the clock, but the necessary security was provided by locks and bars. Usually the tank held petty thieves, joyriders, drunks and brawlers. Today it held only Frank Williams. Jed Barlowe, the drunk who had shot Micah, had been sent off to Casper to a detox program.

Frank Williams, like many of the world's worst people, looked perfectly ordinary. He looked like ten thousand other cops: young, healthy, a little pudgy around the middle from spending too many hours in a patrol car. He was nothing special, nothing frightening.

Except, Micah thought, for a strange wildness to his eyes. They were the eyes of a Charles Manson. Looking into those eyes, he found it possible to believe everything he had heard about Williams, and possible to suspect there was plenty more as yet untold.

"You're sure a unique-looking deputy," Williams remarked, half smiling as he watched Micah approach.

It was a friendly smile, Micah noted with detachment. From anyone else, under other circumstances, he would have accepted it as a friendly overture. From this man, friendliness was bound to be manipulative. "I'm a unique man," Micah answered levelly. He stopped two paces away from the cell and simply stared at the other man.

Finally Williams began to get unnerved. "What are you doing?"

"Memorizing you."

"Memorizing me?" Frank came to his feet. "What for?"

"So I'll know you the next time I see you, whenever I see you, wherever I see you."

Frank shifted uneasily. "Why? What difference does it make?"

"Well," Micah said slowly, "I spent twenty years in the Special Operations branch of the army. It's a habit to know my target."

"Target?" Williams backed up a step. "What do you mean by that? I'm not your target."

"Not at the moment." Micah took a step toward the cell. "I'll tell you something, Williams. If you so much as lay one finger on Faith ever again, if I ever so much as catch wind of your stinking scent within fifty miles of that woman, I'm going to track you down and teach you the meaning of fear. I don't care how far you go, I'll follow you. I'll track you to the ends of the earth and I'll get you. I swear it." Turning, he started to walk away.

"You threatened me!" Williams shouted after him. "I'll sue you for that!"

"Prove it," Micah said flatly without looking back, then disappeared through the door.

Nate insisted that Micah take desk duty, so the day dragged. He finished all his own paperwork and half of Nate's, while listening to Charlie Huskins tell old jokes and talk about his wife and baby daughter. Charlie liked to talk. All in all, it was a quiet day in Conard County.

Just before five, Gage Dalton showed up. Wearing his usual black from head to foot, Gage entered the office like doom on an already gloomy day. Charlie gave Gage the kind of uncertain look people always gave him, even when they saw him frequently. Gage nodded to him and looked at Micah.

"Got a minute?"

Micah nodded and followed Gage into Nate's office. Gage closed the door behind them.

"What now?" asked Nate when the two came in, his tone the resigned voice of a man who had found life a little too exciting lately.

"I spoke with a guy I know up at the state lab to see if they've learned any more about Cumberland's cattle. He told me they're having a big fight about it up there, and the lab director is demanding the necropsies be reperformed by someone else."

"Why?" Nate was sitting up straight now. Micah still leaned against the wall, but he felt the tension inside.

"The pathologist is insisting those cattle were cut with surgical instruments."

"Hah!" The sound escaped Micah. He'd known it.

Gage acknowledged the fact with a nod. "There's evidently some more stuff, but my contact doesn't know what it is. I want to go up there and see if I can rattle their cages a little. I don't like the idea that they're sitting on evidence."

"They probably aren't convinced yet that it's accurate evidence," Nate said. "But yeah, Gage, you go ahead, and turn in a travel voucher when you get back. If you have any trouble, give me a holler."

Gage left moments later, and Nate and Micah exchanged looks.

"You were right, old son," Nate said. "But then, you always are. What the hell is going on in my county?"

Micah shook his head. "Wish I knew."

"It used to be so peaceful around here," Nate said. "I could count on handling little stuff, the kind of crap you take care of so your neighbors are happy, the kind of thing you do to keep friends out of trouble. Hell, son, we haven't had a murder in this county since John Grant took it in the chest from that escaped convict four years ago. How many places can say that?"

"Not many."

"Damn straight." Nate scowled at him. "Then we had Mandy Grant kidnapped a couple of months ago by that she-devil who wanted to get back at Ransom. Now we got that Williams character, and cattle being surgically mutilated." He shook his head. "Damn."

"Maybe you ought to kick out all of the outsiders. We seem to bring the trouble. Me, Ransom, Faith, Frank Williams. Gage isn't from these parts either, is he?"

"Nope."

"Where's he from?"

Nate looked up at him. "Hell, Micah. He's been in hell. Anything else, you need to ask him."

A typical Nathan Tate response, Micah thought as he headed back to his desk. Absolutely no information at all. Nate probably said the same damn thing when anyone asked him about Micah.

By quitting time, Micah felt like himself again. One weekend's lovemaking with a woman wasn't enough to throw him off kilter for long. He'd just somehow blown it all out of proportion last night and this morning. Hell, it hadn't even been a whole week since he had rescued the woman from the road. Too short a time to become genuinely attached to her. After forty-three years, he'd suffered from a few hours of craziness, that was all.

Some of the stew Faith had made was left in the refrigerator, so he shoved it into the microwave and headed out for the barn to tend his animals. The work made his ribs ache, but he welcomed the pain. Maybe later he would go for a run.

Pain was a great touchstone, he thought. It reminded him of what was real. It focused and centered him in himself. It was a goad that drove him.

He could feel himself recovering his distance, he thought, as he returned to the house sweaty and aching from his labors. He could feel his barriers rising as if brick after brick were slipping into place, filling in all the chinks. She was only a woman, after all. Just a woman. He'd gotten along just fine before she showed up in his life, and he would get along just as well now.

He was just fine the way he was.

That being true, why did he feel as if he were standing at the bottom of a very narrow, dank, dark hole waiting to be buried alive?

When Faith watched Micah drive away, her initial reaction had been one of relief. She had escaped without harm. Standing alone in the solitude of her father's familiar house, she allowed herself to feel safe. Frank was in jail, and she was never again going to be any man's possession. Never.

Closing her eyes, she pressed her hands to her womb and felt her baby's vigorous movements against her palms. It was just the two of them now. Just her and the baby, and it was going to be all right. In this house, where she had known joy, she was going to make a real home for her child. A home full of love and light and warmth, a home without any shadows of fear.

The smell of pine cleaner was strong, and it grew stronger as she walked back to her bedroom. She was able to see a faintly pink smear where Micah had sponged away the words she had heard mentioned but had never seen. The holes in the wall were still there, but Micah couldn't have done much about those.

Suddenly, without any kind of warning, her legs gave way and she sank onto the bed. Wrapping her arms tightly around herself, she rocked back and forth, and cried and cried and cried.

Frank had followed her here. He had followed her. If she hadn't had that flashback that made Micah take her home with him, she would be dead now, she and her baby both. So what if they came and took Frank back to Texas and put him in prison? So what? How long would it be before he got out again? What if he escaped again? Oh, Lord, Lord, was she ever going to be safe?

At some point she curled up into a tight ball on the bed and fell into exhausted sleep. She hadn't slept last night, but had lain awake staring into the dark, hearing Micah's voice claim her as Frank's once had, trying to deal with the fear she couldn't seem to escape.

At last she left it behind, for a little while, in sleep.

It was dark when at last she awoke. A day had slipped by, lost in the velvet reaches of slumber. She freshened up a little in the bathroom and then answered another imperative call of nature, heading for the kitchen and the refrigerator. She was starved, and the bag of melon balls she had stashed in the freezer on Friday suddenly sounded irresistible.

It wasn't until she was sitting at the table, a half-eaten bowl of melon balls in front of her, that the sleepy sense of well-being slipped away, leaving her horribly conscious of the emptiness around her.

Horribly conscious of missing Micah.

She turned and looked at the phone, wondering if she should call him and explain what had sent her into flight this morning. Surely he would understand? He seemed to have understood all her other craziness. This time she had been running from an idea of men that Frank had pounded into her with fists and words, an idea that had little relationship to Micah. Micah would understand that.

Or would he? Recalling the way he had seemed to harden into granite this morning when she told him she was leaving, recalling how distant and cold he had become and remained, she wondered. For the first time since last night, she was able to look past her fear and consider that she might have wounded Micah, that she might have insulted him by the way she had fled.

And if that were the case, he would never want to speak to her again. Or see her. Or hold her.

Trying to ignore the aching sense of loss that thought engendered, she scooped up her bowl and put it into the refrigerator. Time to get her mind off morbid things, she told herself. Time to read a book. Time to enjoy the total solitude she had been trying to find for ages.

Wasn't this what she'd wanted, to be utterly alone? Wasn't this what she had been telling herself would solve all her problems? That once she was alone she would be safe?

But her solitude mocked her with emptiness, and her heart treacherously remembered how full it had begun to feel.

Uneasiness began to ride Micah like a goad. He couldn't settle down with his book, couldn't sink into the music he put on the stereo. He found himself pacing restlessly through the house, upstairs and down, too often catching a whiff of Faith's elusive fragrance. That would wear off with time, and so would this damn restlessness and sense of loss. Or so he told himself.

Stepping outside, he stood staring up at the starry night sky. He hadn't bothered with a jacket, so the cold seeped through his shirt and made his skin prickle and sting. He needed a good long run, he thought, and turned to run down his driveway, but the uneasiness stopped him.

Somehow, for some reason, he didn't want to be too far from the phone. Shrugging, he gave in to intuition and stayed where he was, studying the stars as if they held some answer to the pain he kept buried in his soul.

Around him he felt the night, the miles and miles of space and distance, the emptiness of Wyoming's wide open spaces. He felt the abiding power of the land beneath his feet, the strength of the rock that had endured for millennia, and tried to imagine himself part of that rock and clay, as strong and as enduring as they were. He drew strength from the earth, he reminded himself, and solace from the wind.

And, like the eagle, he was free.

Gage Dalton found Micah there twenty minutes later. Micah had turned when he heard the approach of a vehicle and waited patiently while Gage's Suburban crunched slowly to a halt a dozen feet away. Gage climbed out and approached slowly, as if he sensed the magnitude of his intrusion into Micah's privacy. For a moment the two men regarded one another silently across a span of about six feet.

"Coffee?" Micah said finally.

"Thanks."

Inside, Gage sat at the table, slouched in the chair, legs loosely crossed. Dark from head to toe. Micah leaned back against the counter, crossing his booted feet at the ankles, and waited.

Presently, Gage looked at him. "I was out wandering the roads, feeling restless. You know the feeling."

"I know."

"I figured you might. Anyhow, I was driving around thinking about the mutilations, about what you found, what the guy at the lab told me, and trying to put it all together in some way that makes sense. When I got near here, I thought maybe we could kick some ideas around."

Micah stared at him. Until this moment, he had thought of Gage Dalton as a near-stranger, someone he would probably respect if he knew him, but someone he would never really know. There were people like that, people who never opened up. Micah was one of them himself.

In that moment, though, he understood that Gage had stopped here not to discuss mutilations, but because he had heard that Faith had gone back to her own place. Gage had come as a friend.

"Yeah," Micah said after a moment, his voice a little rusty. "Yeah, we can kick some ideas around." Coming over to the table, he pulled out a chair and sat.

* * *

Every light in the house blazed brightly. Faith yawned, wondering how she could possibly feel so sleepy after having slept away the entire day—and when every dark corner seemed to harbor a threat.

In the past couple of hours she had discovered that she didn't feel secure here alone, even with Frank safely locked up. Solitude no longer offered protection.

Only Micah offered protection, she thought with a sudden, painful squeezing of her heart. Only Micah had ever made her feel safe. Cared for. The emptiness of this house would never give her that.

It would never give her the strength of his arms around her, or the heat of his gentle loving, or the wonder that filled her whenever he pressed his hand to her womb and felt her child move.

It would never give her any of the things she needed, the things she *really* needed. Things she had begun to believe didn't exist until Micah showed her that they did.

She reached for the phone, refusing to let fear conquer her again. She would apologize. Tell him she was sorry for the hurtful way she had acted. She would . . .

The phone was dead. Blankly, she stared at it, and then every light in the house went out.

Micah broke off in midsentence and cocked his head to one side. Something was wrong. Closing his eyes, he reached out in some indefinable way, trying to locate the source of the uneasiness that had suddenly pricked his mind. After a moment, though, the feeling faded. He looked at Gage.

"What was it?" Gage asked.

"Just a feeling."

Gage nodded, as if he had those feelings, too. Hunches. Intuitions. Something just below the level of conscious thought that you learned to pay attention to if you lived on the edge for any length of time. Gage's acceptance told Micah something about the younger man's shrouded past. It also raised a lot of interesting questions Micah didn't ask because it was none of his business.

Gage wasn't quite as taciturn as Micah, but he wasn't a whole lot more talkative. Somehow they drifted away from the subject of the mutilations, and talk became desultory, the pauses longer, the quiet somehow comfortable.

At some point Micah realized they were both waiting for something. That earlier nibble of unease had left its mark, and apparently his own sense of something about to happen had communicated itself to Gage.

And then he felt it again, only this time it was stronger. Much stronger. Something was very definitely wrong. Disturbed, he didn't hesitate any longer. He went to the phone and dialed Faith's number.

With each unanswered ring, his trepidation grew. Visions filled his head, none of them reassuring. She could have slipped in the tub, or fallen down her basement stairs, or...

He slammed the phone into the cradle. "I'm going over to the Montrose place," he told Gage.

"I'll come with you. If something's wrong, you might need help."

Micah was in no mood to dally, but some things needed doing, like it or not. He got his vest, his gun belt, his jacket, checked his .45, made sure his speedloaders were ready. There was no reason to suppose that Faith was in danger from a person, but he supposed it anyway. Instinct. Gut feeling.

Gage must have felt the same way, Micah realized as he stepped outside. The other man was at his Suburban, pulling on his own body armor. Better safe than sorry.

They took Micah's official vehicle, and as they raced toward the Montrose ranch, Micah tried to think of other things to keep himself from dwelling on what he might find.

And that was a dead giveaway, he realized. A dead giveaway. He'd been through hell many times in his life, and he'd never before found it necessary to play mental hide-and-seek with reality. If this were a routine call, he would be *trying* to imagine every possibility before he got there, so that he would be as prepared as possible. He wouldn't be trying to think about the fact that Gage had body armor and had just asked if Micah wanted him to call for backup, two clear betrayals of the fact that Gage had a long background in active law enforcement. No, he would be focused on the task at hand, not wallowing in a sense of dread.

With a sharp, inward mental yank, he forced himself to do this right, to think clearly about every potential threat. He owed that to Faith.

This was the second time in less than a week that he'd made this drive in the middle of the night in a near panic about Faith. The second time.

"When I get my hands on that woman," he heard himself say aloud, "I'm going to shake some sense into her."

"Might be a good idea," Gage agreed easily. "Seems like a damn fool thing, living alone all the way out here when she's pregnant."

Micah thought so, too. And this crap about independence... Faith wasn't meant to be independent and alone. She was meant to be loved and cherished, not to stand by herself in the cold winds of the world. He would willingly have bet that if she was asked, she would confess to wanting more than one child, and damn it, she would make a wonderful mother.

If he had to shake her until her teeth rattled, he would make her see that she had no business burying herself like this. She needed a life, a full life.

But he wouldn't shake her. He wouldn't lay a finger on her, because he knew that if he did, she'd run away like a scared rabbit—and probably for good. And he also knew that if he touched her again, he probably wouldn't be able to let her go.

She was a song in his blood, the sunlight in his soul.

When the lights went out, Faith froze into instant immobility. With the phone already dead, she didn't for an instant think this was a simple power outage. Were the doors and windows locked? Oh, God, she couldn't be sure, because she hadn't checked them yet. Frank might have unlocked them, or the deputies might have, after Frank broke in here. The only door she knew for certain was locked was the kitchen door, because she had locked it when Micah left.

Bending slowly, she lowered the receiver until she could let go of it without leaving it to swing and bang against the walls. Then, carefully, she stepped out of her pumps, knowing her stocking feet would be quieter.

The circuit breakers. Where was the breaker box? To throw off all the lights at once, the main had to be thrown or the power line had to be knocked down, and she seriously doubted anyone would attempt the latter. The basement? Could Frank be in the basement?

Her mouth felt as dry as Death Valley, and her heart was hammering so hard it seemed loud in the silence. The baby stirred, kicking gently and turning over. Please, God. Please, please, please!

If she could get her car keys, maybe she could get to her car and get out of here before . . .

The thought drained away as she looked at the door to the basement. It was dark, but her eyes were just beginning to adjust, just enough to see the pale gleam of the doorknob. If she stuck a chair under there . . .

She grabbed one of the kitchen chairs and carried it swiftly to the basement door, keeping quiet until the very last moment, when she needed to wedge it into place beneath the doorknob. The sound was excruciatingly loud in the utter silence of the house. With the power out, not even the refrigerator hummed, and the hot water heater had stopped groaning.

Her car keys were in her purse on her dresser, all the way back in the bedroom. She refused to allow herself to consider that he might already have disabled her car. She had to try.

How had he gotten out of jail this time? she wondered desperately as she held her hands out and tried to feel her way through the impossibly dark house. How had he managed to get away again?

In her mind, Frank Williams was taking on the character of a supernatural force. He just kept coming and coming and coming, and not even prison bars seemed to be able to hold him. And this time there would be no Garrett Hancock to break the door down and come to her rescue. This time she couldn't call Micah.

This time she was utterly alone.

As she eased along the counter, her hand came up against the storage block that held the butcher knives. Instinctively, she pulled out the ten-inch chef's knife and carried it with her. If he came at her again with a knife, she vowed, she wasn't going to be the only one wounded.

In the midst of her terror, as she tried to ease down the hallway without making a sound, she was suddenly drowned in a burning wave of shame over her flight from Micah that morning. It had been a reflexive reaction to his claim that she was his, but only to a point, and that was what shamed her now. Frightened or not, she was guilty of putting Micah Parish in the same class with Frank Williams, and there was just no comparison between the two. Even as scared as she felt of being a man's possession, she surely should have been able to see that Micah wasn't anything like the man she believed was pursuing her now.

She hoped she would have a chance to tell him that, to apologize, but as she took another gulp of air and slid another step down the hall, she wasn't sure she would ever again have the opportunity to do anything.

Finally—finally—she reached the door of her bedroom and slipped inside, closing the door behind her. Now for her purse, and then she would climb out the window.

Maybe it wasn't Frank, she thought as she moved cautiously across the room toward the dresser. She hadn't heard anything, after all. Maybe it was just coincidental that the lights had gone out. Maybe she was acting like a frightened idiot, and she'd better be damn careful she didn't fall on this butcher knife. Wouldn't that be ironic, to die of a self-inflicted stab wound in an empty house because the lights had gone out?

Suddenly there was a banging from the other end of the house, and the unmistakable sound of something being forced across the kitchen floor.

Oh, my God! Oh, my God! He was coming for her!

Forgetting all about car keys and the window, she scurried for the huge, old oak armoire that had been one of her favorite hiding places as a child. It had survived the fire that gutted the original house, and her dad had kept it, even though the new house had adequate closets. In it now were sheets, blankets and pillows, and she crawled quickly into it. In moments she had closed the door behind her and listened to the latch catch. Then she burrowed into the blankets and quilts until she was sure she was covered from head to toe. In the dark, perhaps all the blankets would fool him. Perhaps.

Her heart raced, and her oxygen-starved lungs drew great gulping breaths as she strained with every fiber of her being to hear.

An eternity passed while she huddled and waited, the knife in her hand, her ears straining for any sound other than the hammering of her heart. Disconnected prayers and pleas raced through her mind, and she felt herself trying to reach across the desolate distance to Micah. If only some pinprick of uneasiness could reach him ... if only some prayer or wish could summon him.

"I know you're here, bitch!"

Frank's voice shattered the terrifying silence with the incontrovertible evidence of his presence. Clapping her hand over her mouth to smother an instinctive cry, Faith bit her knuckle hard.

"I'll find you. You know I'll find you!"

Faith curled up even tighter, trying to wrap her womb in the protection of her body.

"You stupid whore! Did you really think I'd let you go? Did you really think I'd let anybody else have you? Nobody's going to have you, Faith. Nobody. You're mine."

Faith swallowed another whimper and fought to keep from shaking so hard that she lost her grip on the knife. Oh, God, God, God, *please*...

"After I take care of you, bitch, I'm going after that redskin who's so fond of you. When I'm done with you, I'm going to cut him into little pieces and laugh all the time I'm doing it."

Profound terror gripped Faith, fueled by her vivid memory of the last time Frank had come after her. She could still feel each blow, each stabbing thrust of the knife.

This time, she thought in the instant before her mind went totally blank, this time she was going to die.

Chapter 13

The sight of a pickup truck pulled off to the side of Faith's driveway was all the additional evidence Micah needed that she was in serious trouble. A visitor would have pulled up to the house, not left his vehicle a good quarter mile away.

He jammed on the brakes and looked at Gage. "Call in and let 'em know we've got trouble. This looks planned. I'm going ahead on foot."

"I'll be right behind you."

Micah ran, keeping to the side of the driveway so the snow would muffle the sound of his steps. It was an easy run for a man with his training, a man who often ran a couple of miles just to clear his head a little. His breathing hardly deepened, but with each step he sank more profoundly into the inner stillness that brought him to the peak of preparedness.

It was the night of the new moon, and there only starlight to guide him, but the snow reflected that little bit of light, magnifying it, making it just possible for him to see enough.

The basement window near the front of the house had been knocked in. A piece of glass had fallen outside onto the snow, and the glint of the dim light on the perfectly smooth surface drew Micah's eye instantly. He must have used a cloth to muffle the sound and made a silent entrance.

Faith was alone in the dark house with an intruder.

Rage struck him like a thunderclap in his head, leaving a deadly clarity in its wake. Time was of the essence, but he had to get into that house without alerting the intruder, who might hurt Faith if he became alarmed.

Although in truth, Micah thought grimly as he fell to the ground and began shimmying backwards through the small window, there was no doubt in his mind who had broken into the house. No one else in all of Conard County would come after Faith like this. Oh, it might be some drifter, but Micah would have bet his life savings that Frank Williams had managed a jailbreak. With only one deputy on duty as a jailer, it would have been easy enough to accomplish, and until the shift change took place at midnight, nobody would even know Williams had escaped.

What a great time, Micah thought acidly, to realize that jail security needed a good beefing up.

Once his feet hit the floor, he pulled a penlight out of his jacket pocket and scanned the basement quickly. In the shadows he saw that the door of the breaker box was open. If the guy had thrown the breaker, then there had been lights on when he got here—otherwise he wouldn't have bothered. That meant Faith had been awake. Had known someone was in the house. Was probably even now in his clutches. Micah bit back a curse and headed for the stairs, flashlight in his left hand, .45 in his right.

At the top, the door was wide open. A chair lay overturned nearby. Micah doused his light and paused, listening, and heard a sound from farther back in the house. Taking two steps, he reached the kitchen door and unlocked it, opening it wide in invitation to Gage. Then he turned and headed toward Faith's bedroom.

"I'm going to cut that baby out of you, bitch!"

Micah froze, but no sound answered Frank's vile threat. That meant Faith was either hiding or already unconscious. Micah prayed it was the former and began creeping down the hall.

"You're mine, you filthy tramp! Did you really think I'd let you walk away from me?"

Suddenly Faith screamed, and Micah quit worrying about silence. In an instant he reached the bedroom. As dark as it was, he could still make out their shadows, and he saw that Frank had Faith on the floor in front of him as he towered over her and held her by her hair. In his hand, a knife gleamed coldly.

Micah took aim. "Let her go."

Frank jerked Faith closer. He laughed. "It's all over for me anyway, but I'll be damned if I let some redskin have her!"

He lifted the knife and jerked Faith back yet again. Micah hesitated an instant, just an instant. It was dark, and though he'd never in his life hesitated to pull a trigger, he hesitated now, just a fraction, because Faith was one of those shadows. Then he fired.

Frank jerked and dropped the knife. He let go of Faith and pulled a gun from the waistband of his pants.

"Drop it, Williams," Micah ordered. "Next time, I won't just graze you."

"Go to hell." He pointed his gun directly at Micah.

A report sounded, and Frank Williams staggered wildly and then fell to the floor. Micah hadn't pulled the trigger. Slowly, he turned and found Gage right beside him.

Gage shrugged, a barely perceptible movement in the dark. "Figured you wouldn't want to be the guy who killed the father of her child." He slipped into the room past Micah, gun ready, and approached Williams. Micah covered him.

Gage knelt and felt for Frank's pulse. "He's gone and good riddance," he said with patent disgust. "Deader than a doornail, Ms. Williams. This bastard will never trouble you again."

Faith didn't answer. Freed from the necessity to be a cop, Micah closed the distance between them in a flash and knelt beside her on the floor, reaching for her, trying to hold her close, but finding she was curled up into a tight ball and wouldn't unfold.

"Faith, baby, it's over. It's over. You're safe now."

Shudders rippled through her, shaking her from head to toe. "Micah?"

"I'm here, Moonbeam. I'm right here." His voice was little more than a husky whisper as his throat closed. "Did he cut you?"

"No..." The word was a groan of anguish. "Micah, I'm losing the baby!"

The distance between Faith's house and County Hospital was 33.6 miles. Micah covered them in under twenty-five minutes with the Blazer's lights flashing and the siren howling across the desolate countryside.

"Maybe it's for the best." Faith's whisper pierced his heart.

"No," he said. "No."

"No man wants another man's child," she argued, her voice rising as another cramp seized her. "No man. And can't you just imagine the stories this baby would hear about her father? Oh, God, Micah!"

"Shh...shh..." Reaching out, he found her hunched shoulder and squeezed. "It's going to be all right, Moonbeam. You want this baby, and we're going to save her. We're going to save her."

Hell, he found himself thinking as he made promises he couldn't keep, he wanted this baby, too. He'd become attached to the little pokes and flutters and the whole damn idea of the kid. And newborns—well, hell. Newborns were the whole point of living and loving. The best part of humanity. There was a space in his heart already waiting for this child to take up residence, and it had been there from the moment he had felt the child move.

Once again he wanted to stake his claim on this woman and child, to tell Faith that the only father this kid was going to know about was going to be him. He kept the words locked up tight, though, because this wasn't the time, and because he remembered all too well how she had fled from him just this morning. She didn't belong to anybody, she had said. He wondered how long he would let her go on believing that.

When he lifted her out of the Blazer and placed her on the waiting gurney, she was still doubled over, but he was relieved to see no evidence of blood or water. It wasn't too late. Not yet.

Bending, he kissed her on the forehead. "You need me, just holler my name. I'll be here."

Then they took her away, out of his hands, and left him with nothing to do but wait. With a cup of terrible vending machine coffee, he settled down in the waiting room.

At some point he realized he was no longer alone. Looking up, he saw Ransom seated across from him.

"Mandy wanted to come, too, but I wouldn't hear of it," Ransom said.

"Good. She needs her rest."

Reaching into a nylon bag on the floor beside him, Ransom pulled out a large insulated bottle. "I know about hospital coffee," he said, and proceeded to fill two disposable cups. "I sure drank enough of it."

"Thanks." Micah accepted one of the cups and tasted it with pleasure. "Mandy makes the world's best coffee."

"How bad is it?"

Micah met his friend's concerned blue eyes. "Don't know. She was cramping, but... I don't know. They haven't told me anything."

"When Nate called me, he said he didn't think Williams had hurt her."

"No. He didn't have time." Thank God for that. Now, if they could have just one more small miracle, just one tiny little miracle... He closed his eyes a moment against a surging tide of feeling. "I wonder how that bastard got out."

"Would you believe," said Nate's familiar voice from the door of the waiting room, "that Williams conned Lou into going into the cell? Lou's in here with a dented skull, by the way. He's going to be okay."

"How'd he get Lou to do that?" Micah asked. He wouldn't have thought Lou was the gullible type.

"We may never know. He's concussed and can't remember anything past the point where Frank called him over." Nate smiled faintly. "Hell, son, this is Conard County. We're not prepared for serious criminals and jail breaks. Guess we'll be a little better prepared after this, though." He settled onto the sofa by the door. "Gage said to tell you he'll clear up the paperwork before he heads out to the state lab this morning.

"You know," he continued, "now that we've got Frank Williams taken care of, all we need to do is put a stop to the cattle mutilations."

Micah nodded. "Maybe Gage will bring back something we can go on."

"Maybe," Nate agreed. "How's Faith?"

Micah shrugged. The hours just kept ticking by, and nobody had told him anything. Years of training kept him patient, sure only that sooner or later Faith would ask for him. Until then, he didn't want to force himself on her, not even that little bit. Not after what he'd heard tonight.

Nate popped back up from the couch. "I'll go ask questions."

If anybody could get answers, Micah thought, it would be Nate. When he returned ten minutes later, though, he simply shrugged. "All they say is they're doing what they can."

The same thing they'd told him earlier, Micah thought grimly. It wasn't enough.

But with nothing else to do, he sat with the two people closest to him in the world and tried to absorb the cracks and crevices that the earthquake of today's events had made in his deepest places. Faith had been scared of him this morning. Maybe, after what had happened tonight, she would never be able to be with a man again. Maybe she would lose more than her ability to trust. Maybe she would never be able to stand being with a man again.

Maybe, he thought, he would have to start all over again with her. Maybe he would have to begin at the very beginning and show her little by little, day by day, that she need never fear him. And maybe she would never believe that.

And maybe he would just keep on trying, for the rest of his days if necessary. This morning, he admitted, he had reacted to his own old fears the same way she had been reacting to hers. His own defenses, the carapace of ancient scars he wore like a shield, had stood between them as surely as her fears had. If he hadn't been reacting to his own scars, he would never have let her go. He would have stood there and insisted they talk it out, work it out, love it out. He would have put his arms around her and held her gently until she understood that she had no need to fear his possession.

Well, that was what he would do from here on out. For the next forty years if he had to, because, by God, life was worthless without her.

It was nearly dawn when a weary Ben MacArdle appeared. "Micah? She'd like to see you."

Micah sprang to his feet. "Is she . . . ?"

"She's just fine," MacArdle said as they walked down the hall together. "As miscarriages go, this one never even got started. The baby's fine, no distress, and Faith's comfortable now. We'll keep her until tomorrow as a precaution, but physically, she's just great." He paused at the door of her room and looked up at Micah. "The rest of it is going to take time."

"I've got time. Plenty of it."

"Then give her some. She's not ready to handle anything more right now."

Thus warned, Micah entered the room cautiously. She lay on the bed, looking so small and fragile that he ached. Her pale curls made a silky halo on the pillow, and her small hand looked as pale as the sheet on which it lay. So fine, so delicate, so fragile.

He reached her bedside without making a sound and watched her sleep. God, he wanted to gather her up and hold her close and make sure no harm ever came to her again. He wanted to stash her safely away and guard her like a dragon protecting his treasure. Such a thing was impossible, of course, but that didn't keep him from feeling protective enough that he wanted to do it.

"Micah." She spoke his name without opening her eyes.

"I'm here, Moonbeam." When he saw her hand stir on the sheet, he took it in his and held it. "How do you feel?"

"Better. The baby's okay."

"I know. I'm glad. I'm so glad."

Slowly, she opened her eyes and looked at him. "Micah?"

"Hmm?"

"I'm sorry."

"There's nothing to be sorry for."

"Yes, there is. I ran from you. I hurt you. I know you're not anything like Frank. I know it, but I ran, and I'm sorry...."

"Shh...shh." He gathered her into his arms and held her to his chest. "Don't worry about a thing, Faith. Not a thing. As soon as you get out of here, we'll talk, okay? But right now, don't you worry about a thing. Not a thing."

A ragged little sigh escaped her, and she softened against him, leaning into him. "I missed you," she murmured, then fell asleep once more.

He held her until they made him leave.

The following morning at ten, Nate appeared in the doorway of Micah's office. "Micah? Get over to the hospital. MacArdle's about to let the little lady out, and she'll need you to take her home. And don't come back here until you get her straightened out, hear? I don't want any solitary pregnant females out in the back of beyond in my county, and you can tell her I said so."

Micah almost smiled, but he was too busy grabbing his hat and jacket to realize it.

She was standing with her back to the door when he arrived, packing the small overnight bag he'd brought her yesterday. A shaft of sunlight fell through the window, catching her hair and making it gleam like pale gold.

"Need a ride, little lady?"

She swung around, frowning, then laughed when she saw the teasing sparkle in his dark eyes. "You know I hate that, Micah."

"I know." He crossed the room and grabbed her overnight bag. "I took care of the paperwork before I came up. You're free to leave." He didn't tell her that he'd paid the bill. She would find that out soon enough. For now he didn't want her angry, and he didn't want to ruffle her independent feathers.

The day was beautiful, without a cloud to mar the perfection of the blue sky. Snow gleamed and sparkled so brightly that it hurt the eyes to look at it. Micah helped her into the Blazer, then joined her.

He put on his mirrored glasses again, and Faith leaned her cheek against the headrest and simply watched him. She didn't think she would get enough of the sight of him if she had a million years to simply sit and stare. He was so masculine, so exotic, with his long dark hair and harshly featured face. He was a man, he was a cop, and he was big, and the thrill that realization gave her was no longer one of fear. Not at all. Not even remotely.

She expected him to take her to her house. After the stink she had made about leaving, after the way she had run and insisted she needed to be independent, she didn't expect him to turn down his own driveway. But he did, and he didn't say a word. She considered questioning him, but his mouth was set in a grim line, so she kept quiet.

He lifted her down from the Blazer, then reached for her overnight bag, saying more clearly than words that she was staying. Her heart took a leap, and her mouth turned dry.

"I moved your stuff back over here last night," he announced as he ushered her into his kitchen.

"Micah—"

"Hush." Gently, he urged her onto a chair. When she was seated, he tugged her boots off, then reached for the buttons of her jacket. "Get as mad as you want, Moonbeam, but I'll be double-damned if I'm going to let you live alone. Sure as hell not while you're pregnant." He glanced up at her from dark eyes as he struggled with a button. She didn't look mad, he realized. Not mad at all. He wasn't quite sure what her expression was, but it wasn't mad. "Nate said to tell you he doesn't want any pregnant women living all alone in the middle of nowhere in his county."

"He did, did he?" She pursed her lips. "And that's why you dragged me here without asking? Because Nate said I can't live alone?"

There was something in the tone of her voice that disturbed him, but he was no coward, and he wasn't going to back down this time, no matter how angry she got. "No, that's not why. It's because I'll be old before my time if I have to make one more mad midnight dash up that road to your place wondering if you're hurt or...or..." He couldn't finish. After a moment, he cleared his throat. "You're turning my hair gray, Moonbeam."

She lifted a trembling hand and touched the dark silk that reached his shoulders. "I'd hate to do that to such beautiful hair," she murmured.

Her touch was like a blessing to his aching soul. Of her own free will, she had reached out to him. He wanted to catch her to him and sweep her upstairs, but he restrained himself. His heart needed some signs from her, and this was but a first tentative move. Turning his head, he brushed a kiss on her palm.

She cupped his cheek then, touching him with the gentleness he so deeply craved. "*You're* beautiful, Micah," she murmured. "I tried to tell you that once before, and you didn't like it, but it's true. You're beautiful."

He closed his eyes for a moment against the welling tide of feeling, then returned to the task of removing her coat. She let him pull it from her shoulders, and she offered no protest when he leaned forward and rested his cheek against her womb. Instead, her gentle hands held him there, stroking his cheek, his hair. This was a touch he had been seeking for his entire life, he realized.

"I had a lot of time to think last night," Faith continued softly, stroking his hair, calming him. Soothing him. Soothing herself. "For the first time in years I was completely free of my fear of Frank, and I realized that all my other fears were just reflections of my fear of him."

The baby stirred and kicked Micah's cheek, a soft little poke. "I must be squashing her," he said roughly and started to raise his head.

Faith's hands stopped him. "No," she said. "No. She likes you there. *I* like you there. It makes us feel safe and warm and cared for."

Micah caught his breath, and this time he did raise his head to look her squarely in the eyes. "You were afraid of me."

"I was afraid of a word, Micah. A word that Frank abused." Her blue eyes were steady, unafraid, as they returned his searching gaze.

"'Mine,'" he said. "That word. That's what scared you. I heard him say it just before I got to you the other night."

She nodded. "He was always saying that, saying he could do whatever he wanted, because I was his. He claimed he could kill this baby because it was his."

"And I claimed you both, just as he did."

"That's what scared me," she admitted. "It was stupid, I know, but—"

"Not stupid," he interrupted her. "Not stupid at all."

"But I'm not afraid of you, Micah," she said. "I'm not one bit afraid of you. That's why it was so dumb that I managed to get you mixed up in my mind with him...." Her voice trailed off, and she looked away for a few seconds. When she looked back, her eyes were sad. "And I can't promise never to mix things up again. I don't always seem to be able to control the way my mind and feelings work."

He drew a deep breath and took her hands in his. "Moonbeam, I can handle the mix-ups if you just promise not to run again. We can always work it out."

"W-we can?" Her voice broke, then rose on a note of hope.

He heard that hope, and a vise that had been gripping his heart for two days now suddenly let go. He gave her one of his very rare smiles. "We can. All you have to do is try to talk to me. I'll get angry sometimes, and sometimes I'll probably remind you of him, but, Moonbeam, I'd burn alive at the stake before I'd ever lay a hurtful finger on you or our child."

She drew a sharp breath, and her grip on his hands tightened. "*Our*... child?"

He tugged one hand from hers and laid his palm against her stomach. "This child. Our child. I told you that when I spilled my seed in you this child became mine. I wasn't kidding."

"But..." She searched his face almost desperately. "How can you...? Is this some kind of Indian thing?"

He shook his head. "I don't think so. It's just my thing. I've always felt that loving a woman included loving the fruit she bears. It doesn't matter who plants the tree, Faith. The apple still tastes just as good."

"Oh my," she said softly. Her lower lip quivered, and one huge, silvery tear appeared on her lower lash. "Oh my." Leaning forward, she threw her arms around his neck and clung tightly.

This woman's absence for the last couple of days had been like a hole in his heart, and now that hole was being filled in by her sweet warmth, her gentle touch, her personal fragrance. He released a long sigh and gave up the battle to remain patient. He needed her, and he needed her now, hot, warm and willing beneath him. There was a lot that they would have to settle, but it was just going to have to wait, because emotions were locking up his throat, and there was only one way he could show her all his feelings. Words had never been his way.

He lifted her easily and started up the stairs. Faith buried her face in his neck, her breath a hot caress on his skin. "Don't you have to go back to work?" she asked him, hoping against hope that he didn't.

"Nope. Not until I get you straightened out, anyway."

Once, such a statement would have thrown her into a tempest of fear, but Micah made her feel so safe that she could discern the teasing note in his voice. "Straighten me out how?"

"Flat on your back," he said huskily. "Under me. Making appropriate sounds of pleasure."

"What if I want *you* flat on your back under *me?*"

The question, sounding so coquettish even as her voice quavered at her unaccustomed boldness, caused Micah to laugh. "Moonbeam, you can have me any way you want, any time you want."

Knowing he would have to be cautious because of the baby, he lowered her gently to his bed and just as gently began to undress her. And while he removed her clothing and tempted her with the light caress of his hands, he talked as he had never talked before.

"I've been lonely my whole life long, Moonbeam. I just never admitted it to myself. I told myself that my solitude was a fortress, that as long as I stood alone no one could hurt me."

"Oh, I know," she breathed. "I know. I told myself the same thing. Oh, Micah, it's not true!"

"I finally realized that." His dark eyes, like blazing black fire, devoured her. "When I held you, I realized I had some big holes that needed filling, big holes that were aching with emptiness. You filled my arms, Moonbeam, and I knew for the first time that they'd been empty."

She lifted her hand as if to touch him, but he rose and pulled her pants from her, leaving her completely naked on his bed. Then, standing over her, he began to strip his own clothes away. She watched every one of his movements in a way that told him she hadn't been kidding when she said he was beautiful. That understanding made him ache, too.

At last, at long, long last, he was beside her and they were pressed together from head to toe, bare skin on bare skin, warm sunlight illuminating every moment of their joining. She smiled as he claimed every inch of her with his hands, and that smile grew when he groaned at the gentle touch of hers.

When he finally sank into her liquid heat, he knew he had come home. The last barrier fell, and as he moved he told her, "I love you, Moonbeam. I love you body and soul."

"I love you, too, Micah," she answered. "Oh, I love you!"

"Stay...with...me," he gasped.

"Yes...yes..."

"You're mine." The words slipped past one of his lowered barriers, and as soon as he heard them in the air, a fist squeezed his heart. He stopped moving and opened his eyes, almost afraid to look into Faith's face. What if he saw panic, or fear, or...?

"I'm yours," she told him, her eyes wide open and steady, without a shadow of fear in their depths. "I'm yours for as long as you want me."

Cautiously lowering himself to his elbows, he kissed her on the mouth. "I'm *yours,*" he said huskily. "I've never belonged to anybody before, but I want to belong to you."

"Oh, Micah," she breathed, lifting her hands to cradle his face. "Oh, I do like the sound of that. You're *mine?*"

"All yours. One hundred percent. Forever."

Her breath caught, and then suddenly she was laughing and crying and hugging his neck so tightly that he was afraid he would fall on her, and damn it, he still needed her....

She still needed him, too, and with a gentle, beckoning roll of her hips, she let him know it. "Love me, Micah," she whispered in his ear. "Love me."

"To my dying breath," he vowed, and lifted her with him to the most intense expression of his love that he could give her.

"You are the song in my blood," he told her. "The light in my soul. My Moonbeam."

* * * * *

MARIE FERRARELLA

The babies are coming! Six, to be exact, and you'll meet these bundles of joy in THE BABY OF THE MONTH CLUB, RITA-Award-winning author Marie Ferrarella's latest miniseries. Your first appointment is scheduled for December 1995: *Baby's First Christmas*, Special Edition #997.

All Marlene Bailey wanted for Christmas was her baby's safe arrival. To her dismay, Sullivan Travis's holiday list included the same wish—only he'd come to claim his late brother's child. So why was she allowing Sullivan into her life, into her dreams...into her heart?

Your next checkup is January 1996 as THE BABY OF THE MONTH CLUB continues in the Intimate Moments line with *Happy New Year—Baby!*, IM #686. Don't miss a single month of fun, only in— ᵀᴹ *Silhouette*®

Silhouette ROMANCE™

What's a single dad to do when he needs a wife by next Thursday?

Who's a confirmed bachelor to call when he finds a baby on his doorstep?

How does a plain Jane in love with her gorgeous boss get him to notice her?

From classic love stories to romantic comedies to emotional heart tuggers, Silhouette Romance offers six irresistible novels every month by some of your favorite authors!
Such as...beloved bestsellers **Diana Palmer,**
Annette Broadrick, Suzanne Carey, Elizabeth August
and **Marie Ferrarella,** to name just a few—and some sure to become favorites!

Fabulous Fathers...Bundles of Joy...Miniseries...
Months of blushing brides and convenient weddings...
Holiday celebrations... You'll find all this and much more in
Silhouette Romance—always emotional, always enjoyable, always about love!

SILHOUETTE®

Desire®

Do you want...

Dangerously handsome heroes

Evocative, everlasting love stories

Sizzling and tantalizing sensuality

Incredibly sexy miniseries like MAN OF THE MONTH

Red-hot romance

Enticing entertainment that can't be beat!

You'll find all of this, and much *more* each and every month in **SILHOUETTE DESIRE**. Don't miss these unforgettable love stories by some of romance's hottest authors. Silhouette Desire—where your fantasies will always come true....

DES-GEN

If you've got the time...
We've got the
INTIMATE MOMENTS

Passion. Suspense. Desire. Drama. Enter a world that's larger than life, where men and women overcome life's greatest odds for the ultimate prize: love. Nonstop excitement is closer than you think...in Silhouette Intimate Moments!

WAYS TO *UNEXPECTEDLY* MEET MR. RIGHT:

♡ Go out with the sexy-sounding stranger your daughter secretly set you up with through a personal ad.

♡ RSVP yes to a wedding invitation—soon it might be your turn to say "I do!"

♡ Receive a marriage proposal by mail— from a man you've never met....

These are just a few of the unexpected ways that written communication leads to love in Silhouette Yours Truly.

Each month, look for two fast-paced, fun and flirtatious Yours Truly novels (with entertaining treats and sneak previews in the back pages) by some of your favorite authors—and some who are sure to become favorites.

YOURS TRULY™:
Love—when you least expect it!

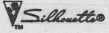

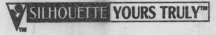